Somewhere in Germany

Terrace Books, a division of the University of Wisconsin Press,
takes its name from the Memorial Union Terrace, located at
the University of Wisconsin-Madison. Since its inception in 1907,
the Wisconsin Union has provided a venue for students, faculty,
staff, and alumni to debate art, music, politics, and the issues of the day.
It is a place where theater, music, drama, dance, outdoor activities, and
major speakers are made available to the campus and the community.
To learn more about the Union, visit www.union.wisc.edu.

Somewhere in Germany

AN AUTOBIOGRAPHICAL NOVEL

Stefanie Zweig

Translated by MARLIES COMJEAN

TERRACE BOOKS
A trade imprint of the University of Wisconsin Press

The translation of this work was supported by a grant from
the Goethe-Institut,
and its publication was made possible with financial support from
the National Endowment for the Arts.

NATIONAL
ENDOWMENT
FOR THE ARTS

Terrace Books
A trade imprint of the University of Wisconsin Press
1930 Monroe Street
Madison, Wisconsin 53711

www.wisc.edu/wisconsinpress/

3 Henrietta Street
London WC2E 8LU, England

Originally published as *Irgendwo in Deutschland*
© 1996 by Langen Müller in der F. A. Herbig Verlagsbuchhandlung GmbH, München

Translation copyright © 2006
The Board of Regents of the University of Wisconsin System
All rights reserved

1   3   5   4   2

Printed in the United States of America

Library of Congress Cataloging-in-Publication Data
Zweig, Stefanie.
[Irgendwo in Deutschland. English]
Somewhere in Germany: an autobiographical novel / Stefanie Zweig;
translated by Marlies Comjean.
p.   cm.
ISBN 0-299-21010-3 (cloth: alk. paper)
1. Zweig, Stefanie—Fiction.   2. Jews—Germany—Fiction.
I. Comjean, Marlies.   II. Title.
PT2688.W45I713   2006
833'.914—dc22   2006006963

In memory of my dear brother,
Max

Somewhere in Germany

1

ON APRIL 15, 1947, the express train from Osnabrück arrived with unexpected suddenness in Frankfurt on the Main despite a two-hour delay at the control point between the British and American occupation zones, after a travel time of close to nineteen hours. The travelers in the compartments and corridors were not prepared for the abrupt stop, which felt like a sudden shock rather than a release. Still numbed by the coldness of the night and the unusual warmth of the morning hours, and their view blocked by the cardboard screens on the glassless windows of the train, the passengers lost their orientation, and for a few minutes their senses deprived them of the long-awaited certainty that they had reached their destination.

They hesitated before putting their rucksacks, bags, and suitcases on the floor, exposing their belongings to the dangers that were unfortunately typical for the new times, which in the most aggravating way had dispensed with the moral concepts that had still been intact during the last years of the war when, in spite of all the suffering, things had after all been less chaotic. The lucky few passengers who had robustly fought for their comfort, which they considered just and democratic, were not willing to relinquish their seats or standing room in the passageways by getting out too early.

Only those travelers on the running boards and roofs of the train, already envied for their excellent physical condition, realized immediately that the blackened beams of the open hall, the loose hanging wires, the

3

piles of shards glittering in the sunlight between the tracks, and the stones that had been piled up from the rubble were indeed the heart of the Frankfurt Grand Central Station. At first only a few people dared to get off the train. Almost simultaneously, men with backpacks climbed off the roofs; women with headscarves and determined, sooty faces jumped off the running boards.

Those passengers spilling out of the train had a much better vantage point for conquering Frankfurt than the Redlich family, which was returning from exile in the last car. That one was locked from the outside and first had to be opened by a remarkably well-nourished American corporal with a tendency toward slow leg movements but fast jaw motion.

Wearing the heavy gray coat that he had received three days earlier as a last gift from the British Army in London when he was released from the military, Walter Redlich hesitantly stepped off the train. He carried the two suitcases that originally came from Breslau, had left German soil ten years ago, and were now touching it again. His wife, Jettel, followed him in the dress that had been sewn by the Indian tailor in Nairobi especially for her return to the now foreign homeland. In one hand, she clutched a handkerchief that was wet from crying all night, and in the other, a hatbox she had been unable to be separated from during the ten years of her emigration in Kenya.

Their daughter, Regina, whose fourteen-year-old body had trouble filling out one of her chubby mother's dresses that had been altered for her, concentrated on the task of not crying like her mother while she got off the train and, above all, of not annoying her by allowing a trace of the hopeful smile that her father expected to steal into her face. She carried her one-year-old brother, Max, who missed the decisive moment of his arrival in the new homeland. He had dealt with the hardships of the journey and a stomachache, caused by an unaccustomed diet of lettuce leaves between slices of white bread, by incessantly screaming with a vehemence that had not let up the entire night. Now he was asleep, rocking on Regina's stomach, his head on her shoulder. When the first breeze of the Frankfurt air touched his face, he only slightly clenched his fist but did not wake up.

The British army had carried out its obligation of releasing a soldier to his homeland in a circumspect and responsible way. After arriving at

Hoek van Holland, the Redlichs had been brought to Osnabrück and housed in a refugee camp for the night, with the admonition to avoid any contact with enemy Germans as best as possible.

In Osnabrück, Walter, Jettel, Regina, and the baby had been put into the locked train car with rations to which a soldier without special physical exertions was entitled for one day. Their fellow travelers included a British major and a Canadian army captain who had boarded the train with two bottles of whiskey each and had very quickly emptied one of them. Except for some orders addressed at regular intervals to the "bloody baby" to "shut up," and the occasionally uttered observation "fucking Germans," when Jettel was sobbing too loudly or Max cried too self-confidently for a baby on the losing side, there were no further contacts. The major and the captain had already left the train when Walter took a first look at Frankfurt.

"We were supposed to be picked up," he said. "That is what they told me in London." Ten minutes after their arrival, this was the first sentence he uttered in the town he wanted to be his home.

"I thought the Germans were always on time," Jettel answered. "That used to be their best feature."

"Nobody rolled out the red carpet when we arrived in Africa, either. And at least here people do understand us. Give it time, Jettel."

"They are taking their time," Jettel sniffled. "I cannot go on any longer. The poor child. How long is an innocent little child supposed to endure such hardships? I cannot even face him."

"You don't have to. After all, the poor child is asleep," Walter said.

Regina stared at her feet. She tried to focus on not feeling the hunger, thirst, or fear that had caused her body to stiffen after she saw the first destroyed houses upon crossing the German border and the one-legged men on crutches at the train station in Osnabrück. She rubbed her face on her brother's warm skin and resisted the temptation to whisper the few Jaluo language words to him that would have given her the strength to fight her fears. It was not good to wake the child of a mother who could not keep her own eyes dry. Only when Regina realized that her parents had stopped fighting and were staring in the same direction did she permit her eyes to relax and look around.

Her father was no longer standing next to her; and her mother had put her hatbox down, stretched out her right arm, and called out loud,

"Good God, Mr. Koschella. What is he doing here? He was at our wedding."

Regina saw her father running. He stopped in front of a man in a gray suit, shook his head for a moment, extended both arms, and suddenly let them drop again. It was the stranger who grasped Walter's hand. He had a deep voice and Regina could hear from a distance that this voice was used to traveling far.

"Walter Redlich," the man said, "I could not believe it when I was told yesterday to go and meet you. I still cannot believe that someone would be crazy enough to return to this country. Where in the world are you coming from? Oh, well, I know. The entire justice department has been talking for days about nothing but the madman who has abandoned the fleshpots of Africa so that he can starve here as a judge. Good heavens, don't tell me the baby is yours, too."

Regina very closely observed how the man held out his hand to her mother and how all of a sudden the smile of those dead days, before she had known about their return to Germany, lit up her mother's face. Regina tried to extend her hand to the man, too, but did not succeed because her brother became even heavier and started sliding down her hip. She tried very hard to shape the name Koschella in her mouth and, at the same time, to follow her parents' excited talk and the hastily spoken, somewhat sharp-sounding words of the man; she took too much time deliberating what the words "attorney general" might mean and if they were important to all of them.

Regina finally managed to translate the happiness her parents expected of her to the regular movement of her legs and the challenge of keeping pace with the men and her mother. She noticed that her father walked quite differently here than in Africa. She listened to the sound of his shoes and saw the dust they kicked up: it was dark and dense, no longer light and transparent as in the good days of warmth.

The group exited from the gray of the station, stepped into the light of spring, and crossed a street lined with bombed-out houses on either side. Old women pushed carts piled high with their belongings. Small children sat on cardboard suitcases and gray blankets. They had the lackluster eyes of the leprous beggars that Regina had encountered in the streets of Nairobi. The bell of a light yellow streetcar chimed in high notes. The doors of the streetcar were ajar; the tightly crowded people on the running boards seemed like the old trees that the wind had caused to grow together on the farm in Ol' Joro Orok. Robust bushes of yellow flowers grew on the rubble mounds of the dead houses. Birds were twittering. Walter said, "Even the birds sing differently here than in Africa." Koschella laughed and shook his head.

"Still the same old joker," he said.

Her father pushed Regina into a big, clean room that was very dark and smelled of antibacterial soap, which reminded her of her school at Lake Nakuru. She forgot for an instant that she had hated the school and smiled at the thought that she was becoming just like her mother, confusing the good memories with the bad. Still, she saw the flamingoes rise and had to prevent her eyes from getting immersed in the pink cloud.

A young, very blonde woman with bright red lips was sitting behind a long table. Her blue dress had a white collar. Her head, its hair coiffed in evenly shaped waves, was on the same level as the highest of the yellow roses in the blue vase in front of her.

Koschella's strong voice increased in volume when he announced, "Attorney General Dr. Hans Koschella." After a slight pause, which the woman filled with an annoyed glance, he added, "This is district court judge Dr. Walter Redlich from Nairobi. Yesterday I reserved two rooms for him and his family."

The woman ran a finger through the lowest wave of her hair. Even though she hardly moved her red lips, she could be heard saying, very distinctly, "Sorry. The Hotel Monopol is off limits for Germans."

"What are you saying? You should have told me that yesterday when I reserved the rooms."

"But," said the woman, smiling long enough for the upper row of her teeth to become visible, "you did not give me a chance to do so. You made the reservation and instantly hung up."

"Well, then refer me to another hotel. Do you think the justice department can afford to have a judge come all the way from Africa and not provide him with accommodations? What are you thinking?"

"There are no hotels for Germans in Frankfurt. You ought to know that, Dr. Koschella. All hotels have been seized by the American military government."

"Let me talk to your hotel director then."

"The Monopol is one of the hotels directly managed by the military government. We do not have a director. I also have to inform you that it is a punishable offense for me to have Germans sitting in the hotel lobby."

Dr. Hans Koschella looked at the woman for some time and then even longer at his watch. He made a small movement toward the baby on Regina's stomach; she held the baby, who was playing with her hair, out to him so that he could touch it, but he withdrew his hand. Then he looked at Walter and said, no longer as forcefully as before but still in a voice that was used to being heard, "I am terribly sorry, Redlich. Something went wrong here. Unfortunately I have an urgent appointment and cannot help you any further. Well, you will soon find out for yourself that the few jurists who are still permitted to work these days are quite busy."

"But what are we supposed to do now?" Jettel said quietly.

"Don't worry, Mrs. Jettel. Your husband's best bet is to go to the housing authorities right away and have them assign an apartment to you. He must have the necessary declaration of urgency from the justice department. Come along, Redlich; don't look so dejected. I will take you to the streetcar. I will take the time to help you. And do not let the officials there intimidate you. They are required to give repatriated applicants preferential treatment. You can no longer afford to be polite these days."

Regina went to the door with Walter. Her feet were heavy and her mouth was dry. She knew that her mother was watching her and so she did not dare ask her father where Jettel, she, and Max should wait for him. She followed Koschella and him with her eyes until their silhouettes dissolved in the bright sunlight. Then she returned as slowly as possible to her mother. She had just come back to the table with the roses when the blonde woman pointed to a leather bench in the darkest corner of the room and said to Jettel, "Sit down over there till your husband comes back. But for heaven's sake, keep the child quiet. If anyone finds you here, I will get into trouble and have to put you out into the street."

The streetcar was so crowded that it took Walter two stops to move inside from the running board. Even though he had hardly eaten anything since their departure from Osnabrück, in order to save the military rations for Regina and Max, and therefore felt dizzy and nauseous, he welcomed the stress as an opportune distraction from his state of mind, which consisted of a bewildering mixture of outrage, numbness, and shock.

He had been under no illusions when he insisted on his decision to return to Germany against Jettel's resistance and Regina's never openly voiced despair, and he had known that the homecoming would present him with problems that he could not even imagine in the hours of his deepest depression in Africa. But he had never envisioned that an irony of fate would instantly burden him with the same kind of shame as in January 1938, when he had arrived desperate and penniless in Kenya. The shame had started to undermine his self-confidence the moment he had to leave Jettel, Regina, and Max alone in the hotel lobby. He knew from experience that this new humiliation was sure to stay with him for a long time.

Walter, expecting that it would take him quite a while to find the house that Koschella had described, unhappily got off the streetcar. The first man he asked for directions, though, pointed to a gray building with inadequately boarded windows and a wooden door. A cardboard notice, affixed with thumbtacks, read "Municipal Housing Authority."

An old man with a black eye patch sent Walter to a room with the sign "Moves"; four younger men with movements similar to the first perplexedly stared at him, rejected him, and sent him on with very curt words. None of them gave him the chance to do more than mention his name and the fact that his wife and children were sitting in the lobby of a hotel where they were not allowed to be.

The sign on the fifth door said "Refugees." An official was sitting at a small, wooden table covered with files, three pencil stubs, and a slightly rusty pair of scissors. Next to those was a tin mug with some steaming liquid. Walter seemed to vaguely remember that chamomile tea smelled this way. Even the word had not occurred to him for more than ten years. The thought occupied him in a way that he considered inappropriate at this moment of utmost tension.

The man was flipping through a pile of gray papers and chewing on a thin, strikingly yellow piece of bread when Walter approached him. He did not seem any different from his colleagues and Walter prepared himself for the tired motion of rejection, but to his surprise the man first said, "Good morning," and then, "Please take a seat."

His voice had the singing intonation that instantly reminded Walter of his friend Oha in Gilgil. He resisted the randomness of his memory when he remembered that most likely all people in Frankfurt sounded like Oha who, after all, had been from Frankfurt. His stomach, which had turned into a knot when he saw the official chewing his bread, quieted down a bit. Walter smiled and was embarrassed by his own timidity.

The official's name was Fichtel. He was hoarse, wore a gray shirt with a collar much too big for his neck, and, in spite of his Adam's apple and sunken cheeks, his face exhibited a trace of good humor that Walter found encouraging.

"Well, why don't you tell me your story," Fichtel said.

When he heard that Walter had just arrived from Africa, he whistled in a long, almost absurdly youthful way, and said, "Oh boy, oh boy," which Walter at first did not understand. Made confident by the alert expression that all of a sudden illuminated Fichtel's face, Walter began to report in detail about the last ten years of his life.

"And you want me to believe that you voluntarily returned to this damned country? Man, I'd rather emigrate today than tomorrow. Everyone here wants to. Whatever made you come back?"

"They did not want me in Africa."

"And they want you here?"

"I believe so."

"Well, you must know. Everything is possible these days. Did you at least bring some coffee along from those Negroes?"

"No," Walter said.

"Or cigarettes?"

"A few, but I already smoked them all."

"Oh boy, oh boy," Fichtel said. "I always thought the Jews were clever and got through anything."

"Especially through the chimneys at Auschwitz."

"That is not what I meant, certainly not. You can believe me," Fichtel assured him. His hand slightly trembled as he pushed the stamps from one side of the table to the other. His voice was uneasy when he said, "Even if I immediately classified your request as an urgent priority, I would not be able to give you an apartment for years. We have none.

Most apartments have been either bombed out or taken over by the Americans. You will be much better off with the Jewish community at the Baumweg. People say that they can work miracles and have entirely different possibilities than we have here."

The sentence confused Walter so much that he did not allow himself to contemplate the emotions that crowded in on him.

"Are you telling me that there is a Jewish community here in Frankfurt?" he asked.

"Of course," Fichtel said. "After all, a sufficient number did return from the camps that everyone is talking about these days. And we hear that they are not doing too badly. They even get a bonus for heavy labor. You are entitled to that, too. Look, I am going to write down the address for you, Dr. Redlich. You will see; you may be able to have an apartment of your own by tomorrow. As I always say: Your own people will take care of you." It was already after four o'clock when Walter returned to the Monopol. At the Jewish community he had only been able to see a woman who had asked him to come back the next day. At the hotel, he expected to find Jettel, if at all, in tears. He saw her from a distance and believed that the hallucinations that had threatened him since he took leave of Koschella had finally gotten to him.

Jettel was sitting in a jeep next to a soldier in an American uniform, Regina in the back with Max on her lap. Walter was certain that they were in the process of arresting his family because they had remained in the hotel. He hurried toward the car, his stomach in cramps, making gestures that seemed as absurd to him as the entire day.

"Hurry," Jettel cried excitedly. "I already thought that they were going to take us away from here before you returned. Where in heaven's name have you been? The child does not have a single dry diaper left and Regina has a constant nosebleed."

"Sir," Walter called out, "this is my wife. And my children."

"Well, then don't leave your beautiful wife sitting in a seized hotel, you fool," the sergeant grinned.

His voice distinctly betrayed the fact that he was originally from Baden; his name was Steve Green, formerly Stefan Grüntal, and because of his linguistic skills he was in charge of all problematic issues involving Germans. The secretary of the Hotel Monopol had called Steve

Green when she realized that she would not be able to get rid of the lamenting Jettel, her sobbing daughter, and the crying baby in her usual way of just displaying intimidating arrogance.

Until 1935 Steve's parents had owned a small hotel in the vicinity of Baden-Baden. His mother cooked the best chicken soup in the world and hated the Germans. In New York his father had worked his way up from a night porter in Brooklyn to a salesman in a jewelry store on 47th Street; he went to synagogue every Shabbat and also hated the Germans. Steve hated above all Frankfurt, the bloody army, and the PX store's German employees, who shifted the supplies to the black market before the GIs could buy them.

He communicated all of this in a mixture of fluent German and incomprehensible American English while he drove the jeep at breakneck speed and with curses—much coarser than anything Walter had ever heard in the British military—through streets lined with burned-out houses in Frankfurt's inner city. If streetcars or men with wheelbarrows forced him to stop, he threw, depending on the situation, a cigarette out of the jeep and amused himself watching the people fight over it. Or he forgot that he hated the Germans and surprised stunned young women, whom he called "Fräulein" or "Veronica," with a bar of Hershey's chocolate.

Steve gave a packet of chewing gum to Regina, while speeding mistook Jettel's knee more and more often for the gearshift, and answered Walter's questions about their destination with a wink and by pointing out "off limits." About fifteen minutes after their start, he turned from an alley with chestnut trees in bloom into the small but remarkably well-preserved Eppsteiner Straße. He jumped out of the jeep, gallantly helped Jettel out of the car, somewhat roughly hurried Walter and Regina, still with the baby on her arm, to get out, took a pistol from his pants pocket, stormed into the corridor of the house, ran to the third floor, and rang a bell.

A gray-haired woman reluctantly opened the door and anxiously cried, "Oh!"

Steve screamed "Seized!" in the direction of the startled woman and "Okay!" down the staircase. The woman turned pale, wiped her hands repeatedly on an apron with a flower print, and lamented, "But I have only two rooms left."

"One too many," Steve shouted. "These people are going to stay. Housing for one week."

The woman opened her mouth, but instantly closed it when Steve said, "Shut up," and asked her, "Did I lose the war or did you? And you'll provide some food, too. Or I will be back, and not alone."

After that he patted Jettel's hair, slapped Walter on the back, pushed Regina aside, and stuck into Max's mouth a piece of chewing gum, which Jettel tore away from him in a panic and began to chew herself. Max started to scream. The woman groaned and said that her name was Reichard, that she herself did not have anything to eat, and that she had lived in a flat with five rooms before the occupation of Frankfurt.

At the back of her neck, her hair was braided into a bun, which made her look stern and intimidating, and she held her arms crossed in front of her stomach; for a moment it seemed as if she was going to push Jettel out the door, but then Walter said, "We are very sorry to cause you any trouble."

"I will show you the room," Mrs. Reichard sighed, "but I want you to know right away that I only have vegetable soup. I am not obligated to do any more."

Of all the mysteries of the day that they were never able to solve later on, she remained the most inexplicable one. The vegetable soup turned into a casserole; a cardboard box was transformed into a child's bed; there was a thin slice of bread for everyone; and, after that, in cups of Dresden china appeared some hot beverage that Mrs. Reichard referred to as coffee. She called Max "Bobbelche," rocked him on her lap, and cried. She got a cot from the attic for Regina. After dinner Mrs. Reichard spoke about her husband, whom the Americans had arrested, and her only son, who had been killed in Russia. Jettel said that she was sorry, and Mrs. Reichard looked at her in surprise.

The four of them slept in Mrs. Reichard's room. Over the bed hung a picture of two chubby-faced angels that fascinated Regina. There was a big, light rectangle on the opposite wall that interested her father. He maintained that a picture of Hitler must have hung there.

Jettel said, "What a shame that you are always so clever about things that really don't matter." Her voice was not malicious, though, and Walter said, laughing, "Your mother used to say that, too."

Regina was glad that she did not have to catch any poison arrows before they hit their prey. She fleetingly thought of the chocolate that Steve had thrown to the young women and for a long time of the scent of the guava tree in Nairobi. Her stomach was not full enough, though, and her head was too empty to enjoy the safari.

Shortly before falling asleep, she heard her parents fight after all, but it was, almost like in the best hours of the days gone by, only a harmless squabble and then a quickly reached peace. First, they were unable to agree who had invited Koschella to the wedding, and at the same time, they were sure that they had probably mistaken him for someone else and that most likely he had never been to Breslau in all of his life.

2

Hurrah. Today for the first time I am (almost) happy in Frankfurt. Finally, we have been able to move out of Mrs. Reichard's apartment. At
the end she really made our lives miserable. Until an apartment is assigned to us (that may take a long time) we can live at 36 Gagernstraße.
Three days ago, Papa was finally able to reach someone—the world's
nicest man—at the Jewish community. His name is Dr. Alschoff and he
managed to find a place for us at the former Jewish hospital. It is extensively damaged and no longer a hospital but rather a nursing home. We
have a room with three beds, a table and three chairs, and a hotplate.
We wash ourselves in a bowl that is standing on a three-legged stand
that I like a lot. The toilet is down the corridor. We get one meal a day
from the cook of the nursing home, but only for three persons because
Max has food stamps for infants; that is, too many for milk, too few for
fat. That is what the cook says. Our clothes stay in our suitcases. For the
first time in my life I am glad that I do not have much to wear. A truck
brought us to the Gagernstraße. We could have come on Saturday but
we were not allowed to do so because Jews do not drive on a Shabbat,
and the nursing home is kosher.

I am glad that I can keep a diary. I have to thank Dr. Alschoff for
that. He gave me three notebooks and two pencils as a welcome gift,
and now I finally have someone to talk to. I am only going to write in
English in this diary. Then I will feel at home. But I have to write really

small and not every day either because paper is scarce in Germany. Who knows if I will ever get more?

I have to write something else about Dr. Alschoff. He was in a concentration camp. In Auschwitz. When Mama heard about it she cried terribly. Her mother and sister died there. But he had not met them.

He has very sad eyes and wants to stroke Max over and over again. He says there is only one purely Jewish family with children in addition to ours in the community. Papa told me later that Jews did not get sent to the concentration camps if they had a Christian spouse. Like Koschella. Mama said God did not have to save him. Papa became angry and told her that saying that was a sin. Then they fought terribly. Max always laughs when our parents are getting loud. He has not talked since we arrived in Frankfurt. But he already knew how to say *kula, aya, lala, toto, jambo,* and almost "Owuor" before. For the first time tonight, Max is not going to sleep in a cardboard box, but in my bed instead. I am very happy about that.

THURSDAY, APRIL 24

There is a big lawn here with many benches. Today I sat on one of the benches for the first time. A very old woman sat down next to me. Her name is Mrs. Feibelmann and she started talking to me right away. I was terribly embarrassed, but she did not laugh at all at my English accent. She said she got rid of her laugh in Theresienstadt. That was a concentration camp, too. Almost all of the people who are living here were in Theresienstadt. Frau Feibelmann took Max on her lap and sang to him. Then she limped away and returned with two cookies that she put into his mouth. She had three children, but only one son is still alive. In America (that is why she has the cookies—he sends packages to her).

Her two daughters and five grandchildren were killed. I do not know how a person can talk about this without crying. I never heard as many sad things in all my life as in our first ten days in Frankfurt. Many people here have a number on their arm. That means they were in Auschwitz.

There are three sheep in the yard. I envy them a lot; they have enough to eat. The cook does not like us. The portions that he gives us are much smaller than those for the old people. We are not allowed to eat in the dining room because Max disturbs the old people. All of us have gotten thinner already. Except for Max. We give him a lot of our food.

FRIDAY, MAY 2

Today Papa went to court for the first time. He is now a district court judge. He was terribly excited and even paler than usual. Mama gave him her second piece of bread for breakfast. He hugged and kissed her and said, "Jettel, this is the happiest day of our lives since we had to leave Leobschütz." Too bad that Mama said, "How happy we would really be with a full stomach." I thought Papa would get angry, but he just gave her another kiss. When he came home, his cheeks were all red and he looked much taller than in the morning. He reported that everyone had been really nice and everybody wanted to help him get used to his old profession again. If they only knew that he never forgot his old profession at all. Otherwise we would not be here in Frankfurt, but in Nairobi instead. Or even better: on the farm in Ol' Joro Orok. Tonight we are all going to the Shabbat service. Mama wanted me to stay in the room with Max, but Papa laughed and said, "At home in Sohrau the women always brought their babies to the temple." It is strange how we all mean something different when we talk of *home*.

SATURDAY, MAY 10

In spite of the fact that paper is in short supply, I have to write today. Max is talking again. He has just said "Herta." That is the name of the black shepherd dog that belongs to the cook. I am very happy and will try not to speak English or Swahili with Max any more. Mama says that it only confuses him.

MONDAY, MAY 12

Since yesterday it does not get dark until eleven o'clock at night. Double daylight saving time. It means that we go to bed later and have to be hungry longer. Papa calls it the victors' revenge, but I have heard that it is supposed to save electricity. You can go to jail if you use too much.

WEDNESDAY, MAY 21

Papa has been singing "Gaudeamus Igitur" for the past hour, has completely forgotten about being hungry, and has found a fraternity brother. It happened like this: He talked to a (very beautiful) young woman in the yard. She told him that her father had been a member of a college fraternity, but had to leave because he married a woman who was not Jewish and had not brought up his children as Jews. Father immediately knew that the man must have been a member of the *Kartell Convent deutscher Studenten jüdischen Glaubens* (K.C.). His name is Dr. Goldschmidt and he is a physician. He comes to the Gagernstraße every Wednesday. When he was looking for his daughter in the garden, Papa greeted him whistling the K.C. tune. He is going to invite us to his home. For a cup of real coffee (he gets it from one of his patients).

MONDAY, JUNE 2

It is hotter here today than in Nairobi. Mama moans a lot, but she still came to take my place after I had been standing in line for an hour at the grocery store to get milk. We were only able to get eight ounces. Still, it was not a completely bad day. As of today we are getting a newspaper. The *Rundschau* (Frankfurt Review). Victims of racial persecution (that is, us) receive it without having to be on a waiting list. Finally, we do not have to worry about toilet paper anymore. It is a pity that we are not able to get the *Neue Zeitung* (New Post). It is supposed to be much softer.

THURSDAY, JUNE 5

Good news again. The pram we bought in London for Max has arrived. It was sent to the courthouse. Now I don't have to carry Max anymore when we go for walks.

SATURDAY, JUNE 7

Germans are very nosy. Everyone wants to know where I got the beautiful pram, and when I tell them "London," I have to talk on and on. About Africa, our return, etc. Almost all of them then say, "How can one possibly come back to this country?" and keep on asking questions. Many tell me that they once had Jewish friends and were always against Hitler. It embarrasses me.

SUNDAY, JUNE 8

Papa did not watch Max and did not notice that he ran out of the yard. We searched for two hours. Max sat in only his underpants and without shoes on the streetcar tracks in the Wittelsbacher Allee. Luckily, street-cars are not allowed to run on Sundays, and nothing happened.

MONDAY, JUNE 9

We had to go to the police station to be fingerprinted for our identification cards. Mama raged, "Just as under Hitler," but Papa said it was the Americans' fault. Mama later told me that she has been terrified of German officials in uniform ever since Hitler's time. I found the men quite pleasant. One of them gave Max a slice of real white bread. Strange, when people here in Frankfurt speak German, they talk quite differently from us. I have a hard time understanding them.

FRIDAY, JUNE 13

Real joy. We have an apartment. Nuß-Zeil in Eschersheim. Three rooms, a kitchen, and a bath. Papa arrived with the assignment from the housing authority and was so overjoyed that he was unable to eat even the little bit the cook is giving us (it is becoming less and less). Mama says that she needs a maid now.

MONDAY, JUNE 16

A day of tears. When Papa and Mama went to the new apartment this morning, it was occupied. By a Mr. Hitzeroth. He had already moved in on Thursday. The superintendent whispered to Papa that H. is a paper merchant and has bribed the people at the housing authority. Papa does not believe him and says that the whole thing must have been a mistake. German officials cannot be bribed. At any rate, Mr. H. has more than enough paper to give away. I now have five new notebooks (in case I am ever allowed to go to school), but they do not bring me any happiness. After all of us had calmed down somewhat, the cook came by and told us that he could not keep us here much longer.

FRIDAY, JUNE 20

Mama's 39th birthday. Papa painted a cigar box (from Dr. Goldschmidt) and put a gift certificate in it for a maid (to be redeemed when we get an apartment). I gave her a small bowl of raspberries that I picked in the Ostpark. Mrs. L. (she is from Breslau, and she walked from there to Frankfurt) took me there yesterday as a special treat. I think that was really decent because she has a child of her own. Max said "Mama" again for the first time since the boat ride. I taught him.

THURSDAY, JULY 3

When we were standing in line in front of Spannheimer's store, a woman said, out of the blue, "We have to stand here forever while everything is thrown at the Jews." Mama shouted, "Do you think I am standing next to such a damned Nazi shrew out of my own free will? I am Jewish. And if you want to know what has happened to us—our entire family perished." Everyone looked at us but nobody said a word. One woman ran away even though she was far ahead in line. I admire Mama a lot.

WEDNESDAY, JULY 9

Now we really do have an apartment. On David Stempel Street on the other bank of the Main in Sachsenhausen. Again, three rooms, a kitchen, and a bath. At the moment, a former Nazi is still living there with his wife, but he will have to move out by August 1.

FRIDAY, JULY 11

Today Spannheimer first attended to everyone else who came into the store after me. I was starting to get annoyed but then, all of a sudden, he took my bag and put oatmeal, sugar, and a piece of cheese into it. I was so startled that I could hardly thank him. Mr. Spannheimer said that he respects Mama and finds her very courageous. He has only one leg and hates the Nazis. He saw how people were taken from the Jewish hospital. Papa was very happy about this story.

SUNDAY, JULY 13

I finally share a secret with Papa again. When I came into the room today (Mama was having a conversation in the yard), he sat on the balcony with Max on his lap and sang *"Kwenda Safari."* I said *"Jambo bwana"* and we talked for a while without words and then about Kimani and Owuor and the farm. Later Papa sang *"Kwenda Safari"* once more and said, "Your mother does not have to know about this." I felt the way I used to feel as a child again. Only then I did not know that love could even get rid of hunger.

WEDNESDAY, JULY 16

Papa brought the address of a woman from Upper Silesia home from court; she lives in the East Zone, wants to come to the West, and is looking for a position as a maid. Mama instantly wrote to her.

THURSDAY, JULY 17

I got enrolled in the Schiller School. Like our new apartment, it is in Sachsenhausen I am afraid. After all, I am almost fifteen and hardly know how to read, at least not in German.

FRIDAY, JULY 18

A few days ago, Papa told a policeman that in Africa he had always raved to me about cherries and that I still did not know how they tasted. There is no fruit for sale anywhere. Yesterday the policeman brought him a bag of cherries from his garden. When Papa told us this story, he had tears in his eyes and said that nobody had ever been this nice to him in ten years in Africa. Of course, I did not tell him that I thought that cherries were sour and I would rather eat mangoes.

MONDAY, JULY 28

We are not getting the new apartment. The Nazi displayed a certificate saying he had not been a Nazi after all, and he can stay. He is a butcher. Now even Papa is starting to believe in bribery.

MONDAY, AUGUST 4

I was sick all week. Stomach cramps and nausea. Acute appendicitis. But this is not enough to go to the hospital because there are not enough beds. I was glad. Mama applied compresses, and Dr. Goldschmidt came every day. Once he had to treat Papa, too. He had collapsed in the courthouse. Malnutrition. He has lost fifteen pounds. Mama and I have only lost ten. We always go to the train station on Sunday. There is a scale there.

TUESDAY, AUGUST 12

Great excitement. The maid has arrived. Her name is Else Schrell and she suddenly appeared in front of the door with her suitcase. She used a good opportunity to cross the border. Mama was happy. Papa was not. Else will sleep in his bed and he on the balcony. Luckily it is very hot. Now we have to divide the food that is intended for three among five people. But Else has brought along onions. She is from Hochkretscham. That is very close to Leobschütz. The three of them talked far into the night.

SATURDAY, AUGUST 16

Yesterday was the first day of school for me. I do not know where to start. I was terribly scared. It is a miracle that I even found the school. The Schiller School does not exist at all. It is a pile of rubble. The pupils of the Schiller School have to go to the Holbein School. Classes start at two o'clock. I was half an hour early and asked the first girl I saw about the eleventh grade. Luckily, she was in the same class. Her name is Gisela and she instantly wanted to know if I was Catholic or Protestant. I became quite alarmed and said, "I am Jewish." She became even more embarrassed than I was and murmured, "Oh. Excuse me. I only asked because we have religion now." I did not understand her and she said, "Religion class." She was a Protestant and I went with her.

The teacher was very nice to me. Quite different from the English ones, who could not stand new students—especially when they were different from the others. She asked about my last school. I said, "Kenya Girls' High School, Nairobi." It took forever until she understood that I am from Kenya. Then she asked if I had gone to boarding school there. She used the German term "Internat," and I said, "No, only my father was interned." Everyone laughed really hard. I was mortified and am still not quite sure what was supposed to be so funny.

In the second class a rather old teacher came up to me. Her name is Dr. Jauer and she said, "I am very happy to meet you, child." I said the same to her because I thought that this was the German equivalent of "How do you do?" Obviously I was wrong since the girls laughed again. Dr. Jauer did not laugh. She teaches English and read something to the class. I almost giggled. Not even the refugees spoke such poor English at home.

During the other classes I did not understand a word. The German teacher's name is Dr. Dilscher. He was particularly friendly. He asked me about my favorite authors. It seemed that he had never heard of Charles Dickens, William Wordsworth, and Robert Browning.

The girls are incredibly inquisitive. During the break they gathered around me and asked me one question after another. They are all very friendly. And very elegant. Many are wearing skirts made of two different materials and wonderful white knee-high stockings. Most of them have long braids and look like Heidi.

TUESDAY, AUGUST 19

Else is like Aya. She only has to take Max on her lap and he stops crying. She has a big bosom and stays with Max in the evening when we want to go for a walk. Yesterday we even went to the movies. We had to stand in line for the tickets longer than at the bakery, but it was worth it. The movie was called *In Those Days* and was very sad. Mama and I tried to outdo each other crying. I realized once again how good our life had been in Africa.

THURSDAY, AUGUST 21

The girl I like best at school is named Hannelore. Everyone calls her Puck, though, because she once played the role in *A Midsummer Night's Dream*. She wears beautiful clothes because she has a grandmother, a mother, and two aunts, all of whom can sew. They make blouses and skirts from old curtains and even shoes from uniform jackets. Puck always tells me what the teachers previously used to say.

Yesterday, for instance, the headmistress had me called into her office and said, "You will have to let me know if any girl is rude to you. I am not going to tolerate that. The Jews have suffered enough." I only stared at her silently. No teacher would have thought of anything like that in an English school. I was quite impressed and immediately told Puck the whole story. She started laughing uncontrollably and reported that previously the headmistress had firmly punished anyone who said "Good morning" instead of "Heil Hitler." I think I will never be able to fully understand life here. Everything is so terribly complicated. I did not talk about any of this at home. Papa does not want to hear this kind of thing and Mama would only have called him a fool again.

FRIDAY, AUGUST 22

Else came home crying. When standing in line at the butcher's a man had said to her, "You gypsies from the East are just what we have been waiting for here. You had nothing to eat at home and here you want to steal the little bit that we have left." Mama, who likes Else very much because she always addresses her with Papa's title, was furious and consoled her very nicely. Else's father had been one of the richest farmers in Hochkretscham. Else, therefore, knows a lot about plants. She often goes to the Ostpark very early in the morning and picks stinging nettles that she uses in a salad. They do not taste too bad and even take away the hunger. Only Papa always says, "It is a good thing that Owuor cannot see that his *bwana* has turned into an ox that eats grass."

SATURDAY, AUGUST 23

Trouble again. Else hung the diapers out to dry on the balcony. She did not know that one is not supposed to do that here on a Shabbat and, of course, we did not think of it either. The superintendent's wife was enraged. Papa became furious as well and shouted, "My son also poops on a Shabbat." The entire nursing home is talking about it.

MONDAY, SEPTEMBER 1

During the break, we get school lunches from the Americans. Mainly noodles in chocolate sauce or tomato paste. I do not eat much of it and always take the leftovers home for Max. Papa does not like me doing that because I am weighing less and less while Max is gaining more and more. The long way to school is partly to blame for that—one and a half hours there, and one and a half hours back. There is only one bridge leading to Sachsenhausen and you have to walk across it. My fellow students are lucky because they all live in Sachsenhausen. I would be there, too, if the Nazi had left the apartment.

FRIDAY, SEPTEMBER 5

Papa's 43rd birthday. Only Else had a present for him (blackberries from the Ostpark). I was sad that I had nothing, but he said, "You do not know how much you give me every day." I think he means that I never complain about our life here. That makes me happy. We still have our secret and sing songs to Max in Swahili when we are alone with him. I never would have thought that Papa knows so many songs.

FRIDAY, SEPTEMBER 19

My 15th birthday. Mama gave me an elephant-hair bracelet for good luck. She bought it in Nairobi especially for me and had been hiding it all this time. Papa gave me *The Old Curiosity Shop*. In English! I had no idea that he knows how much Dickens means to me, especially this book. He did not want to tell me how he got a hold of this treasure, but when he went to court, Mama told me. He got the book from a judge in exchange for his tobacco ration for the next month. I will never forget this birthday and my parents' love. It is too bad that we cannot all live together (just the four of us) on an island. In Lake Naivasha!

Everybody wished me a happy birthday at school. I could not really enjoy it all that much though, because Puck, unfortunately, has made sure that I now know exactly which girls were previously enamored with the Nazis. It makes me feel awkward. This time last year it never would have occurred to me that I would have such thoughts some day. We were still in Nairobi then. Owuor had baked the little rolls that he was so proud of and I did not know what hunger was. It all seems to be years ago now.

SATURDAY, SEPTEMBER 20

The people in the nursing home constantly ask Papa to come to prayers. They need ten men before they can begin the service and there are never enough men. Papa considers it an obligation of honor and always goes even though he complains.

WEDNESDAY, SEPTEMBER 24

This week we can get only 900 calories on the food ration cards, but luckily there is a special addition from the Jewish community. A quarter pound of fat, one pound processed foodstuffs, 200 grams milk powder or one can of milk, and 200 grams egg powder. All of a sudden, people who were never Jewish claim to have been persecuted by the Nazis. They are called milk-can Jews. The K.C. in America (Papa's old fraternity) wrote that they would send us a CARE package even though this is against the regulations because Papa voluntarily returned to Germany. They are going to make an exception because of Max and me. Papa has not been this furious in a long time. He immediately wrote that he was not about to accept any charity. Mama tore up the letter. A huge fight ensued. I think Mama is right. Pride does not fill your stomach.

THURSDAY, OCTOBER 2
Even though it is still warm, everyone is starting to talk about winter. Papa is afraid that he is not going to be able to sleep on the balcony much longer.

MONDAY, OCTOBER 6
There is a Jewish camp in Zeilsheim. Puck told me about it. Groceries are sold on the black market there. I think she goes there with her mother. When I asked Papa why we could not do the same, he got really angry. A German judge cannot do anything like that. Unfortunately, a German judge cannot do anything but be proud of being called "Your Honor." Last week a man wanted to give Papa a pound of bacon, but a German judge has to have integrity. The flint stones, which we had brought from London and could exchange for groceries, are still in the suitcase. A German judge does not make deals. I am the only one in my grade whose father is a German judge and who has no relatives who live in the country. This is worse than being a Jewish girl in an English school.

THURSDAY, OCTOBER 16
Three days ago some German Jews who have returned from Shanghai came to live here. They were already as thin and pale as we are now when they arrived, but they are much more courageous than we are and constantly complain about everything. Mama admires them a lot and says, "At least they have elbows and do not say yes to everything." They immediately received clothing from the community and told everyone that they were not going to live in the nursing home for any length of time. The cook threatened us once again. He is not going to keep us any longer. But Dr. Alschoff says we can stay until we get an apartment. Else suggested that we slaughter one of the cook's sheep. She knows how to do that because she comes from a farm; of course, Papa was against it (German judge).

THURSDAY, OCTOBER 23

In spite of thirty-three spelling errors, the German teacher marked my essay with "You are making remarkable progress." I was very happy because German is the only subject I really enjoy. Dr. Dilscher is also the only one who understands that English schools are quite different from German ones. He was not surprised that I had never heard of Schiller and Goethe before I came here. The French teacher acts as if her ears are hurting when I read aloud. The French we spoke in Nairobi was pronounced very differently from here. The same is true for Latin. And we did not even study physics, chemistry, and biology. In addition to German, I like history. The teacher was actually quite interested when I said that the Seven Years' War had taken place in India and Canada. All my life, I worried because I used to be the best student in my grade and attracted unpleasant attention for being overambitious among my English classmates. That will never happen here, but I am not happy, often even quite depressed. I am also sad because the girls consider the blue cardboard case, which I use to carry my school utensils and the glass jar for the school lunch, incredibly funny and will not stop talking about it. We did not have schoolbags in Kenya, but I am tired of explaining this over and over again.

WEDNESDAY, OCTOBER 29

We have been assigned another apartment. For November 15, in the Höhenstraße. Three rooms, a kitchen, a half-bath, and furniture. The proprietor lives there. He was a Nazi and is supposed to leave. We do not believe it. At least we will not be disappointed this time. Mama said, "I hear the words, but lack the faith." That is supposed to be by Goethe.

MONDAY, NOVEMBER 3

The most beautiful day since we arrived in Frankfurt. When I came back from school, Mama had picked up a parcel from America at the customs office. Her friend from Breslau, Ilse Schottländer, sent it. A pound of coffee, ten packages of pudding mix, two chocolate bars, two pounds of flour, a tin of cocoa, four cans of corned beef, a pound of sugar, a package of oatmeal, three tins of sardines, a can of cheese, a can of pineapple, three pairs of pants for Max, and two blouses for me. We put everything on the table, sat in front of it, and cried (even Papa).

SATURDAY, NOVEMBER 8

We visited the Wedels in the Höhenstraße. They are quite nice and do not look like Nazis at all. They are supposed to move into a couple of attic rooms. Their furniture does not fit into those and so we can use it. Mama and I are sure that this is only a trick, but Papa says Mr. Wedel works for the gas company and most likely does not have anything with which he could bribe the people at the housing authority. Who knows? . . .

FRIDAY, NOVEMBER 14

Papa went to see Mrs. Wedel again, and all of us are full of hope and stomachaches. We are supposed to move tomorrow. The cook all of a sudden became quite friendly when he found out and sent us four portions of the Shabbat meal, even though we only used to get the midday meal till now. If I am not here at this time tomorrow, I will believe in miracles again. And I will start praying again, too.

3

KARL WEDEL WAS A MID-LEVEL EMPLOYEE at the municipal gas company. He was hardworking and frugal, and he liked to tinker around in his free time. As long as the situation had permitted, he had built German castles and fortresses with matchsticks and with the same kind of meticulousness that his superiors valued in his work. For most of his life he had relied more on the sense of reality that his courageous wife displayed than on the promises and pressures of the times. Up to the lethal attacks on Frankfurt, he had never been interested more than absolutely necessary in events that he felt he could not change anyway. After the war he found it all the easier to concentrate on his own affairs because that attitude seemed to be the only one feasible for people who did not want to stand accused of being too intensely involved in politics again.

The eviction notice came at a time when he no longer expected it. The postwar period had brought general deprivations like hunger and a short supply of electricity and coal but had demanded fewer sacrifices of the Wedels than of other people in similar circumstances. They also did not have to deal with any of the bothersome acknowledgements of guilt.

Appearing in court for a denazification trial had not been easy for Karl Wedel, who had a hard time standing up for his own interests and found it even more difficult to talk about himself. Before the trial he had been in a state of permanent anxiety. Yet the outcome had not been entirely unsatisfactory. He had been categorized as highly incriminated because of his early entry into the party, which had been influenced more by his wife's urgent pleas than by the definitely persistent and unmistakably threatening recommendations of his superiors at work. But in early 1947, because of a shortage of experienced and qualified people, his place of employment had been able to get special permission for him to keep working at the same level as those of his colleagues who, through clever corrections to their life's histories, had attained the desired status of nominal party members.

The order to give up his apartment at such a late time seemed too harsh a punishment for a man who, even considering the new democratic ideas, had never exposed himself to criticism. Once again his wife turned out to be the stroke of luck and stabilizing force in a series of circumstances that he felt were as unfortunate as unjust.

In contrast to him, she had not been blinded by the apparent calm and was prepared. Through connections that Karl Wedel was unable to fathom and as a municipal employee would have been unable to endorse, Frieda had had the two attic rooms finished in such a way that they were ready to be occupied at any time. In spite of this, and because he knew that his tenants were not exposed to an equal fate, he considered the planned move of the returning emigrant Redlich family into his apartment a personal defeat.

He would have felt less oppressed if lodgers had been assigned to one of his three rooms as was customary for the times. Then he could have talked about this daily sacrifice and could have complained without any fear of the misunderstandings that were so typical for the new times. Also, he would not have become, as he imagined he was now, the secret laughing stock of people who had never acted any differently from him but had been luckier in the current so-called democratic times.

When it became obvious that all protests to the housing authorities were futile and might in the future even lead to incriminations that were difficult to predict, Frieda Wedel went back to her old habit of accepting the inevitable and making the best of a bad situation. Her experiences as the eldest of five children with a prematurely widowed mother; the deprivations of her youth during World War I; her relationship with a constantly undecided husband; her dealings with two stepdaughters who, despite all her efforts, had remained strangers; and, above all, the long dispute over the inheritance of the house in the Höhenstraße, had at every turn in her life kept alive a natural talent that enabled her to come to an arrangement with fate without worsening the situation through her own actions.

When the inescapable became a fact, Frieda Wedel made the final preparations for the two attic rooms with the same energy that she had invested as a young woman in fixing up their first apartment. She mobilized, quite successfully, the hope that the uninvited guests might disappear as quickly as they had come. There were the corresponding rumors, in this case quite encouraging, that the Jews in Germany were sitting on packed suitcases anyway, and were only waiting to move to countries where they were not the cause of such problems.

Even though Frieda Wedel considered it an irony of fate that she could not fully understand—why she of all people had to relinquish her apartment to a Jewish family returned from emigration—she still found it a blessing that she personally did not have anything to reproach herself for in this regard. Even during those years when it would have been understandable and opportune, she had never taken part in any of the events that today, rightly so, were designated as cruel.

Apart from the Isenbergs, who had disappeared suddenly and had owned a house in the Rothschildallee, which she had been able to see from her window, and the unfortunate wife of the mailman Öttcher, to whom Frieda Wedel had given bread and sausages a few times when it was dark and even after the woman had been forced to wear the yellow star, Frieda Wedel did not know any Jews. Yet, she was apprehensive about meeting the Redlichs. People like Frieda, who were interested in current affairs, could not be as uninhibited at the prospect of Jewish tenants as of people whose customs and reactions were predictable.

The first meeting with Walter Redlich was unexpectedly pleasant for Frieda Wedel. He had not, as she had anticipated and feared, confronted her as a man who was certain of his rights, but instead had acted rather shy and almost as if he had trouble with the fact that he was driving her out of her apartment. Two weeks later, Frieda Wedel was satisfied to find that the favorable impression of the first encounter of two such disparate worlds had not been false. On the contrary.

Frieda Wedel liked the Redlichs whether she was pleased about it or not, whether her acquaintances understood her or not, whether she could explain her feelings to herself or not. It was not only that she considered a university-educated man, who would not have rented an apartment in the Höhenstraße in normal times, an enrichment for the middle-class housing community. The Redlichs obviously had even less than most people although there was all that talk that Jews were doing well again. Frieda Wedel was touched by the Redlichs though she was unable to account for her emotions and softheartedness, which at the beginning of autumn, and in view of imminent problems like cold and hunger, seemed ridiculous and not at all in step with the times.

Walter Redlich was reserved, friendly, obviously grateful for every conversation in the staircase, open to suggestions, and surprisingly receptive to the situation of the Wedels. His modesty and the totally unexpected pleasure that even after moving in he still talked about "your apartment," as if he were aware of the temporary nature of their relationship, made this clear in an almost delightful way.

Jettel Redlich was to Mrs. Wedel the embodiment of the lady she would have liked to be, and she admired Jettel without reservation. She found that baffling. Jettel's helplessness in practical matters, her thoroughly engaging lethargy, and her absolutely astonishing naiveté whenever an emergency had to be faced with experience and ingenuity, held for Mrs. Wedel the kind of special appeal of a culture that had disappeared completely from the times and was longed for. The oddity alone that Jettel had a maid in a three-room apartment and had told Mrs. Wedel, during their first conversation, that she had never been without household help in all her life and could not be either, impressed Mrs. Wedel. She also liked the fact that Jettel was not aloof or even arrogant, but was always ready for a conversation and would then talk about her life in Africa in the same matter-of-fact way as Mrs. Wedel about her garden plot in nearby Seckbach. That she was able to help this bird of paradise with her practical advice gave a boost to her self-confidence, which otherwise certainly would have been undermined by the forced expropriation.

There was more. Frieda Wedel envied the Redlichs' family life, which she had not been allowed to experience in this way. Even though Walter and Jettel became so loud at times during their fights that Jettel's accusations and Walter's equally violent answers could be heard in the two attic rooms, Mrs. Wedel could sense the bond that, as she had already heard before, was typical for Jewish families. Mrs. Wedel was utterly fascinated by the fact that Regina came home immediately after school, did not meet her friends, pushed the pram every afternoon to the Günthersburg Park, and almost insisted on taking care of her brother, who would not only say "Mama" to his mother but often also to Regina.

In spite of the happiness to have escaped the nursing home and with that the malice of the cook, the caretaker, and the fellow lodgers from Shanghai, Walter, Jettel, and Regina found adjusting once again to new surroundings more difficult than they had originally envisioned. With the cold weather, which set in very suddenly at the end of November after the steaming summer, came the worries about coal, restrictions in the use of electricity and gas, and above all the lack of winter clothes.

Jettel alone was all set with her black wool coat from Breslau. She had only kept it during the hard times of the emigration because winter coats could not be sold in Kenya anymore after the beginning of the war when the rich British farmers' wives did not need them any longer to travel to England.

Walter's gray winter coat from the British military had been stolen on the first cold day at court. He was left with a dustcoat that was too big for him and he got so cold in that his old rheumatism acted up again. He often pondered if his pains were bothering him more than his hunger, and he did his best to hide his state from Jettel and Regina.

Regina got an old ski outfit of her mother's that was almost completely new because it had only been worn once during her honeymoon in the Riesengebirge, but it was so old-fashioned that it stood out as strange even in destitute postwar Frankfurt. On the first cold day she came home with frozen hands; for the rest of the winter she had to protect herself from the elbow down with woolen cloths, and she felt like the tattered men on crutches whom she met on the bridge. On rainy and stormy days she would remember how a pregnant Jettel had been sitting under a tree in the glowing heat of Nairobi, the rains long overdue, and had said, "You can protect yourself from the cold, but not from the heat." The anguish of her memories discouraged her even more than the realization that she did not have the strength to defend herself against her despair.

Else still had a winter coat that she had bought before the war in Leobschütz, but no shoes except for a pair of sandals that she had worn all summer long in the Gagernstraße. This only became evident when she refused over and over again to leave the house, which led to the first serious conflict with Jettel, who did not want to stand in line in front of the stores while Regina was in school.

Walter's old military boots, which he had not turned in during the demobilization, saved the situation. Else even wore them in the kitchen, where only the coal stove, which because of a lack of electricity was also used for cooking, was heated. Walter taught her to say, "A present from King George" and her trouble with the pronunciation amused the whole family during their most dismal hours.

Without Mrs. Wedel the mood would have plummeted even more precipitously than the thermometer. She put in the good word that was necessary for people without connections with the coal dealer so that he at least delivered the fuel that they were entitled to on their ration coupons. She revealed to Jettel the addresses of halfway sympathetic merchants who on rare occasions would surrender some articles against clothing coupons, and she talked to the neighborhood greengrocer. Without the encouragement of a woman who was well informed about her past, the owner would not have even surrendered turnips, let alone a potato, to the Redlichs.

Regina not only learned how to knit from Mrs. Wedel, but also how to unravel old sweaters from her supply, use the wool over again, and furnish her brother with sweaters, caps, and mittens. Else got such useful recipes for turnips from her that she only occasionally still muttered, "At home only our pigs used to eat these."

The axe, cooking utensils, blankets, needles and mending yarn, ink and the little bag for soap scraps, mason jars for grocery shopping, little zinc tub for bathing Max, clothespins, coal shovel, pail, broom, and all those other things for daily use, for which politically and racially persecuted people got special coupons, but that could not be found in any store, came from the Wedels' well-equipped household.

In the beginning Mrs. Wedel was confounded by her compassion, but after that more by the fact that just at a time when the only important thing seemed to be one's own survival, she was, in spite of her tough sense for the practical, unable to combat her continually growing readiness to help.

It was not, as most of her neighbors and acquaintances surmised and sarcastically remarked, that Frieda Wedel had recognized the signs of the time and sensed personal advantages when she took the obligation to right wrongs literally, which was publicly endorsed but usually considered superfluous and burdensome. She just had not been prepared for the fact that these people, rumored to be doing better than everyone else, were in even more dire circumstances than the many envious people who believed in their own rumors.

For Hans Puttfarken's visit, Mrs. Wedel, because she was impressed by the fact that the head of a ministerial department from Wiesbaden was going to sit on her sofa, not only contributed the recipe for the cake made of oats, artificial cocoa, and honey, but also the cake mold and an apple from her garden. The result was a personal triumph for Jettel. She wondered if the Puttfarkens might like the taste of a piece of the gray cake mound, which had luckily absorbed the aroma of the roasted apple peel, or if a man in high office like Puttfarken might be used to better food than a judge and would, therefore, have to force down every bite. This question occupied her even more than the anxiously anticipated reunion itself.

After Puttfarken's letter to Nairobi announcing Walter's appointment as a judge in Frankfurt, there had only been one further contact. Walter and Jettel had received a postcard to welcome them to Frankfurt, and this gesture had actually hurt them more than it pleased them. The few sentences had been more formal than friendly, even stiff, just the way the two of them remembered Puttfarken from his time as a judge in Leobschütz and quite different from his heartfelt, open letter to Kenya that Walter for a long time had called "the beginning of my third life."

"Jettel," Walter had said when he brought the card home from court, "we have to get used to the fact that a mere judge is only a nebbish for a man in high office." It was one of those rare moments since arriving in Frankfurt that Jettel agreed with her husband.

Now Hans Puttfarken stood in their living room: tall, blond, hardly changed at first glance, only thinner and with the gray skin tone that corresponded to the shabbiness of the times, in a jacket that was too big and a shirt that was too loose. He was as embarrassed as he had been when he had come to bid them farewell in Leobschütz and had been afraid it could be rumored that he was still visiting Jewish friends.

He moved his hand as if he just had to straighten out his hair, which prevented him from taking a clear first look to check and collect himself.

But then he surrendered utterly to the surprise that Jettel was still the beautiful woman he remembered with the thick, midnight-black hair, the perfect skin, and that trace of discontent in her soft brown eyes, which had always made her seem capricious and, in a disquieting way, desirable to him. He was searching for words to tell her about those of his emotions he could disclose, but his throat was dry and his tongue was heavy.

He wanted to draw his wife, whose unease he could sense even though she was standing behind him, into the circle of mutual expectations, but he did not succeed in that either. Then he noticed Regina with her sunken cheeks, but still not without the kind of harmony that he was no longer able to interpret, and a happily crowing baby on her stomach who was clapping his hands and blowing tiny bubbles of spit from his mouth. Relieved, because he was too shy to embrace the father, Hans Puttfarken closely hugged the laughing package in the gray terry towel.

"Too much has happened," he murmured.

"Too much," Walter agreed, relieved that the emotions of the moment made them mute.

They sat down at the table. Else served the malt coffee from the well-traveled coffee pot with the floral pattern that Owuor had once loved and bathed in the sun of Ol' Joro Orok. Regina saw a black arm glisten, heard the shuffle of bare feet on the thick wooden floor boards, and smelled the sweetness of Owuor's skin. Startled and hurriedly, she swallowed the salt of the memory before it could get into her eyes.

Mrs. Puttfarken, with tired eyes marked by suffering, her hands shaking, which she tried to suppress in vain, praised the cake and timidly stroked Max. Jettel smiled, but the uneasiness, frozen onto the rigid faces like ice-flowers to a window, remained an unwelcome companion for people who wanted to recapture the years but did not know how.

Max reached for his cup with one hand and with the other for a small pin that gave a shimmer of light to Mrs. Puttfarken's dark brown dress, when Regina said in the best Silesian dialect, "Careful with the mug!"

"Good God, Regina speaks Silesian," Puttfarken exclaimed. "Just think about it; she grows up in the bush and speaks Silesian."

His laughter reminded Regina of the long buried echo that was warmed by the sun in the mountains around Ol' Joro Orok. She readied herself once more to fight her tears. When she opened her eyes, she saw that Puttfarken was still laughing. Her father, too.

Once the hearts had been opened so suddenly and in such an unexpected way, the words could not be held back anymore. They tumbled with unrestrained force from the silence; even the briquettes, wrapped in moist newspaper in the oven and already given up for the day, seemed to struggle for new life. The wind shook the windows but its voice had lost its fury and bitterness.

Puttfarken spoke of the anxiety and fear about his Jewish wife during the years when every day was a renewed gift and yet at the same time an extension of the anguish, of his call to forced labor, of the misery of the flight from Upper Silesia, and of the difficulties and hopes of a new beginning. His voice had become calm, but not his eyes.

Jettel and Walter fought about Africa. She talked about the farm and Nairobi, of friends and joys she had to leave behind; he spoke about the despair of those years in a foreign country.

Jettel said, "Walter was always a dreamer."

"And you only liked to be where we were not at the moment," Walter reproached her.

Hans Puttfarken smiled faintly and said, "The two of you always fought with such gusto. How nice that that is still the case."

Regina was trying to understand the word "humiliation" that her father spat out in the same way she had once spat out the hot berries of the pepperbush, but her thoughts first went on a safari that she did not want to start and, after that, her ears traveled into a country where the words that she did not know could no longer bother her.

Later she sat with her brother, who warmed her limbs the way the dog Rummler had done once, asleep on her lap, and Mrs. Puttfarken in the darkest corner of the room that was illuminated by only one light bulb. The day turned out to be a good one because Mrs. Puttfarken wanted to know everything about Africa, tried to pronounce Owuor's name, and while doing so laughed in such a way that her eyes changed color. She was even interested in the guava tree fairy that had accompanied Regina when she was still a child and had been allowed to believe in fairies.

"Do you know Swahili?" Mrs. Puttfarken asked. "My son really wanted me to ask you that. He is fifteen, too. Just like you."

"I can say everything in Swahili," Regina assured her.

"How do you say," Mrs. Puttfarken whispered and laughed a second time, "I hate the Germans?"

"I do not know the word for hate," Regina perplexedly realized. "I think we did not hate at home. I was only allowed to hate the Nazis," she remembered, "never the Germans."

"Lucky child," Mrs. Puttfarken sighed. "I learned to hate and I cannot forgive." Her eyes were very small in large hollows. Her hands were trembling again.

"I hate the Germans, too," Jettel said.

Else carried the dishes into the kitchen and did not return, even though the Puttfarkens asked for her when they were leaving and called out, "See you in Hochkretscham."

Regina put Max to bed by herself. She softly sang the song of the jackal that has lost its shoe, waited until Max was asleep, crept out of the small room, and went looking for Else. She found her sitting without any color in her face, with her long blonde hair matted and wet, and her small eyes red from crying at the kitchen table. Her shoulders were shaking.

Regina tried stroking her but Else's body was as limp as the top of a thorn acacia that has been broken by a storm, and she reacted as little to the tenderness of the touch as her ears responded to fearfully whispered questions. Regina tore the door to the living room open and called for her parents. "Else, what on earth is the matter?" Jettel shouted, alarmed. "What has happened?"

"Who hurt you?" Walter asked.

Else clutched her hands together and started to cry again. When she was finally able to speak between two bouts of crying, she sobbed, "My father." Later she screamed, "They beat him to death. Like an animal."

Walter was very pale when he asked, "Who?"

"Why?" Jettel asked. "Why your father, of all people, Else?"

It was almost midnight when Else—wrapped in Mrs. Wedel's blanket and supplied with malt coffee that Jettel warmed up again and again and held out to her—was again able to control her body and voice.

"The Poles beat my father to death," she said and stared at the stove. "They came to the farm, dragged him outside, and killed him."

"Why?" Regina asked.

"Because he was a German," Walter said.

They went to bed in silence. Regina tried to revive the old incantation to protect her against terrifying images, but it had not been able to survive the long journey and had lost its power. The words, and above all the devils that she had tried to kill with the balm of her childhood days, mocked her like a warrior who meets an unarmed opponent and is not satisfied with the arrow alone from a taut bow.

From her parents' bedroom she heard the first, still-muted sounds that preceded the war, then she heard her father say, very clearly, "If you hate all Germans, do not forget Else either."

Jettel's voice, full of the bewilderment that Regina loved in her mother and would never be able to understand, said, "But not our Else. I do not hate her."

"But you are allowed to hate Mrs. Wedel," Walter said. "She was even a Nazi."

"I will not have anything said against Mrs. Wedel. Not against her! Where would we be without her?" Jettel angrily asked.

Walter's laughter, strong enough to bounce against the wall, and not losing any of its sharpness in the process, reached Regina's ears a fraction of a second before she was sure that she had been wrong. The old magic of the God Mungu, whom she had been forced to leave, was not dead. Only Mungu dried tears before they hardened into salt and turned them into laughter.

4

DISTRICT COURT PRESIDENT KARL MAAS was an exceptional individual. He was pleasant toward everyone, but also suspicious—without letting his distrust become offensively obvious—of people who considered it opportunistic to vie for his friendship too quickly. He was neither taken in by continual complaints about the present nor by people's constant compulsion to prove their innocence in the past. He used the kind of straightforward language that was considered typical for the comfortably simple and unaffected way of life in the old Frankfurt. Even in February 1948, when provisions had become as meager as never before, Maas appeared as well nourished as in peace times.

That a person could manage to look healthy, well-fed, and above all as if he were able to concentrate on things other than butter and ration cards for meat, and could even be content, gave hope. It could not be overlooked that Maas had very nourishing connections and obviously also the courage to use them in spite of his office. Contrary to the common practice of envying others' well being, no one begrudged the corpulent district court president his satisfying sense for practical affairs. In addition to his sense of humor, which was always down-to-earth but never crude, and his quick answers that balanced sharpness with wit, it was his ample girth—so atypical in these times of need—that actually contributed to his popularity.

All of this made many people forget how strongly the events of the Nazi period had shaped Maas. The general consensus at court was that he had been let go from the legal profession because of his courage and his unwillingness to reach a compromise with a regime that he had recognized for what it was very early on. But in reality he had a Jewish wife whom he only knew to be safe when the American troops marched into Frankfurt.

The humiliations he had suffered and the fear of the long years without hope made Karl Maas sensitive to the fate of people who had been forced to endure the same shame of defenselessness; since their first meeting, he had felt connected to Walter. At first he had only been touched by the younger man's disheartened demeanor, his palpable fear of not being able to fulfill his old job after years in exile, and the almost frightening eagerness of the outcast to be an equal among equals again.

But when Karl Maas realized that Walter had the same kind of personal courage as he did, and that he reacted temperamentally and very harshly to consciously insulting or even involuntarily voiced slights from his colleagues, the spontaneously felt sympathy turned into a relationship that younger men certainly would have interpreted as friendship.

At first they took every meeting in the corridors of the courthouse as an excuse for a conversation, but very soon they no longer left those encounters to chance. Beyond the obligations of his office and considerations for a man who was missing ten years of professional experience, Maas felt responsible for Walter. Walter, in turn, was able to speak with Karl Maas about his plans and hopes without his usual fear of revealing too much about his feelings and sometimes even about the despair that in his darker moments, he felt as foreign in Frankfurt as he had in Africa.

The two men only met twice outside of the court: once at the Maases' apartment, once at the Redlichs' in the Höhenstraße. Both invitations turned out to be just an oppressive exchange of civilities. It was obvious that Mrs. Maas was irritated by Jettel's complaints and helplessness and especially by the persistence of a woman who put strangers in the position of a referee in her domestic squabbles. The daughters, too, even though they were almost the same age, did not have much in common. The Maases' daughter, robust, athletic, and sociable, was unable to relate to Regina's reserved behavior, her seriousness, and her concern for her little brother, a feeling that was unfamiliar to an only child. She did not leave any doubt that she had no intention of following her father's recommendation to accept Regina into her circle or even become friends with her.

The bond between the two men became even stronger without the restraints of a social etiquette that Maas would have considered a hindrance. Walter gave up the habit of using the warm stove in Maas's office as an excuse for his frequent visits. Maas no longer disguised his conversations with Walter as business-related. It was only natural therefore that Maas was the first one Walter told that he did not want to be a judge any longer than absolutely necessary. He had expected objections, even feared that Maas would think him ungrateful, but did not delay the conversation once he had made up his mind.

But Karl Maas only said, "I am not surprised."

"Why?"

"You are not born to be an employee."

"I had enough time to learn, but I did not succeed. I want to be free. In all those stolen years I dreamed of being an attorney again. I never thought of being a judge."

"Have you told your wife yet?"

"Not yet. She hates change."

"Wait till it is all settled then," Maas advised him. "It is not easy these days to get established as an attorney. Office space is in even shorter supply than bread."

Walter was relieved. His plans were not yet concrete, almost illusions still, but it had bothered him not to tell Maas about them. The conversation seemed to him a first, important step toward the kind of freedom that he was, in spite of all efforts, unable to find as a judge. For the first time since his arrival in Frankfurt, he gave in to the pleasure of his true dreams. He saw himself sitting in his own office, reading files, composing briefs, dictating letters, and giving advice to clients: an independent man who is only accountable to himself—and has finally reached his goal.

Walter was so occupied with his fantasies and his flight into the future, which all of a sudden seemed no longer so far out of reach, that he only slowly became aware of a silhouette in the corridor in front of his room. He was able to make out, quite clearly, two rusty pails next to a big suitcase that was held together by some string. The bigger pail was filled with potatoes, the smaller one with onions. The thought of a plate heaped with home fries full of fat and smothered in a brown onion gravy came quickly and uninvited. It tortured Walter's nose and tormented his stomach, which immediately reacted with cramps; anxiously he tried to fight off the yearning for steaming bowls in a cozy kitchen.

Walter imagined in too much detail, with too much pleasure, and for too long how he would feel if he were ever full enough again to leave leftovers on his plate. He only noticed that the man with the pails had gotten up when he saw that the stocky figure in the gray coat was no longer sitting on the chair in front of his room. After some time, in which Walter once again only thought of fried potatoes, he realized that the man stretched his body, lifted his head, and slowly put one foot in front of the other. He advanced three steps toward Walter and stood still.

Only his gray hair, strangely light in the dark corridor, seemed to move; it stood upright and crowded together like young plants that stubbornly push out of the ground before their time, on a head that seemed especially big and angular and in an almost bizarre way familiar to Walter. The veil in front of his eyes became thick and the pictures that he allowed to get through ambushed him with a suddenness that rushed his memory through the years. Walter was able to see clearly now that the man had a red face and arms with powerful hands that he stretched out to him. It was the voice, so hard and yet so incredibly soft, so long gone and yet never forgotten, that made Walter run.

"Dr. Redlich," the voice said, "do you still recognize me?"

Walter swayed as he reached for the gray coat, but he did not fall when the flame of recognition started to burn his body. The rough cloth chafed his face and caught the tears that started to flow. He made no attempt to defend himself. The happiness that flooded him made him blind and mute, and yet through the emotional upheaval he very clearly heard his own deafening scream.

"Oh, my God," Walter shouted. "Greschek. Josef Greschek from Leobschütz."

He registered, even though his head and heart were already racing backward into the past, how the doors around him opened and his colleagues rushed into the corridor, perturbed and uncomprehending; he felt their astonishment without seeing anyone but the one whose picture had accompanied him for so long.

Walter could not take his eyes off Greschek. He pushed him through the corridor, shook him, clapped him on the shoulder, grabbed his gray mop of hair, and stroked every line in the face that he pulled close to his own again and again. When Walter, after a while in which he only heard the beating of his own heart and the rattle of his breath, was finally able to at least control his hands, he let go of the gray coat, ran to the door of his room, took a pail into each hand, clanged them together, and hurried back to Greschek.

"Greschek from Leobschütz," Walter shouted into the line of curiosity and disapproving bewilderment in front of each room. "We are both from Leobschütz. Take a good look at the man who was not afraid to come to a Jewish attorney up to the last day. He accompanied me all the way to Genoa when I had to emigrate and not even a dog would take a piece of bread from me anymore."

"The onions and potatoes are for you, Dr. Redlich," Greschek said. "I brought them from Marke. You know that I made off to the Harz. I wrote that to you in Africa. Did you ever get my letter over there?"

"Oh yes, Greschek. You cannot imagine what that day was like. We cried like children. Before that we did not even know if you were still alive."

"The Missus, too? She cried, too?"

"Yes. She, too."

"That is nice, the way you said that," Greschek smiled. "I sometimes dreamed of that."

The reunion made it impossible for the two men to express their thoughts. They walked from the court to the Höhenstraße past ruins and black walls, wheelbarrows, trams, and leafless trees with contours that in the light rain of the afternoon seemed deceptively subdued. As soon as the two friends stood still, they looked at each other and simultaneously shook their heads. Greschek was carrying both pails and, grumbling, repeatedly refused Walter's attempts to help him. "A man like you does not lug potatoes."

Walter kept on saying, "That I live to see this."

He stayed on the stairs and had Greschek wait alone in front of the apartment till the door was opened. A plate fell from Jettel's hand, and she heard the high sound of her own voice at the same time as the hollow sound of the broken dish. She screamed, "Greschek!" She sobbed and laughed as she opened her arms, and she pulled Greschek close and danced through the kitchen with him—the way she had once danced with Martin at Ol' Joro Orok when the friend of their youth had come from South Africa and had released her and Walter for two unforgotten weeks from the trauma of abandonment.

Later, still reeling from the shock of the encounter, Jettel insisted on preparing the fried potatoes, which Else had already peeled and salted with her tears.

"My husband likes them just the way my mother used to make them," she said and bent over the cut onions when she started to feel the pressure in her eyes.

Greschek's tempestuous welcome also reminded Regina of Martin and her first, long-buried, but never forgotten love. She sat in the kitchen and was unable to stop the journey into the good days because her nose had already started to rule her head. The images became clearer with every piece of onion that was thrown into the hot fat. She saw Owuor standing in the kitchen; she watched his arm with the gleaming skin move the pan, heard the sound of his voice when he sang, and felt his breath that formed small circles in the smoke.

"I never realized," she sniffled, "that Greschek really exists."

"Greschek," Walter said and bit into a piece of raw onion, "is the embodiment of the decent German for me."

"Then you have not met many decent people in Frankfurt yet, Dr. Redlich," Greschek said. "I was not decent, only not as bad as others."

Before it got dark they sat at the table, Greschek between Jettel and Walter, a little embarrassed and even more awkward in his movements than at other times. He had traveled for three days by train, had to defend his pails for a very long time at the border between the occupation zones, and now he was distressed that he had not listened to his wife, Grete, and had not taken a fresh shirt.

"The lard was more important," he said and put the knife into his mouth.

"Man, Greschek, can you imagine that I am full for the first time since we arrived in Frankfurt?"

"Yes," Greschek answered. "I only have to look at all of you to imagine that. Miss Regina is not going to survive much longer."

As soon as Regina wiped her brother's greasy hands, he would put them back into the dish. He had to stand up on the chair to reach the mountain of home fries and, bursting with happiness, was looking for fresh prey while he was still chewing.

"Regina, don't let him eat too much. He is going to be sick. A two-year-old cannot take that much."

"Let him be, Jettel," Walter said. "My son has not been able to get sick to his stomach for a long time. Who knows when he is going to have this opportunity again?"

"Just let me take care of that, Dr. Redlich. I am going to stay for a while, if your Else washes my shirt and it is all right with your wife. One cannot leave a man like you on his own at a time like this." Since he did not know anything about the laziness of a full stomach, Walter also forgot to shut off his head and throat in time. While he listened to the sounds of his stomach, which was pleasantly extended, he tried to catch the images of the day. It became a long journey that expanded into one of those confusing safaris, which, as Walter now realized, no longer ensnared only his daughter with their appeal. Alternately he stopped in Leobschütz, Genoa, and Ol' Joro Orok and then found himself, too unexpectedly to be cautious, standing at the warm oven with Karl Maas and talking about plans in which hunger was no longer the measure of life.

"You know, Greschek," he said in the direction of the dozing head in the easy chair with the flowery upholstery, "one of these days I will be an attorney again. And then we will sue everyone in Marke who upsets you."

Jettel heard her husband's words just as she was in the process of giving herself over to the confusing feeling that her body did not have any more demands, but she did not make an effort to understand those sentences. She only moved her head. She, too, was too full, too unaccustomedly content, and above all too tired to sense, even remotely, any danger of change.

Later, when Greschek was snoring on the couch and Else was letting water run into the bowl in the kitchen while putting up her field bed, softly singing, Regina heard the bed in her parents' bedroom squeak. At first she smiled knowingly as in the days when she did not yet have a brother and wanted nothing more in the world. Yet when she noticed that she was listening for every sound and tried to interpret it as in her childhood days, she was ashamed that she had ever been able to think that her parents might have forgotten the only part of their lives that came without a fight.

Greschek, physically lazy but with a mind that was all the more active when it came to the climate of the times, which called for men like him, did not waste any time changing his friends' lives and making them more nourishing. Even during the days when his electrical appliance store in Leobschütz was flourishing, he had taken more pleasure in conducting business outside the ordinary channels than in those that were deemed appropriate and the norm in a small town and which he found monotonous and not profitable enough. The long, arduous escape on foot from Upper Silesia and especially their life afterward as unwelcome "Eastern scum" in the small village in the Harz Mountains, where people had to accept them, had brought Greschek's talent for improvisation and his business acumen to new heights. Since he was shrewd and above all knew people, he made Jettel his confidante for those undisclosed ways that he knew Dr. Redlich would not approve of.

Jettel, who considered herself a businesswoman, was delighted. She was flattered that Greschek praised her street smarts and she concurred from the bottom of a full, long-suppressed heart with his opinion that decency was just a lack of courage to claim one's own. Most of all, she recognized Greschek as a jewel—rough and grumpy, it was true, but above all as devoted as she was used to men being toward her. The first day she showed Greschek the green coffee beans from Kenya in the little bag that Walter was saving for a special occasion. He took it wordlessly, shaking his head, and returned just as mutely with a pound of butter and a pack of cigarettes. The second day, he took half a pack of cigarettes with him and came home with a radio.

"You are not among the Africans anymore, Dr. Redlich. Cut off from the whole world. I still remember how happy you were when I sold you your first radio in Leobschütz." At the end of the week Greschek had procured a side of bacon, a small tub of liquid soap, half a pound of roasted coffee, four cans of corned beef from American supplies, and two pairs of nylon stockings, with which Jettel danced around the apartment as happily as if they were diamonds.

To the general bafflement of all, Greschek was able to trade in the unwanted, bitter cornmeal that had been distributed as food rations for weeks for the coveted white flour; he exchanged the dates they had gotten as meat rations for two bananas for Max. From his rucksack he proudly produced two Hershey's bars for Regina and suffered his first defeat. She only licked the chocolate and then happily stuffed it in her brother's mouth.

"Miss Regina is just like her father," Greschek complained to Else, whose earrings he had traded for shoes. "Too good for this world."

Jettel, although without hope, brought out a little sack of tea from Kenya. During the passage a bag of detergent had split open and made the tea forever unpalatable. This was the only time Greschek laughed out loud.

"Don't you know that good tea always tastes a little bit like soap?" he asked. Late that night, when Walter, who saw doom coming any day, believed that he had been arrested, Greschek returned home without the tea, but with two meters of flowered fabric for a dress for Jettel.

She was ecstatic and gave Greschek a kiss. (This had never happened before.) Nobody knew how he got the things that so radically changed their life. He could neither be persuaded to tell where he conducted his beneficial transactions nor how he, who came from a village and did not know the city, had found the right access routes to the black market so quickly.

He did not even tell Jettel that on his way there he used the trained eye of the electrician he had been in his youth and the expertise of the junk dealer he had become to remove electric cables and pipes from bombed-out houses and even from a few buildings that were being reconstructed. He considered it an ill-timed waste to disappoint the large number of fences who were already counting on his deliveries.

Greschek reserved the evenings for the real kind of happiness that had driven him to Frankfurt. As soon as the women had gone to bed, the two men talked as in the old days when Greschek had been Walter's only sounding board. But Greschek never talked as much of Leobschütz as Walter would have liked. Instead, work, duties, and especially the moral principles of a German judge interested him much more than the memories of Upper Silesia. He enthusiastically listened to Walter's reports about Karl Maas, whom Greschek had met and whose position he held in the kind of respect that was otherwise foreign to him. He obtained salami for Maas on the black market. Walter was very embarrassed when he brought the gift, Maas not at all.

With every nightly conversation Walter felt more strongly that Greschek was the only one who really understood why he had returned to Germany. One night Greschek told him that he had visited Walter's father two times in Sohrau even after the Germans had marched into Poland, had brought him some groceries, and had seen him at the railroad station in Kattowitz when he had to flee, but had not dared to speak to him anymore.

"I do not believe in God, Dr. Redlich," Greschek said, "but He will punish me for that one of these days."

"If only one out of every ten had your conscience, Greschek, I would be happier here," Walter answered. All at once he noticed that he had just taken away years of hope with a single sentence, and he was not even able to talk with Greschek about his father's death. He went to bed dejected.

At the end of the third week of Greschek's visit and just as the well-filled bowls on the dinner table had started to become a habit, Regina became ill. What at first looked like a bad cold developed into a state that Walter called the flu, Jettel labeled pneumonia, and Dr. Goldschmidt claimed to be the result of malnutrition.

Greschek got milk and butter for her on the black market, a chicken for a real soup, the kind his mother used to make when one of her six children was sick, and to lift her spirits a lipstick that made her mother much happier than Regina. When the high fever persisted, Greschek arrived home with penicillin and the news that this was a wonder drug that would cure any illness overnight.

Dr. Goldschmidt refused to inject Regina with the penicillin and with that made an enemy for life out of Greschek. Instead, he repeated once again, "Regina is suffering from malnutrition." He vaguely spoke about the possibility of sending her to Switzerland for three months. Regina refused, horrified. She had heard about the Swiss aid for children long ago at school, and had been afraid her parents might find out about it.

Regina was not suffering as much from being sick as was apparent. She rather welcomed the opportunity to go on safari undisturbed, free from the daily household chores and her self-imposed ambition to reach a goal in school that was as unattainable to her now as on the first day. As soon as she was alone in the apartment, she happily summoned the pictures of the days gone by in spite of fever and weakness.

She lay down at the edge of the flax fields with Owuor and smelled the sweet scent of his steaming skin, enjoyed his silence, heard the drums beating and the monkeys calling, dug her bare feet into the red soil, and let time run through her hands until Owuor's laughter thundered back from the trees like an enormous echo and caressed her ears. On other days she climbed onto the guava tree in Nairobi, numbed her nose, and woke her fairy from the eternal slumber to which she had been condemned on the day when Regina no longer needed her because she now had a brother.

During those quiet days between waking and sleeping, sickness and recovery, Regina discovered that she still had the ability to find refuge in her own magic. But her sense of reality, which she had developed early on, remained as acute as a newly sharpened bush knife. She realized more intensely than ever that she needed both the escape and the return to a world that she did not love but accepted because her parents and her brother lived in it.

At any rate, for the sake of a few pounds, Regina did not plan on giving up the familiar miseries of Frankfurt for being rootless again in a country she did not know much more about than the fact that it had as many mountains as cows and, therefore, milk and chocolate.

Coincidence and the timing of the discussion about her health were against her. Dr. Goldschmidt had hardly planted the seed when Walter found out that Jewish families in Zurich wanted to take in children from the Jewish community in Frankfurt, but the community did not know how to respond to this offer. The community did not have enough children for the action: Most children had been born after 1945 and were, therefore, too young for the philanthropic aspirations of the Swiss foster families.

Although her father said nothing, Regina gathered that he would register her with the community for a journey to Switzerland so she tried very hard to appear healthy, content, and busy with the task of finally catching up with the schoolwork for her grade. Her situation, however, deteriorated rapidly when Greschek all of a sudden had to return to Marke and it became clear that a renewed period of hunger was only days away. Indeed, Walter talked to her the night Greschek left.

"Dr. Alschoff promised that he will personally make sure that you are going to stay with a good family," he said.

"Mine is good enough," Regina furiously replied.

"But you no longer are."

"I am getting better every day. If I did not have to be afraid that I will have to leave home, I would already be completely well."

"Dear God, Regina, what are you afraid of? That you will eat too much chocolate? You didn't complain when you were seven years old and had to leave us, and now you are rebelling because of three months."

"I had to go to school then, not to Switzerland."

"Are you starting to become like your mother? No changes ever."

"That is not fair. I have never complained."

"There is the problem; you never complain. In that you are just as stupid a fool as your father. Heavens, Regina, don't make it so hard for me. I am simply afraid for you. And I am not used to fighting with you, either. I'm not going to force you to go. I am only asking you to take the pressure off me."

This time the never-vanished pictures came without invitation to Regina. She relived the day once more on which her father had become the crafty hunter in the fight for her heart and she had decided once and for all to give it to him. He still knew how to draw the bow to shoot his arrow.

"It is all right, *bwana*," she murmured, "you are winning, but I want you to know that I do not like to go."

"You don't have to like it, *memsahib kidogo*," Walter smiled. "The main thing is that you gain some weight."

5

On the trip from Basel to Zurich, in a train with small, neat curtains in front of gleaming clean windows, Regina succumbed to the delicate flowers of the forsythia bushes that glowed in provocative yellow on the hills; the black-and-white cows, well-nourished as in old picture books, on soft green meadows; the small houses in their spotless cleanliness; daffodils and primroses in tiny gardens; and the spring exuberance of young dogs. In parting she had defiantly been determined to shut herself off from a world she had not wanted to enter because she knew that the promised paradise would turn her into a child again, exposed without protection to the loneliness of a strange place.

Yet her eyes had stubbornly insisted on their old right to drink, and since the days in which the voracious monster had swallowed Europe as rapidly as a hyena eats its unexpected prey, Regina knew that people who do not want to damage their relationship with the black God Mungu forever should never fight their eyes.

Even during the short time that she did not know who was going to pick her up at the station in Zurich and what she was supposed to do except stand next to her suitcase and look for the unknown rescuer whom her father had announced, she felt secure in her tremendous amazement. The station platforms were as clean as the trains that arrived and departed. There were people with smooth faces standing at the windows or sitting in dining cars on velvet-covered seats at tables with white tablecloths and in front of well-filled plates. Those people were talking to one another as if it was not important to them to suppress hunger, and some only opened their mouths to laugh. This carefree attitude, which she watched through shiny windows, turned by the reflection into a fiery ball of colors that she had forgotten existed, fascinated her most. She was just about to notice that the people around her on the platform — men in shiny shoes of real leather and women in shimmering nylon stockings under light-colored, bouncing dresses of weightless material that went to their ankles — were distinguished by the same lightheartedness. At that moment a woman in a blue silk dress and matching jacket and white gloves of angel's skin touched the yellow puffed sleeve of Regina's dress and again turned her, even though she would celebrate her sixteenth birthday half a year from now, into a child, who in a whirl of relief believes in fairy tales once more and knows for all eternity that a single touch can bring a person from the sleep of death back to life.

In the prickly, melodic pattern of a language that tickled Regina's ears and made her consider whether she had ever heard a similar one or not, the splendid queen said, "I am Margret Guggenheim and you must be our little charge from Germany."

Regina did not know this word and was thinking hard if charges usually had to be giants and whether she, therefore, seemed little to the woman. She tried to open her mouth without looking as silly as she felt. She was glad when she could at least move her head and nod. Very slowly, as if she had to scan the distance first, she extended her right hand.

After a while, which seemed very long to her and in which she silently followed the scent of roses in full bloom that emanated from the blue dress, she let her stiff body be pushed into a taxi. Yet even in the soft upholstery of the car she remained as stiff as a dried-out tree and the numbing confusion had her so firmly in its grasp that every breath became embarrassing to her. Regina found it impossible to clearly capture even a single picture although she knew that she had to do just that to report to her parents about a world in which cars had the color of flowers, people the appearance of knights and princesses, and even the dogs on their thin leashes of supple leather seemed freshly washed and looked as if they had never experienced what hunger might be. As hard as Regina tried to understand, to answer questions, and to put the splendor of satiety in her head and store it, she could not remember anything but the name of her rescuer.

The taxi drove up a steep hill and stopped in front of a house in the midst of a small garden, in which high, flowering trees and thick green hedges blocked the view from the windows. The blue sovereign with the singing voice laughed and said, "You have made it, child." She gave the taxi driver beautiful silver coins, touched Regina's shoulder again, grasped the small brown suitcase that was held together by a rough string with a white-gloved hand, and pushed Regina into a corridor that was very bright and smelled of heavy hyacinths that were blooming toward their decay.

Even after the first two hours in this house, which Regina could not determine to be a castle or only a mirage, she was unable to say more than yes and no, and, frightened by the possibility of unpleasant mis-understandings, had to concentrate on not answering too quickly or especially too slowly.

When Mrs. Guggenheim led her through the house, she felt as lost as a Kikuyu child who steps on a wooden floor for the first time and is afraid of getting hurt. The big rooms with curtains on which flowers were whispering, light wallpaper, and dark furniture made Regina si-lent. The many pictures on the walls, demanding like the demons in the dark nights of Africa that were hunting down the sun and never let go of their prey, and the long rows of books with dark leather backs and gold inscriptions in big glass cases, confronted her eyes like a storm and made her unable to distinguish shapes and colors.

In a kitchen with white tiles there was a woman, dark-haired, with two thick braids around her head, in a black dress with a flowered apron. She had very white teeth, but when Regina started to thank her for her smile, the furniture began to whirl around and the one big white refrigerator changed into two powerful giants.

Regina was soon sitting on a small sofa with a cover that resembled moss in a forest after the first night of the long rains. The windows around her were as big as doors. The sun rushed in and drove the white pictures within the center of a bright fire into a dance of light. As soon as even the tiniest sunbeam made the pictures even lighter, the white became as transparent as glass and caught the colors of the vanishing rainbow.

"Utrillo," Mrs. Guggenheim said. "Have you heard of him?"

Regina shook her head. She heard Mrs. Guggenheim laugh and say,

"You will learn about that here if you have eyes." Regina made an effort to laugh, too, but was again unable to move her lips. Even her fingers were stuck to each other. She reluctantly took the glass that Mrs. Guggenheim held out to her and only then noticed how thirsty she was, and she was amazed how the water, as white as the pictures, tasted sweet and sour at the same time. She happily drained the glass in one gulp, heard herself swallow, then wanted to apologize and put the glass on the table, but held it undecided in the air because she had to think about the sequence of her actions first.

"Not on the table," Mrs. Guggenheim called out, warning her, and closed her eyes for a moment as if she expected great pain.

She hastily held out a newspaper to Regina the same way Regina did at home for her brother when he had eaten too quickly and was retching. Regina noticed too late that she too had begun to get sick and bit her lower lip.

"Do you want to freshen up, child?"

"Yes," Regina whispered.

"I will show you the bathroom," Mrs. Guggenheim said.

She led Regina into a brightly tiled room with a big washbasin, shiny silver faucets, and green towels with a white trim, stood for a moment undecided, pulled a chocolate bar out of the pocket of her blue skirt, handed it to Regina, nodded at her, and quietly closed the door.

Regina did not dare turn the faucets. She also could not imagine that she was allowed to use the towels or the soft white paper that was dangling from a silver holder next to the toilet. For a while, she only stood there and stared at the small window with the tiny curtain. She was even afraid to use the mirror. Her helplessness made her furious and made her throw all caution to the wind.

With a suddenness that incensed her even more, she tore open the silver foil and smelled the chocolate. She had wanted to lick one corner of it, the way she had done with Greschek's chocolate, just to get a taste and then to keep the treasure for Max, but her tongue and teeth refused to obey her. She discovered too late that nothing was left of the chocolate. Struck by the fact that she had succumbed to her greed at just the moment when she had been thinking about the needs of her family, she started to cry.

A few minutes later, Mrs. Guggenheim heard her sobbing, gently opened the door, and led Regina out of the bathroom.

"Come," she said, "lie down a little bit. This is all too much for you."

On the bed, with its duvet of yellow silk and pillows that had the same scent as the hyacinths in the corridor, lay a long white nightgown with lace and next to it a little black and brown cloth dog with a round belly and a tiny wooden keg at its red collar. Regina was so surprised that she only touched him cautiously as if she first had to find out whether he was alive or not, but she had not yet forgotten how to feed her ears with imagination.

While she swallowed the laughter in her throat like her tears earlier, she already heard the dog bark. When she noticed that he also winked with his right glass eye, she realized that she had been asleep with open eyes the entire time. Her hosts had expected a child and had gotten her instead. The Guggenheims most likely were as confused as she was.

Relieved and amused, she took off her dress and put on the child's nightgown that was too tight for her. She only wanted to lie down for a moment to think, but she immediately fell asleep, and therefore did not meet George Guggenheim till the next morning.

The small chubby man, with the first signs of balding and eyes that betrayed calmness and at his best moments the wit of a skeptic, was a well-known personage in his native town. He was on the board of the Zurich Jewish community, a lawyer by profession, and above all a man of understatement. People who did not know the name George Guggenheim, which happened rarely in Switzerland and hardly ever in Zurich, would have drawn the wrong conclusions from his demeanor and frugal way of life, and never would have gotten the idea that he was immensely wealthy. His modesty and strictly middle-class lifestyle made him popular with friends, colleagues, clients, and the people who worked for the many charitable organizations on whose boards he had served for many years. He was easily able to establish contact with people who talked on an educated, tolerant, and humorous level similar to his own temperament.

Since he did not interact or have any experience with children, they frightened him unless they looked at him out of a frame and were painted by Cézanne, Renoir, or Picasso. He had, therefore, only very reluctantly given in to his wife's wishes to host a child from Germany because this had all of a sudden become fashionable among the rich families of the Zurich Jewish community. George Guggenheim did not approve of fashionable trends—not in art and even less in charitable causes.

When Regina sat at the breakfast table this first morning—pale, thin, and with dark rings under her eyes that touched him and reminded him in a disturbing way of the pictures of Otto Dix—George Guggenheim had to fight against an embarrassment that was normally unknown to him. He wanted to be polite and cordial, but could only think that it was probably customary to talk to children about school. Thinking back to his own childhood, this seemed to him as silly as it was commonplace. He considered whether he should ask his intimidated guest about her parents and Germany, but the first question struck him as inappropriately curious, and he also felt the typically Swiss reluctance of those years to speak about Germany.

Even though he could clearly see that Regina had a roll with jam on it on her plate, he passed the jam to her. She looked at him with consternation as if he had already said something wrong. When the doorbell rang and his wife got up from the table, he took the silence as an unwarranted provocation. George Guggenheim pulled his chair closer to the table, coughed slightly, and asked with a determination that he considered as exaggerated as ridiculous, "Who are your favorite authors?"

Regina had not expected the taciturn man to speak to her anymore. She was startled, dropped her roll onto the plate, and hesitated with her answer because she doubted, after her experiences in German class, that he had ever heard of Dickens and Wordsworth.

While she hurriedly swallowed the last bite, she fumbled with her dress and unhappily wondered which German writer she could name without making a fool of herself because she did not know any more than merely his name. At that moment she was saved by her memory that in school they had just read *The Tailor Makes The Man* and with much more enthusiasm had learned by heart the ballad of "The Feet in the Fire."

"Gottfried Keller and Conrad Ferdinand Meyer," she said, relieved.

"My, my. Our Swiss writers. I would not have expected that from a child."

"I am not a child," Regina heard herself say. Her skin immediately started to burn, and the muscles in her face became rigid. She was terribly ashamed because she was not used to being forward and bold.

Above all, she could not explain to herself what caused her to let her tongue run away at such an uncertain, alarming moment. Embarrassed, she stared at the spot of red jam on her plate and kept her head lowered. Suddenly a deep sound reached her ear.

"Great," George Guggenheim burst out laughing. "Wonderful! You don't even know how afraid I was of you. In my nightmares I only saw chocolate fingers smeared all over my paintings."

"Your beautiful pictures," Regina wondered. "I don't even dare look at them too closely."

The sentence marked the beginning of a friendship that lasted only three intoxicating months, but changed Regina's feeling and thinking as definitely as the arrival in Africa and the terrible death of all familiarity after the departure. On this morning, after the silent breakfast, George Guggenheim pushed open the door to a world that Regina never would have discovered with such intensity without him and for which she would be grateful to him all her life.

The connection to a teacher, whose patience was only surpassed by his passion to share with her what was most precious to him, was instantaneous. At the very beginning, the giver presented the recipient in an African way. He entrusted her with a secret that she kept locked in her heart like the gentle, always reassuring memory about the small, hidden, mischievous jokes that united her with Owuor across two continents.

"Come along," George Guggenheim said. "I want you to get acquainted with Zurich. And do you know where we are going to start? I will show you where our Gottfried Keller was born."

They walked past clean houses adorned with the respectability of their owners, bursting forsythia branches, impatient daffodils with nodding heads, and freshly washed children on roller-skates, down the spring-intoxicated Restelberg. In spite of his compact build, George Guggenheim was a fast walker and Regina had trouble staying at his side. Once, she forgot that she was no longer a child and skipped up to the sky and back. A blessed moment long, he lifted both feet off the ground.

"Do you ever eat ham?" he asked.

"Never," she said.

"Is your home kosher then?"

"But no," Regina laughed, "we just don't have any ham."

"Neither do we. My wife comes from a religious family and we have a kosher household. Didn't you see the two refrigerators in the kitchen?"

"Yes," Regina replied, "when I got sick yesterday and the furniture began to whirl around me."

"You know what kosher means."

"No pork, and milk never together with meat."

"Right. That is why there are two refrigerators, clever Miss. One for milk and butter, and one for meat. And kosher means a lot more than that. No cheesecake for desert if you have eaten meat before, no cream sauce like my mother used to make, no venison, no shellfish, no butter under cold cuts, and never any ham. Remember that and shake your head if a religious man ever asks for your hand in marriage."

They were standing in front of a butcher shop. Regina could hear her stomach talk when she saw the sausages, schnitzel, sandwiches, grilled chickens with brown skin, and bacon in the display case. She finally understood the meaning of the land of milk and honey in the German fairy tale in which sausages hung from the trees and grilled pigeons were flying overhead.

She felt the sharp stab of a troubled conscience when she thought of her father, how thin he was, and how he used to love to eat in the good days, but George Guggenheim did not give her any time for guilt. He pushed her toward the counter and greeted a robust salesgirl in a white apron. She laughed and asked, "For the little one, too?" George Guggenheim impatiently nodded and instantly both had in their hand a roll with ham protruding from the edges, and both were chewing.

"My wife is never to know about this," he whispered and looked like the cloth dog with the keg at its neck.

"Never," Regina promised.

"Do you keep other secrets as well?"

"Yes," Regina giggled, a second roll in her hand, and talked about Owuor in Africa and about her father, with whom she spoke Swahili when nobody was around.

"Why did he return to Germany then if he lets his heart talk in Swahili?"

"Because he wanted to work in his profession again," Regina said. She was not talking fast enough to suppress the final sigh and felt that she had betrayed her father.

"He had to come back," she repeated.

"I can understand that," George Guggenheim said. "Yes, one has to understand that," but Regina noticed that he had not understood anything at all. After that incident she talked as little as possible with him about her father.

When she became aware that she was describing the meals at the George Guggenheims and how much and how quickly she was gaining weight in far greater detail than what really occupied her so much, namely the new fascination of the pictures, she began having a hard time with her letters home. She knew only too well how much her father distrusted imagination and all knowledge beyond logic and professional advancement. For the first time in years she remembered an incident at the farm.

She had tried to paint a picture. Even though she knew that she had not succeeded, she had had fun choosing the colors, mixing them, and creating magic on paper, but her father had hardly looked at the picture and only grumbled, "You are able to read; why do you want to paint?"

When Mrs. George Guggenheim told her, "The pictures are originals" and informed her about their material value, she dared even less to mention Renoir, Cézanne, and Utrillo in her letters. She was certain that her father would not hold in high esteem a man who spent his money on pictures. She only mentioned the frequent visits to the theater after a performance of *The Devil's General* and wrote so extensively about the "decent German" that she felt disloyal and dishonest again because she pretended that only this aspect had been important to her and she did not mention at all that the genius, language, and atmosphere of the play had carried her away.

Staying with the Guggenheims had made Regina obsessed with the theater and pictures. She lived in feverish expectation of the performances, just as she had done as a child with the books of Charles Dickens. She learned about life based on deception from Ibsen's *Nora,* and about the love of life and confidence in one's own character from

Goethe's *Egmont*. She was hardly able to bear *A Midsummer Night's Dream;* the imagination and beauty of the language were almost too powerful for eye and ear.

The Guggenheims took her to gallery openings and taught her to have patience with pictures she did not like. On Sundays they took her to museums in Bern and Basel where she saw the glowing colors of Franz Marc and Marc Chagall for the first time. Maurice Utrillo remained her passion. She had the motifs explained to her over and over again, listened to stories about his life, and became devoted to seeing and comprehending.

When Regina was going to bed one night, George Guggenheim had had the pictures in her room changed. Instead of the two etchings by Picasso, two landscapes by Utrillo hung on the long wall opposite the window. She sat in front of them, the little cloth St. Bernard on her lap, and knew that this was her first declaration of love. She surmised, not without sadness, that in the future her escape from the miseries of the world would no longer always take her to the forests of Africa.

When George Guggenheim realized that Regina was interested in history, he no longer permitted her to see Switzerland solely as a paradise of pictures and benefactors, of full plates and secret ham rolls. He told her about the Jewish refugees who had come to the Swiss border in deadly peril, had been sent back to Germany by the officials, and had perished there. He also angrily told her of rich Jewish families in Switzerland who had been afraid that too many refugees would enter the country; how he had tried to fight the narrow-minded, barbarous behavior of the well to do; and how little he had been able to accomplish.

"Be glad that you were too young in idyllic Africa to learn about death and destruction," he said.

Regina told him about her grandparents and the two aunts who had been murdered in Germany.

"How does one live in this Germany?" George Guggenheim asked.

He looked at her doubtfully, but she returned his glance and said, "Well, everyone there was always against Hitler and did not know anything."

"You have grown up very fast."

"I was born a grown-up."

In mid-June George Guggenheim visited his mother in Lugano and took Regina along. Sunshine, blue sky, the lake with its white swaying life, the mild evenings, the splendor of the flowers, and a lightness that intoxicated all senses rivaled for the illusion of unending happiness. The three of them drove to the mountains, sat on meadows, talked to flowers and cows, and had picnics at the lake. Regina borrowed Renoir's eyes so that the beauty would dissolve into light and shadows. Only at night, under the enormous down comforter with the red and white checked cover, did she realize that she had forgotten her family and had to atone for it because her shame did not know about the benefits of mercy.

With old Mrs. Guggenheim, from whom the son had inherited his sense of humor and talent for giving, Regina went into the cool town with its narrow, winding streets. She ate ice cream in all flavors and drank in a never-before-experienced cheerfulness with colorful sodas; she indulged her tongue with cake, her palate with spices, and her nose with the smells of this summer of abundance; and in a store with dark wooden panels she was allowed to choose two kinds of fabric—one of them with blue and white checks, the other dark red with white flowers. Within two days, an Italian tailor, who sang even when speaking, sewed two dresses with tight bodices and long, swinging skirts. They went down to her ankles and turned the *bambina* who had come to the tailor's shop into a *signorina*. Regina savored the word and tasted vanity.

Regina, who had never been interested in clothes before, said "The New Look" to her image in the mirror and realized that her body also started to show that she was no longer a child.

On her return to Zurich she found a letter from her mother.

Sunday, on my birthday, of all days, the currency reform took place. The good mood was gone. But you cannot imagine how life has changed. We could not believe our eyes when we went out on Monday morning. All of a sudden the butcher has cold cuts, and Mrs. Heckel next door has fruit and vegetables and is suddenly quite friendly, asking me what I want to buy.

The stores in town are full. There are dresses, hats, baby clothes, plates, pots, light bulbs, thread, furniture, and lamps; everything you can imagine. One can even buy cigarettes and coffee now. But we no longer have any money. The old money is gone and everyone got just forty marks per person. We have no idea how things are supposed to go on.

Unfortunately we did not get the forty marks for you, even though we said that you would come back soon. Your dear father now wants to give up his safe judge's compensation and become an attorney. I am trying every day to talk him out of this nonsense, but you know how stubborn he is. I am looking forward to having you back. Maybe you will be able to talk to him.

Reality had caught up with Regina. She did not fight it. She even welcomed her longing for Frankfurt and agonized over and over again if Max would still recognize her, how big he might be, and what he might be able to say already. She saw his big, black eyes and already smelled his skin after he had just been bathed.

Utrillo and Renoir were already in the process of losing their colors. The Guggenheims were talking of a farewell present and wanted to know what Regina would like to have. She asked to keep the small stuffed St. Bernard, and wished for a bar of chocolate and a ball for Max.

The ball, as blue as the lake and as red as the poppies in Lugano, was lying on the luggage rack of the train. Regina was wearing her new, checkered dress with the long, swinging skirt. Mrs. Guggenheim had packed a big basket with fruit, breads, cakes, and chocolate for her. Regina knew that she would not touch anything and would bring everything home. She was as embarrassed and helpless as at her arrival.

"Thank you," she stammered, "and not only for the food."

The whistle was announcing the train's departure when George Guggenheim passed a package through the window. He laughed and said, "So that you won't forget us." Regina saw him winking but was too excited to return his last greeting.

To prolong the anticipation she only started to open the package when the train drove into Basel. There was a box with a book about Utrillo, photographs of all of his paintings that were hanging in the Guggenheims' house, and, tightly wrapped in a light blue napkin, a roll with ham. Regina broke into tears.

6

THE BATHTUB HEATER, which was behind the curtain in the bedroom, was old, hard to operate, too expensive because of its inadequate airflow and enormously high coal consumption, and had only been used once, when Regina had a severe flu. The kitchen, with a big flowered washbowl on an iron stand, therefore, also served as a bathroom. The soap was on the windowsill, and the towels were draped over the stove. Only Max, who was being washed between bed and table in a small zinc tub, for which he had grown deplorably big for some time now, did not have to leave the house for a bath. The rest of the family used the public bathhouses.

Else went to a bathhouse in the inner city on her free Wednesday afternoons and was gone till evening. She did not consider the large expenditure of time a sacrifice since she was able to cleanse her body and soul at the same time. The bath attendant had been sent to Hochkretscham on a farm work program during the war and she always had a sympathetic ear for Else's longing memories of her native village. Most of the time she also had leftover pieces of soap to put in the practical little bags in which they were collected and that one was able to buy again lately without having to give up the soap, which one needed so desperately, in exchange for them.

Walter, Jettel, and Regina went on Saturdays alternately to the shower baths at the Merianplatz or the Hallgartenstraße. At the latter, an old brick house offered the possibility of taking a full bath in bathtubs that were definitely up to pre-war standards. Until her visit with the Guggenheims, it had never occurred to Regina that healthy people could take a bath at home.

After the currency reform, the shower baths were more popular with the Redlichs than the previously loved full baths. In contrast to Else, they liked walking there but did not care for the destination. The way to the Merianplatz led through the Berger Straße, which had recovered remarkably fast from its wounds. It was the heart of Bornheim, was called "Bernemer Zeil" again, just as before the war by the much-envied inhabitants of the quarter with their many connections, and had many small stores that held the promise of a beginning prosperity.

For two weeks now the dry goods store at the big intersection displayed fabric, needles, thread, and even a few packages of nylon stockings with wonderfully transparent covers. The grocery store next door, its window up to a few weeks ago only decorated with a yellowed photograph of the employees in the founding year, now featured coffee, chocolate bars, and boxed chocolates, which alone made every detour worthwhile.

The household goods store no longer offered wooden spoons and, above all, no more steel helmets converted into saucepans. Instead, there were gleaming, very expensive dream kitchen utensils made of new sheet metal. Even the undertaker on the other side of the street was showing off the changes and miracles of the times—instead of an empty picture frame decorated with a black crape band, there now stood in the window a coffin crafted of excellent oak.

Seeing such splendor and, especially, thinking that it might some day be within reach of the majority of "average consumers," pushed the newly revived imagination to euphoric heights. Ever since the changes in Frankfurt's business life, Jettel had become unusually peaceable during the Saturday shower bath excursions, which seemed to have the appeal of the enjoyable family outings of former times. She only rarely complained about the things she did not have and when she talked about the future, it was without the otherwise inevitable allusions to lost happiness and wealth left behind in Africa.

The first Saturday in August of 1948, however, differed painfully from this beautifully optimistic scheme of things. Between the bedding store with its extraordinary eiderdowns in the window and a laundry that had recently switched from liquid soap to a real detergent, Walter stopped and said that he now had prepared everything so that he could establish himself as an independent attorney.

He thought that the time and place for his message had been cleverly orchestrated, and as if he were just about to fulfill one of Jettel's long-held wishes, he put a hand on her shoulder and laughed. Regina did not even dare look at her mother and closed her eyes.

Since her trip to Zurich she had come to fear those smoldering fires that suddenly erupted into a blaze much more so than before she had come into contact with lightness and abundance. But when she finally looked at Jettel, who had not even shaken Walter's arm off yet, she immediately became aware of an impending change in her family's life. Regina recognized, amazed, that her mother, like a Masai warrior in a decisive battle, had obtained new arrows for herself.

"That is fine with me," Jettel said quietly. "I don't care. But where are you going to have your practice? After all, there are no offices available."

"I know. In the beginning, it will have to be in the apartment. Mrs. Wedel has no objections. I have already talked to her. She even encouraged me."

"Not with me. And if I have to personally throw every client out. You do not open a law practice in three rooms."

"Many start with less these days."

"They do not have a small child. Max needs his own room."

"Jettel, after ten years of emigration you cannot be presumptuous enough to insist on a child's room when the founding of our existence is at stake."

"You have an existence and we have everything we need to live."

"Too bad that you have never told me how happy you are, Jettel."

"Well, I am telling you now. I don't have any big ideas. I only need a little bit of security. And there is no use to keep on talking. We are only going to have a fight."

In no other situation of her life had it ever occurred to Jettel to avoid a fight. Because she thought highly of her own spirit and courage, she often provoked the storm even before Walter did and considered it the only constant in their marriage. It was one of the rare instances in which Walter and Jettel were in agreement.

To achieve his goals he, too, needed the open war with loud words and illogical accusations, Jettel's stubbornness, and Regina's conciliatory attempts at mediation. But Jettel did not respond to pleas or threats and Walter felt betrayed by even his daughter when Regina said, "This is strange; all my life I was told to pray that you would not lose your job and now that you have one you don't want it."

The silent war was long and oppressive for all. In the Höhenstraße, the Iron Curtain, which everyone was talking about at the time, descended between the kitchen and the living room. When Jettel finally became aware that she had turned herself into a very unhappy prisoner through an approach that she disliked intensely and that contradicted her passionate nature, she signaled the start of the peace negotiations everyone had been longing for.

As suddenly as she had become silent, she now talked to Walter again. She shouted; cried; implored; called him a cruel father; and threatened first suicide, then divorce, and finally, triumphantly, that she would return to Nairobi, take Max with her, and marry a rich farmer. She had expected anything but Walter's relieved laughter and him taking her in his arms and saying, "Thank God, my Jettel is her old self again." Pouting, but also flattered, she gave in and sighed, "Go ahead; open your damned office here then."

"If you are going to be hungry for just a day, I will pack your suitcases myself," Walter promised.

He also made a promise to Mrs. Wedel, who he believed—rightly— had played a decisive role in Jettel's late change of mind. "As soon as I can, I am going to move out of your apartment and you can move in again."

At the beginning of October he started as an independent attorney and one hour later he received his first client. She was the daughter of a tobacco store owner whose business was in the house. She wanted to have her husband, who was missing in the war, declared dead and did not know how. That night, Walter put the first fees his new independent profession had earned him on the table—a pound of bacon, which was still considered the most stable currency, half a pound of real coffee, and a pack of cigarettes.

Jettel was not embarrassed about her enthusiasm and could not be drawn into any conversation about the most recent past. She brewed the coffee, even though Monday was still the day for ersatz coffee, finally sang Carmen's signature aria, drank two cups in a row, and said,

"If necessary, I can occasionally write a letter for you. After all, I used to work for the best lawyer in Breslau."

"And just don't forget to mention that he called me the greatest idiot of all time," Walter said. He beamed as if Jettel had ever been able to appreciate his sense of humor. Max instantly learned the new word and said first to his father, then to his mother, and finally to the picture of a policeman on his plate, "Idiot."

His linguistic development, in combination with a strongly developed awareness of his irresistible charm, progressed as quickly as the law practice, and in retrospect turned Jettel once again into a Cassandra with an absolutely infallible sense for catastrophe. Walter had considered the difficulties of working undisturbed in an apartment with a curious two-and-a-half-year-old, but he had never anticipated his son's enthusiasm for strangers in general and for his father's clients in particular.

Only for a short while did Max limit himself to the traditional habits of his age group, such as showing his toys to friendly adults and luring them into the spell of innocence and blind confidence. Unpleasantly fast he began to try out his atypical vocabulary on them and to enjoy the sweetness of applause. Max greeted clients with either the question, "Do you want to get a divorce?" or the statement, "You won't get away with that." He reacted to any attempts to remove him from the center of the action with the kind of persistent howling that went even beyond the modest scope of what Walter had expected for his work. Jettel could not have asked for a better ally than her determined son to get the apartment free again. After two months Walter gave up.

At the bar association he learned about a colleague who was looking for a partner for his practice, which was described as well-established and very reputable. Attorney and notary Dr. Friedhelm von Freiersleben lived in the once-renowned West End and received Walter in an imposing old residence that had survived the times as safely as its main inhabitant on the second floor.

He was sitting in a dark green leather chair in front of a desk of extraordinarily fine mahogany, wore a jacket of mixed gray and white tweed, and annoyed Walter right away because he not only looked like an English colonel, but also had the habit, widespread in British military circles, of speaking of "your people" when he talked about Jews.

Other than that, Friedhelm von Freiersleben talked very little about his practice and too much about the Jewish friends he somehow had lost track of to his amazement and great regret. Walter thought about his howling son and that he needed a filing cabinet, typewriter, telephone connection, and room for a typist. He suppressed his pride, instinct, and revulsion, and agreed to bring Jettel for coffee the following Sunday afternoon.

"It has always been my rule to look at my partners' wives," Friedhelm von Freiersleben laughed, "for a wife tells you more about a man than a thousand words." He kissed Jettel's hand and called her "a small feast for the eyes," told her about his father's estate and that his sisters had already ordered their linens from Paris in the thirties, invited her to his summer house in Kronberg, gave her a long-stemmed rose when they were leaving, and asked her to see to it that her "talented husband," for his own benefit, came to a quick decision.

Walter was so completely convinced that his wife had succumbed to the advances of a man whom he could not imagine ever seeing eye-to-eye with on any important point that he got stomach cramps on the way home. Trembling and with his face chalk-white, he had to lean against a wall next to the destroyed opera house and he knew that he would never be able to look into a mirror again without blushing if he agreed.

Jettel declared that Friedhelm von Freiersleben had an evil eye and bad breath, and she had always disliked long-stemmed roses. In addition, the coffee had been terribly watery, tasted of roasted chicory, and was clear evidence that he had to be a con man.

"That whole to-do with the little summer cottage," she groused. "You cannot fool me. My mother always used to say that. I have never heard of Kronberg. I bet that place doesn't even exist. If you work with him, you will make us all miserable."

Walter nodded so unhappily that Jettel did not take the time to play any more of her trump cards. Instead she asked, not without real sympathy, "Why don't you talk to Maas? He is from Frankfurt. Maybe he knows someone you could get together with."

It was one of those rare occasions in his marriage when Walter, without objections, gratefully and instantly accepted Jettel's advise. Karl Maas was horrified when he heard of Walter's visit with Friedhelm von Freiersleben, called him a sleazy fraud, and reported that he was a passionate anti-Semite and had already been a fervent follower of the Nazis when nobody else was taking them seriously yet, but the Nazis had not accepted him in the party because of a dubious great-grandmother in the East. For this reason Friedhelm von Freiersleben had also, in spite of the general indignation in judicial circles, survived the denazification trials as "not involved."

"You have more *massel* than brains," Maas told him. "At least you could not have asked me at a better moment. If it is true that there is a lid for every pot, I have exactly the right thing for you. An attorney just started in the Neue Mainzer and he could most likely use an associate. A decent fool like you. His name is Fafflok and I know you will like him. He is from the East."

They shared the same language, the same concept of integrity and duty, tradition and responsibility, the same wit nourished by a harsh tongue and soft heart, the same reluctance to show emotions, and the same view of the landscape and the rough, warm people when they looked back to Upper Silesia.

Fritz Fafflok was tall and very slim. At first glance he seemed smaller than he was because of his bent shoulders. This alone corresponded to his credo in life. In everything he was a man of understatement who did not betray his experience, intelligence, or extensive professional knowledge. His eyes spontaneously revealed his kindness; his self-conscious gestures that did not have anything awkward about them expressed his modesty. Tolerance was not part of his vocabulary, but it was one of the basic requirements of his soul. He was a Catholic and he honored his faith the same way that Walter honored his. Fafflok was from Kattowitz, and knew Sohrau, the Princes' School of Pless, and Leobschütz. He was not embarrassed by the word homeland. He used the regional expression for Saturday and said half-ten instead of half-past-nine when the clock showed that time of day. His wife used the Silesian names for the sausages and cabbages she bought at the butcher shop or greengrocer's store.

After the Poles arrived in Kattowitz, they let Fafflok, who during the last years of the war, after having been injured, had attempted to defend those who were displaced and enslaved in court, keep his apartment. Walter did not have to know anything else. With the exception of Karl

Maas and Greschek, Fritz Fafflok was the first German Walter met in Frankfurt who did not talk about his inner resistance and the many Jewish friends he had helped. Rather, he said, "I knew about all of it."

They talked about poppy seed cake, carp with brown sauce, the demise of Breslau, excursions to the Riesengebirge, and the times in which one did not ask and sometimes did not even know who was German, Polish, or Jewish. Fritz Fafflok told Walter that he had lost three fingers in the war and that at the moment he was wounded, he had only worried that he would never be able to play the violin again.

Walter spoke about his black friend Owuor on the farm at Ol' Joro Orok, how he had taught him to greet visitors by shouting "Arschloch," and that he was able to sing "Ich hab' mein Herz in Heidelberg verloren." Fafflok's pleasant smile turned into laughter till he cried and he surmised that Walter's moist eyes, in spite of all he had revealed about the emigration, were the manifestation of a farewell he had never recovered from.

They agreed without any contract or pomp "to try it with each other" and both knew at that moment that they were establishing more than just a legal practice together. Walter told Fafflok about Friedhelm von Freiersleben and his principle "to have a look at the spouse" and invited the Faffloks for dinner the following Sunday.

On the way home Walter became aware that he had talked more about his children than about Jettel. Gloomily and unhappily he asked himself how her demanding ways, her complaints, her unwillingness to compromise, her love of provocation, and her habit to air marital troubles immediately and without restraint would strike a woman who had been forced to flee from Upper Silesia to Frankfurt with two children.

"He is such a nice person," he said. "It would mean a lot to me if you made a good impression on him."

"I am going to buy Roquefort. It has become available again recently."

"Jettel, I am not talking about the food."

"How am I supposed to know? You always talk about food otherwise."

Without having to say anything to her, Regina once again gave her father her head and her heart. She wore the Bordeaux red dress from Switzerland even though it had short sleeves and the December day was particularly cold, and she practiced, in front of the mirror, a smile that would not immediately betray her awkward shyness. She also gave her brother an exceptionally thorough bath; brushed his hair till he screamed; calmed him down with a poem by Wordsworth, a Shakespeare sonnet, and chocolate; draped him in a light blue blanket that looked good with his skin; and carried him in as proudly as Else carried the soup bowl, sporting a new apron and the first perm of her life.

Max, elated from the caresses to his ear and the sweetness of the chocolate in his mouth, and longing for applause, first clapped his hands and then after a short pause spat from the high position on Regina's hip directly at Mrs. Fafflok's forehead. "You will not be able to get away with that," Max said.

Mrs. Fafflok dabbed her face dry and said, laughing, "My children only knew how to spit at that age." She had conquered Jettel's fortress with a single sentence and was treated to precisely the stories that Walter had dreaded. Jettel told in great detail and very enthusiastically about all the attention that used to be lavished upon her, how her mother and all the young men at the dancing school had adored her, and that her husband had to promise her in Nairobi that she would have a maid in Frankfurt.

"Otherwise I would not have set foot on German soil," she declared. Walter suffered further tortures after the soup when Jettel, in the middle of a discussion of their difficult start in Frankfurt, put her knife and fork down on her plate and announced, "My husband is particularly unfit for survival and on top of that as stubborn as a mule."

"All men are like that," Mrs. Fafflok agreed and reported that her husband was very slow, terribly idealistic, and never on time.

"He was even late to our wedding," she said.

Käthe Fafflok was a determined, smart, honest, and understanding woman. She had great respect for her husband, whom she called "Lumpsele," even though she was completely different from him in temperament and in contrast to him offered her opinion, and instantly, even if she had not been asked to do so. She was flexible, very practical, and did not have much patience with people who wallowed in self-pity, moaned about the present, and embellished the past.

Jettel became the great exception.

Käthe Fafflok thought her beautiful and charming, and as capricious as she would have liked to have been herself as a young girl. Jettel's domineering nature did not disturb her because it matched her own courage. Moreover, she was tolerant enough to consider Jettel's lack of logic spontaneity and her lethargy as part of her self-confidence. Käthe Fafflok was to become one of the few people who tried to look at the problems of a difficult marriage from Jettel's point of view, and she was full of sympathy when she considered how the years of their emigration had impacted and worn out the Redlichs. Most of all, she was aware of the tightness of a bond that was completely different from the way it appeared. Jettel's assessment of people was actually quite astute, a fact that she constantly had to point out to her husband and Regina. Jettel immediately recognized the understanding that came her way and did not hesitate to turn it into an uneven friendship.

The evening became one of hope, cheerfulness, and accord. Even Regina stifled her fear of strangers, talked about Africa, and let herself become so enmeshed in her dreams that she almost betrayed the secret she still shared with her father, namely that they spoke Swahili to each other when they both heard the drums and the monkeys in the forests of Ol' Joro Orok at the same time.

It was Else, however, who gave both families their first common memory. On a tiny saucer she carried a few crumbs of the precious Roquefort and, shaking her head, declared, "I cut off all of the mold, Mrs. Redlich."

On January 2, 1949, Fritz Fafflok and Walter Redlich opened their law practice together.

7

F ROM THE SMALL BUT QUICKLY GROWING CIRCLE of spectators,
Regina gathered that the two Volkswagens that were standing with
open doors in the Höhenstraße must have collided. She was no more
than thirty feet from home, and because of a completely filled milk jug
in one hand and her heavy briefcase in the other, she had no intention
of stopping. At that moment, though, the driver of one of the cars came
to her attention.

Even though she was normally not able to remember faces, she
immediately recognized the extraordinarily short man with the unruly
black hair and gold incisors. She had seen him at the synagogue during
the High Holidays. At the end of the service he had stepped on her
foot by accident, first smiled at her, afterward very solemnly extended
his hand to her, and wished her all the best for the New Year. He had
not spoken to her more than the few traditional Hebrew words for the
occasion.

While he was now standing in front of his car, getting more and
more excited, slamming his fender, and unmistakably searching for
words, Regina noticed that the man spoke in broken German. It was
not only the spontaneous sympathy for a human being who was not
equal to another because of his linguistic inability that made her stop.
The man, who was obviously from the East, touched her because he
was small and timid, and appeared unable to assess the situation he had
gotten himself into and was quite aware of it.

The other car's driver, who was big, robust, and dressed in one of those recently fashionable colorful shirts with palms and birds printed on them, shouted and stood with arms akimbo. The small black-haired man perplexedly looked around several times, raised both hands, pointed at his fender again, and nervously stammered that he wanted to call the police. He did not say, as Regina noticed instantly, "police," but "the German policemen."

Windows were opened in the houses and pillows were put into place. The practice of getting comfortable while gawking had previously only surprised Regina because of its undisguised display of curiosity. Now she felt an irritation that quickly turned into revulsion when she looked at the men with their cigarettes or newspapers in hand and the older women who occasionally still held a dusting cloth. In contrast to other times, she felt that she could read in the voracious faces an unusual kind of hatred for this kind of scenario. The voices grew louder.

First Regina had trouble finding out if only the two people involved in the accident were talking or if the bystanders were already voicing their opinions. All of a sudden, however, she clearly heard the man in the multi-colored shirt piercingly shout, "They forgot to gas you, too."

The doubt if she had really heard what her ears tried to make her believe was mercilessly short. It only lasted until Regina felt the retching in her throat and the coldness in her hands. A sharp pain seemed to be tearing her apart and she did not know in which part of her body it had started. Her first impulse was to keep on walking as long as her legs would still carry her, but she realized that it was already too late to escape and that it was not only the shock that overwhelmed her, but also shame because she was standing there as if nothing had happened and was silent as if she had not heard anything.

Regina had known for quite a while that she did not have her mother's courage to instinctively defend herself against insults and defamation, but she had never before considered her dislike for confrontations as weakness or cowardice. She had accepted her habit of never offering an opinion prematurely or unasked as a typical result of her English education and the kind of pride that she thought would make her invulnerable. Now a single short sentence had taken away her self-confidence and dignity.

In spite of her excitement, she did not have any illusions when she looked up to the apartment. She was hoping her mother would be at the window. The urge to call Jettel and hand over the responsibility for protection to her became so painful that her heart started to race and her eyes to sting. Dismayed, Regina realized that she would not be able to fight her tears much longer; her head was only able to hold on to one thought: She wished it had all been nothing but a bad dream and she would wake up soon in her mother's consoling embrace. At that moment of defeat, she saw her father.

Walter stood in front of the man in the multi-colored shirt. In her fear and confusion, he seemed quite small and very weak to Regina, but to her amazement his voice was strong.

"Say that again," he shouted.

"I am going to tell that to anyone who wants to hear it. After all, we are living in a democracy. Someone like him would have been gassed before."

"I am going to bring charges against you," Walter said. He was very quiet now. As a child Regina had often seen him like this when he felt lost and still refused to give in to his despair.

The man with the large hands looked at his feet for a moment as if he had to find new ground, but then quickly looked up again and suspiciously said, "What is that Yid to you? Why are you getting involved?"

"Because I am such a Yid, too, whom they forgot to gas. And I also know how to bring charges against swines like you. Unfortunately for you, I am a lawyer."

Regina longed for her father as strongly as just a few moments ago she had longed for her mother. She ran, the milk jug still in her hand, toward him and realized only then that she was able to breathe, see, and feel again, and that the people, the masks of hatred, and the indifference had disappeared.

Only the small dark-haired man was still there—and a few steps and a thousand years removed from him, the shrunken giant. Walter, his hat tilted backwards, his lips pressed together tightly, stood between them and silently wrote down the license plate numbers. Regina noticed that sweat had formed on his forehead. She let her briefcase drop to the ground and grasped his hand.

"I was here and heard everything," she whispered.

"I am sorry, Regina. I didn't want this to happen. Come on, we cannot go home like this. We better sit down on the bench over there. Your mother doesn't have to know about this."

They sat among the trees and blooming roses of the broad street, exhausted and burned out from their anger, and were both unable to speak for several minutes. They did not even dare look at each other.

"I am sorry, Regina," Walter repeated. "I would have liked to spare you. I had always hoped that you would never experience anything like this today. Until today at least you didn't know that such things exist."

"Oh, yes. I have known for a quite a while. But usually it is different."

"Different? How?"

"Quieter. Not so brutal."

"I am glad that you are not like your mother."

"She has courage. I don't."

"Yes, you have courage. Only in a different way."

"I don't know," Regina said, doubtfully. "Anyway, why did you stop?"

"I immediately saw that the man was a Jew."

"So did I," Regina said.

She felt the trembling in her father's body and, even though she did not want to at just this moment, she remembered their last day in Africa when the two of them had been sitting on the kitchen floor and had said goodbye to Owuor. Her ears had opened too far and too wide. "Your father," she heard Owuor say, "is a child. You have to protect him." Even though her eyes were still wet, she was able to smile again and to prepare herself to help her father keep the dreams he was unable to give up.

"We are a great pair," Walter said, "sitting here like two children who are in trouble and don't dare to go home."

"And we didn't do anything. Only the others."

"It is always the others."

"In my childhood I would have learned such a beautiful sentence by heart," Regina said. She reached for the jug on the ground because it occurred to her that her mother needed the milk and would demand an explanation, but her father put his hand on her arm.

"Wait a moment," he said. "You have to promise me something."

"I already did. Mama is not going to find out from me."

"There is something else. Promise me that you are only going to marry a Jew when the time comes."

"What makes you think of that all of a sudden?"

"Not all of a sudden, Regina. You are going to be eighteen this year. I should have brought this up long ago. But on days like this one I know that I would not be able to stand it."

"Stand what?" Regina asked, although she knew what he was talking about.

"Not to be certain that some man in some fight would not call my daughter a dirty Jew. In fact, I sometimes ask myself why my daughter never goes out with a young man."

"Just because of that," Regina answered, embarrassed.

Dinner consisted of potato salad with herring, apple, pickles, and homemade mayonnaise, and garlic sausages from the new Silesian butcher in the Berger Straße, and for dessert there was the traditional conversation that people in Frankfurt had no idea of a good potato salad and were generally unable to cook. In contrast to other times, however, Jettel herself had to point out her culinary mastery because Walter, as she noted reproachfully, was far away with his thoughts and Regina had to have a headache on a Wednesday of all days.

Wednesday had been a special day for a while. It was the day the magazines arrived from the reading club. First everyone devoured his or her favorite publication and at the end Walter always read the romantic novel, which was illustrated with photographs, aloud and with such a deliberately wrong pronunciation of individual words that Jettel and Regina kept on infecting each other with bouts of laughter because Else was not aware of Walter's ironical supplement. She listened earnestly and always said at the end, "It is so nice and cozy here, just like at home on the farm." After the events of the day, though, Regina noticed for the first time that the sad heroine was a young girl who, because of her noble father, had to decide against her heart and in favor of duty.

The deeper meaning of the sudden invitations to the Jewish nursing home by people who frequently had visitors from abroad, and whom her father hardly knew himself, became more obvious as well. Previously he had always disguised those visits laboriously and not very convincingly as related to his new position on the board of the Jewish community. Now he declared openly and—only to Jettel's amazement—with a determination that precluded any contradiction, "We are going. A man has surfaced for Regina."

Regina was less angry about the fact that she had always had to decline any invitations of her classmates on Sundays, and could not even tell them why, than about her own naïveté before the decisive conversation with her father.

For months she had not realized that the strange afternoon coffees, which were as boring for her as for her four-year-old brother, were linked to a Jewish tradition that she had not expected to find in her own liberal home. Neither her father's tolerance nor her mother's romantic notions about love and marriage, which were documented every Wednesday afternoon by reading the magazine stories, prevented the two of them from parading their daughter like a prize-winning cow in a meat market. Regina was baffled, furious, and unsure of herself.

Had her life been more like that of her contemporaries, who were able to liberate themselves from their parents without ever thinking of family and tradition, without feelings of guilt, and full of the kind of happy optimism unsupported by experience, the men, almost all of them considerably older than her, probably would have touched her. Most of them came from countries where it was apparently just as difficult to find a Jewish spouse as in Germany after the war; the ones from England or America usually lived socially isolated in small towns without Jewish communities.

This rootless generation of men was so extraordinarily alike because they had all escaped from a hell of homelessness and persecution and were determined to revive their murdered dreams of vitality, youth, and family.

They had melancholy eyes, which did not match their bravado not to waste time on conventions and courtesy. They all talked about a tragic fate in a mixture of broken German and Yiddish, and openly stated that they were looking for a capable wife, and immediately. Only Regina had not caught on for a long while that she had been chosen as prey for these lonely hunters.

Over the course of one month, a businessman from Chile, a farmer from New Zealand, two American sales representatives, and the owner of a grocery store in Liege appeared on the scene. The businessman from Chile was especially in a rush. He had even called on Sunday night to find out if Regina had made up her mind so that he could reserve a second ticket for the boat.

Regina lost her nerve, humor, and composure. Max cried along with her and shouted, "I want a divorce." Jettel called her husband a heartless fool and Walter finally had to admit to himself that he could not use the methods of the Old Testament to provide for the future of a daughter whom he had raised according to his own ideals of independence and pride. He no longer accepted invitations to the nursing home, but he continued to talk, glum and obsessed, about his responsibility to find a husband for Regina before she had a chance to fall in love with a non-Jewish man.

"We are not living in the Middle Ages anymore," Regina protested. "I never thought that you were in such a hurry to get me out of the house."

"I am not," Walter admitted. "I cannot even conceive of life without you."

"So why are we performing this kind of a rigmarole?"

"If I only knew. What did Owuor say? My tongue is faster than my head."

Even though the conversation had no consequences at first, Regina already felt better because Walter had mentioned Owuor at just the right moment. Now, she was able to remember her childhood and, above all, that her father had never been able to resign himself to waiting. She made peace with him because she understood that he suffered some guilt he could not even speak to her about. He was unable to forgive himself for bringing Regina to a country where she would never have a chance of finding a Jewish husband and, at the same time, he felt guilty for asking her to promise to marry only a Jew.

The Jewish community in Frankfurt was small, yet all the more quickly did people, to whom matchmaking was still a traditional way of life, see their chance. Regina was introduced to the owner of a café in Zcil, an agile widower who had just opened his second sausage stand, an optimistic scrap metal dealer with a humpback and his own car, and a clothing store owner, whom Jettel was enthusiastic about because he sold dresses that she would not be able to afford even years from now. Walter most liked a rabbi from Bremen because he suspected that he at least had the level of education that he longed for in his daughter's husband. In her newfound, relaxed state of mind, Regina almost betrayed the secret of George Guggenheim's ham sandwich. But she only said, "Well, just make sure that you give up smoking in case you want to celebrate the Shabbat with me and my husband."

Walter happily laughed as if she had indeed made a good joke and Regina realized that he was finally tired of his farce. The last doubts about her father's charade disappeared when she noticed that Walter never missed informing his four-year-old son about the newest events in the marriage trade, and told everyone that he had laughed so hard that he had to cry when Max had tugged at the sleeve of a young man, absorbed in prayer in the synagogue, and asked him, "Do you want to marry my sister?"

When the year 1950 came to an end, Regina also felt outwardly relieved from the threat of an arranged marriage and the humiliating evaluation of her person and her father's fortune. Even the most eager matchmakers were no longer able to find any candidates. The old basic intimacy of secret hints and keen understanding, of sentimentality and irony, blossomed stronger than before. Regina was even able to laugh again when Walter said, "You will remain an old maid and run your brother's household."

Regina, therefore, did not arm herself with any suspicion, which was left over from the most recent experiences, when Walter said, "I met a fraternity brother from Mainz and have invited him to come over Friday night." It was already that period of time when Walter, constantly on the lookout for contacts who truly warmed his heart, discovered people who came from Leobschütz, Sohrau, or Breslau almost every week, or was contacted by fraternity brothers from abroad who were passing through Frankfurt.

He strenuously ignored Jettel's objections that the people he invited were strangers and only made work for her. Guests, with whom he roamed through the never-forgotten world of yesterday as if it had never ended, were fulfillment for him and the only confirmation that his dreams had come true.

Dr. Alfred Klopp was not like the other guests with whom Walter had much better conversations than his wife and daughter. He was a strikingly good-looking, quiet, polite man, about fifty-four years old and unmistakably content and well to do. Hidden by good friends in

Holland, he had survived the persecution and soon after the war settled in Mainz as a pediatrician.

He mentioned that he did not have a family, but he did not talk about wanting to start one. Instead, he spoke of his patients, of books he liked to read, and that he loved Flemish paintings, ever since his stay in Holland, as a piece of home. After that he conquered Regina's heart because he talked to Max as if he had only come because of him.

She reflected, a little dismayed, on the irony of fate, and admitted unusually fast to her heart that she would have instantly married the thoughtful man, whose profession and education impressed her, if he had appeared on one of the hated Sunday afternoons in the Jewish nursing home. During dinner, she changed from the gray sweater with the mended sleeves into a new red blouse, put her hair up, used Jettel's lipstick and rouge, and caught herself wishing Dr. Klopp would pay as much attention to her as to her brother.

But when she returned to the room, she heard Jettel say, "Our Regina is really a very capable girl. Always busy with housework, and the way she takes care of her brother! Everyone envies me. She sews beautifully."

Regina, who fastened loose hems with a safety pin and had frustrated sewing teachers on two continents, immediately got the picture. Her skin turned as red as her blouse and she was glad that she was able to offer, with a steady hand, the vegetable bowl to Dr. Klopp, who was intensely busy with his pot roast and seemed all of a sudden embarrassed and distracted.

She tried to smile at him, but she was unable to answer his question about her journey to Switzerland because Jettel was just telling him how Regina never minded getting up at night when her brother needed her. "The man who ends up with our Regina is a lucky one," Jettel said and laughed as coquettishly as if she were part of the catch that the guest could not possibly let pass.

Dr. Klopp took his leave immediately after dinner, somewhat abruptly and deeply embarrassed. He had just remembered that he still had to visit a little patient of his and had to take care of some "urgent paperwork." He stood at the door in his coat and hat and waved at Max.

"Curtsy, Regina," Walter said.

"You couldn't have found a better way of telling him that I am too young for him," Regina later hissed at her father.

Even though he had at least had a good time during the earlier part of the evening, Dr. Klopp was never heard from again. Regina was grateful to him nonetheless. Without him she would not have found out until much later that her father dreaded nothing more than the moment when he had to give up his daughter to another man.

"You don't want me to get married at all," she reproached him.

"By everything that is holy to me, that is not true," Walter insisted.

"*Bwana,* you are lying like a monkey."

"Yes, but it is your own fault."

"Why?"

"You," Walter sighed, and imitated Owuor's voice, "have stolen *my* heart, *memsahib.*"

8

Max was able to catch the quietly blowing wind and turn it into a transparent cool washcloth for his burning face when he rotated the crank and held one hand out of the open car window. As soon as he moved his head just a little bit from one side to the other, trees with big round trunks became as thin as a thread, just like Kaspar, the little boy who would not eat his soup in *Slovenly Peter* on the fifth day. The trees, topped with green hats, flew into the blue sky and scratched at white soap-sudsy clouds. But most of the time Max just sat quietly next to his father and looked at him through the black curtain of his long eyelashes. The great miracle kept rolling on. It was like being in one of those fairy tales, which silly little children believed in. Only a thousand times better and as real and sweet as the red lake of strawberry jam on a breakfast roll.

Max was the first to learn that his father had turned into a rich giant who was able to honk the horn with one hand and with the other to give orders to the gearshift, which had to be obeyed immediately and with a great howl. The giant could have ridden on a golden horse in the sun above the houses. If he had wanted to, he could have flown to the moon and back in an airplane of pure silver, but he did not need such tricks because he sat in a big, wonderful car with dark red metal fenders and shining glass windows.

The giant with the dark brown, wavy hair, who looked like Max's father had looked only yesterday, was singing, "The Eunuchs are sitting crying in the harem," "Who is supposed to pay for this?" and

"Gaudeamus Igitur." Foaming bubbles emerged from his mouth. Between the songs and powerful shouts of "hurrah," the king took his hands off the steering wheel and clapped. The thunder was very short and quite hard. But when he did not sing, honk the horn, or clap, he called out loud enough for the windows to vibrate, "This car belongs to me and my favorite son."

"Not to Regina?" the mighty son asked.

"Women do not have cars. But they can come along for a ride if they are nice."

"Why is Regina not coming with us then?"

"There is no place for women on a maiden voyage. It is bad luck to take them along."

"What is a maiden voyage?"

"This here. We are driving our own car for the very first time. This is for men only."

"Only you and I," Max happily said. "Me and thou. And miller's cow."

"We are not taking the miller's cow along either. A lawyer doesn't pay attention to cows. That was once upon a time. I only talked to oxen in my other life."

"Did you live once before, Papa?"

"And how, my son. I was a little gray mouse then and afraid of every cat."

"And now," Max realized, "you are the Puss 'n Boots."

"Nonsense. I am an attorney and notary."

"I am going to be an attorney and notary, too. With a big office and lots of clients."

"You do that, Maxele, my son."

The miraculous carriage was a used Opel Olympia, a wheezing prewar model, only insufficiently recovered from many injuries. It had been a bargain from a client who, on his way up the social ladder, had quickly switched cars and had sensed Walter's desire for mobility—and at a speed the car itself had not been able to achieve for years now.

After that the robust little Opel with the magic powers became above all the triumph of a man who had been imprisoned on a farm in Africa and had dreamed of a donkey with a saddle when the fever shook him and he needed a physician. The singing giant and his chosen son stopped between Königstein and Kronberg, sat down on a meadow of green velvet, ate potatoes made of marzipan and bread made of nougat, smoked cigarettes made of tobacco and chocolate, and decided to name the car "Susi Opel."

Max, who attended a Catholic kindergarten in the Eichwaldstraße and was quite taken by the mysterious stories that Sister Elsa retrieved from the depths of her black habit, wanted to baptize Susi Opel with three drops from the small bottle of blueberry liqueur in the glove compartment.

"Jews don't get baptized," his father told him, "and neither do Jewish cars. You should never forget that."

"Never," Max promised.

In a life that permitted miracles again, Susi Opel was a shining heroine when she stood red and squat in front of the house, and she became the panting mistress of father and son when she had to negotiate hills and curves. Just one look in her mirror overshadowed the new miracle of the slim, heavily made-up *Fräuleins,* the young women in their long skirts and high, clanking heels. The rooster that was crowing about the economic miracle, which was just about to start and would make bank accounts and new houses grow, was less audible than their own squeaking wheels and coughing motor. Those sang of a dream that Walter had believed in for such a long time, and that now had so obviously taken shape that Jettel no longer mourned the fixed salary of a judge.

The practice of attorneys Fafflok and Redlich prospered in such a way that people at court no longer talked in a vague and patronizing way about the "two stubborn mules from the East," but said respectfully and often even enviously, "Those two have made it."

In addition to his industriousness and professional brilliance, perseverance, and astute business sense, Fafflok had also brought his old, amply proportioned secretary, who handled all tasks to perfection, ranging from Kattowitz to the new attorneys' union. Part of Fafflok's dowry consisted above all of two industrialists with roots in Upper Silesia and great need for a notary. Walter initially was only able to offer his energy, quick thinking and action, a passion for the profession he loved and had never forgotten, and the obsession to seize from the present what the years of emigration had taken away from him.

Very soon clients came for his sake, too—Jewish people from abroad who hoped for restitution for lost homes and businesses, and Jews who had ended up in Frankfurt, had lost family, health, and all means to gain a livelihood in the concentration camps, and still remembered the word "justice."

Refugees from Upper Silesia came in droves. Even the drums in the woods of Ol' Joro Orok could not have been faster in spreading the news about a tribal war or a bushfire than the happy Upper Silesians were in telling each other the news that at 60 Neue Mainzer Straße there was a friendly man behind his desk whose sense of justice was as pronounced as his kindness. He spoke the same language and had the same sense of humor as the people, who—like he before them—had lost their homeland, faith, and belongings. Because he was unable to forget his own fate—being cast out and dispossessed—he was never just the legal adviser he had to be, but also someone who gave them sympathy. He felt that every case that was entrusted to him, no matter how small, demanded his full attention. More than anything, this man, with the vehement, choleric temper and eyes that immediately betrayed his kindness, knew how important it was for people who had been humiliated to go to court and to sue for respect. When the unwanted refugees from the East were called "gipsy pack" or "dirty refugees" and were accused of offenses that incensed and insulted them, he was not concerned about the negligible fees for the legal battle, but burned with the same indignation they felt.

When it became known that almost every week Walter wrote a letter for his friend Greschek in Marke so that no accusation would remain without a rebuttal, others were also encouraged to defend themselves against the provocations of the well-to-do. They came with the defeatist attitude of an outsider from the small surrounding villages where they had been banished, and left the practice with their heads held high.

Although it was no longer customary in these times of a growing economy, Walter also still took payment in kind, just as he had done a long while ago from the peasants around Leobschütz. The refugees, who lived in the villages and were able to buy produce cheaply from the farmers, could spare groceries more easily than money. Some of them already owned small stores. Walter considered vegetables, potatoes, geese and rabbits, wood for a living room table, cheap tin toys, fabric for dresses, and blankets as sufficient payment for his services. The only important thing for him was that the wares, which piled up in his office, could be equitably divided between him and Fafflok.

Occasionally, though, Fafflok mildly, and not on his own accord, had to remind Walter about the rent, insurance, salaries for the office personnel (in addition to Mrs. Fischer from Kattowitz there was also a young intern now), and other necessities besides kitchen and household. His wife, first occasionally and later more and more often, encouraged him to such objections after he brought her the sixth tablecloth from a dry goods store in Friedberg.

This rebellion also encouraged Jettel to protest when she and Regina kept getting, from the same store, aprons and blouses that did not even live up to the modest requirements of the times, and moreover were made from the same material as the tablecloths. Since Walter desperately wanted a car, Jettel could not have found a better time to persuade him to finally give up his beloved bartering.

Anyway, Susi Opel offered an opportunity to find new outlets for his connections to Upper Silesia. Almost every Sunday Walter drove with Jettel, Regina, Else, and Max to find the lost homeland—for a few hours at least. The trips into a gilded past led to Bad Vilbel and Kleinkarben, Friedberg, Bad Nauheim, and to villages that could rarely be found on any map and also to farms where refugee families had been taken in.

As soon as it became known that Dr. Redlich and his family had arrived, small feasts were improvised, and they turned into melancholy gala celebrations. There were always cakes with streusel and poppy seeds, mountains of whipped cream, and "real coffee." In addition, "decent schnapps," mustard pickles, and herring salad made from an old family recipe were never missing. The roast was accompanied by a sauce and mashed potatoes, which were all served under their original Silesian names. The green beans were prepared sweet and sour, "just like at mother's," and with raisins, and if Dr. Redlich had announced that he would come, baked calf's feet and brains were dished up because everyone knew that he had made the trip just for them.

Walter believed all of this himself. Jettel and Regina were not that easily deceived. They very quickly realized, and were even more baffled by the silent accord of their misgivings, that it was not his homesick stomach that he wanted to indulge on Sundays. He was healing his wounded heart.

Only with people from Leobschütz and even more so with friends from his youth in Sohrau was he able to immerse himself without prejudice, uncertainty, and restraint into a world he had to believe in if he wanted to look at his return to Germany in the merciful light of a boost to his ego. When people from Sohrau innocently asked about his father and his sister, as if those two had just gone on a trip and had forgotten to write the promised postcards, he took the question itself as an interest in his fate.

When he then told them that his father and sister had been murdered and they asked amazed, "But why?" and said with the same kind of innocence and bafflement, "They were such good people," he never lost his patience, never got embarrassed, and never became suspicious. If someone from Leobschütz asked after former Jewish acquaintances, he never intimated that they should have known what had happened to people who did not emigrate in time. Walter, who at least since his emigration to Africa detested escaping into illusions and dangerous expressions of sentimentality, lost all sense of reality if someone was able to evoke the pictures and sounds of the homeland.

Not once did Walter ask himself in those hours, when he drank the balm of forgetfulness with each swig of schnapps, why the people of Upper Silesia, specifically, would not have known what had happened to their Jewish neighbors. He never doubted the integrity and honesty of their outrage, and it never occurred to him that his beloved fellow Silesians could, like so many people in postwar Germany, have a past they did not talk about either. Until someone was able to prove the opposite, Walter would believe the best of everyone and was not interested in knowing anything that might have undermined his belief in integrity.

He was firmly convinced that he could not find a better place to present a picture of a decent Germany to his daughter and little son with the Frankfurt dialect than in the circle of complaining and tearful people who had experienced the same injustice of expulsion as he had. He was deeply hurt when Regina asked, "Didn't the synagogues burn in Leobschütz and Sohrau, too?" And he was outraged when Jettel, after a

Sunday outing that he felt had been especially poignant, said, "Greschek told me quite a different story."

Yet it was Max who—with a single question—made his father stop looking for his lost homeland every week. In the synagogue Max fell spontaneously and undyingly in love with a curly-haired beauty of his own age with big eyes in a round doll's face. He reproachfully asked his father, "Didn't you know that there are Jewish children in Frankfurt?"

It was one of the rare occasions when Walter did not give an honest answer to his son, whom he had enlightened very early and extensively about persecution and emigration.

The enchanting girl, who was already as clever as flirtatious and self-confident, was called Jeanne-Louise and conquered Max with her white socks, Parisian elegance, and an invitation to visit her on the Shabbat. He would be able to eat as many chocolates as he wanted and could pet her dog. Jeanne-Louise's father was born in Frankfurt, had returned as an attorney to his hometown a year ago, and was well on his way to becoming a wealthy man. Walter told neither his son nor the rest of the family that he had already known all this for quite a while.

After his emigration, when Josef Schlachanska returned with his wife and daughter from France to Frankfurt, where many people still remembered him from before, and just as many soon started noticing him, he had a common acquaintance ask Walter if he would be interested in becoming his associate. This happened half a year after Walter had opened the practice with Fafflok. Walter had refused Schlachanska's offer, and heard immediately afterward that he had said, "That fool from Africa will truly be sorry. From now on he is not even going to earn the butter on his bread."

Hurt and upset, and not completely without envy of the quick success of a man who did not even have to fight for victory, Walter avoided any kind of personal contact with Schlachanska although he was with him on the board of the Jewish community and liked him well enough there. Josef Schlachanska, with his mustache that made his full, round face even softer than it already seemed, was remarkable not only because of his astonishing corpulence in a time of just-conquered hunger. He was triumphant in a baroque manner. His ready wit and humor, and a calculated blend of comedy, derision, and self-effacing irony, were as infectious as his energy and titanic temperament.

He possessed that contemporary good nose for profit and speculation that Walter considered beneath him. He was an attorney with an immense talent for acting, which Walter also rejected as unprofessional and which created quite a stir because he habitually and with expressive gestures refused judges as prejudiced, and thus created the impression that he was fighting for his clients with the full force of his two hundred and fifty pounds.

Josef Schlachanska talked to the people in Frankfurt in their easy-going, earthy language; made the same jokes they made; and immediately gave them the confidence that he was one of them. He did not bother the Jews from the East, who chose him for their advisor as quickly as if they had just waited for him to get established as an attorney, with the details, precautions, and legal subtleties that they viewed as typically German. Walter was unable to do either.

Josef Schlachanska, who was always willing to come to a compromise with secular moral principles and was never shy to admit this and, moreover, in a way that people appreciated, was a pious man. In spite of everything he had experienced when he and his wife had to find shelter with a young physician's family in Paris, where they only dared to go on the street for a few minutes after dark, he had no doubts about a God who had allowed millions of his people to be murdered.

Josef Schlachanska's father had been a teacher at the Philanthropin, the renowned Jewish school in Frankfurt; his brother, headmaster of a Jewish school in Cologne, had returned shortly before the outbreak of the war from the safety of England and had been deported together with his pupils. But just like Walter, Schlachanska had realized that he could work in his profession only in Germany. He spoke of his return, but never of a homeland.

Schlachanska's household was kosher, his daughter received a strictly religious upbringing, and he and his family never missed a service. When he sang in the synagogue in a deep warm voice, draped in his white prayer shawl and his face lit with ardor, nobody saw and heard the cantor, but everybody just saw and heard him.

He was big enough to admit his mistakes and did not deny the rude comment he had made about Walter, apologized with a charm that was just as fetching as his kindness, and extended both hands to Walter after the ice had finally been broken. He felt the necessity to share the abundance he needed to live and was a passionate host.

Well-informed about the situation in Frankfurt, Schlachanska could only tolerate for a short while the apartment that had been assigned to him in the modest Frankfurt North End after his return from the French exile. He moved to a suite of six rooms with a large terrace on the prominent Eysseneckstraße, which had survived the war in good condition. There he resided under spectacular lamps and crystal chandeliers, amidst luxuriously covered armchairs and heavy, dark furniture. He owned French china and expensively framed pictures with Jewish themes, and had a maid, a nanny, and in everything the pompous taste that matched his magnificent appearance. Schlachanska knew of no inhibitions or limits to ostentation. His generosity ensured that his vanity and flamboyance were accepted with the same unqualified mind-set that common people exhibit toward an extraordinarily popular king.

The pralines that his daughter had promised Max and that Schlachanska stuffed as freely into the mouth of his slobbering setter Seppl, as if he had never experienced hunger and the fear of death, tempted Walter to accept a second invitation after the first. With a bluntness in language and judgment, which, in spite of all differences, was in accord with Walter's character, he was able to cut all barriers as quickly and decisively as Alexander the Great severed the Gordian knot.

Josef Schlachanska represented to Max all he wanted to be himself some day—he was a rich, mighty, magnificent giant in Frankfurt with the biggest car: a Maybach. This lover of children, who could frolic like a clown and change the world like a magician, helped himself from glass bowls filled with mountains of sweets, and only had to clap his hands and everyone obeyed his commands. On a Shabbat afternoon he sat in striped pajamas in an ornate wing chair and created the first conflict of loyalties in the life of a five-year-old boy. He corrupted the innocence and modesty, which his own father emphasized daily, first a little with the electric train that the chauffeur had to operate and then completely with the Maybach.

Since Max insisted on his right to play with Jeanne-Louise instead of having to bathe in the caresses and tears of unknown adults, the Shabbat invitations soon became as firm a tradition as the previous trips to the people of Upper Silesia. In the beginning Jettel was just glad that she had to bake only one cake for the weekend instead of two and did not have to worry about anything else till dinner. Yet she was the first who also made contact with Mrs. Schlachanska and was able to see more in her than just a demanding woman who wanted even more glamour than she already had.

Mina Schlachanska was as vain and as sure of herself as her husband, but since she lacked his charm and especially his sense of humor, she appeared aloof and conceited. To take other people into consideration was a religious duty rather than a real need for her. Her originally small talent for tolerance had withered completely during the times when they had to fear for their existence and had to be afraid daily of being deported. After that, her forbearance only extended to the volcano at her side; he generously and cheerfully let her draw from the horn of plenty of his newly found wealth.

Her elegance and the way she accentuated her taste, which had been influenced by French fashion, appeared provocative at a time when other people took their first, very reluctant steps from need to normality. She mistook shabby clothes for a shabby character, regarded the offensive compassion of the haves for the have-nots as genuine sympathy for the fate of others, and allowed only herself to escape from her critical judgments. Etiquette, conventions, and tradition were important to Mina Schlachanska. Wealth and the safety she had been forced to forgo for so long were everything.

She came from a modest background, had met her husband as a young girl in Italy, and instantly married him even though he was divorced. She had a hard time reconciling this situation with her notions of morality and marriage, fled to France with him, and was interned in the women's camp at Gurs when the German armed forces marched in. She hardly talked about that time, which had left her with wounds that could not be healed. Occasionally she mentioned the two years during which she had to live in hiding with her husband and how he had worked in a fish factory in Paris after the liberation.

Mina Schlachanska was obsessed with the desire to make up for everything she had missed in life. Modesty no longer entered her mind—especially where it concerned her daughter, who was dressed far too elegantly and was not allowed to play with children who were poorly clothed. She considered luxury the prerogative of a woman who had not wanted to come back into the country of her persecutors.

Even though Walter admired her industriousness, her discipline, her sense of decorum, her unquestioning love for her husband, and the perfectionism with which she ran her lavish household, he denied her the tolerance that he taught his children. He too often resented her materialism, which in his eyes made her crass and envious.

"Don't talk nonsense," Jettel said. "What do you think I would be like if I had had to suffer what this woman had to suffer?"

"I wouldn't have let you, Jettel, and since when are there people in this world who have suffered more than you?"

"She is a good woman."

"What makes you think that?"

"My knowledge of human nature tells me. You don't have any. My mother always said so."

Walter was most uncomfortable with the thought that the Schlachanska's lifestyle might make his children jealous and seduce them into megalomania. Max was no longer taken in by Jeanne-Louise's white socks and patent leather shoes, but by her room, expensive toys, her father's Maybach, and the chauffeur, who carried his bag to the car.

Regina, on the other hand, very soon relieved her father of the worry that appearances would blind and permanently harm her. After Josef Schlachanska looked at her wistfully one afternoon and said, "A girl like her should not graduate from a German high school, she should be sent to England or Israel to find a husband," she looked at everything he said and did in the future from her usual skeptical and suspicious point of view. Regina, therefore, was also the only one to whom Walter confided, "You know, your father will never be as rich as Schlachanska. But at least he can sleep well at night."

He considered it, thus, a double irony of fate that Schlachanska's tirelessly repeated remark, "One does not live in a seized apartment, and especially not in the Höhenstraße," motivated Walter's ambition in a totally incomprehensible way.

9

"Jettel, by everything that is holy to me, believe me. I went to law school for seven semesters and received my doctorate. You do not need a new hat to go to a notary."

"Don't always act so smart. I was already working for a notary when your father was still paying your bills."

"So why this nonsense?"

"I thought I was going to become a house owner today."

"The house will be registered in your name. That is what you do when you are self-employed. Besides, then you will be in a much better position once you have put me into the grave."

"You yourself said this is a big day."

"The biggest in our lives, Jettel, since we had to leave Leobschütz. Not counting the birth of our son."

"Well, there you go. Do you think Mrs. Schlachanska would wear an old hat on a day like this?"

"Mrs. Schlachanska would even wear a new hat on the day they had to declare bankruptcy. But we have to keep our money together now. So I think you'd better listen to me rather than Mrs. Schlachanska."

"If there is not even enough for a new hat, you won't get far with your construction."

"Our construction, Jettel."

The hat was light blue and had a white veil with tiny white dots, behind which Jettel's skin had the same diaphanous sheen as her old blouse from the Indian tailor in Nairobi. Jettel almost did not come along to the notary because Walter had called the hat "terribly beautiful" and had laughed in spite of his anger. The circumstances required a quick reconciliation that finally took place in the waiting room of attorney Friedrich, whom Walter still knew from their common visits to the tutor Wendriner in Breslau and who transported Jettel into a state of glowing euphoria by not only kissing her hand when greeting her, but by almost simultaneously saying, "What a lovely hat, Mrs. Redlich; a spring poem. It is wonderful that our women have not forgotten how to lead us into the realm of dreams again."

"I found out early on, Friedrich, that you are as much a poet as a lawyer," Walter remembered, "and if you keep on turning my wife's head any more, she is not even going to let me move into her house."

In pensive moments it seemed to him just compensation through fate that the house in the broad, maple-lined Rothschildallee should have a Jewish owner again.

His aversion to an excess of imagination, which he had found dangerous in every stage of his life, however, protected him from inappropriate comparisons and prevented him from overrating the duplicity of events.

Walter had often looked at the heavily war-worn building from the window of his living room and knew about the tragic story of its owners. He had heard that the house was for sale at precisely the moment when he had finally decided to keep his promise to Mrs. Wedel and look for another residence.

The apartment house, built at the turn of the century, with its wrought iron gate, high windows, and massive balconies that, in spite of the bomb damage, still symbolized the bourgeois pride of a self-confident generation, had no roof or upper floor. In the parlance of the times the two floors that were still inhabited were considered "unclaimed Jewish property." After the war, the land and the house on it had been transferred to the Jewish Restitution Successor Organization, which made sure that the new Federal Republic did not profit from any interest on the crimes of the old Germany.

Walter was a consultant and notary for the organization and, because of his patient persistence and Schlachanska's energetic efforts, he was able to persuade the organization to sell him the house for a very good price. He had heard about the Jewish couple, the Isenbergs, who had been murdered in Auschwitz and had no heirs.

Mrs. Wedel had told Walter about the fate of the Isenbergs shortly after they had moved in with her. She had also told him that the house, number 9, had been the first in the Rothschildallee to be bombed and that people had surreptitiously told each other that this was God's punishment.

When it became known that Walter wanted to buy the house, so many people in the neighborhood talked to him about the fate of the Isenbergs who "really had been decent people and were not to blame" that it occurred even to Walter, who hesitated for quite a while before he condemned anyone, that the deportation of the Jewish citizens in Frankfurt could not have happened quite as unnoticed as was maintained again and again after the war.

"I can't wait to see how many people will tell me now how terribly upset they were when the Isenbergs were taken away," Jettel said.

Walter nodded. He would not have contradicted her even if he had not agreed with her. His energy for arguments with his wife on this important day had already been spent by the early afternoon. In attorney Friedrich's practice, Jettel had to be persuaded by the combined efforts of Friedrich, Fafflok, and Walter to go along with the necessary legal formalities. When she heard that Walter was not going to pay cash for the house, which incidentally was not the custom anyway, she angrily picked up her handbag and told the perplexed trio, "I have never had any debts in my life and I am not going to start having any now."

"Without you, Jettel, we would all be in the debtors' prison," Walter said.

A blue parrot with a big beak said "Oh" twice in a row, while a tiny monkey chewed on a banana and demonstrated in its own way that life had changed—three years ago nobody would have thought that there would ever be enough bananas in Frankfurt and then for monkeys.

Walter and Jettel were sitting in the Cafe Wipra at the Liebfrauenberg, and were already agreeing again on an important point of mutual interest: This was the only place where one could eat real poppy seed cake. The owner and his wife were from Silesia and, in contrast to the inhabitants of Frankfurt, knew that poppy seeds had to be ground twice and had to be soaked in milk before baking. Cafe Wipra, with its blooming, real tropical plants, birds, monkeys, and the many other animals, which were happy enough in their cages to give the admiring guests a feeling of vacation and exotic climates, was a special favorite among children. Walter and Jettel often went there alone as well. On this happy day Walter had dreamed not only of poppy seed cake but also of another pastry, the hard to digest "Liegnitzer Bomben," and Jettel felt the desire to introduce her new hat to a place where hardly any lady appeared hatless.

Both ordered two portions of whipped cream with their cake, Walter a double cognac afterward, and Jettel an egg liqueur that put her in such a good mood that she tried to smoke one of Walter's cigarettes. Both remembered simultaneously that she had done that last during an excursion from Leobschütz to Jägerndorf and had coughed in the same way then as now in Frankfurt.

The times in which they had been hungry were not yet far enough removed to consider a full stomach to be unpleasant. To be more than just satisfied smoothed the hard edges of life. The fullness made Jettel tender and Walter pensive. Even though they had just traveled to Leobschütz, they arrived in Africa.

It was Walter who looked for too long at the little monkey in the cage in front of the small marble-topped table and was unable to protect himself. He first thought about the farm at Ol' Joro Orok and how the Indian Daji Jiwan had had a house built there from freshly felled cedars. Initially Walter only smelled the wood, but his nose urged him on and he saw how Owuor fed the fire in the fireplace with his breath, slowly rose, and looked around with satisfaction. When the picture finally lost its colors, Owuor started to sing "Ich hab' mein Herz in Heidelberg verloren." His voice carried to the huts near the river. Walter felt his neck getting stiff and the cognac burning in his throat. "Strange," he sighed, "at least I knew what I was afraid of at the farm."

He was startled when he realized that he had just elicited an answer from Jettel that was sure to lead to an argument that would still ruin the day, but to his surprise she took his hand and squeezed it.

"We are going to end up as a couple of love birds yet in our old age," Walter laughed, "and I have to admit, I do like your hat."

In the following weeks he also got to know Jettel from another, quite welcome side. With the recurrent remark, "It is my house after all," and already dressed early in the morning as if she were going to call on the mayor himself, she turned the renovation of 9 Rothschildallee into a personal mission. Adorned with a hat and white lace gloves, without which a lady could not be seen in the street, she stomped through the rubble of the building site with the fighting spirit and self-confidence of an Amazon, exhibiting the coquettishness that, during the time of her dancing lessons, had made all the young men notice no one but her in the ballroom.

She enraged the architect with her demands, suggestions, and unexpected flow of tears, and calmed him just as quickly with her charm, cherry cake, and truly fascinating stories about her experiences as a builder in Ol' Joro Orok. She got workmen, whom she rendered defenseless with her temperament and enchanted with her helpless smile, to come from their place of work and she enticed them with complaints, many promises of a taste of specialties from her kitchen, and ingenious appeals to their honor to come to the building site. All of this was necessary because Walter had once again succumbed to the lure of his old habits before the currency reform and had hired carpenters, plumbers, painters, masons, electricians, and roofers who had not paid his fees and were quite unenthusiastic at the prospect of working off their debts, and could only be motivated to show up in the Rothschildallee by Jettel's varied appearances.

The house that originally had been three floors high grew to four. The uppermost floor was divided into two small apartments. One had been promised to Greschek, who wrote every week that he could not stand life for another day as an ostracized refugee in the village where he was exposed to outrageous suspicions and even physical violence and that he wanted to work in his old job again.

"Greschek never had a job in his life," Walter remembered. "He always had others work for him. But he needs to get out of that damn village. He is going to perish there. We will give him a position as superintendent. He doesn't have to pay any rent then and Grete can do the little bit that needs to be done."

The thought of Grete's capabilities and industriousness alone gave Jettel renewed energy. She had already been worried that an apartment with five rooms would be too much for one maid alone and especially for Else, who was not familiar with the sophistication that was required by the etiquette of the evermore budding miracle of better times. The anticipation of having Greschek's tireless Grete, who most likely would also be devoted to her, at her side, seemed like a repetition of the happy days on the farm where there had been a man with strong arms for every task.

During this time, when the future meant so much more than the past, Regina's thoughts only traveled in a different direction. When she was sent to the building site in the afternoon with cake, sandwiches, and coffee in a thermos and saw the roof grow, she realized how disturbingly vivid the flood of pictures still coursed within her. Again and again, she remembered the days on the farm when she had seen the house at Ol' Joro Orok get bigger. One last time, before the roof was covered, she had climbed up onto the narrow beam on the top.

While she leaned against the raw walls here in Frankfurt, she was suddenly nine years old again and intoxicated with the happiness of the laughing peaceful people, and the sounds and smells. She saw the snow gleaming far away on Mount Kenya, smelled the freshness of the red soil after the start of the long rains, and heard the drums that told about the new house and its *bwana*. Even worse, she heard her own voice rolling from the mountain into the valley as she cried out jubilantly, "There is no place more beautiful than Ol' Joro Orok." And she knew that nothing had changed for her since then and she would never be able to delude her nostalgia.

"Now," Walter said and looked at the small front yard with the lilac bush that had defied the bombs, "you, too, have something to call your father's house."

Regina thought of the photo album with the worn gray linen cover that had traveled to Africa and back, and of the small, yellowed picture of the Redlich's hotel in Sohrau with the words "My father's house" written under it. She looked at her father. She succeeded in not shaking her head but smiled at him instead, as in the days without beginning and end when she had always been able to summon the balm that healed his wounds.

Regina knew all about close connections to one's father's house, and how it could turn into a prison there was no escape from. But her father, whom she loved so much that she did not even dare to hurt him with one of her thoughts and fears, knew nothing about his daughter. That had not changed, either, since the time when Owuor, at the edge of the large flax field with blue flowers of eternal happiness, had whispered to her, "The *bwana* has forgotten to take his heart along on the big safari."

Grete Greschek, small, wiry, her blond hair with its strands of gray tied into a thin bun at the back of her head, and her hands as red as her narrow face that was lit by the happiness of seeing everyone again and a burning desire to get to work, arrived a few days before the move in Frankfurt. After the first shared meal, she retrieved from her worn gray cardboard suitcase a washboard that she called by its Silesian name, "Rumpel." She also produced a can of lard ("the real thing with greaves, the way our Dr. Redlich always got it from me"), and a blue apron dress. She took the plates that Jettel was about to collect out of her hand and said, "That is not for you." She had not forgotten anything else, either, since 1938, the year in which the "Doctors" had had to "make off."

At every move in Leobschütz, Grete had been an active consoling force who, without being able to put it into words, had known the sorrow of separation from the people she was connected to in the same reliable, familiar way as to her siblings. She could remember what the kitchen in the Lindenstraße, the curtains at the Hohenzollernplatz, and the bed of winter pansies at the Asternweg had looked like. She also still remembered that Walter became hungry when he got upset and that Jettel started to cry when there were unexpected challenges or excitement and would talk about her mother, who had recognized her sensitivity early on.

Greschek's Grete, as she still referred to herself when talking about those times in Leobschütz, when room and board were still payment enough for her, was undauntedly convinced of the healing powers of hot soup. As soon as Walter and Jettel started one of those battles without beginning or end, she put the pot on the stove and began to cut the bread. With the call, "Soup is ready," she brought the soup terrine to the table. Grete called slippers "pampooshes" and had them ready as soon as Walter rang the doorbell and started whistling "Ich weiß nicht, was soll es bedeuten." When Max ran around between the cartons and boxes, disturbing Grete while she was packing glasses and dishes, she fished in the pocket of her apron for a ten-pfennig piece, told him, "Here is a Groschen," and sent him to the street vendor in the Allee to buy himself a treat.

She called Else a "dumb goose" when she squashed a cordial glass with her big hands and once said the same of Regina because she considered modesty in people she valued as too much baggage for life. At night she talked about Greschek, who wanted to stay a few more months in Marke to settle some important business transactions he had started. Under no circumstances did Grete want to move into the superintendent's apartment by herself. After the move she insisted on sleeping on a cot in the kitchen. While she was making the coffee for breakfast, she told Max about her goat, Lemmy, that she loved so much that she started crying when she described it jumping around in the garden as soon as the rooster, which she seemed to love as much as the goat, started crowing. Grete thought the eggs in Frankfurt were not fresh enough and the people too fresh.

Regina was the first to realize that the Grescheks were not planning to move to Frankfurt, but as hard as she tried she was not able to find the words that would protect her parents from their illusions and desire to turn back the clock.

Beds, tables, chairs, a sideboard, a bookshelf, closets, a stove, a sofa, easy chairs, a console, and a dressing table with a three-part mirror, the kind Mrs. Schlachanska had, needed to be purchased because Mrs. Wedel not only got her apartment back but also her furniture. And, as Jettel heard from the greengrocer's wife, she also got money for the renovation. Walter denied that, called the greengrocer's wife an old gossip, and refused to have radishes on his bread.

Grete washed out the furniture (which had all been bought secondhand) with vinegar and scrubbed the new linoleum with liquid soap till it looked as if several generations had already run across it. She waxed the parquet floor until one could slide on it, in the backyard beat the moth-infested carpet that Walter had received from a client as a fee, and put the three rubber trees, which had been delivered for the housewarming party and were used for airing out her dust cloths, into the sun room.

There a snakeskin, a souvenir of an unforgettable day at Lake Naivasha, crawled along a wall painted in a sunny yellow. Below that Masai warriors with tiny arrows and shields of genuine buffalo hide marched on a white plastic shelf that was just becoming the clean, handy symbol of the new times. Among the carved men with fine metal rings around their necks, a bald Kikuyu woman made of light wood sat on a stool nursing her child.

Jettel had given the Indian shopkeeper at Ol' Joro Orok two plates from the fruit set for the figures. Walter had gotten so mad that he threw the remaining four against the wall. Now, however, both were talking admiringly and tenderly of their "African corner" and greeted the wooden elephants with *"jambo, tembo"* in the morning.

An "Ice Günther" truck had come to the Höhenstraße three times a week to deliver two blocks of ice for the icebox. In the Rothschildallee, a refrigerator stood next to the window—"a real electric one from Bosch," as Jettel never forgot to mention. In front of the magnificent white marvel she and Walter ended the longest battle of their marriage. It had gone on since the day when Jettel, contrary to her husband's advice to bring an icebox from Breslau, had instead arrived on the farm with an evening gown.

"You always knew everything better," Walter said and happily stabbed his knife into a piece of cold, hard butter. "That was the great tragedy of our emigration."

"The evening gown was exquisite. I don't care what you say. I will never find one like it in Frankfurt."

On the first Saturday in the new apartment, Walter opened the bottle of wine that had traveled to Africa and back. On the day of his emigration his father had given him two bottles for good days but there had only been one good day.

"Do you remember," Walter asked, "when we drank the wine?"

"When the baby was stillborn," Regina said.

"Was that a good day?" Max asked.

"Yes, because your mother did not die."

"Fine," Max said, and let an ice cube tumble into his glass.

Since the move Max had started to add ice water to his sherbet powder and had dreamed of a refrigerator in the Maybach he would drive to court once he became an attorney.

The harmony of the moment had rendered Regina idle; she let her head have its way and remembered the fairy that had lived in her colored cordial glass and had shared pleasures with her of which her parents were unaware. The thought of the magic that had served her for so long warmed her even more than the wine, but her good mood did not have the same stamina as the fairy. All of a sudden she felt sorry for Max because he had not known the adversity and anxiety that had made her resilient and because he did not know anything about the power of an imagination that goes beyond material desires. She got up to get a glass for Grete and touched his head in passing.

"Careful with my ice cubes," Max admonished her.

Grete emptied her glass in one gulp, fumbled at her apron, got out a letter, and said, "I will have to leave soon. Greschek wrote. He needs me."

"To pack?" Walter asked.

"But no," Grete laughed, "to clean. He cannot manage by himself."

"But you are going to move to Frankfurt," Walter said. "Josef wants to leave Marke. He writes in every letter how unhappy he is."

"Don't you believe it, Dr. Redlich. You cannot believe Greschek. He is full of talk. He could never live in Frankfurt. Everything here is much too big and too dirty and too noisy. He certainly wouldn't like the people here. And the superintendent's apartment is no good for him. He needs his freedom."

"And you, Grete?"

"My goat is waiting for me, Dr. Redlich, but I will always come to you when the missus needs me."

"It would have been so nice," Walter sighed. "I am going to drive you home and have a talk with your Josef."

Two weeks later, on a Saturday, Walter, Jettel, Grete, and Max departed for Marke and Else went by train to visit her sister in Stuttgart. Regina, who had sprained her ankle and had not told anyone that it did not bother her anymore, stayed home by herself. When she saw the car leave and waved with a handkerchief in each hand, as she had done as a child when she had to leave the farm, she remembered the two black oxen at Ol' Joro Orok. They had always seemed much stronger and younger at night when the yoke was taken off than in the morning. She was ashamed of her happiness, but the relief remained.

Regina determined that she was going to spend the weekend, which seemed very long and precious in her liberation, as if she were just like any other young woman. She very seldom had a chance to visit her friend Puck without having to take her brother along.

Puck lived with an old, deaf aunt and she enjoyed all the freedom that Regina was denied, the experiences of life beyond school and middle-class prudishness that Regina longed for, and a born winner's attractive charm, which she admired without being jealous. On this weekend, without pressure, Regina longed more than ever for the happiness and cheerfulness that waited for her at Puck's; for uncomplicated conversations about clothes, hairstyles, and movies, which the times had made possible once again; and for the natural confidences among girlfriends.

She stood for quite a while in front of the built-in closet that the architect had labeled "Girl's Room" in pencil on the door, first put on a white blouse with the blue skirt, then a yellow one that corresponded more to her good mood, and tried Jettel's rouge and lipstick in the bathroom that still smelled of Grete's soapsuds. She smiled at her reflection in the mirror and laughed aloud at the thought that some of her classmates were allowed to come home as late as they wanted, but were not allowed to put on makeup and did so only after leaving their house. With her it was just the opposite. Regina could have put on as much makeup as the vamps in American movies without upsetting her father. He offered her cigarettes and liked it when she drank a glass of schnapps with him, and he was tolerant in his conversations and thoughts, but felt insulted, upset, and dejected when Regina wanted to go out. In most instances she gave up her plans before even talking about them.

She had just locked the apartment when the doorbell rang. Since she was only able to reach the buzzer from the inside and had already put away her keys, she quickly ran downstairs. There was a man in a blue uniform standing next to the mailboxes, and for a short moment she assumed he was a policeman. She needed some time till she understood that he was handing her a telegram. Her hand turned cold when she took it, but she was still able to swallow the first wave of fear and was even able to follow the messenger with her eyes when he left the yard.

The pain in her chest paralyzed her body and her head. Regina was so completely convinced that her parents and Max had been in an accident that she did not dare open the telegram. She hurried back up to the fourth floor before she found the strength to tear open the yellow envelope.

The letters pierced her senses like newly sharpened arrows and burned her throat with the hot salt of a pain she had forgotten was still in her. The long-gone days attacked her and shook her with merciless passion, but when she opened her eyes and started to breathe again, it was triumph that made her howl like a hyena, erasing all other emotions.

"Arriving frankfurt saturday 6 o'clock, martin barret," the telegram said.

10

"Good God, Jettel, how young you still are," Martin sighed and pressed Regina so close that she immediately knew what was going on. Time, the merciless thief, had not been able to rob him, but had left him with the habit of the fleeting glance. Martin had confused her with her mother when she was still a child and he a king.

His hair, too, had remained victorious in the fight against the curse of change. It was still the color of African wheat that has shot up too fast toward the sun. The man, who in earlier days had crossed the gulf between past and present with giant steps, had eyes that were shining in the same bright blue as in the beginning of the bewildering story without end. Even in a dark German corridor, smelling of floor wax and vinegar, those eyes instantly became as light as the fur of sleeping dik-diks in the midday heat of Ol' Joro Orok.

When she first met him, Martin had shown up in Nakuru, had released Regina from the prison of her school, and on the way home had given her the magic of early knowledge. Back then he had worn the wrinkled khaki uniform of a British sergeant and a crown that only Regina was able to see.

Now he had disguised himself as a successful businessman on a trip to Europe, wearing a starched white shirt, a blue blazer with an emblem and gold buttons, a yellow and white striped tie, and a light-colored duffle coat. It was as if he had fallen out of the skies to embrace the friends of his youth. He had not, however, made too much of an effort to get used to his new costume in time. His hands still held too much of the strong grasp of the world he had come from. The light pressure of his lips on her skin scorched away any doubt. Regina had forgotten nothing of the unsettling crush of her childhood days although she had, years ago, buried it more carefully than an experienced dog hides its bone.

"I am not Jettel," she said when laughter no longer tickled her throat. "I am Regina."

"That is impossible. I know for sure that Regina is a child."

"A child without parents. They left this morning and will only be back tomorrow night."

The whistling, as sharp as the wind that has lost its way between two trees standing too close to each other, reached Regina's ear even before Martin said, "I once knew someone called Lucky Hans. Is he still around?"

"Sure, but he is called Martin now and sends his telegrams too late."

"There you go, you can see now how lucky that Martin is. May he come in? Or have you been warned to be wary of men?"

"Only of strangers," Regina said and pulled Martin into the hallway.

When he hung his coat on the hook, she saw his face in the mirror and also noticed that he quickly swallowed the words his lips had already begun to form and rubbed the skin on the back of his nose with two fingers. She remembered that he had done that in her first life whenever he was embarrassed and needed time to think. Her mother had told her his secret then; now Regina was able to rely on her own eyes. "You must be hungry. Do you want to have something to eat?" she murmured and became as insecure as Martin's hands because she realized that she was talking with Jettel's voice.

"For God's sake, do you still talk like this here when you haven't seen a person for years?"

"I believe so. Where are you actually coming from?"

"South Africa. I have been living in Pretoria for the past two years. Don't tell me you didn't know that. I write to your father on a regular basis."

"No. I didn't know that."

"What? You didn't know that I moved from Cape Town to Pretoria or that I write to your family every month?"

"Neither," Regina realized.

"Good old Walter," Martin said. "Still the same. And the better of the two of us when he is in love. I think he never quite forgave me that your mother robbed me of my wits before I even had any."

"There is another thing he has not forgiven you for, namely that you promised me on the farm you would come back when I was a woman. And unfortunately, I have never forgotten that either."

"Why 'unfortunately'? I did arrive in time, didn't I?"

Martin Barret, who, when he was still called Batschinsky, had shared with Walter and Jettel his youth, hopes, and a friendship that did not even break when he desired Jettel and Walter knew about it, as well as later the fate of emigration, touched his nose once more. He noticed that his skin was getting moist, and that he was starting to behave like one of those aging men whom he despised when they prepared for the hunt without looking into the mirror and looking even less at the victim.

For a long time, as if he had to remember their color and form exactly, he looked at the easy chairs covered in brown corduroy and the broad sofa on which lay a teddy bear with two glass eyes of different size and a picture book between pillows of dark red velvet. Only one meaningless breath still separated him from the many questions that would certainly have come to him easily if Walter and Jettel had been here. Yet his thoughts freed themselves from logic and concentration in a way that seemed all the more absurd to him because he was no longer used to breaking away from the secure walls of reality.

At the same moment Martin remembered that he was only three months away from his fiftieth birthday and that he had been very impressed in his youth by the story of the man whose picture was aging while he stayed young and radiantly beautiful. For a short while he was deceived by the illusion that he could read in Regina's eyes the confirmation that the same might have happened to him, but he did not give in to the temptation of looking at her and glanced at his watch instead.

He heard it ticking and saw how the golden hand caught the light and quickly became dark again. With a sharpness that irritated him as much as his silence before, he remembered that a flood of carelessly summoned fantasies had once before swept him onto a shady shore. He saw a powerful tree in the dark African forest and a light piece of skin when Regina, who was still unaware of the traps she was setting, had unbuttoned her blouse. The thought of the irretrievable innocence changed him back into the man who had discovered early on that it was always the coincidences and never the morality that demanded renunciation.

"Come," he said and tried to look more cheerful than he was, "I am going to take you out to eat. An old fogy and a young girl don't belong together under the same roof. Especially not when the beautiful, innocent child is the daughter of his best friend."

Only in the dining room of the Frankfurter Hof, where he stayed because his travel agent had recommended it as the best hotel in Frankfurt, did Martin realize how clever and prescient his suggestion had been. He had banned temptation with three sentences before it was able to extend its choking hold and had turned Regina back into the child he had hoped to find.

There was no doubt that the guests, most of whom were from abroad, were not accustomed to an atmosphere of distinguished, just recently revived old-world bourgeoisie and luxury and were quite impressed by the splendor and elegance, which stood in stark contrast to the everyday life in town. Regina furtively looked around as if she were ashamed of her curiosity, only dared to whisper, and looked in total surprise at the bowls and platters that were carried past her till they disappeared.

The black dress, which was too big for her with its tight-fitting sleeves, tiny buttons up to her neck, and the white lace collar that reminded Martin of the tablecloth that his mother only put on for visitors, made Regina look like one of those dressed up, giggling, prim young girls of his student days. Martin moodily anticipated that she would order lemonade and, most likely, instead of an appetizer a double portion of strawberry ice cream with those mountains of whipped cream that he remembered from Breslau, just like the upper-class daughters who mistook the smell of lavender for sensuality and whom a man could only touch while dancing.

Martin tried to escape from the undergrowth of the tangled details that bothered his memory. As he looked at the menu without enthusiasm he ordered, in a sharp voice that struck him as unpleasantly exaggerated, "A martini, but dry." He was annoyed when the waiter asked, "Also for your daughter?" but afterward even more annoyed that he had let himself be irritated by a man who had to wear such thick glasses.

After the first sip he waved the waiter back to the table with a movement of his hand, which most conspicuously proved him to be a man from South Africa who is used to giving orders.

"I said dry," Martin complained and twirled the olive around.

Regina actually started to giggle and held a hand in front of her mouth. He looked at her glumly and opened the button under his tie.

"See," she laughed, "nothing has changed. You fought with waiters all your life."

"How do you know that?"

"I knew that even before I met you. The sentence 'Martin would not have put up with that' was quoted daily on the farm."

"Who said that?"

"Mama."

"If I believe anything, I believe that. I never envied your father. What do you want to eat?"

"Everything. I mean I better have what you're having."

"Are you always that easy to satisfy?" Martin smiled.

"With food, yes. We were hungry for so long, we are still happy if we have enough to eat every day."

"I would not have had your father's courage to go back to Germany this early. Is he at least happy here? And what about you?"

"Those are two questions at once."

"With different answers?"

"Yes."

Martin ordered a selection of appetizers from a cart; turtle soup that he expressly wanted to have prepared with cognac, not with sherry; filet steaks that he assumed in advance a German cook would overcook; and a Cape wine that was not on the wine list and the waiter had not even heard of. The manager was called to confirm this. Martin extensively discussed the matter with him and, on the outer limits of politeness, wanted to know why a hotel that had been recommended to him in Pretoria did not carry wines from South Africa. He finally asked with a sigh, "Is there anything at all one can drink here?"

"Maybe a glass of champagne with the appetizer," the manager nervously suggested.

"A bottle of champagne," Martin decided, "but properly chilled."

After the first glass it occurred to him that he was no longer used to champagne and Regina not yet. He had heartburn and she had red circles on her face, but her flushed cheeks seemed to bother her less than his stomach bothered him. She held her glass, which she had drained in one gulp, out to him and emptied the plate with the appetizers at a speed that perplexed him. The fast movement of her jaws reminded Martin of the hamster that one of his classmates had given him and he had not been allowed to keep. He was amazed that the disappointment had not abated for over forty-four years and he realized that the alcohol was attacking his head much faster than during the many drinking sprees in Pretoria. There he only had to contribute the good spirits of a man who had experienced more than most and knew the art of a good punch line.

He was hardly able to catch his thoughts before they accumulated into an avalanche of discontent about things that had not been of any importance for a long time now. The waiter was just about to fill Regina's plate with another selection from the appetizer cart. She had overcome her shyness and pointed, animated by the flatteries of the waiter, to the silver bowls with delicacies she had never seen before.

The waiter called her "Miss"; Martin's expression changed from discontent to irony, but the two did not notice. He usually appreciated women with a good appetite and wanted to smile at Regina, but at just that moment he remembered how much his first wife's habit to send the plate back to the kitchen after a few bites had always exasperated him.

When he climbed out of the deep valley of his last youthful folly and needed unexpectedly long to remember when it had happened, he realized that his heartburn was gone and that he had come to a false conclusion. Regina was not a child anymore and above all not a squeaking girl from a good family, but a young woman who undoubtedly baffled him more than was good for him. Three of the small buttons of her dress were open. The lace collar now surrounded her slim neck like a fine veil and seemed to him the embodiment of a lightness that he had longed to see for quite a while.

Martin felt an absolutely unfamiliar impulse to protect her, then caught himself with fantasies that he considered ridiculously adolescent and, finally and very abruptly, with the thought that he not only looked a lot younger than he was, but that his attitude toward life was not yet worn out by all those years that had demanded a lot of strength. He put his hand on Regina's shoulder and noticed with satisfaction that the light touch excited her. He asked himself for the first time what Regina knew about him.

He only rarely, and then always without regrets, thought of the fact that he had gone to law school and because of the Nazis had hardly been able to practice his profession. Because of his time in the British army, his emigration to South Africa had quickly been followed by the acquisition of citizenship. After the war he had experienced some painful financial disappointments with a garage and a textile company, but he had joined an export firm just in time and—just at the right time again—had taken it over. The revitalization of business with Europe and especially with Germany had made him a prosperous man. In sentimental moments like the one he was experiencing right now, he felt a slight need for German work ethics, efficiency, and culture, but he also knew that he had lived in South Africa for too long to seriously think about returning to Germany. Africa had given him the freedom to count the hours, not the days.

"What are you doing?" he heard Regina ask.

"Whatever one does in the wholesale business. At the moment I am trading oranges for machines."

"I am talking about your hand."

Regina immediately realized that she had asked Martin once before, under the tree at Ol' Joro Orok, what he was doing. Then, too, she had only spoken about his hand and he had given the wrong answer. She talked without embarrassment about the encounter and did not allow her eyes to avoid his. The old invigorating spell—that she was talking about a strange child she had once known fleetingly—only lasted for a short moment. Then the certainty arrived that Martin would not leave her with unfinished pictures this time.

He had started out like a young Masai who has not yet drawn his bow too often, and in his eagerness he had forgotten to protect his own body. Martin had not noticed the danger he had exposed himself to, but Regina's eyes had taken exact measure.

"Did you really not know that I thought you were a king and that I fell in love with you then?"

"Do you always ask such damned open-ended questions?"

"No. Never. Only when the glasses and plates are starting to dance around me, and the waiters all look like penguins," Regina replied. Her throat was dry but her voice was firm when she said, "And when a king has finally come to fulfill his promise."

"Dear Lord, you have been drinking too much and I am a complete idiot that I let you. I hope you are not feeling sick and are not going to collapse here. Old men don't like complications."

"I have never felt better and you're not an old man."

"Two years older than your father if I am not mistaken."

"Thirty years older than me, but you are not my father."

"Dear God, Regina, do you even know what you are saying?"

"Yes."

Martin pushed his plate toward the small vase on the table and watched attentively how the pink and yellow pieces of the half-eaten ice-cream cake got submerged in the chocolate sauce. It seemed important to him to interpret the pattern of the running colors, but he had never had a tendency toward abstract contemplation and was unable to understand the randomly chosen symbol. He only knew that he had to fight if he wanted to protect himself from illusions and the long-overdue recognition that no man has the right to repeat his mistakes.

He realized that, at the least, he had to take his hand off Regina's shoulder. He succeeded in this one move and in such a quick and sure way that his lips were already starting to form a comment that appeared appropriate to him; however, he had only prepared his body for flight and could no longer prevent the furious battle in his head between vanity and wistfulness.

The weight of his memories already stifled him on the first part of the path that he did not want to take. He saw Jettel in her ball gown—black-haired, laughing, attractive, almost ridiculously impudent in her demanding coquettishness—but he did not want to long for her again because Walter had fallen in love with her first and he was Walter's best friend. Only he did not know the second time around either if he had passed the self-imposed test or not.

The images of yearnings and experiences from later years got confused too quickly to restrain his emotions. Martin only became aware that he had spoken when Regina moved her head, but he could not remember what had entered his head in this moment of need. The knocking at his temples became louder.

"Did your mother teach you how to unsettle a man?"

"No. Owuor did."

"You mean the strange boy on your farm?"

"He was not a boy. And not strange either. Owuor was Papa's friend and the giant who held me in his arms when I flew up to the clouds. He lent his eyes to me. He also taught me to hear things that do not come from someone's mouth."

"How did your great magician do it? What did he tell you?"

"You have to make your ears really big, *memsahib kidogo,*" Regina laughed. "That's what I did today. I listened carefully. You talked about Lucky Hans when you saw that I was alone. You said that you didn't want to be alone with me. That's when I knew that you were afraid of me. Your fear has made me courageous."

"I was afraid of myself, you depraved child from Africa."

"Owuor used to say, 'fear is fear, and whoever is afraid is going to be hunted. And caught.'"

"Your Owuor was a clever man. I am sure he also told you not to leave the house without a toothbrush when a man asks you out to eat."

"No, he only said, 'always take your head and your heart on safari.' But I also have a toothbrush."

Regina was already lying in bed when Martin came out of the bathroom and again he was wearing a crown that only she could see. She was eleven years old once more and heard the monkeys chatter in the woods, but this time she was clever enough to think of the magic of the wise God Mungu in time. Only He was able to kill a budding wish before it turned into a lethal plant that burns the intestines.

But when she touched Martin's body and he touched hers, and when she felt his breath at her ear, felt the hand on her mouth, and stifled the scream that was still caught in her throat, she understood that she had dared to get too close to a fire that neither Mungu nor time would ever be able to extinguish.

She had taken her heart on safari, but had left her head behind. Much later in the eternity that lay between desire and fulfillment, Owuor sent his knowing laughter to the mountain, for he alone was clever. His little *memsahib,* however, lay in the arms of a sleeping king and had offered herself to the hunter.

"I always thought," Martin called from the bathroom the next morning, "a woman at least wants to know if a man is married before she seduces him. German women always asked about that. I do remember that."

"I am not a German woman," Regina laughed. She was still lying in bed, numbed by the brevity of happiness and the weight of wonder.

"You are an African witch. I felt it over there," Martin said, "but I didn't remember it in time."

He sat in front of the mirror and thought, like the day before, of the man who was allowed to stay young while only his picture aged.

"Of course you are married," Regina knew. "Why should I ask you? All men your age are married."

"I am not. I have been divorced for years. A second time. I do not know why, but it is important to me that you know that."

"To me, too."

"Why?"

"Just because. You don't have to be frightened right away."

"Will you promise me something, Regina?" Martin said to his picture in the mirror. "That you will not be sad when I have to leave again."

"You told me that once before."

"Will you promise?"

"Yes, but not because of you. And not because of me either. How could I explain my sadness without speaking of this night? I could not hurt my father. He loves me so much that he will never want any man to have me. And certainly not you. He has still not forgiven you for the blue blanket that you lay under with my mother."

"Is that part of your magic, too? What makes you think about a blue blanket?"

"As long as I can remember, the two have never been able to agree if the blanket was really blue."

"In those days," Martin said, "your father really only saw ghosts."

He was even able to laugh when Walter and Jettel returned in the afternoon from the Harz and the trip to Greschek, saw him sitting in the living room, and Walter, after an emotional hug, instantly asked, "You did not harm my daughter, did you?"

11

IN THE EARLY MORNING of the second Tuesday of April 1952, Max took his parakeet, Kasuko, off his head before the inky blue bird could even say *"Jambo"* and unfurl its wings, put it on the rim of his plate, and informed his friend about a future meant to become as sunny as the day itself, with a sentence that had finally been released for use by a six-year-old boy: "Today life begins in earnest." After breakfast Max climbed onto the little stool in the bathroom to look into the mirror undisturbed and free from unsolicited advice that was no longer in keeping with his new status in life.

Even though he was unable to detect the anticipated changes to the extent he had hoped for, he smiled, knowing that he had finally arrived at the turning point in his life for which he had yearned for so long. From now on there would be only a short, manageable path before he, too, would be an attorney and notary and, above all, would be as rich and famous as Josef Schlachanska and drive to court in an even bigger Maybach than his idol.

Max was wearing a long-sleeved white shirt with a tight collar that still needed some getting used to, and a tie matching the shiny red cone-shaped bag with school supplies and goodies for the first day of school. He also sported the longed-for cap with the rounded shade that turned a kindergarten child, previously just wrapped in bright blue woolens, who at most might have been allowed to go to the milkman or the playground by himself, into a first grader whose independence was not only expected, but demanded. Standing in the familiar spot between door and washbasin, he already knew that his first long pants—gray, soft, and with a black leather belt—had forever relieved him of the shame of the hated long brown stockings that had been attached to girl-type suspenders. Even more important and irreversible things had happened. On the day before, his father had told his mother not to call her son "Maxi," "Darling," or, of all things, "Pumpkin" anymore; not to kiss him in the street without any particular reason; not to cut his meat and mash his potatoes at the table; and not to tie his shoes or button his coat when in a hurry.

Max had gotten the confirmation from his father that he was a real man from now on; he could no longer cry because of a hurt knee or when he was fighting with other children about possessions or privileges, but he also could no longer be bothered by insulting demands to carry plates from the dining room to the kitchen, to hang up his coat, or to carry out other ignominious duties from the world of women.

The child—who had called for his mother or his sister, or in dangerous situations for both at the same time, whenever he fell in the street or could not defend his toys or reputation alone in the sandbox, and who had been limited to looking at pictures in books and newspapers—now separated himself from Jettel and Regina in a room that smelled of sharp scouring soap, vinegar, and chalk, and with determination sat down at a desk in the first row. After three hours, Max emerged from the classroom again. He was accompanied by a blond boy with accurately parted hair, very short gray lederhosen, and a resolutely clenched right fist. This boy was a year older but luckily not yet much taller to significantly impair Max's own self-confidence. Max called out to his mother, who was standing at the school entrance with other excited parents in their Sunday dresses and dark suits. He yelled from afar and loud enough for everyone to hear that she had been wrong once again and that he would—contrary to her assumptions this morning—not have to learn single letters and could already read and write a lot, "a real, real lot" as he declared.

On his first day of school Max managed, without any detriment to his strongly developed self-confidence, to get over the insulting way that older students knocked the cap off his head and teased him with some doggerel about being a first grader. After all, he was able to not only write his name, but also his address and the two sentences, "I

am going to the Lersner School. My teacher's name is Mr. Blaschka" —
the first success of the "whole word method" that many parents said was
too challenging for the children and a typical example of the deplorable
tendency of a democracy to endorse experiments at the expense of innocent creatures who were unable to defend themselves.

With the anticipation of a person with an early awareness for the
triumph of initiative and the result of surprise effects, Max sat at the
kitchen table after school while his mother carefully unpacked his
schoolbag and angrily noticed that he had not eaten the expensive banana and an exercise book and pencil were missing.

Max could not be convinced to give the explanations that were due
for such a loss of property. Instead, he was happy that in addition to his
mother, Else, his father, and his sister would simultaneously become
aware that he was not a student like all the others, who were satisfied
just to copy the nice yellow cards that Mr. Blaschka had put on their
desks in the morning. He had immediately understood and used the
power and possibilities of the written word.

His schoolbag no longer had on it the name his mother had written
in blue ink, but instead read "Dr. Max Redlich." For some weeks and
after repeated study of the small golden plate on the apartment door, he
had practiced the two decisive letters and the important little period,
which had been added in strong black pencil lines. He now considered
it a special bonus for his hard work that his parents would discover
his idea before lunch. He licked his lips in sweet anticipation as on the
otherwise deplorably rare occasions when his mother took a second
helping of vanilla ice cream out of the freezer.

The excitement and moreover the prospect of the praise that was
due him made his ears deaf to any noise that did not concern him. His
eyes were unable to concentrate on the events in the kitchen. Max,
therefore, did not realize right away that the happy voices that were appropriate for the festive occasion had become silent, nor did he notice
that his father's face had already changed color. He also heard his
mother's cry too late, and the plaintive accusation, "The rascal has already smudged his new school bag." Almost simultaneously, he got a
slap in the face from his father — not painful, but embarrassingly hot
because it was so unexpected and unusual.

Only after the raspberry pudding, which tasted strangely bitter, did father and son resume their communications. Max got fifty cents that Walter termed "compensation for personal suffering" and to which he added the surprising promise that his son had a credit for a slap in the face on any occasion when he was aware that he was doing something wrong at the time of the infraction. The conciliatory handshake common among men was followed by an extensive lecture about the unlawful acquisition of academic titles.

The slap in the face did not remain the only lasting memory of his first day of school for Max. Much more impressive than his father's angry outburst and his legal teachings was the confusing admonition that wealth could not be put on the same level as academic achievement and that Joseph Schlachanska, in spite of the Maybach, chauffeur, and spectacular appearances, in contrast to his own father, did not have the title "Doctor."

A week later Max had an opportunity to enjoy his father's wealth, too. Since there were no schoolbooks for the "whole word method," the teacher, Mr. Blaschka, distributed his own handwritten texts on separate sheets of paper. After Walter had seen his son do his homework once, he offered the teacher with the likable Silesian name the opportunity to copy his manuscripts on the new copying machine of the practice of Fafflok and Redlich. Max considered this a personal merit and instantly forgave his father for not occasionally sending him—like many of the other children—to school with a bottle of schnapps, flowers, or even chocolates to make the teacher well disposed to the bearer of such gifts. Max, therefore, came home from school daily in the best of moods and fully enjoyed his parents' repeated praise that he was finding friends much faster than his sister.

All the more remarkable was a lunchtime meal, three months to the day after the beginning of school, when the first grader, until then spoiled by success, came home very quietly and so dejected that he did not even take the parakeet out of its cage. He was pale, had red eyes, and, even though they were having the scrambled eggs and spinach he had asked for in the morning, pushed a half-eaten plateful aside with a small sigh and shook his head. Only after repeated questioning—and when his mother's assumption that he was sick turned into the serious threat of using the thermometer—did Max realize that this was his last chance to break his silence if he did not want to end the day with one of those hated moist throat compresses that his mother considered the only weapon in the fight against all ailments except a sprained ankle.

"Is it true," he asked, "that the Jews were all burned in one big oven?"

"Who said such a thing?"

"Klaus Jeschke."

"You have never talked about him before."

"He is the tallest in the class because he has already had to repeat it twice," Max said and gloomily looked at his mother. He noticed that his skin was burning as if he indeed had a high fever and he felt the start of the violent beating of his heart all over again as if he had just heard the words, which had hurt him in the same strange way that a too-vehemently-thrown ball would hurt one's head. Now that he had decided to talk, all of a sudden it became important to him to tell the story as fast as he could and without any bothersome questions that would force his tongue to make detours. It had confused him since main recess in school and had shamed him in a way that he only knew from having a bad conscience and being unable to defend himself without getting tangled in an ever-growing web of lies. He angrily stabbed his fork into the yellow mass of cold scrambled eggs.

"He said that all Jews stink. That is why Hitler burned them. And then he pushed me over and said that he likes Hitler best in the entire world. Is it true that all Jews stink?"

"Your father—" Jettel started, but when she realized how shrill her voice had become, she pushed the fury back into her chest because she realized, at the moment when rage was her only strength, that she had to stifle the fire for her son's sake. She kept silent till she was able to relax her hands sufficiently so that she could put the thermometer back into its case. Realizing that she could not expose Max to the feeling that something unusual had happened, she suppressed the desire—which hit her like a physical pain—to take her son in her arms. She was surprised how easy love and lying had become for her.

"You know," she said, "that Klaus Jeschke is just a very stupid boy. He doesn't even know what he is saying."

"I always know what I am saying," Max insisted.

"Not everyone is as smart as you. Many children only repeat what they hear from their parents. He only said this without thinking about it. He doesn't even know what it means."

"So what does it mean?"

"We have," Jettel said and forced herself to look at Max, "often told you about Hitler. You know that he was a very evil person. You also know that we had to go to Africa because otherwise we all would have died here."

"In an oven?" Max asked. "Would they have burned us all like the witch in Hansel and Gretel? Regina, too?"

"Yes," Jettel said. Only after some time, when Max looked at her expectantly, but also with a curiosity that she could not interpret, she added, "I would not play with Klaus Jeschke anymore if I were you. Then he cannot say such nasty things to you. And you do not have to get upset."

Max touched his head and sniffed, "I never played with him. Not with that one. He stinks. When that Onion-Klaus comes into class, we all hold our noses."

"Tonight you can tell your father the entire story," Jettel said. "Let's see what he is going to say."

But Walter had a municipal council meeting and came home so late that Max was already in bed and not allowed to get up. He was, therefore, unable to check any further if his first encounter with this new kind of hostility, which had paralyzed his fists and tongue so that his head could not forget it, would embarrass his father as much as his mother.

But he was still awake enough to find out that Klaus Jeschke was the cause of one of those huge fights in the bedroom that were almost always taken up again at breakfast the next morning—without words, but apparent for a boy who had been trained early to detect the exchange of looks between his parents.

While Max let the last cookie melt on his tongue and happily anticipated the moment when the taste of chocolate would mingle with that of the toothpaste, fighting noises started that were too familiar to frighten him. First his mother shouted, "Your damned Germany," and shortly afterward, "You had to come back to the country of the murderers at all costs." And his father screamed angrily, "Not even you can be stupid enough to take the jabbering of such a brainless brat seriously. Do you really think Regina never encountered any anti-Semitism in her fine British boarding school?"

Before he fell asleep, Max decided to remember the word that he had heard for the first time in the pleasant state between waking and sleeping, and to ask his father about it and about the size of ovens in which people were being burned. But the next morning he forgot about both because he had to look too long for his pen and his gym bag. The next one of those serious father-son conversations, which gave Max the uplifting certainty that the major problems in life could only be solved by men, would only take place at the Bethanien Hospital at the Prüfling. There, however, Klaus Jeschke was not mentioned anymore.

On the Wednesday when Walter received a warning that the times of hope were past, they had sauerkraut and the kind of sausages he loved for lunch. Before the big fight, Jettel had gone out of her way to the Silesian butcher in the Berger Straße and was now, to her regret, unable to change the menu according to the tense atmosphere at home. But Walter, who had only eaten one of the sausages without touching the skin, had not even asked for the mustard that Else had forgotten to put on the table and he also left most of the sauerkraut uneaten.

During the silent meal, Jettel had made every effort, as required by the special circumstances, not to look at her husband and through an unguarded look to give him the idea that she might be ready for a reconciliation. When she noticed that Walter pushed his plate toward the bowl with the potatoes the way Max had done the day before, she thought that he was giving her a hint that the fight would be resumed. But while she was beginning to formulate the sentence that boiled within her, she looked up and saw that he had pearls of sweat on his forehead, very dark lips, and an unusually pale face.

"What is wrong?" she asked.

"Nothing," Walter said. "You do not have to be concerned. We can go on fighting."

His voice was strange and weak, his gasping breath too loud, and when he put both arms on the table and let his upper body slide forward, he groaned quietly and pressed his lips together.

"For heaven's sake, something is wrong. Did you eat anything on the way home? Shall I call Dr. Goldschmidt?"

"Let it be, Jettel; we cannot afford a doctor till we have saved enough for Regina's tuition."

For a short moment Jettel thought with relief that he was feeling better already and had just made one of his usual jokes, reminding them of the time of their emigration when there had not been enough money to think of medical help even in life-threatening situations. Her instinct, however, had become as sharp and suspicious through the pictures that this one sentence evoked as during dangerous times on the farm. She understood, overwhelmed by terror and also tenderness, that Walter had actually confused the times and scenes of his life. She saw the fear in his eyes and the fluttering eyelids, helped him get up from the table while murmuring, "You will feel better in a moment," and led him to the wing chair in the living room. Then she ran to the telephone.

Half an hour later Walter was in the hospital. On the first day the physicians diagnosed a heart attack, on the second day they suspected severe diabetes and spoke about acetone, and on the third day, the leading physician recommended that the infected teeth in his upper jaw be extracted. When Max was finally allowed to visit his father on the fourth day, the teeth were lying in the sink and Walter was giggling in bed.

"Your Papa," he said and began to swing the empty bedpan toward the window, "bit a nurse to death and now has to eat porridge as a punishment for the rest of his life."

"Mama says you will never be able to eat chocolate again."

"Women's talk," Walter laughed. "You know how women are. Long hair, little intelligence. Go look at my teeth."

"Regina says one should put the tooth under the pillow and wish for something. During the night a fairy will come and get the tooth."

"Don't let Regina tell you such nonsense. You are a man."

Max was just about to admire the seventh pulled tooth when the head nurse, Clementine (the other nurses did not dare bring the patient, who had been classified as unusually difficult, his meals), arrived with a bowl of grits and applesauce and was sent out again by Walter with the grumpy remark, "The doctor can eat that stuff himself."

"Are you allowed to do that?" Max asked, impressed.

"Just remember this, son," his father told him. "If you believe in the diseases the doctors want to convince you of, you are lost. If I had had money for a physician in Africa, I would be dead by now."

Except for malaria shortly after arriving in Kenya and black-water fever in the military, Walter had never been seriously ill. On the farm, he had been determined from the very beginning to fight illness with willpower and fearlessness, and during the time of loneliness and hopelessness, he had become as fatalistic as the people in the huts who did not interpret the signals of the body as warnings because they entrusted their life and death to the black God Mungu without resisting fate.

Even though he had experienced the fear of death before he had been checked into the hospital and had not forgotten his panic, he was not willing—and because of his experiences in Africa, which had marked him for all times, also no longer able—to consider a collapse, for which the physicians only suggested rest and a special diet, a serious illness. He had his files brought from the office, composed letters and briefs by hand sitting at a little round table in his room, insisted that Fafflok come to visit him daily and tell him about the practice, and did not allow being spared even the smallest professional annoyance or any major agitation.

Even though the physician had recommended that only family members should come to visit him, Walter called his friends from Upper Silesia four days after being checked into the hospital. They instantly arrived in droves to sit at his bedside, unload their problems, and get free legal advice. He greedily drank in the rough wit of the straightforward language of home and ate with relish the fat sausages and heavy cakes they brought along.

He fought with Jettel as in healthy days when she carried the chocolates home before he had a chance to open the box. He made fun of her when she read the dietary prescriptions the doctor had given her and maintained that she had waited all her life just to take the chocolates away from him. He told the doctors and nurses over and over again that he had been hungry for too long to have them rob him of the only pleasure in life that was left to a man his age.

When Jettel, Regina, and Max were in his hospital room at the same time, he would paint them a picture of his funeral with an imagination that in pensive moments surprised even him. It would be a solemn ceremony with mourners, some of whom, Jettel among them, of course, were about to throw themselves into the grave. Walter, in a white nightgown with a red sash wrapped around it in memory of the outfit in which Owuor had served large meals for special guests and occasions, composed graveyard speeches for Karl Maas, who had become district court president; for the representatives of the bar association; for the board of the Jewish community; for Schlachanska in tux and cylinder hat; and for the Territorial Association of Upper Silesia.

He promised that Jettel would have a new black hat with a large veil and that his son would be allowed to wear his grandfather's gold pocket watch for the funeral, sit in the first row, and never have to go back to school because he had to earn the livelihood for his incompetent mother and shy sister. Jettel was furious, Regina unhappy, and Max enthusiastic.

The conscious escape from reality, provoking of the physicians, melancholy grim humor, and constantly crossing the gulf between irony and suppressed fear only protected him during the day. At night, unable to sleep and brooding, he felt old and was tortured by the idea that he did not have enough time to leave the house in the Rothschildallee free of debt for Jettel and his children.

The existential worry of the emigration, which he had thought would only be a memory of happily conquered times after the powerful rebuilding, returned to him as a hissing monster with talons and sharp claws and he returned to Ol' Joro Orok to sit with Kimani, the thoughtful judge of human nature, at the edge of the flax field. In his color-drenched waking dreams he heard the friend of years past say again and again, "No man dies, *bwana*, unless he says, 'I want to die.'" Before Walter turned off the light, he removed the mask of the clown who deceived the world with his cheerfulness. Then he only saw Kimani's face with his perceptive eyes and white teeth that shone in the midday sun, and he fell asleep, confused but consoled.

Regina, who brought him the newspaper every day before she went to school, found her father one morning with closed eyes, his hands folded on his stomach. *"Na taka kufa,"* he said quietly.

"You shouldn't say that," she cried, horrified, and crossed her fingers. "You do not joke about that. It is bad luck."

"Why? Kimani said it, too, when we left the farm, and they found him the next day dead in the woods. He said, *'Na taka kufa.'* I know that for sure even though I was not with him."

"He wanted to die; you don't."

"I am an old man, Regina. My time has come."

"You are not even fifty yet."

"Much older. Hitler stole years from me."

"And now you are stealing them from yourself once again. Don't you want to see your son grow up?"

"Yes," Walter said, "but the good Lord is not going to let me."

"How can you talk about God and not trust him? Has everything you taught me as a child been only a fairy tale you did not believe in yourself?"

"You are right, *memsahib kidogo*. I have only been on safari."

"But you forgot once again to take your head along. Owuor told me before leaving that you are a child and I have to protect you. Don't make it so hard for me."

"Don't you understand me anymore, either? I want to make it easy for you when the time comes. You are supposed to sit at my funeral and laugh because everything has happened exactly the way I predicted it."

Even before Regina felt the first kernel of salt scratching her throat, she understood that the old, never-forgotten story was about to repeat itself. Nothing had changed since the days that were dead. Her father was again the cunning Cupid from the Masai tribe who in the fight for her heart carefully took aim before letting his arrow fly from the bow. She was once again the child who turned into a woman and was unable to defend herself against the avaricious flame of love that he had ignited.

Regina saw herself standing under the guava tree in Nairobi and heard her father talk about returning to Germany. He asked her not to doubt him and to come with him on the safari without return, and she promised to go along.

Only for a short moment, during which she felt that she could not carry the new burden, did she hesitate. Then she took the newspaper off the bed and embraced Walter. She felt his tears on her lips, heard his heart and hers beating, and knew that she was ready to go with him the way that neither of them wanted to follow.

"Let it be a long safari, *bwana*," she swallowed. "We have a lot of time."

"As long as possible, *memsahib kidogo*. I promise. And now give me the fine chocolates from Mrs. Schlachanska that your mother hid in the closet."

12

AT THE BEGINNING OF HER LAST DAY, which Regina had looked forward to with an intensity that could only be explained by long-pent-up loathing and her inability to talk about her own troubles, she experienced a double surprise at the Schiller School. She found out that she was going to have oral examinations in English and German. Without joining the complaints of most of her fellow students, who used their self-doubts as flirtatious demonstrations of modesty, Regina immediately knew that she would pass the high school finals even though she had handed in an empty sheet for the written mathematics test and had also gotten an F in biology.

The English teacher had never really forgiven Regina for her unusual entry into life at a German school—the stuttering girl from Africa had used the familiar form of address for her and thus exposed her to the ridicule of the class—but her vanity was more strongly developed than the kind of imagination she would have needed to muster sympathy for frightened children from a different world. At this point she had not been able to resist the temptation to suggest that Regina, in spite of language skills that so unpleasantly surpassed the class level, would get a B as an overall grade, which she could possibly bring up to an A through an oral examination. She saw this as a chance to present to the observing teachers, and especially to the representative of the Hessian Ministry of Education, who was known to be quite critical, a student who would be proof of her excellent teaching abilities. After all, the difficult girl from Africa spoke English without an accent, knew about literature that had not even been read in class, and presented the Hamlet monologue as if she had written it herself.

Regina, for her part, had never forgiven the English teacher for her intolerance toward a student who, at age fifteen, sentenced to speechlessness, had stood at the edge of an unfamiliar culture that, at best, had condemned her to mediocrity for all times. Even less could she excuse the fact that the teacher had let the naïve initial misunderstanding over time turn into a very conscious aversion, which she was unable to express in bad grades only because the unloved student had spent years in emigration and was, therefore, performing too well. Regina abandoned the temptation of tasting the sweetness of revenge with a slight hesitation when she considered that the school was about to attest to a certain degree of moral maturity in her. Reluctantly she did not use her talent, trained so early by Owuor, to imitate voice and gestures. She deprived the celebratory community of the experience of hearing her speak English with the same bad pronunciation as her teacher.

Regina had given the German teacher—who had fascinated, encouraged, and promoted her from the start, and who was the only teacher she would part from with the feeling that their encounter had been a worthwhile and lasting one—credit for those caring characteristics she had profited from ever since her first day at a German school. Only when he did not ask her a single question about *Faust II,* in spite of the fact that they had studied Goethe extensively in the last two grades of high school, but immediately encouraged her to talk about the author she had chosen as her specialty, did she suspect that even this humanitarian, whom she admired, might have special reasons for placing a student whose development was somewhat out of the ordinary into the spotlight.

While the other graduating students had limited their own choice of authors whose work they wanted to independently study to Rudolf Binding, Manfred Hausmann, and, at most, Hermann Hesse, Regina had chosen Stefan Zweig. Now, during her oral examination, when she talked about his inability to forget his mother tongue and roots and to develop new ones in exile, she saw with amazement and even shock that several of the teachers, and among them some she certainly never would have expected it from, were wiping their tears away when the topic of homelessness was mentioned. Regina particularly noticed the dismay of the French teacher, who was generally praised as a capable educator and was surprisingly cosmopolitan. She had never been able to understand why a child who had been educated in an English school would speak French with an accent that she regarded as an insult to her ears. She had covered them theatrically whenever Regina started to speak.

The biology teacher, who had misconstrued Regina's dislike of the thorough study of genetics as laziness and malice, suffered so noticeably when she heard about Stefan Zweig's suicide that Regina, had her in-born skepticism not been heightened by the Schiller School, almost would have forgiven her the F in her report card and the insults that had been evident only to her.

Even though she passed the German exam with the coveted B, she felt awkward about the suspicion that she had just been set up as an actor in a skillfully staged play in which her teachers had been able to demonstrate the kind of tolerance that she had not encountered over the years. The events of the last school day caused Regina, without the wistfulness that young people generally experienced at a crossroad in their lives, to take leave from a community to which she, in spite of the friendliness of many of her fellow students and the friendship of a very few teachers, had never completely belonged.

When she stood undecided and unmoved in the Gartenstraße and looked, lost in thought, at the school's gray walls, whose stones had been salvaged by students, ready for sacrifice and motivated by eloquent teachers, with their bare hands from the rubble, she even found herself shuddering. All of this increased her desire to share this day of happiness and liberation with only her parents and to enjoy it in an atmosphere where there were no hidden allusions or the exhausting need to clear up misunderstandings.

In contrast to her usual school days, when an acceptable amount of dawdling had resulted in the delay of unpleasant domestic chores, Regina now ran, without stopping to enjoy the old houses or the newly built-up houses on both banks of the Main, across the Eiserner Steg. She chased the tram to Bornheim at the Konstabler Wache and hurried to her destination in the Höhenstraße like an exuberant child expecting its due reward.

It was a mild, March day, full of the anticipation of spring. In the tiny front yard of 9 Rothschildallee, the first crocuses had sprung up in yellow, white, and purple, surrounded by chickadees. The lilac that

Walter loved and tended carefully, and that every May again symbolized for him the natural events he had dreamed of in Africa, already had buds. In a round bed the first green went into the strong stems of the carnations, which had been grown from seeds that originally came from Sohrau and which Owuor had carried from Rongai to Ol' Joro Orok in a white envelope.

Regina only permitted herself a short encounter with Owuor among the healthy carnations at home—yet it was long enough to smell her friend's skin and to feel his arms while he lifted her up to the sun and told her that she was as smart as he was. She still felt his light breath at her ear when she rang the doorbell. On the stairs she could already smell that her parents had waited for her with lunch.

"Did you flunk, my daughter?" her father shouted from the fourth to the first floor in a voice that would have been well suited for the beloved echo from the mountains. "Never mind; that happens in the best of families."

"Not in ours," Regina shouted back. "I passed." She simultaneously embraced her parents and pushed their bodies together the way she had always done as a child when she had returned from school to the farm and could not decide whom to give her love to first. The emotional tears her fellow students had shed finally came to her, too, when her mother said, "We are having Königsberger Klopse. I always made them when you came home from your boarding school."

"And then you always used to say, 'There are no capers in this damned country.' And I asked, 'What are capers?'"

"Why don't you look at your plate," Max said impatiently.

With the money he had asked her for last night he had bought his sister a gold-colored coin on a ribbon and he had painted her a picture with a red car, blue sun, two green stick figures, and the sentence "Regina has her Final exxam. Now you'll not Be with Us much longer." She took him on her lap and squeezed him tight till his laughter and hers had become one. Then she asked, "Why will I no longer be with you just because I am not going to school anymore?"

"Because you have to go to England."

"What am I supposed to do in England?"

"Get married," Max explained.

"Who has been telling you that?"

"Mr. Schlachanska. He told Papa that there are a lot of husbands for you in England. I listened carefully."

"Is that starting again?" Regina said and tried in vain to look the way she had looked just a minute ago. "What's going on?"

"Nothing," Walter tried to calm her down. "Your brother is just proving once again that he is not yet ready to give an accurate witness report. The only true thing of the whole story is that we want to celebrate the day by having coffee with the Schlachanskas in Gravenbruch."

"Well, what do you know," Regina said and searched for anything suspicious in her father's face, but he returned her glance without averting his eyes. She stuck her fork into a piece of potato and swallowed her anger with Jettel's especially delicious sauce.

The popular Forsthaus in Gravenbruch was a favorite destination for excursions, which Walter had previously suggested only on special occasions and not at all anymore after his illness because he had started to classify all unnecessary expenses as irresponsibility toward his family. The cakes were more expensive in Gravenbruch than in the cafés in town. Coffee was only served in little pots and playing in the open air made the children price-increasingly thirsty.

Their mothers, dressed in clothes that stood in stark contrast to the rustic surroundings, not only allowed them to order more drinks but they themselves tended to surrender to the persuasion of the well-trained personnel and concluded happy afternoons with expensive Danziger Goldwasser or egg liqueur.

Mrs. Schlachanska was dressed in a new white hat with a wide brim and a big dark-blue tulle rose, and a blue silk suit with white polka dots that had been bought on her last trip to Paris. Jeanne-Louise wore a dress of yellow taffeta with ruffles, the white socks that Max still loved as much as on the first day of his fateful encounter with female beauty, and white patent leather shoes with delicate buckles. Jettel wore a black dress with a pink veiled hat and matching gloves, and Regina still wore the white blouse with a bow and the blue suit that she had worn for the oral exam.

Walter had been able to get Jettel's dress as a special deal from the textile merchant whose hand Regina had refused years ago; he had become a client of the practice of Fafflok and Redlich in the meantime, was married to a woman from South America, and was the father of two daughters.

The gentlemen had been less particular about their attire. Joseph Schlachanska had stuffed his bulk into a white tennis sweater; Walter was wearing his British military khaki pants, which he had only had started to like in Frankfurt; and Max sported a red and white striped sweater and gray leather pants that had become too short for him. Max's outfit elicited an ever-so-slight movement of Mrs. Schlachanska's eyebrows; her daughter's playmate looked too American on top and too German on the bottom for her pronounced sense of style.

Jeanne-Louise, too, was amused. At age seven she had already learned enough from her mother to pay critical attention to outward appearances, but she was not yet adequately sophisticated to exhibit the necessary discipline that corresponded to her mother's ideas of appropriate behavior. After coffee and an instant reprimand for a small spot of cream on her dress, she stumbled with her patent leather shoes into a puddle while playing catch and, on top of that, used a rather vulgar word that she had learned from Max just fifteen minutes ago.

Free of the curious children and the pressure of responding to questions, which were never discouraged by the parents although the children could in no way understand their meaning, Joseph Schlachanska, after a third piece of cake and a second cognac, began to address the topic that had been the reason why he had suggested the excursion. He briefly spoke of his own final high school examination, mentioned his turbulent student days in passing, and suddenly asked, "Well, Regina, what are you planning to do now?"

"I haven't really thought about it yet."

"You are not planning to stay in Germany, are you?"

"Oh, yes, I am going to," Regina replied, and this time she knew without even having to look at Walter that a net had been put out for her. But Joseph Schlachanska was not the man who could be put off by the abruptness of an irritated young girl. He smiled at her with the charm of innocent friendliness that hardly any woman could resist.

"I have suggested to your father that he should send you to England for a year. A young thing like you needs to get out of here for a while and meet new people."

"The ones I know are enough for me," Regina said, and she did not take any time to catch more of a breath than she needed to get rid of her built-up anger that had just been revived. "You are not just talking about people, but about a husband I am supposed to find. But I have not gone to school all these years just to be married to some man whom I don't know and who does not have anything to offer me except that he happens to be Jewish."

She impatiently waited for the storm she had just set in motion, and stared uncomfortably at her hands, which she suspected had the same color as her face. She let herself be shaken by helplessness and fury, and felt betrayed and humiliated. But when she looked at Walter, she caught the old, familiar, infinitely touching panic in his glance.

When the first wave of tenderness started warming her, she realized that nothing had changed since the first days of the unwanted suitors. Her father feared nothing more than a separation from his daughter. He only had not had the courage to admit the truth to Schlachanska. Regina slowly dabbed the perspiration from her forehead. She had to concentrate so that she would not wink when she asked her father in a voice that trembled, only audible to her, "Could we discuss my future tomorrow? I do not want to spoil this beautiful day right now."

"Kessu," Walter said with Owuor's innocence in his eyes, and pressed Regina's hand softly under the tablecloth. *"Kessu,"* he explained to Joseph Schlachanska, "is a wonderful word. It means tomorrow, soon, sometime, or never. I sometimes miss *kessu* in this country."

"Oh, Redlich, your damned Africa has messed you up. If you had stayed there, in the end you would have married Regina to an African."

"Is Regina allowed to marry an African if he is Jewish?" Max asked, and when he saw that his father laughed more loudly than on most other occasions, he used the chance to lick the last of the Danziger Goldwasser from a glass. He was then the only one who had an indelible memory of Regina's last day of school.

The little Opel, worn out by its years of service and Walter's temperament, stood next to Schlachanska's mighty Maybach on a meadow that had been dry in the early afternoon but after the first little rain shower had gotten wet surprisingly fast. Walter had almost reached the road with his family when he noticed in the rearview mirror that the Maybach had gotten stuck and sank in deeper every time the gas pedal was pushed. Schlachanska sat cursing at the steering wheel with a bright red face and moved his body toward the windshield every time he turned the motor off and on again as if he wanted to propel the car forward with the weight of his massive body, but the Maybach did not budge.

Walter got out of the Opel whistling; loudly slammed the door; asked Mrs. Schlachanska and Jeanne-Louise to get out, which they did without the expected contradictions; and tried to push the metal colossus forward.

"Don't do that, you fool," Jettel cried out in alarm after having gotten out of the car with Max. "A man with a sick heart does not push cars."

"Help me push, then."

All of them pushed — Walter gasping, Max shouting encouragement, Mrs. Schlachanska in high-heeled shoes, Jettel with her pink hat sliding, and Regina in the delicate outfit of her special day — but before getting totally exhausted they had to admit that their attempts were futile.

"Come along, my friend, I am going to give you a ride home if you know how to get into a small car."

Joseph Schlachanska did not find enough room for his stomach in the passenger seat and when he pushed himself backward groaning, he got stuck with his nose pressed to the rear window. His feet, in the newly fashionable suede moccasins, dangled out of the car.

"Just like Winnie the Pooh," Max cheered.

"Be quiet," Walter scolded.

He had to dismantle the passenger seat before he was able to push Schlachanska onto the backseat. With the windows turned down and Walter loudly singing *"kwenda safari,"* he started driving an hour later.

Mrs. Schlachanska, mad because her silk dress was full of spots, and Jettel, with her veil askew, shared the torn seat of the Opel on the meadow between daisies and a black-headed sheep, in a first mild and later very strong spring wind. Jeanne-Louise sat silently on her mother's lap. In spite of his mother's and sister's admonitions, Max could not be dissuaded from dancing around the freezing quartet and periodically shouting, "My father is the best driver in the world."

When Walter returned with Rumbler, the chauffeur — who had been summoned on his day off and was obviously animated by a large dose of malicious glee — to pick up his passenger seat and family, mother and daughter Schlachanska refused to wait for the Maybach to be freed from its ignominious state. They crowded, unusually subdued, into the Opel.

"I will never forget this," Max promised his father that night, still impressed by the victory of the David he had not recognized before over the Goliath he had admired for years.

The somewhat overdue conversation between father and daughter took place two days later. Regina was embarrassed in a way that irritated her and became even more embarrassed when she realized that Walter felt the same way.

"I am not a rich man," he said with a formality that he immediately recognized as being exaggerated and foolish, "but I have enough money to let you study. You can choose any field you want. What have you been thinking of?"

Baffled, Regina asked herself if her father really did not know that almost immediately after entering the Schiller School she had not wanted to study anymore and especially not at a German university. She felt oppressed by a feeling that she was duty-bound to be grateful for a favor and could not disappoint the benefactor for the simple reason that she could not feel anything when thinking about her future but the desire, which had become even stronger over the years, to be in an easily comprehensible world with people who thought the same way she did. She remembered just in time that it still might be possible to make her father happy with the answer that he most likely had been expecting from her for years. She smiled, full of regret when she realized that she had been negligent and had made her eyes blind and her mouth silent for such a long time.

"Law school," she said with satisfaction.

"You can't be serious, Regina. Only ugly girls go to law school. Real bluestockings who will never get married."

"We would have one less problem, then," Regina deliberated and intensely reflected whether she had perhaps not understood the point of some joke, "but I don't insist on law. It was just an idea because I am interested in everything you tell me about your work. Actually," she said, briefly chewing on her relief and encouraged to tell the truth, "I don't really want to study at all. I am almost twenty-one and have been a financial burden for you long enough."

"Don't talk such nonsense. I told you I can afford to send my daughter to the university. Only I am not too excited about law school. And not only because you are a pretty girl. I found out what law means. You can work nowhere in that profession but in Germany. An attorney is a prisoner for life."

Confused, Regina asked herself what kind of an effort it had been for her father to make this confession. She knew that she could not look at him so she stared fixedly at the picture of the town hall in Breslau the way she had done as a child when the words had not jumped fast enough from her head to her mouth. "You want me," she said, and all of a sudden it became easy for her to allude to the agreement of their eternal pact, "to stay here. How about becoming a kindergarten teacher?" she suggested. "After all, I like children a lot."

"Do you really still want to play 'Ring-around-the-Rosies' and sing 'I'm a Little Teapot' when you are going to be an old lady of fifty?" Walter asked.

"You are too smart for me, *bwana*. Seamstress would not be too bad either. People always need clothes."

"I did not know that you like to sew."

"Neither did I," Regina laughed. "How about selling books? Many in my class want to do that."

"An attorney's daughter is not going to be a salesgirl. You did not go to school for years on end to stand in a store. Good God, Regina, there must be something in this world that an intelligent girl like you wants to do."

"Writing," Regina realized. "I never really liked to do anything else as much in my life."

"Don't tell me you want to write books. Didn't you see in your father what it means not to be able to make a decent living?"

"I have been thinking of becoming a journalist for some time now," Regina said too quickly and even more perplexedly, but she considered it a lucky break that she had just been thinking about her German teacher who had annotated most of her essays with "too journalistic." "But I have no clue how one goes about becoming one."

"Neither do I, but the idea is not as bad as the others. I can make some inquiries at court or in the Jewish community if anyone knows someone who has something to do with newspapers."

"The main thing is that the newspaper not be in England or some other country with a huge number of Jewish men intent on marrying," Regina sighed.

"I suppose you would not be that opposed to South Africa?"

"How did you know?" Regina wondered aloud. "What made you think about that? Why did you never mention anything?"

She was too confused and relieved to be angry with her father about the fact that he had gone hunting without first presenting her with the weapon he had sharpened with so much cunning and that had caught her unaware. For a heartbeat that made her skin warm and her head hot, she allowed herself the escape to a carefully hidden shore, and enjoyed the quiet of the moment and the taste of a memory mixed with salt and honey, but then she heard the hunter laugh and cut the dream with an equally sharp knife as at the moment of parting.

"Did you really think I don't know about you and Martin? Martin was never able to be with a woman for more than an hour without getting her."

"With me it was a night," Regina said, "and I am glad that you know."

In the days that she had yearned for since her first hour in a German school and that now seemed to her as senseless as they were long, she tried to justify her lack of enthusiasm for the future and her even more annoying lethargy as the normal state of mind of a high school student who has been protected from life for too long in a community of equals. But she was not skilled enough in self-deception and not naïve enough either not to know better. Regina had never been able to overcome the fear of a child, who with irreparable suddenness and devastating vehemence, had been pushed out of its own world to permanently live among strangers.

She considered it a special irony of fate that it was Joseph Schlachanska, of all people, for whom Regina's wish to stay in Germany was a sin against experience and faith, who finally released her from the stranglehold of her self-doubts. He had connections to a publisher in Offenbach and persuaded him, without even telling Walter beforehand, to take a look at Regina.

13

AFTER TEN MINUTES OF NERVOUS WAITING, a petite, reddish-blonde woman with strikingly green eyes behind equally striking gold-rimmed glasses ushered Regina into the office of publisher Brandt and toward an empty chair in front of his imposing desk. Regina tried to smooth out her pleated skirt and to move as little as possible while doing so. She was wearing the blue suit that had accompanied her through her final oral exams at school and since then had had to ensure on all occasions of greater importance that she did not have to be embarrassed about looking too young. Still, she was convinced that her eyes and her mouth, even before the first word of the interview, revealed her uncomfortable tension, which she considered as much of a burden as the doubt that she ever would be able to explain to her parents her first defeat on the way to an alluring independence.

The publisher had one of those smooth, round faces that usually freed Regina of her shyness in front of strangers because widely spaced eyes and a broad forehead, even in white-skinned people, immediately made her think of the good-natured openness of black people. He was sitting in a tweed jacket—reminding her of her childhood, that is, her first headmaster—in front of a desk of dark wood on which yellowed newspapers were stacked up into a high, wobbly mountain next to a vase filled with lilacs.

Regina realized that she did not have much time left to utter at least one intelligent sentence if she did not instantly break the silence, but she could not even remember the small platitudes that she had formulated and practiced over and over again on the long tram ride from the Konstabler Wache in Frankfurt to Offenbach.

Despite all heart-pounding efforts to concentrate on the reason for her visit and especially the task of creating the impression of a smart young woman who was dying to take a hold of pen and paper and portray life, Regina let the time pass by with thoughts that she considered absurd but could not easily abandon. She imagined, with an attention to detail that she classified as remarkable in view of the circumstances, that with such mountains of paper her family would have been able to afford the diarrhea that they all feared more than a reduction of the fat rations every day.

Regina only realized that she must have moved her lips while thinking of those days, when the printed word was far less important than the paper it appeared on, when Uwe Brandt said, "I like that. This happened to me all the time, too, when I was young. I just smiled and people considered me friendly."

"Thank you," Regina said.

"What for?"

"For saying anything at all."

"The famous first word," Brandt laughed. "All journalists have a hard time with that."

Regina realized before the publisher that he himself, even though most likely unintentionally, had mentioned the reason for her visit. She searched in her handbag, too long as she instantly registered, handed him her final school report at last, and wondered if it was too early and too much of an exaggeration to mention that her German teacher had recommended journalism to her.

"Oh, just forget about that, lovely lady. I do not put much stock in report cards. The top student in my class only got to be a supervisor at the railroad and ended up in a mental institution."

"I hope something like that is going to happen in my class, too," Regina said. She became embarrassed again when she realized that she had laughed, but to her amazement she found the courage to keep on talking. "I have not been the best in my class. Not since Africa."

"What makes you mention Africa all of a sudden?"

"I lived there," Regina said. She unhappily asked herself how it could have happened that, without the slightest provocation, she had been tempted to talk about herself and then immediately about something this important. She did not want to drop the thread of her conversation right away either, so she explained, "I mean, we emigrated to Kenya when the Nazis came."

When the publisher, spontaneously and with the kind of attention that Regina had not encountered often, asked her about her family, emigration, and life in a foreign country, and she told him without reservations and with increasing happiness about Ol' Joro Orok, the flax fields, Owuor's wisdom, and the night sounds, she was certain that she had summoned the black God Mungu just as she had done as a child when there was no way out. He had come to her aid and had thrown his stroke of lightning into her tongue.

"You can tell a good story," Uwe Brandt said after Regina had also described their return to Germany and even the desire to stand somewhere and not to see a house or a human being, and that she was still waiting for that moment. She heard him laugh and then speak.

"That is more than most journalists can do. Tell a good story well. What were you thinking of, the *Offenbach Post* or the *Evening Post?*"

Regina had to take an immense detour to return to the present. She thought with much more effort than matching results if she had ever heard of the *Offenbach Post* and if this was even the name of a paper. Relieved, because at least it gave her a clue, she thought of the young men at the main station who held the *Evening Post* up high and cried out the most recent news in an amazing volume although one could read the huge letters of the headlines even from far away. She tried to concentrate hard, but was not sure why she had to pick one of two possibilities.

"The *Evening Post,*" she haltingly said.

"Well, you have taken on a huge bite. Tabloid journalism is not easy for a woman. By the way, do you know Mr. Schlachanska well?"

"Very well," Regina said, happy that Uwe Brandt obviously did not expect a comment on the first two sentences.

"An interesting man."

"Very," she agreed.

"But that just makes me think."

"Why?"

"You see," the publisher began but became silent too quickly and also changed his face too noticeably not to put Regina into a state of heightened alert. He carefully moved the vase with the lilacs from the right to the left side of his desk, searched some time for his handkerchief first in his jacket pocket and then his pants pocket, and dried his forehead.

"May I tell you a little story?"

Regina forced herself to nod. She let the weight of her discomfort press her deeply into the chair and asked herself if the publisher knew Joseph Schlachanska well, and especially since when, and to what extent he would make her feel responsible for his Maybach and appearances. Only too discouragingly clear did she hear her father's reprimand, "That is going to affect all of us, the way good old Schlachanska behaves."

"Two weeks ago," Uwe Brandt said and looked at Regina with a glance that she interpreted as skeptical, "a paper salesman came by and made me an offer. A really nice young man who spoke German well. I looked over his offer and found it too expensive. And you know what happened when I told the good man?"

"No."

"He made a terrible scene right here in my office and screamed that I was only denying him the order because he was a Jew. Just ask my secretary how terrible this was for all of us."

"Yes," Regina said.

"I don't know if you can imagine why I tell you this story."

"I think so."

"If I now decide not to employ you as an intern in our house because we do not have an opening, you will most likely assume that I am rejecting you for racial reasons. I mean we can't even talk normally about these things anymore these days. That is the problem with our times."

Even before she had heard the last sentence, Regina knew that she had actually summoned the God Mungu and that He had lent her for a short, revitalizing moment the magic power of His right arm, which weak people asked for when a thief threatened to forever steal their face and strength. As she took her report card from her lap, folded it very slowly, put it into her handbag, and afterward got up with the sly suddenness of a water buffalo blinded by lethal danger, she was not yet quite sure if the beams of Mungu's deadly fire were also caught between her teeth. But the wish burned strongly in her humiliated senses and drove her to a shore she had never reached before.

"If you think this way," Regina said and could not believe that her voice was as calm as a dying wind, "there is no point in talking to me any further. At home we refer to this as the liability of the whole family for the actions of one of its members."

When her eyes were searching for the door she felt how the rage in her gave way to a great comforting feeling of release. Finally liberated from the day—which had troubled her for so long—when her father had confronted the anti-Semitic driver in the Höhenstraße, she now only thought with the delight of the magically empowered about the cowardly wasted minutes when she had known nothing but silence and fear. She even thought that she heard herself laugh, loud and heartily, but then she realized that the laughter that had reached her ears was not hers.

"For heaven's sake stay, you temperamental Miss," Uwe Brandt called out. "That was not what I really meant. On the contrary. I like you. I find it fabulous how you just told me what you think of me."

"Yes," Regina said and was annoyed that she was only able to produce a whisper at this point. She was not able to decide fast enough if she should sit down again or would immediately have to say more than just one word, but the way to the chair seemed too far for her and she also recognized that her eyes were unable to focus on a single destination. She remained standing and after a few seconds, during which she was still searching for an answer that was appropriate under the circumstances, she settled for the fact that she had at least succeeded in closing her mouth.

"Journalists need courage," Uwe Brandt explained with the kind of goodwill that was generally regarded as infectious. "I learned that when I started at Ullstein. I better send you to the editor-in-chief of the *Evening Post*. If you can get along with him, nobody here is going to be happier than I. I am also happy to do a favor for my old friend Schlachanska. You better have a cup of coffee with me first. We should give our friend Emil Frowein a little time to recover from the shock. He is having a hard time accepting women, you know. Just go ahead to the secretary's office. I am going to be right there."

Emil Frowein put the receiver down with a sigh and examined very thoroughly, and, as usual, mercilessly, the reason for his mood change. It was not the common aversion of the editor-in-chief against the interference of the publisher in things that concerned the editorial office that bothered him. He considered himself diplomatic enough not to show his weariness of the repeated intervention and was always ready for a patient and sympathetic conversation with people who were interested in his profession.

Emil Frowein always made every effort to find out if the young people in the chair in front of his desk were only the victims of romantic illusions or, on first impression at least, seemed to be capable of following a path that had not spared him, for one, from some painful admissions regarding his own talent and, even worse, the dangers of being ready to accept compromises too quickly, as well as from an ambition that he had considered unhealthy for quite a while now. It was the way that Brandt had announced the young woman that bothered him—not the fact that editors-in-chief were better off by not rejecting the personnel suggestions of their publisher without any really sound reason.

"I am sending over something very special for you to review," Uwe Brandt had said on the phone. "A strikingly attractive person. Female. She has beautiful black hair, the kind only Jewesses have." "Uwe," as he was known in the editorial offices, had ended the conversation somewhat abruptly but not quickly enough to leave his editor-in-chief in doubt about the fact that he had laughed jovially.

It was well known—in fact a joke in the business, accepted by all—that Emil Frowein had reservations against women journalists unless they stayed with the established subjects of church, kitchen, children, and lately, of course, also fashion. He had little trouble and used only a few ironic remarks to give a sound defense for an attitude that was no longer considered quite appropriate for the times. Frowein considered women—even though ambitious enough to live up to his high expectations—too sensitive, jealous, argumentative, and thus almost always a problem in an editorial office that was dominated by men. They also had a tendency—which in his opinion aggravated a continuous working relationship beyond any reasonable measure—to put too much emphasis on personal security, which he basically understood and even welcomed. They let their private lives distract them too much from their professional ones and often got married just at the time when they were about to become useful members of the staff.

Frowein used the regrettably short time that remained until he had to meet with Uwe's dark-haired beauty to recognize clearly and relentlessly that this time it was not the prospect of a disturbing female presence in his office that irritated him. Dear Uwe, with the sure instinct of a man who knew a lot and said nothing, had laughed at exactly the right moment. He might as well have asked his editor-in-chief, "And how about your religion?"

It was not as if Frowein, after his experiences in Poland, Holland, Belgium, and France, had specifically avoided the confrontation with a past that he did not gloss over in any way and was even less able to understand. If there was a man in the new, oblivious Germany who was unable to get rid of the pictures he had seen, and who was burdened by the guilt that his early-benumbed conscience tortured him with in all eternity, it was Emil Frowein.

There had not been a day in his life after the hour zero, which he considered as such with all his intelligence and ready insight, on which he had forgiven himself for the weakness and blindness of his youth. After the war, however—and that became obvious to him only now as he stared at the door of his office and waited for the expected knock— he had never had any contact with Jewish people beyond the strictly professional requirements and had not anticipated that he might ever have a personal conversation with them again.

Frowein had, of course, attended the dedication of the rebuilt synagogue in the Freiherr-vom-Stein-Straße as an invited guest because this was natural in his position as editor-in-chief. Although it would have been easy for him to delegate this to a reporter, he himself had even written about the event, which had moved, had depressed, and had actually driven him to face that part of his personality that he wanted to make ever fewer apologies for with every hour of soul searching.

He did not miss any Society for Christian-Jewish Cooperation events, which journalists were invited to, he gave extensive coverage to reports about the Brotherhood Week, and he considered it more than just his duty as a chronicler to participate in the annual commemorative ceremonies for November 9, 1938, at the site of the burned-down synagogue in the Friedberger Anlage.

Now, at this moment that deprived him of his peace with an intensity that he was unable to explain in spite of all he knew about himself, he felt like a frightened child who does not know how to get home. He clearly saw that his theoretical exercises in remorse had lifted only a very small burden from his penitent soul. He shuddered.

Frowein poured some coffee for himself from a thermos and took a cigarette from a mangled pack of Lucky Strikes. He had just discovered that his hands were as unsteady as his head when he heard the knock. He energetically untangled himself from the web of his emotions and called, "Come in!" with great determination. He jumped up, which he had not planned to do, saw Regina standing in the door, saw that she actually had very black hair just like his tomcat, and said, "I have been expecting you. Come in; sit down. I do not bite. I just look as if I do."

Routine immediately took away his embarrassment and he asked her the usual questions about her school, her high school diploma, her special interests, and her ideas about a profession that he was somewhat reluctant to recommend. He did not get the usual answers. Regina did not hide her ignorance about journalism or the fact that she had arrived in the room she was sitting in now more by chance than inclination.

The rigid tendency of her English schooling to understatement and restrictive modesty attacked her in an uncompromising way that she had not experienced for a long time, and guided her head and tongue. She talked, amused and ironical, about her mediocre accomplishments in school, the German teacher and his aversion to any over-simplification of complex topics, and—because she could not think of any other details about her mental development but wanted to keep up the conversation—about her time at the Guggenheims. Slightly embarrassed, she also mentioned her enthusiasm for art and the theater, adding that her father suspiciously held his own enthusiasm for art and the theater in check.

"Does he want you to be a journalist, then?"

"He is not opposed to it. In any case he thinks it is better for me than painting pictures or becoming an actress."

"Oh, you paint?"

"Well, no."

"And did you ever consider acting"

"I would have been thrown out of my home a long time ago. Besides, I have been much too shy to even recite a poem all my life."

"I have too many unfounded fears, too, as a father."

"Then you should meet my father sometime," Regina said.

Frowein noticed her voice, and above all the precision with which she articulated every word with the unusual hardness of a language that did not correspond to her reserved manner and in addition offered memories of a long-hidden cheerfulness. He needed more time than he had expected to tell himself that it was only Regina's language that concerned him, and asked, "Where are you from?"

"From Africa. I mean," she quickly corrected herself, "I lived there for a long time."

"Were you born there?"

"No. I was born in Germany."

"Where?"

"Oh," Regina said and blushed, "you will not know it. I have never met anyone in Frankfurt who knows this funny place unless he happens to be from there."

"Try me," Frowein smiled.

"From Leobschütz."

"In Upper Silesia. My wife was born there."

They both laughed and Regina laughed so much that she had to bite her lips so that she would not talk about Owuor and tell how he had enchanted her as a child with the wisdom that the hearts of two people would immediately grow together if they laughed at the same moment. She had often and always without luck tried to catch the sounds of a sudden laughter in time. It was important to steal the stranger's glance instantly. Regina discovered in Frowein's face that expression of persecuted concern that she knew from her father. She also realized that the man in front of her had shadows in his eyes and in his conversation often protected himself with wit and irony, and this reminded her a lot of Martin. She had to prohibit her thoughts to break away from her head.

"What are you going to do," Frowein asked, "if I send you to the theater to write a review and the theater starts to burn?" Regina hurried back to the gate of the labyrinth and looked at Frowein, taken aback. "I am going to make sure that I get out and run home," she said.

"And you don't call the office to report that the theater is on fire?"

"I never would have thought of that. At least not before I had assured my family that I was still alive."

"This was actually," Frowein said, "the decisive question to determine if you are suited to be a journalist."

"I must have flunked that one."

"That's right," Frowein said. "But not as a daughter. I want to give you a try anyway. Only you better start right away at the feuilleton. It is the only section of the newspaper that allows journalists to have a heart."

He asked his secretary for fresh coffee and a second cup. Regina did not dare tell him that she was still feeling sick from the first one with Mr. Brandt and she dared even less to ask him what he meant by "giving her a try." She stared at the coffee and said she always took it black because she saw that was the way he drank it, and then she had a hard time explaining why the remark "No milk, again!" amused her so much.

They lifted their cups at the same time as if they were about to toast each other and put them down again. Regina thought about her brother and a game that he had loved for a long time. Whoever spills the first drop loses. Frowein was thinking about a black-haired girl, with raised hands and dead eyes, whom he had once seen in Holland. Only a minute, an eternity. He cleared his throat and said, "I want to tell you something else."

"Yes?" Regina asked.

She sensed—when she looked at him and detected his pallor, which she had not noticed before, and also alarmed by his serious, formal tone—that she would now experience something similarly painful as with Uwe Brandt. She tried to numb her senses, but her heart beat so violently that she caught herself thinking of the old childish question of whether a heart that was beating too loudly could betray a person, but she managed to hold her eyes in check.

"I was a Nazi."

Regina was so sure that she had become the prey of her fears too early that she actually turned into a child again. She pressed her lips together till she felt the pain, for she knew that a human being on a precipitous flight had to close her mouth if she had already been foolish enough to have her ears deceive her.

She looked unperturbed at Emil Frowein, fixing her gaze on the white spots on his temples, the teeth in his open mouth, the knot on his gray tie, and the cigarette smoke, which moved in tiny clouds to the light-colored curtains. Her fear had not found an echo.

"Why did you say that?" Regina quietly asked.

"Because you would have found out anyway. Everyone in the office is just waiting to tell you the nice story. I will do it myself."

"Go ahead."

He used words and terms that Regina had never heard before. He spoke of armchair culprits, opportunists, and the German front newspapers that he had saturated in the occupied countries with an ideology that forever prevented him from looking into a mirror without shame. He was his own accuser and judge, and he talked about the stupidity of intelligent people, the ambition and blindness of the young man he had been at one time, the despair of early recognition, and the insight that came too late.

Regina did not let his words deceive her heart. She liked Frowein. She thought of the second of their shared laughter, felt his honesty, admired his courage, and knew enough.

"You are the first Nazi I ever met," she said with a smile. "At any rate, the first who admits it. Usually I only meet people who have saved Jews and have said 'good morning' instead of 'Heil Hitler.' My father will be amazed when I tell him tonight. At home, we have been looking for a real Nazi for years."

"What is he going to tell his daughter?"

"Oh," Regina said, "my father is like you. Honest through and through. He always says that he perhaps might have been a Nazi, too, if Hitler had let him."

"A remarkable father," Emil Frowein said. "I am not surprised that he also has a remarkable daughter."

Regina did not hear the telephone on the desk ring; she saw no movement. So she did not realize at first that the honest wolf, which had not wanted to change its fur, was no longer talking to her. But then his voice became thunderous and swallowed his breath, and for the second time this day she was unable to understand the words that whipped her ears.

Excited, Frowein shouted into the receiver, "But not the Schlachanska from Frankfurt? Don't tell me they arrested good old Schlachanska."

14

THE LITTLE SILVER-COLORED MERCEDES, which Regina had searched for in every corner of the apartment the day before to stop her brother—who had given up all hope of ever seeing his favorite toy again—from crying, lay on the small piece of grass between the round bed of carnations and the lilac. Relieved, she unlocked the black wrought iron gate to the front yard. When she bent down, smiling, to pick up the little car and thought of the happy face that would greet her in a few minutes, her senses finally freed themselves from the confusion of the overwhelming day.

She allowed enough air to get into her chest and head to feel better through the conscious movement of her body, and smelled, until her nose could hold no more of the intoxicating sweetness, the lilacs that were warm from the afternoon sun. Only at this moment of final release did it occur to her that she was returning home unscathed, proud, and above all happier than she had been in years.

Because she wanted to drink in the happiness of her liberation for another moment before sharing it with her parents, Regina sat down under the lilac bush, looking at the light walls of the house, without even hearing the noises from the street. She took off her shoes, pushed her feet into the moist soil, rubbed her back on the thin sturdy stem of the bush, and closed her eyes.

She quite distinctly saw herself sitting in the publisher's office, pedantically watched how he moved the vase from one side of the desk to the other, and heard him talk about the salesman with the inflated prices for paper. With the pleasure of the winner she had never been before in her life, she once again enjoyed her angry eruption from the world of long-held silences and, after that, the precious units of a new time in which she had become courageous and outspoken.

Later, in the soft, cozy state between satisfaction and beginning sleepiness, she saw the sharp contours of Emil Frowein's office with the light curtains and thin billows of smoke from his cigarette, and finally his gray eyes, which had not been able to contain their shadows when they met Regina's glance. She lifted her cup, this time animated by cunning and the pleasure of knowledge, and waited for the laugh that he did not know the meaning of. But she knew when she let the scent of the lilacs fill her nose for the last time that her heart would linger a long time before it returned from this safari.

Dreamily, Regina considered how much of all of this she could tell her father and, above all, how she could avoid frightening him without taking away the taste of happiness and pride. She looked up at the windows on the fourth floor before she had had enough time to bring the last pictures and words into a comprehensible panorama. Max stood on the balcony, shook the bars, and excitedly called her name.

"A fat man with a big car is in prison. But I am not going to tell you who he is. I am not allowed. Papa says that that is attorney-client privilege," he shouted into the garden.

Regina jumped up, took her shoes into her hand, hastened up the stairs, noticed that her father was wearing his hat, and asked breathlessly and reproachfully, "What kind of nonsense is this?"

"Don't be scared Regina. Schlachanska has been arrested."

"I know. But why did you have to tell that to a seven-year-old boy, of all people?"

"He was here when I got the call. I was in such shock, I repeated everything out loud and if there is anything I regret in my life, this is it. Explain to him that he is not supposed to talk about this. Jeanne-Louise is not supposed to know."

"Where is Mama?"

"At Mrs. Schlachanska's. You have no idea what has been going on here since the call came from Schlachanska's office. I have to leave right away, too. We are going to try to have him declared unfit to undergo detention. Then he won't have to go to jail and can lie in a hospital. How do you know about this already?"

"I heard about it in Offenbach. At the editorial offices," Regina said. When she realized that she had pronounced the words with the pride of a child who is only aware of herself, she sadly pushed her hair out of her face.

"I am sorry Regina. I am a bad father. Did it go okay?"

"Yes, *bwana*," Regina said and laughed off her embarrassment. She embraced Walter till his gasping breath sealed her ears. "You are a good father," she said. "All good fathers have moist eyes when their daughters are happy."

"I still have a moment," Walter said. "Have a cigarette with me, Regina."

"But you have given up smoking."

"He only does not smoke when Mama is around," Max announced cheerfully. "Attorney-client privilege. He always smokes in the office. I have known it for a long time."

"Me, too, unfortunately," Regina sighed. "You never had any luck being dishonest. Just like me."

They sat in the sunroom with its yellow painted walls that glowed in the evening sun like the maize fields at the edge of the woods. A scaly black-and-white snakeskin lay across the sofa, a big spear shone reddish-brown behind white wicker chairs, and on the plastic shelf little Masai soldiers carved of dark wood declared a permanent war on each other among grazing elephants and light-colored wooden gnus. A yellow rubber ducky had swum to Africa and sat next to a buffalo with just one horn. Max rubbed his silver-colored Mercedes on the hem of his blue and white checked shirt and let it race around the ashtray. The smell of the tobacco was heavy and sweet; the last drops of a deep red blackberry liqueur sparkled in the pink shot glasses from Leobschütz.

Regina let the tip of her tongue glide into the glass and, recalling her own childhood, allowed her brother to do the same. She was too tired to decide if she was still content or already in the claws of the excitement related to Schlachanska's arrest.

Sadly, she realized that she had only had a few opportunities since Walter's illness to share with him the magic of an accord that bound them so closely together. When she talked about her visit to Offenbach she was no longer the chronicler she had wanted to be. The old pain and always new yearning for the dead days, when it had been enough to let the hours run like sand through one's fingers and only open one's ears, came unexpectedly. Determined, because she was about to miss the connection, she returned to the present.

Her voice was as smooth with care and caution as the naked body of a thief with oil when she talked about Emil Frowein and how she instantly found him agreeable. She actually succeeded without any effort and even with delight in pronouncing the word "agreeable" as if it were the only one that had occurred to her.

"I hope he is not planning on having an affair with you."

"What has happened to Schlachanska?" Regina answered.

"You are not supposed to say that name out loud," Max admonished her. "Nobody is allowed to do that except Papa and me."

"It had to happen at some point. I am not able to see through the whole thing yet. He obviously helped to transfer abroad some money that his clients got as restitution and were supposed to spend here. It is called a currency offense. I will have to explain that to you in detail sometime."

"And you?" Regina asked, taken aback. "Aren't you also opposed to the fact that Jews have to travel to Germany first to get their money?"

"Yes, I am. I don't agree that people should be forced to come here for money that is owed to them. I think it is immoral that they are being told: 'If you want our money you have to forget what we have done to you.' At least Schlachanska fought against this."

"Are you going to do the same?" Regina insisted.

"No. You know that your father is a fool. An honest Prussian nebbish, law-abiding and with a concept of justice that Schlachanska laughed at."

"And what does that mean?"

"That I am driving an old Opel, don't buy enough hats for your mother, and don't buy new shoes for myself. I just want to be able to sleep in peace and not have my children visit me in the Hammelsgasse."

"The Hammelsgasse is where the prison is," Max said. "Is Jeanne-Louise allowed to go there now?"

"Why don't you talk to your smart little brother and tell him to be quiet," Walter laughed and got up. He took his hat off the table, gave his son a slap on the shoulder and his daughter a kiss, and was already at the door of the apartment when he turned around. Regina knew this movement only too well.

His voice was not able to deceive her either. She had realized during the last five minutes that his throat had become too tight and his eyes restless.

"Oh, Regina," Walter said, "I have to ask you a small favor. I have an appointment with a client at the Hotel National at eight o'clock and I'm not sure that I will be able to be there on time. I know you don't like strangers, but just make an effort. I don't want *this* man, of all people, to spend the evening alone in Frankfurt."

"So many words, such a small favor. What is the matter with you?"

"I know you. But I am sure this client will interest you. Just ask for Otto Frank from Basel at the reception desk and tell him you are my clever daughter, big *memsahib* of the printed word. By the way, he is the father of Anne Frank. I already told him I am running late. He is expecting you."

Even though Regina had, early on, and after that again and again, followed the traces of Anne Frank, she had never realized that it had been her father's fate to survive. While she waited for Otto Frank in the dark foyer of the hotel and contemplated, annoyed, why Walter, contrary to his usually open ways, had never told her that he knew him, she was unable to imagine meeting the father of the murdered girl.

She stared at the faded wallpaper and envisioned an old, marked man with a bent back and cane, a broken voice, and trembling hands. She was sure that she would not even be able to think of a courteous greeting and that he would feel the same way. She repeated the name several times like an incantation, and was scared and exhausted from her fantasies.

Otto Frank was tall, slim, and white-haired, elegant in an understated way, and looked younger than he was. He wore a light-colored jacket that emphasized the friendliness of his narrow, slightly tanned face. He had remarkably straight shoulders and a quick, firm step when he walked toward Regina. His handshake was firm, too. He smiled and said, "You don't have to be embarrassed if you stare at me, frightened. I am used to it. Most people do stare. They think I am a ghost. I am very flattered that my attorney is sending his enchanting daughter to meet me."

"I thought you might be annoyed," Regina replied and realized with relief that she had been able to remember the little bit that she had doggedly rehearsed in the tram to the main station. "I am sure you have things to discuss with my father," she continued, encouraged by her unexpected nerve. "I am supposed to tell you that he will be here soon."

"Everything is going well in my case. Your father is an excellent lawyer. I just wanted to meet the man who never wrote me a single letter without a personal note. He must be a very goodhearted person, your father."

"He is," Regina agreed and asked herself how she ever could have been afraid of meeting Otto Frank. She was about to tell him about her confusion, and no longer had any difficulty finding the right words, but he was already talking again. She liked his voice. It was soft like his glance, but firm like his handshake.

"You are coming at just the right time," he stated. "I don't like to eat alone and if I know something about young ladies your age, they are usually hungry around this time."

"That is true. I could eat an ox. I think that is what they say here in Frankfurt."

"That's right," Otto Frank confirmed. "I lived here long enough."

They sat in a small corner of the big, brightly lit restaurant that had more waiters than guests. He ordered eggs in "green sauce" and explained, making a face as if he had done something laughable and had to apologize, that unfortunately his stomach, too, had never been able to forget Frankfurt.

The last trace of insecurity left Regina even before the arrival of the eggs in a bed of watercress and a silver sauceboat. Otto Frank spoke of Basel and how he had only gradually been able to get used to the dialect there; he discussed his second wife, whom he had met after being released from Auschwitz; and he told Regina about the trips he did not like to take but was unable to avoid because he did not want to disappoint the young people who wanted to meet him. He talked a lot about Amsterdam and affectionately about their friends there, but all of a sudden, as if he had been carried away by inappropriate details, he asked Regina to talk about herself.

She reported about the return to Germany, hunger, the long hunt for an apartment, and finding their own house. She was amazed how well he knew the Rothschildallee and how often he had been there in his life. She spoke briefly about her years in school and longer than she considered polite about her professional goals. This led her to her visit in Offenbach. She did not even skip the publisher's story of the paper salesman. She was now able to talk without uneasiness and even ironically about the event. He considered it as bizarre as she did, but "unfortunately typical." When Otto Frank laughed for the first time, Regina looked at him for a moment too long and with wide-open eyes.

He noticed it and laughed a second time. "Everyone thinks," he said, "that I am not able to laugh anymore. Maybe people even think I should not be allowed to laugh anymore. As if I had no right to be alive. But I find laughing easy today."

"Why?" Regina asked.

"Just look into the mirror."

She instantly put her knife and fork on her plate without being disturbed by her confusion, and took a small mirror out of her handbag, which still held the folded high school diploma. She lifted the mirror up high and tilted her head a little to the side like the parakeet at home when he tapped against the shiny glass of his cage.

Regina looked at her face, which was framed by dark hair, high cheekbones, a sharply defined nose, and a small mouth. She saw her pale skin and the eyes that were marked by an early understanding and never without a veil of sadness, and she knew. Since she had first read Anne's diary and had seen her picture, she had felt what Anne's father had just confirmed for her.

"She looked a little like me, didn't she?" she asked quietly.

"Yes. Very much so. I have never before met anyone who reminded me so strongly of Anne."

"I am sorry," Regina murmured, "I didn't want that. It must be very hard for you. So suddenly."

"No. I do not want to forget. I want to be able to imagine what she would have looked like if she had been allowed to live. That is the difficult part. Anne always remains a child to me. We had no time for a farewell. Faces slide away then. There is no way to fight against time."

Regina thought about the farewells that lay behind her, but for once the claws of sorrow were shortened to the softness of grateful amazement; she understood how merciful life had been to her. At every parting she had been allowed to take a long look. She knew every trace of the face that she did not want to forget: She only had to close her eyes to see Owuor, only had to open her ears to hear him laugh. His laughter bounded back from the snow-covered mountain like a mighty thunder whenever she summoned it.

"What did you feel when you read Anne's diary?"

She was not able to return from Ol' Joro Orok in time to restrain her tongue, to admonish her head to be careful. "I was sorry that I learned so little about your other daughter. I mean," Regina said, horrified when she heard herself talk, "she was your child, too."

She had not expected that Otto Frank would react so spontaneously and would get up this fast. She wanted to tell him that she had not meant to insult or hurt him, that she had only been an ignorant, curious child when she read Anne's diary. She was unable to utter aloud any of the explanations that raged within her. Otto Frank pushed his chair back, quickly walked around the small table, and stood behind Regina, bent down. Then he pressed her close and kissed her. When her tears came, she also felt his.

"Thank you, Regina," he whispered, "for saying that. I have waited for so long to hear this just once. It has always pained me that the entire world talks about Anne and nobody speaks of Margot. She was a wonderful girl. So generous, so understanding, and so modest. I never heard her complain in all that time. We understood each other perfectly She was her father's daughter."

After sitting down again, he talked with the obsession of a man who has hemmed in the flow of his memories for too long—of his older, forgotten daughter, whom he could only speak about to the few people who had known both his children. He showed Regina every nook of the small house in Amsterdam where things had happened, which people thought they knew well, and he spoke with tranquility as if time could offer the solace of understanding to a father.

She, too, was calm. At times she felt as if her heart had stopped beating. Then she closed her eyes but could not stop pursuing the tracks that became as fresh as the print of a naked foot in loam. Her questions embarrassed her only at the beginning of the conversation, but soon she no longer considered them to be the curiosity she despised so much, and she understood that Otto Frank expected and wanted to hear them.

Regina realized only then that he addressed her with the informal "you," and in a moment of escalating fear she thought he might also confuse times and faces the way she did when she was unable to hold her head in the present time. Full of compassion, she hoped he, too, would be granted the short, merciful dream of a successful escape, but he looked at her and said, "I have waited for years for this evening. I will never forget it."

"Don't tell me my reserved daughter actually opened her mouth and entertained a stranger," Walter said.

Neither of them had seen him come to the table, and they simultaneously moved their heads as if a door had opened and an unexpected current of air had brushed against them.

"Yes, she did," Otto Frank said. "Fathers never know enough about their daughters. I bet you never realized that Regina is a brilliant listener."

"Oh yes," Walter defended himself. "She had already opened her ears wide as a six-year-old. Children learn to do that very early in Africa."

He looked exhausted, his face gray, too thin, and his shoulders carried a heavy burden, but his eyes lit up when he reached for the menu. He also ordered eggs in "green sauce," said they were the only thing good to eat in Frankfurt, and apologized for letting his guest wait so long.

"I had to have a client of mine declared unfit to undergo detention," Walter said and hit the tip of Regina's shoe under the table with the practiced precision of many years.

"And where is he now?"

"In the hospital. I'd rather visit my clients in the hospital than in prison."

"Your letters had already left me with the impression that you are a kind person. Did you know, Regina, that your father wrote to me in detail about your time in Africa?"

"Oh," Regina said.

"You see," Walter laughed, "as soon as her father shows up she leaves the talking to him."

Free of Jettel's watchful eye and exuberant like a child, who at the moment of his action already knows that he is safe from punishment, Walter ordered a bottle of Mosel wine. He had another portion of eggs and green sauce brought to him, drank as fast as he talked, and enjoyed speaking, as never before, of the time of his emigration, drawing on an abundance of experiences that Regina had never suspected to still be in his head. On this night of remembrances Walter only told of the happiness and beauty of Africa, and with such joy and at times even longing that he occasionally got caught up in the soft, dark sounds of Swahili that floated in the empty restaurant till they disappeared.

"Are you happy here in Germany, then?" Otto Frank asked.

"Very happy, just not *glücklich*. If you know the old emigrant joke."

"I do, but the other way around."

"I, too, only heard it the other way around, before," Walter said and emptied his third glass. His face was red, his eyes full of delight.

"If you keep on drinking like this," Regina said and borrowed Jettel's voice, "you will hit your clients on the head with their files tomorrow morning."

"Not the files, not the clients either. The head is wrong, too," Walter enumerated. "My daughter has no clue as usual. Do you know, Mr. Frank, why I was able to have your claims processed so quickly? I was lucky enough to be assigned a particularly anti-Semitic judge."

"And what is lucky about that?"

"He picked his nose with one finger and with the other he poked around in my brief, the way these gentlemen do, because they do not yet dare to say what they've thought for a long time. But then this fellow did say that he needed more witness statements to prove the entire story. He actually said 'the entire story.' The next day I slammed Anne's diary on his desk and told him to call me if he had any further questions. He had none."

"Thank you," Otto Frank said, "for the slam. And also thank you for Regina."

It was close to midnight when they left the hotel. The street was empty. An old man was asleep on a bench, wrapped in his coat.

"He is lucky," Walter said.

Regina had to dissuade Walter from going to a bar with her and then she had an even harder time preventing him from running back to the hotel, calling Jettel, and asking her if he should bring home a bottle of wine. Walter finally managed to start the car at the third try. When he put it in reverse, he nicked a street lantern and called Regina a hysterical goat when she screamed. She was quiet and reproached him only in front of the house, labeling him a cruel father who was turning his children into orphans.

"Half-orphans," Walter corrected her. He was sober enough, too, at this point to say, "Don't tell your mother."

"She is going to find out anyway that you have been drinking. If she is still awake."

"I am not talking about the wine, you silly goose. I mean the judge. Your mother will be gloating. She is so full of glee when my eyes are occasionally being opened, too."

15

BENT OVER, HIS FACE CONTORTED AND ASHEN, Walter unsteadily walked through the abandoned garden. Groaning, he dragged himself to a bench and let his aching body slide forward and his head fall onto his arms. It was three o'clock in the morning and precisely three months before his fiftieth birthday.

"I am not going to make that anymore," he quietly complained but sat up straight again. "I hope they have not yet bought any presents."

"Don't talk such nonsense," Fafflok said calmly and with conviction. "We don't have far to go."

He had raced to the Rothschildallee when he got Jettel's panicked and barely intelligible call, and after that he instantly drove Walter, who had refused to bother Dr. Goldschmidt in the middle of the night because of a condition he flippantly dismissed as a stomachache, to the university hospital. Fafflok's equanimity was challenged even further at the emergency department.

With a suddenly revived voice, Walter called a startled young doctor with a small beard a stupid goat because he had talked about a fracture and had tried to put the patient in a wheelchair. Walter angrily shouted, "Not me!" and insisted on walking to the surgery department.

"Only three more minutes," Fafflok encouraged him, "if the goat is right. Most likely it will not take heroes like you even that long." When he pushed open the surgery department's old, heavy doors, he too was only able to breathe with difficulty. He had to prop Walter up.

The physician, old and sufficiently well shaven to be considered competent by Walter, diagnosed a strangulated hernia. In addition, on the patient's chart he noted some mental confusion, which, even considering that he was suffering severe pain, seemed atypical. Walter had acknowledged the necessity of an immediate operation with the remark, "Sir, I am telling you right now that I am going to speak German under anesthesia."

"Naturally, you do that," the physician tried to soothe him, "if you get to talk at all under our efficient modern anesthesia."

"It is not natural at all," Walter explained during an interval between two painful attacks. "They were quite offended by my mother tongue when I had black-water fever."

"Black-water fever? Where was that?"

"In Nakuru. The Nakuru Military Hospital. 'Sergeant Redlich, we are at war with Germany. Do not forget that!'"

"Dr. Redlich was an emigrant," Fafflok clarified, "in Kenya."

When they put him on a stretcher Walter asked to speak with Fafflok for five minutes in private in the white-tiled room.

"You should not," the surgeon murmured, but he did leave the room.

"Take care of my Jettel," Walter said and energetically removed his arms from under the thick cover, "if I don't come back. She is so unfit for life and is not even aware of it. Someone has to take care of her. Regina is not ready to do that yet."

"Man, a hernia operation is not a big deal these days."

"It is if one has a weak heart. It is if one wants to die."

"Don't say such a thing."

"One does in Africa. One says *na taka kufa* and they put you in front of the hut. And then the hyenas come. Marvelously practical for the people who are left behind."

"We are in Germany. That means no pain, no gain," Fafflok said. "We even have to earn death the hard way. I learned that myself during the war. And besides, I already bought your birthday present."

Fafflok wondered, while quickly walking back through the garden into the day, if Walter had still been able to hear him. He wished for it so much that he thought himself naïve and frivolous. He realized, amused but not fully relieved of the ghosts Walter had conjured, that he himself was truly a man who could not be frightened easily and had survived a

hernia operation a long time before those had become routine proce-
dures. To his surprise, Fafflok found himself talking aloud.

When he saw a stray dog in the street and immediately thought
about hyenas, even though he had only seen pictures of hyenas and
those only long ago, he smiled and shook his head. Yet he drove so fast
and absentmindedly across the Friedensbrücke to get Jettel to the hospital that he had to rein in his imagination before decreasing his speed.

The operation was completed without complications. On the following day Walter was thirsty and called the nurse a *mjinga mingi* because
she would not allow him to drink anything. Any child on the farm would
have recognized the term as "fool," but she, however, patiently took it for
a Yiddish expression. On the second day he was hungry and swore so
rudely—in German!—that even the hospital personnel crept out of the
room on tiptoe. On the third day he was bored and harassed Jettel and
Regina—because they had forgotten to bring him the newspaper—so
persistently that both dissolved into tears.

On the fourth day Walter had files brought in from his office despite
the chief of surgery's protest and Jettel's threat that she would never visit
him again. He angrily declared that he owed it to Fafflok not to leave
him alone with all the work; otherwise he would terminate the partner-
ship. Fafflok, called in to help again, managed to remove at least half of
the files the secretary had lugged to the hospital. At the end of the week
Walter had an embolism. Max was home alone when the call from the
university hospital came.

"I am not allowed to ride the tram by myself until I am nine," he
reported into the phone.

"Wait till your mother comes home," the nurse told him, "but tell
her to come to the hospital right away. Tell her it is urgent. Your father
is not doing well. Did you understand me?"

"Yes," Max said impatiently, "I have known how to use the telephone for quite a while."

He took the money that his mother secretly used to put aside from
her household money (she thought he did not know where it was hidden) from a tin labeled "Personal" on the upper shelf of the kitchen cabinet, cleaned two ink stains from his hands, and smoothed his hair with
water. He ran down the Höhenstraße as fast as he could, got into the
streetcar, and changed at the right stop. An hour later he stood, very

breathless and even hotter from pride than from running the last part of the way, at his father's bedside.

"Where is your mother?" Walter asked.

"At her afternoon coffee party at the Kranzler."

"What, she is at a café while her husband is dying? This is proof again, son, that women have no brains."

"But she doesn't know that you are dying. Regina doesn't know it either. She is at work. And Else has her day off."

"Your Papa is not going to die," the doctor said, giving Walter an injection and patting the son on the head. "We discovered at exactly the right time that he was going to play a very bad trick on us."

"What kind of a trick?" Max asked.

"You spoiled all the fun for my son," Walter said. "I had promised him that he could sit in the first row at my funeral."

"You should not talk so much. You need a lot of rest now. I already got a hold of your wife. She is going to be here soon."

"And how am I going to get any rest then?" Walter asked and winked at his son. Max knowingly returned the look of their beautiful conspiracy.

Since Walter had never been interested in medicine and even less in sickness, and that on principle, because he considered it wise and a measure of self-defense and could not be dissuaded from his opinion that doctors had a tendency to exaggerate, he was the only one who did not know that his condition was actually quite critical for a few days.

The physicians admired his spirit, courage, humor, and craziness. They considered the way he provoked them original and likeable, and regarded it as the secret weapon of a man who had experienced adversity and knew how to talk about it with the kind of jovial wryness that even most healthy people could not muster.

Jettel spoiled the difficult patient with a lot of affection that both had not thought possible any more and above all she spoiled him with boiled sausages, herring salad, and poppy seed cake. The head of surgery and the medical director had to taste the delicacies to convince themselves of the superior quality of Silesian cooking. The fishmonger sent a bouquet of flowers that was even bigger than the one from the Jewish community.

Max, who had proved beyond a doubt that it was unreasonable to restrict him from using the tram by himself until his ninth birthday, insisted on his new privileges. He would arrive unaccompanied in the early afternoon to help Walter with the files that had been returned to the hospital, and he was particularly interested in criminal law and difficult divorce proceedings. When he put a chocolate bar on his father's bed, both laughed and said "attorney-client privilege."

"I would like to live to see two things," Walter said.

"Which ones?" Max asked.

"My birthday and your bar mitzvah."

"Your birthday first," Max decided. "My bar mitzvah is not going to be for another five years."

"At least I have one child who is able to think logically and is standing with both feet on the ground. Maxele, my son, you have to go to law school."

"I am going to, and I will only marry a Jewish girl."

Regina came to visit her father at ten o'clock in the morning before driving to the editorial offices in Offenbach. During the first days after the embolism she tried to restrict their conversation to topics that she thought would not excite Walter. She never spoke about his illness, never about the future and, consoling herself in her worries about her father, invoked only the soft pictures of the past. Later when Walter was allowed to get up, they played solitaire on the small table in front of the window. It was the first time they did this together since the long evenings at Ol' Joro Orok when it had been a ritual to consult the cards about one's fate. The superstition had remained as strong as the ability to look back and not admit it.

When Walter had become strong enough to go into the garden with Regina, he looked for the bench he had sat on with Fafflok before his operation. From then on they enjoyed the heat of July, the flowers, the many birds to whom they shouted good wishes in sweeping Swahili sounds, and above all the very visible progress Walter made every day.

"It should always be like this," Walter wished.

"It will be," Regina said and crossed her fingers.

Walter saw it and said, "Mental reservations. You always used to do that."

He was peaceable, witty, and exuberant; whistled at young nurses; let Jettel persuade him to get a new robe because, he said, he had noticed that he still had a chance with women; and in long conversations finally abandoned the suspicions he had held against Regina's profession. They were both able to laugh over and over again and aloud about the fact that Max had not gotten frightened at all by the call from the hospital and had only thought about raiding his mother's secret stash.

On the day before his release from the hospital Regina finally found the courage to express the thoughts that had started to oppress her more and more since Walter's first heart attack. "You should not talk so much about death with Max," she said with as much equanimity in her voice as if she had just thought about this reprimand.

"Why? He has to know about his father's condition. He is supposed to be a man when the time comes and he should not stand at my grave like a child. That is the only thing I can do for my son."

"You are taking away his innocence."

"Don't talk so bombastically. The boy doesn't need any innocence. Do you still have yours?"

"You are trying to change the subject, *bwana*. You know exactly what I mean. Max is still a child. It is a sin to burden him ahead of time."

"Not among Jews. We have been doing it for centuries. Had to do it. When the children of Israel went with Moses, they were not told that they were going for a Sunday outing either. Our children are not permitted to grow up and think that they are people like everyone else."

"Isn't it enough that Max knows about Auschwitz and how his grandparents died?"

"You knew all of that, too, Regina."

"Those were different times. I had to know. But I was able to escape into my imagination. You have no idea how much my dream world meant to me."

"Oh yes," Walter disagreed with her, "I always knew. Sometimes I even envied you. And I was afraid to let you escape into your fantasies. I always thought you might not be able to survive in real life."

"And do I?"

"Yes, at least I think so. In your own way. You are very different from your brother. He is already magnificently able to hold his own today."

Regina looked at her father and let Owuor's derision get into her glance. He had never understood why his smart *bwana* only saw people's faces and heard only the words they spoke. "You are sleeping on your eyes again," she laughed, picking up a small stick from the ground and carefully breaking it into two equally long pieces. "I am the strong one, not your son. I have learned things on the farm that Max will know nothing of all his life. He cannot escort you. So play your games with me."

"I am going to try, clever *memsahib*," Walter smiled, "but make sure that you are going to be around."

"I promise. I already asked for a day off for your birthday."

September 5, 1954, was a day filled with summer sun and mild autumn air. Heavy-headed dahlias, Walter's favorite flowers after vetches and roses no longer bloomed, stood in his mother's crystal vase and lured him into the dining room during the night.

At five o'clock in the morning he was unable to control his impatience any longer. He first woke his family, then Else on the fifth floor, and finally the screeching parakeet, Kasuko, under his embroidered cover. He called out several times, "I made it. I am a real quinquagenarian," and sang "Gaudeamus Igitur" after that.

In a new robe and with a crown that he had fashioned from a brown paper bag during his sleepless night, he sat in the flowered wing chair and enjoyed his survival in the sun-drenched living room. At first he disliked the fifty candles, which Regina and Else had stuck into a bowl filled with sand, because some of them were not straight and others were placed too close to each other, but when they were all finally lit, he was happy like a child and laughed with the sound of his healthy days.

"It was the same at my father's birthday," Else remembered. "The candles were all crooked, too."

"What was good enough for your father is good enough for me, Else," Walter decided.

Jettel gave him two new shirts, which he declared were more than he would be able to wear out for the rest of his life, and a gold-banded watch, which surprised him so much that he was silent with embarrassment for a moment. Jettel said that she had pinched and scraped to buy the expensive present.

"From your household money," Walter reminded her but he held the watch up to the light with a serious face, let the parakeet listen to it ticking, and gave Jettel a big kiss. "We are both becoming childish in our old age," he said, "and forget what time it is."

"I am not that old yet."

"What a diplomatic remark!"

"You are not old yet, either," Jettel said conciliatorily.

Max handed his father a huge bunch of asters and was astonished to find that Walter noticed that the flowers came from their own front yard. Max also gave him, with a longing glance, the four-color pen that cost twelve marks and that he himself had wanted for a long time and had actually saved for from his allowance. For the first time this day, and not realizing how often he would have to repeat it, Max recited a poem written by his sister.

The poem had roughly constructed end rhymes and such a poor rhythmical meter that his markedly early feeling for language nearly prevented him from giving a smooth recital. Walter, usually quick to suspect dilettantism in his children and to criticize it, too, appreciated the verse with rare empathy as a declaration of love by the author and remembered with some emotion that she had never been able to rhyme. He dried his tears with one of the six handkerchiefs Else had given him. They were tied together with a pink silk ribbon that Else had braided herself and he had wound around his neck.

Regina had thought about her present for months—in melancholy memory of the first crocheted potholder and the scarf, which Walter had worn without complaint in the African heat because he cherished, most of all, the effort that had gone into the gift. In the same manner, Walter received her first book. It was entitled "Do You Remember?" The pages were typed on the old typewriter that had traveled from Germany to Africa and back and were sewn together by Regina with blue wool. The yellow cardboard cover was decorated with a steamer, its flag fluttering in exactly the opposite direction of the smoke that rose from two smokestacks into the sky. The subtitle was written into the ocean waves in block letters: "From Mombassa to Leobschütz."

To Regina's consternation her father read the end first and thus prematurely learned about the author's intentions. "I have," Regina had written on the last page of the book, "won the biggest prize because I have learned to recognize good fortune when I come across it. For this I have to thank my father, who enriched my childhood with his love and kindness so much that all my life I will pity all the people whom fate has deprived of such a father."

Walter needed the second of Else's expensive handkerchiefs before he was able to speak again. He promised, with an earnestness that moved Regina even more than his tears, that he would read the book after breakfast, and he said that it had just occurred to him that one could actually earn a living by reading and writing alone.

He was just in the process of beheading the second of his hard-boiled eggs, a much-appreciated additional gift from Jettel, who had promised not to mention doctors or dietary prescriptions on his special day, when the doorbell rang. Regina and Jettel looked at each other and let the displeasure of suddenly interrupted hostesses sweep across their faces. Max held a hand in front of his mouth and giggled with such facial expressions that his sister kicked him under the table and his mother elbowed him, but Walter did not notice any of this. With the napkin around his neck, waving the egg spoon, he ran into the hall and told Else, who was there already, "You would like to do that, wouldn't you, to take away my birthday surprise." He pushed the parakeet aside and pulled open the door to the apartment. "Somebody is groaning on the stairs even worse than me," he reported.

"Well, I am not as young as you are, Dr. Redlich," Josef Greschek shouted up from the second floor.

He was lugging the same pail he had arrived with on his first visit to Frankfurt. This time the never forgotten, newly polished magic container was filled with fresh chanterelles and portini mushrooms instead of potatoes. Greschek had replaced the bacon, which was no longer considered healthy for largely immobile urbanites, with two remarkably fat ducks and a rabbit that in honor of the special birthday had a gold ribbon around each haunch.

Later on Greschek retrieved from his suitcase—it was still the old, tattered brown one—a new, dark suit for himself and a package of old postcards from Leobschütz for Walter. He had only been able to accumulate this melancholic panorama after a lot of correspondence with compatriots and the allusion to a good purpose. On the birthday card with a golden fifty surrounded by golden leaves, Grete had written in her neat handwriting "To the esteemed Attorney and Notary Dr. Walter Redlich on his fiftieth birthday," and then with her ability to summarize the essential, she had added, "We think about Frankfurt a lot, and are doing well in Marke."

"That you have come, Greschek, is the most beautiful present of all. I wanted to write to you but my wife said I could not ask you to make the trip because you have been sick, too. Now I know why she acted that way."

"I was not going to come at first. I thought, Dr. Redlich is a fine gentleman now and I am going to be out of place among all the fine guests."

"I should throw you out immediately for that kind of a remark. You never would have thought like that in Leobschütz."

"But Frankfurt is not Leobschütz."

"Whom are you telling that to, Greschek? I long so often for our old comfortable life and the friendly people."

"It was not all that comfortable, Dr. Redlich, when you had to leave. And the people were not altogether friendly either. You spent too much time among the Africans to really know about the whole thing."

Of the guests who had been invited for dinner, only the Faffloks came at four o'clock for coffee, apple and poppy seed cake, and the big butter crème torte from the bakery. In a family that had no relatives anymore, they were considered as such and brought along fourteen-year-old Michael, who displayed his father's quiet patience and instantly realized that he would be spared from Max and his invitations to play as long as he had a filled plate in front of him. Ulla, three years younger than her brother and with the blonde looped plaits that Max adored, as self-assured and honest as her mother, soon got a book from the children's room and, unperturbed, called the host's son a spoiled brat. This only upset the harmony until Max was allowed to recite the poem again.

Fafflok gave Walter an oil painting of an open river landscape framed by large trees that perplexed Walter so much that he remarked, "The painter forgot to put people in the foreground." When his son corrected the omission a few days later with the new four-color pen, Walter was beside himself with anger.

"The 'Tommies' would have paid a fortune for a real oil painting," Greschek sighed.

Greschek particularly enjoyed Mrs. Fafflok; she talked about Rati-bor, Gleiwitz, and the escape from Upper Silesia in the same way as he did, soberly and without longing for a life that Greschek only evoked when he was in Frankfurt. He was quite impressed that the Faffloks not only had a house of their own but were also planning to build an apart-ment house.

"They came into an inheritance," Max explained. "We can't do that because our family was murdered."

When the men drank cognac and the women drank cocoa with nuts, and when even Jettel laughed about the story of the icebox she had not brought along for their emigration, they felt nothing but the relaxed happiness of a close inner bond. All of them sensed that, regardless of the high points, speeches, and ceremonies that the evening's celebration was yet to bring, these were the hours that would be remembered.

"You have become my only friend," Walter said. "Greschek does not count. He is from earlier times."

"I didn't know you then," Fafflok pondered, "otherwise it might have been me then."

In the early evening when the women were all just about to go into the kitchen and share the domestic duties, the postman delivered a tele-gram from South Africa. "To my best friend Walter—may he stay young forever!" Martin had written.

"Nebbish," Walter said and immediately put the telegram into his pocket so that his daughter would not be able to read "A special kiss for my little Regina."

But Regina did see the sentence below Martin's name, turned pale, and insisted that she, not Else, would get the wine from the cellar. She stayed too long in the consoling damp darkness. Walter went to look for her. This is how it happened that he got carried away on his fiftieth birthday to utter a sentence that he would have called an oath of disclo-sure on normal days. He demonstrated to Regina that he was not only her very serious, rigidly moral, and passionately jealous father, but also the only man whom she had ever really permitted to look into her heart.

"I would have wanted you to have him," Walter swallowed, "but only because I have always remained the fool who promised his daugh-ter that he would simultaneously get her the moon and the sun from the sky."

16

I T   W A S   A   C O I N C I D E N C E without special meaning that Walter found
out about the changes imminent in the lives of his two children on the
same day in the late summer of 1956. In the morning came the long-
awaited news that Max had passed the entry examinations for the first
year at the Heinrich-von-Gagern Secondary School. It gave Walter a
lot more peace of mind than Regina's remark that evening that she had
finished her internship at the *Evening Post* and would from now on be a
permanently employed member of the editorial staff.

In no way did Walter pay more attention to his son's development
than to his daughter's destiny. Nobody knew that better than he did
when he took a painfully black view into a future where he would no
longer be able to accompany his children. However, he considered it
better suited to him and certainly much easier to deal with a secondary
school than a newspaper that he had used to call a "tabloid" and whose
popularity in his own law office he failed to understand when he looked
at the red, tasteless headlines that were of no significance whatsoever to
the course of world events.

Walter bought his son a new soccer ball as a reward for his intellectual efforts, now considered much less a child's obvious duty than once
upon a time in Regina's case, and he also gave him the long-yearned-
for briefcase to replace the backpack that was considered too childlike
now. Walter also promised him nightly visits to the six-day bicycle race
and a noticeable increase in his weekly allowance for as long as the success lasted. In case of occasional failures, which he considered quite

likely in memory of his own school years, he threatened his son with physical demonstrations of his displeasure and a cross-eyed tutor with heavy legs.

"When your sister wanted to learn Latin," Walter preached while Max had to scratch his back, "I had no money and she wasn't allowed to learn a word of the world's most beautiful language. This is just going to show you how rich we are today. You are allowed to learn whatever you want, my favorite son."

"Swahili," Max suggested with the long-practiced sense for the danger of obscure promises, "so that I finally understand what you are saying about me when you talk to my mother and my sister."

"Just make sure that you use your practical head in school, too. I was always the sixth in my class; I am not asking more from you either."

"The sixth of seven," Max said and enjoyed the old joke, liberated from his father's misguided hopes about his intellectual ambitions.

Walter had a hard time assessing the change in Regina's life simply because Regina had failed to dispel her own long-held doubts that she might have misjudged her talents, would fail somewhere along the line, and would not be allowed to stay on after her internship. Moreover, he started to notice Regina's new dress at precisely the moment when he found out about her new position in life.

He was, therefore, not able to focus on the news right away. Regina had apparently gotten dressed up in anticipation of her new salary, which she mentioned with unusual pride. Walter considered her behavior wasteful and thought the dress was too tight, too short, too provocative, and too low-cut. The new-fangled expression "sex appeal" entered his mind; he had an aversion to connecting this concept with his own daughter.

He looked at her for only an instant with the attentive eye of a man who observes more than the length of a skirt, but very quickly he turned his newly sharpened view, which had just registered changes that had escaped him before, into a hint of fatherly displeasure by saying, "You will have even less time for your old father now."

"More," Regina contradicted him with an eagerness that at first convinced her more than her father. "You know, editors don't have to write about prize-winning cats and the distribution of Christmas presents at homeless shelters. We send interns to do that."

"What business does a Jewish girl have with the distribution of Christmas presents? You never told me about that. I didn't know that you did such nonsensical things."

"Yes," Regina lied, "I did. At least sometimes."

When she lay in bed she became more pensive than she had intended to be on this happy day. First she realized that she was unable to focus on Saint-Exupéry's much-loved and often re-read book *Wind, Sand, and Stars,* and then she remembered once again how Walter had looked at her, and that she had, at least in the beginning, been flattered. She heard her parents debate about how many new pairs of pants Max needed for his new school. Regina wanted to get up and stop the fight that was going to harm Walter when it reached the anticipated level, but instead she stayed in her room.

The short conversation with Walter took on unexpected dimensions and disturbed Regina. She self-critically asked herself whether she really had only wanted to reassure her father when she told him that he could still count on her in her free time. But it seemed to her more likely that she had been carried away in a euphoric moment to almost allude to her special relationship with her editor-in-chief. Regina was unable to explain to herself what kind of craziness might have nearly compelled her to burden her jealous, choleric, concerned father with that kind of a superfluous confession.

It appeared useful and important to her to find at least some kind of answer to her question, but after barely disentangling these difficult problems, she decided not to bother her conscience on such a good day. Regina told herself that it was the wrong time to justify the fact that she certainly had not behaved differently from any other woman who had caused a man to lose his head. She fell asleep before she found time to think about more than the most important point of her professional life. The way things stood, Emil Frowein would rather go into a monastery than leave her, and she knew it.

From the beginning he had been true to his impulsively given word and he had, to his editors' surprise, albeit after some time not without the nodding agreement of male tolerance, taken the only female in his office under his until-then untested wings. Emil Frowein had not assigned Regina to the kind of tasks that were usually regarded as good job experience for interns. After not being able to get his reason back, and after the balance of his emotions had been upset so unexpectedly by their first meeting, he did not find it too difficult to change his rules of authority and justice either. As he had promised in the unusual job interview, he actually allowed Regina to work only in the feuilleton office during the two years of her internship.

He was very quickly convinced that his decision had been the right one, even though he knew that it soon became the subject of rumors. Regina, excessively encouraged in her one-sidedness by an editor who was obsessed with the theater and defended his resort like a furious giant against even the slightest assumption that there were occasions that required extensive reporting other than just opening nights, learned nothing but to write reviews. They were acknowledged as displaying expertise, wit, and a very palpable love for the theater.

It was, however, a casual remark that resulted in consequences that none of the people involved had foreseen. When Regina was sent to her first opening night and was given two tickets by the secretary, she asked how she should return the one she was not going to use. Frowein was standing behind her and asked her to come to his office.

"The theaters always send two tickets for the critic. But, of course, I cannot allow a young woman to be out on the streets at night by herself," he said and spared neither Regina nor himself the tone of concerned paternity. "If it is all right with you, I will accompany you."

It was the completely natural beginning of an old story—newly experienced by people who were lonely, introverted, in search of a way out of their isolation, and unaware how much they were attracted to each other. Both suspected it and did not protect themselves. Regina's longing for warmth was too big; her interest in the man, who had trusted her in an hour of truth, had already turned into too much fascination and affection to leave her with scruples, which she readily dismissed as small and unworthy of herself.

Frowein, who had always been interested in the theater and had not been able to get to one in years because he considered it a crime not to take part in the headline meetings at the editorial office, had a harder time with morality and conscience.

At first he tried to analyze his behavior, which struck him as most unusual, as the long-overdue revival of an old passion and after that as the duty of a responsible mentor.

Very soon, however, he gave up trying to deceive himself and his editors. When it became a mockingly accepted habit that with Regina he even visited plays that had already been reviewed, Frowein himself, the reserved, hesitant skeptic who had made every effort to stay free from emotions, realized that he had not only the role of an intellectual advisor in mind. During the greater part of Regina's internship, he had managed to maintain, at least in moments of an all-too-merciless confrontation with his conflicting feelings, the illusion that he was nothing but a well-meaning boss who, only because of the subject matter, did not exercise a possibly even outdated restraint.

He was thus actually unpleasantly surprised when he discovered that he had not fallen in love with the theater again, but with the young woman, who sat next to him with wide-open eyes, whom he got champagne for during the intermission, whom he drove home after the performance, and who, in spite of all the years she had lived in Germany, was still a child from a world where enthusiasm and rejection, incredulity and astonishment were expressed in a way that life had made him give up long ago.

Frowein liked the fact that this woman had never learned to distrust romanticism, sweetness, and predictability, and that she was not blinded by beautiful classic words. She cried into Frowein's handkerchief when watching the *Little Tea House*, excitedly pinched his arm during the *Caucasian Chalk Circle*, recited verses in English during Shakespeare's *Measure for Measure*, and asked during the intermission to *The Robbers:* "Did you know that Schiller wrote such extraordinary plays?"

"You must have read *The Robbers* in school."

"No, during the time when German students read Schiller I sat under my guava tree and read Dickens to my fairy."

"What did your fairy and the tree look like?"

"The fairy wore a dress of leaves from a white water lily, the tree smelled like honey, and the bees sang songs only the fairy and I were able to hear."

It was Regina's glance—filled with a suddenly revived longing—more than her laughter that Frowein could not forget. Six weeks later during the *Rain Maker* he accidentally addressed her with the familiar "du" and apologized, stuttering like a high school boy. A month later during Georg Kaiser's *Colportage,* he asked if he could call her by her first name—"only in the theater, obviously."

"But you have done that for quite a while."

"But not in the office."

"No, in your head."

"And you don't mind?"

"Oh, no. My head does not have as much trouble as yours with words that are not allowed to enter my throat."

"You said that beautifully, Regina."

"That was not me. I only translated from Swahili, the language of my old homeland."

"I didn't know that you speak Swahili."

"I don't anymore, *bwana lala,*" Regina said as she got into the car. "I only think in Swahili when it helps."

"Against what?"

"Against almost everything except a sore throat," she contemplated and thought about the long distance their first shared laughter had traveled and that it was not good if laughter reached its destination too early.

"What you said a moment ago with the many beautiful vowels—what does it mean?"

"I spoke about a sleeping man."

"When the man is awake and nobody hears it, may he call you 'du'?"

"Why would he want to say anything at all if nobody hears it?"

When *The Diary of Anne Frank* was performed in Frankfurt and the audience was as moved as if it had only now heard about the tragedy, Frowein had tears in his eyes. Regina sat next to him, her body stiff and paralyzed with pain, and thought about the father who through the fame of one of his daughters had to once more accompany the other to her death.

She told Frowein about the meeting. He only interrupted her once and then with an almost inaudible sigh. It was loud enough to reassure Regina that in this Germany, which so readily and quickly, yet reluctantly, spoke about "collective shame," there was at least one man who approved of the meaning of these two words. This alone was important to her.

When Frowein turned into the Rothschildallee, he upset the dream of harmony a last time and said, "We would like to contact Otto Frank."

"Who is 'we'?"

"The editorial office. Do you have his address?"

"My father does. Why?"

"We should interview him. It would make us look good."

"Unfortunately, I am the wrong person for the job. I am not the type who has her friends grilled by people like the ones in our office. Besides, I am allergic to curiosity."

"Not curiosity, Regina. This is contemporary history. You have to understand that if you want to become a good journalist."

"If that is the price, I pass. I cannot turn death into a current affair. Have you forgotten that I am going to run home from a burning theater to reassure my parents of my safety and will not think about writing a report?"

"How could I?" Frowein asked. "This is how it all began." He knew that this was not the right moment to speak about himself. But he did so anyway. Looking at the windshield, he said, "I have fallen in love with you, Regina."

"I know."

"I have fought and lost."

"I have not fought," Regina realized, "but I am going to lose anyway. You are not a man who can live with the fact that he first lost his head and then his good conscience. Especially not as a boss. Only how are you going to explain it in the office that you have to fire me?"

"Don't ever say that again. Do you really think I would let you suffer because I am an old fool? Nobody in the office is ever going to find out what I have done. I promise you."

"You," Regina said and felt more compassion for him than for herself, "should not count on that. And besides," she said, and was unable to restrain her tongue in time, "you haven't done anything to me yet."

During the months after this conversation, which perplexed her even more in retrospect than she had been aware of at the time, she often asked herself, with a curiosity that she thought disgraceful and that to her horror steadily increased, if she welcomed Frowein's behavior or if it insulted her vanity. He never tried, not even when he went to the theater with her and took her home, to repeat the intimacy of that particular moment.

In the editorial office he was the reserved, mocking boss who had started to treat a young female colleague, after she had stood the test, no different from the men who valued an open word and occasional coarse story. In her presence, he more often now allowed crude male jokes, which he had previously prevented by clearing his throat and simultaneously pointing to the only woman in the office. In the cafeteria he openly called Regina to his table. Most of the time, they talked about the theater.

She admired his skill of perfect concealment and pretext of sovereignty, and she was grateful for the levity of his tone and the way he included her through his wit in the community of her colleagues. But when she was not in the office and allowed her emotions to resist, neither reason nor logic was able to release her from a fortress of provocation. Frowein's behavior then seemed to her like an indifference that deprived her of spontaneity, confidence, and courage. The restriction to such impersonal behavior hurt her pride, which she in melancholy moments and even then vaguely defined as the wish to have the right to make her own decisions.

It took a long time until Regina was ready for the truth. She was surprised when she became aware of the detours she had made before realizing that her reactions were those of a woman who wanted words to be followed by actions. She did not want the openness of the first meeting with Frowein, which still moved her very much; she didn't want his confessions; and she didn't even want his gratifying encouragement when he talked about her talent that she herself doubted.

She only wanted him and not because she loved him. She wanted just once to free her heart and especially her pride from the burden of renunciation. When she realized what had really bothered her since that one night, which had left her with wounds that neither time nor insight could heal, she also understood very quickly that she was not going to wait long to lure Frowein from the comfortable position of a mentor into the reality of a man.

He was faster. The Hersfeld festival started the first weekend in July, the day before the regular critic, who had previously covered the first two nights, broke his leg. After the last editorial meeting Frowein came to Regina's tiny office, which he had avoided for weeks. He stood at the window for a moment, then sat down on her desk and put his arm around her shoulder. First he said, "How about you?" Then, in an extremely good mood, he added "No objections." And finally, in an even better mood, he promised, "I am going to give you a ride. My wife is going to be gone for the weekend anyway."

"It is going to be fine," Regina said.

It is going to be fine," he whispered when Mary Stuart, exactly twenty-four hours later, mounted the scaffold under the open sky of the cloister ruins on a warm night, accompanied by the twitter of birds disturbed by the brightness of the stage lights.

"Why don't they allow any applause at Hersfeld?" Regina asked when they were leaving.

"This was a church at some point. We Germans have great reverence for a house of God. We have always shown that."

Regina enjoyed the derision in his voice and noticed that the connection she felt to Frowein was turning into a feeling that would make it easier for her to look into the mirror after all. "Thank you," she said.

They walked silently, holding hands, released from the days of dishonest glances and dishonest words, down the candlelit path through the park to the Kurhaus, past half-timbered houses to the small hotel where the secretary had booked two rooms. Frowein asked the surly porter for the keys.

Even though the lobby was dark, Regina noticed that his face was burning. His hand was hot and moist when it touched hers. She smiled at him when he opened the door to her room and hoped that he, too, would not say anything. He remained standing for a moment and waited till she had turned on the light and taken off her jacket. Then he spoke after all. His voice reminded her of that of the young birds in the parched thorn acacias that had not yet learned to wait for the first beam of the sun.

"Your room is bigger," he said. "I will be back in five minutes."

"Five minutes," Regina repeated.

"Is that too fast?"

"No, too slow."

Regina pondered, while Frowein reluctantly undressed, if she was not too young to want only to be a hunter or already too old to be allowed to forget that the wrong prey can make a hunter weaker than a dim-witted child for a long time. When his breath became heavy and indicated to her that he, too, knew of the inevitability of desire, she determined that she was not going to mistake tenderness for love, nor excitement for fulfillment. She woke up during the night and was not sure if she had not done it anyway, but the face she saw was not that of the man who was sleeping next to her. The day was already dawning and a trace of deceptive pink shone through the open window when the pain of awareness started and gave her the certainty that she had ended up in her own trap. She had not really forgotten anything that she had wanted to forget.

Frowein heard her sigh and said, "We cannot let this happen again."

Regina was just about to tell him not to worry and that she had experience with nights that leave nothing behind but the power of unwanted images at the wrong time. But without the effort of a long deliberation she succeeded in oiling her throat with the softness of a merciful lie, the way she had learned to as a child when someone was about to steal her face.

"Never again," she reassured him.

When she came back to Frankfurt on Monday, everyone was already at dinner. Her mother had put down a plate with open-faced sandwiches for her and, like every night, said, "One with cream cheese, one with liverwurst, and one with tomatoes. The way you like it best."

Regina saw Ulysses appearing between the glasses and silver bowls behind the freshly polished windows of the cupboard and hesitating for a long while before he moved on. As a child her father had told her that the much-loved Ulysses, too, had found a plate with open-faced sandwiches on his return and only knew then that he would never have to travel again. She repressed the urge to wash the dirt of the day from her hands and the heavy burden of the night from her head, sat down, and said, "I am going to eat the tomato sandwich last. I like that best."

"You always did that as a child," Jettel said.

"Only then," her Walter remarked, "you did not go on random trips with strange men."

"I went to Hersfeld; that is work for me," Regina said, getting prepared for a fight, "and the strange man happens to be my boss."

"A fine boss," Walter said.

17

Jettel was worried and disheartened when Walter rang the doorbell earlier and longer than usual one afternoon in November. She thought that the pains, which he had been complaining about a few days ago but which had disappeared after a hot bath, might have returned again. Concerned, she looked over the railing down the staircase and tried to hear if her husband was gasping more than usual. She called, "What is the matter?" There was no answer.

There was a stool on every floor; Walter usually sat down on the second floor and rested till he was able to catch his breath again. But Jettel saw that he had already reached the third floor. She was amazed. Walter was not gasping at all, he was not pale, and his face also did not show the kind of unhealthy red that indicated exertion. He was carrying a bouquet of red roses and was whistling Jettel's favorite aria from *Carmen* when he effortlessly got up from the little stool.

Without taking even a few seconds to explain to herself why the red roses were more disturbing to her than the heart attack she had expected, she got angry. She spontaneously remembered that Walter had last brought her flowers in Breslau. It had been three days before their engagement and she had been naïve enough not to notice that he had bought the beautiful bouquet (roses, too, although yellow ones) for a hospital visit only to find that the patient had already left the hospital. He had told her about this unromantic point years later—on the farm and moreover during one of those unnecessary fights about her unwillingness to try to pickle cucumbers in brine in a country where gherkins were tiny and completely dry to begin with. Jettel had no illusions.

Even though she still fought the bitter truth that had just hit her fully, she had to smile disdainfully when she thought about how much her naïve husband was mistaken this time. She was no longer the young, merely beautiful, inexperienced bride with the silly dreams of a protected daughter, but was now an experienced woman, quick to react, with an unfailing sense for those situations in a long marriage in which one had to keep a cool head and composure. Thanks to the many articles in magazines, which lately no longer shied away from discussing the most intimate problems between men and women, she knew exactly what she had to do.

Jettel did not doubt for a moment that Walter had deceived her and now wanted to confess his faux pas, but she was perplexed and speechless nonetheless. Before getting married she had realized that Walter's deeply religious beliefs and his strict morals were the best guarantee for his marital faithfulness. She had especially liked this in a man whose character her mother, too, had always termed "very decent."

Over the past years Jettel, of course, had also assumed that his deteriorating health would prevent him from betraying her with anything other than the cigarettes he secretly smoked in his office and the chocolate stashed in his coat pockets. The literature, which Walter derided but which was read by the ladies of the best society, at least, had led her to believe that there was a very close connection between physical health and intact marital relations.

At the same time, Jettel was relieved that at the height of this unexpectedly sudden crisis another article, which she had just read a week ago, gave her clear directions on how to proceed. She was not supposed to show any dismay or jealousy and above all not her immense bafflement that Walter actually seemed to succeed in banning from his face even that small trace of a guilty conscience that, as Jettel knew for certain, was part of the overall picture. His shoulders were straight, and his eyes clearer and more cheerful than they had been for a while. He carried his head insultingly high.

"Jettel," he said, and pressed the roses into her completely calm hands, "I have to tell you something."

She tightened her lips and unfortunately squeezed her eyes tight, too, and thought with some effort how much time the experienced marriage counselors would grant a woman till she could be true to her temperament and at ease in her heart. She had not been feeling well all day and realized now that her headache felt worse than before and that the ground seemed to be moving under her feet.

She only said, "Yes," and tried not to turn the agreement into a question.

"Not here in the hallway."

"Just say what you have to say. I already know what you have to tell me anyway. You cannot pull the wool over my eyes."

"I have deceived you."

"So it is true."

"What do you mean, it is true? You never exactly asked me. I only told you once that I would need three more years and I left you to believe that. But I already did it today."

"What?"

"The house is free and clear. For God's sake, Jettel, that is no reason to cry right away. You would have had reason to cry if I had left you with debts as a widow."

Jettel realized, with a gratitude that left her unusually ashamed, that this was one of the most fulfilled moments of her marriage and one of the rare instances in which she managed to laugh about herself. Warmed by a feeling that she effortlessly identified as happiness, she forgot that she was clever, dynamic, and experienced, and told Walter where her imagination had led her.

With a consciously theatrical gesture she threw up her hands and talked about an abyss. Walter noticed how beautiful her hair was and happily contemplated how she had come up with that word. He also wondered if women shared their husbands' professional secrets during their confidential chats.

They were sitting next to each other on the sofa, and laughed themselves into a mood that invigorated them, drifting in a gentle way into the harmony of lost days. Both remembered simultaneously that they had laughed once before in the same unrestrained way in Leobschütz, but they could not remember why and grew a little sad. The parakeet kept on pulling Jettel's hair and Walter pulled on her ear once.

"My Jettel," he giggled, "still believes in my virility. That is the best compliment you have given me in years."

"Why?" Jettel asked and blushed in a way that made Walter even more wistful.

He drank the Swiss pear schnapps that he had hidden in the bookcase for the days when the pains tore his chest apart and ate, even though it was only five o'clock in the afternoon, a piece of bread with cold beef gravy. After that he kissed Jettel one more time and wiped, without her saying a word, his greasy hands on the living room table's light yellow tablecloth that she never put on without complaining that she never would have bought it had she known how hard it was to keep clean.

With the pleasure of a mountain climber who reaches the peak earlier than expected, Walter told how difficult it had been to get the Rothschildallee debt-free so quickly and how happy the thought made him to have been able to fulfill his obligation. When he reached for the bottle with the pear schnapps again, he became exuberant and asked for two soft-coddled eggs for dinner.

Since Jettel nodded as if it were actually Sunday, as he claimed, the last bit of resistance of the time of great frugality abated. He promised to finally buy himself a new pair of shoes and Jettel the Persian lamb coat she had wanted ever since the severe winters in Leobschütz.

"For our silver wedding anniversary," he promised, "my Jettel will no longer be able to run around and tell everyone that her old man is letting her freeze."

Jettel, once again able to trust her experience in dealing with complex situations and relying on her good instinct for the right timing, told Walter about another of her dearest wishes. "I would really like," she said, stroking Walter's forehead, "to go on a trip for our silver wedding anniversary. On a real winter journey the way so many people do again these days."

"By yourself? Are you going to look for a young man who is capable of more than just gasping?"

"You don't always have to get so indecent right away. Of course, I mean all of us. We have never been away together. We never had a day's vacation. We do not even know what a holiday is. Some people are even going to Mallorca again."

"Why didn't you say right away, Jettel," Walter laughed, "that you just don't want to have to bother with a big party? Maybe you are even right. Few of the people we would invite are real friends. Oh, Jettel, I always dreamed in my first life that we would celebrate our silver wedding anniversary in Breslau. Do you know why?"

"Because my mother was a good cook."

"That, too. But I wanted to take you quite ceremoniously in my arms and say: See, my dear Ina, I have now lasted a whole lifetime with your spoiled daughter. You didn't expect that at our wedding, did you?"

"Yes," Jettel said, "she knew. It was the last thing she said to me when I went onto the boat in Hamburg. 'Be good to Walter, he loves you so,' she said."

"Your mother was a smart woman. You don't know how often I think of her."

"I do, too. Oh, Walter, life has never turned out to be the way it was before the Nazis."

"It would have been an insult to the dead if it were otherwise."

"I didn't know you felt that way."

"There are lots of things you do not know."

An hour later, after Max had come home and found out about the debt-free house, and proved once again to his father's pleasure that he, in contrast to his mother, was able to calculate percentages, Walter put on his coat and declared that he would pick up Regina from the tram.

"I cannot wait," he said, slightly embarrassed, "to tell her about our good fortune."

"You want to go up and down the stairs again?" Jettel asked in her apron, ready to prepare dinner. "You don't even know exactly when she is going to come. Have you gone crazy?"

"I have. There are no stairs for me today. I am able to fly today."

"Can I fly with you?" Max asked.

"Let your father go," Jettel understood. "Not everything in our family is only for men. You'd better help me set the table."

"Only today, my son, a man does not belong into the kitchen. Do you think the Rothschildallee would be free and clear today if I had helped your mother peel potatoes?"

Regina had just gotten off the tram when her father arrived at the stop. She only needed a split second to push back the old fear of a sudden emergency and to read his face.

"I have something to tell you, Regina."

"You don't have to; I can see it in your face. The Rothschildallee is debt-free."

He embraced her in front of a newsstand, told her, still amused and even though he had promised Jettel that he would never reveal the secret, of her doubts about his marital fidelity, and took a small package from his coat pocket.

"A watch," Regina wondered, "and what a beautiful one. Have you gone crazy? What made you do that? It is not even my birthday."

"But it is mine. I was reborn today. I want you to know that I know to whom I owe my courage."

"But you can't do that. What is Mama going to say? She is going to be offended when she sees that you bought me and not her something this expensive. You know how jealous she is. I don't want her to get upset."

"Your father has a sick heart, but a healthy head. Let me take care of it. You will be amazed."

"No humbug, *bwana*," Regina pleaded, "we are getting to old for that." She took off her old watch, put on the new one, and held up her arm. The streetlamps drilled a hole into the damp fog with their yellow light. The golden watchband became bright and for a happy moment reminded her of the green shard of glass with which she had caught the last sunbeams during the hour of the long shadows at Ol' Joro Orok. "You are in charge of humbug, you cunning *memsahib* of the deceitful Owuor."

They walked the short way home even more slowly than Walter's short steps demanded and warmed themselves on their mutual love. To enjoy an extra portion of their closeness, they did not ring the bell at the house door and took long breaks on every floor because the stairs were now becoming hard for Walter after all, and only his joy still had wings. Again without ringing the bell, he unlocked the apartment door and to Regina's surprise stamped his foot so violently that the parquet floor resounded.

"Look at this, Jettel," he shouted angrily, still in his hat and coat. "See what your fine daughter has done now. She takes a gold watch as a present from a strange man."

"It is not gold," Regina stuttered and needed a lot of imagination and strength, and almost too much time to chase the surprise from her eyes, "and besides, I bought it myself."

"Of course it is gold," Walter contradicted her, grasped Regina's arm, pushed up her coat and sweater sleeve and dug his nails into her skin, "and I bet it is from your fine Mr. Reiswein."

"Frowein," Regina corrected him admiringly, "and he does not give me any presents. You should know that. A good father would know that. He would also know that his daughter can economize very strictly to fulfill her heart's desire at times."

"Bravo," Walter mumbled, "you found a good excuse there."

They agreed to drive to the Harz Mountains to celebrate their silver wedding anniversary the day before Christmas in Bad Grund and to stay till New Year's. A man from Upper Silesia had opened a small hotel there several years ago. He immediately answered Walter's letter and wrote that he would, of course, give "our dear Dr. Redlich and his esteemed family" a special price and that he considered it a special honor to treat such dear guests "in a family atmosphere to the home-cooked meals they are familiar with."

Jettel got her Persian lamb coat. It was too heavy and was no longer quite in style, but it beautifully matched her black hair and rejuvenated her face with pleasure. Walter said she looked like the Princess of Pless and since Jettel had heard how wealthy the Prince had been, she considered it a compliment and bought herself a black hat from the money in her private cashbox.

For the first winter vacation of her life, Regina was furnished with one of the new Norwegian-patterned sweaters, which had now become available in moderately priced clothing stores. Max got used ski boots; they were such a poor fit that he also got a sled as a consolation and the assurance that Regina would go sledding with him. Walter let himself be persuaded to get a wool cap, mittens, and a blue scarf, and he called wife and daughter spendthrifts.

At five o'clock on the morning of their departure it was already cold and wet in Frankfurt. On the way the icy windshield had to be scraped free several times and the family had to be warmed with coffee from the thermos. When it started snowing heavily at the foot of the Harz

Mountains, one of the windshield wipers stopped working. Walter cursed a lot because he had not had it repaired, but he did not let anything spoil his good mood, and insisted, in spite of Jettel's bad-tempered protests that the trip would be too strenuous for him and that she was already suffering from frostbite, on making a detour to Marke to invite Greschek and Grete to come to the silver wedding anniversary.

"No, Dr. Redlich," Greschek objected after lunch, "you can't ask me to do that. Sit in a hotel without anything to do? That is nothing for the likes of me. I would go crazy there. And Grete has to stay with our goat anyway."

"So you aren't coming to my funeral either?"

"That's different. Come to Marke on your way back and stay a few days. Then I will also have enough time to get some beautiful mush-rooms for you."

"What, in December, Greschek?"

"He doesn't have a clue," Grete said. "He has never picked a mush-room in his life."

In Bad Grund, "Römer's Hotel," for the last couple of years only open during the summer, was a half-timbered house with broken shut-ters and faded splendor. The hotel received its only guests with a large Christmas tree in the noticeably drafty lobby and with the warm assur-ance of its owner that no one would disturb the family celebration. He had ordered two rabbits and had the stove in the dining room inspected.

"You have central heating, don't you?" Walter asked

"Oh, that does not work too well, Dr. Redlich. You must know all about the workmen in the damned West. All they want to do is make money."

"We can warm ourselves under the Christmas tree," Max whispered on the way to the rooms.

"A Jewish child does not sit under a Christmas tree," Walter grumbled.

"But we didn't put it up. So it doesn't count."

"One cannot deceive God."

The rooms were spacious and filled with furniture, which the yel-lowed hotel brochure that lay on a round table on an equally yellowed crochet doily described as "homey, cozy" and Jettel labeled "old junk." The closet doors were sticking, the beds squeaked once one sat down on them, and the washbowls on the iron stands were all rusty, the water in the pitchers ice-cold.

In the room that Walter and Jettel chose after a discouraging tour of the entire establishment, the stove that had been started by a sullen housemaid glowed fiery red without giving out any heat. In the room Max and Regina were supposed to sleep in, the stove smoked so much that the four of them were already lying in the parental bed at the beginning of the first night: Jettel in her fur coat, the other three in their coats, too, and Walter also in cap and mittens.

"I always dreamed of this in Africa," Walter said.

Max giggled himself to sleep, while his father coughed so much that he had to get up during the night. He sat down at a small glass table, lit a candle, and scribbled with his fountain pen in the exercise book that Max had had to take along to learn some difficult Latin vocabulary.

"What are you doing?" Jettel murmured.

"I am writing poetry."

"You are getting more *meshuge* all the time. You are not even able to see there."

"When I see you everything starts to rhyme."

Breakfast—with invigorating hot coffee, poppy seed cake, and rolls, which Walter for the first time in years called *Semmel* again and thought that they tasted just like the ones from the bakery in Sohrau—found general approval, just like the suggestion by the hotel's owner, with the pleasantly clear Upper Silesian voice, that Jettel's special chair for the night's celebration should be decorated with a silver garland.

"My wife, unfortunately," Walter sniffled, "has another rather immodest wish. She doesn't want to be cold on her special day."

"There is going to be chicken soup as a first course," the host remembered. "My mother always said nothing warms you like a good chicken soup. And we still knew what a real winter was at home."

"I think this one here is real enough," Walter remarked. "I could not have caught a cold any faster in Leobschütz."

He was unable to stand the raw cold and coughed so much that after five minutes he had to give up the walk that Jettel had only been able to persuade him to by pointing out the well-known healing power of the winter air. Even though she, albeit during the summer time, always complained that it was possible to protect oneself from the cold, but not from the heat, she was relieved that she had to go back to the hotel with Walter.

Regina ran on with Max in the whipping wind under snow-covered pines. She realized that she had never experienced a winter landscape and that she did not like it. She told Max how she had imagined, as a child in the scorching heat, that she was Captain Scott on his way to the South Pole.

"Did you have any live friends, as well," Max asked, "or did they all come from the library?"

"I usually had," Regina remembered, "only one girlfriend. I was a very shy child."

"I'm not shy, but I also have only one friend."

"Don't you like being in secondary school?"

"Yeah, I think so. I like the teachers all right, but the boys often say things that I cannot repeat at home if I do not want to upset Papa."

"I know all about that," Regina sighed, "but I did not like my teachers, either."

When she pressed her brother close and he remained motionless for a moment in her arms, she heard his heartbeat and saw his eyes and thought of the day he was born. She was delighted to find that the happiness she had felt then was still within her and she smiled.

"Why are you laughing?" Max asked.

"Because when I was a child I always wished that my deer would turn into a brother."

"And now you want me to turn into a deer?"

"No, but when I think of the Harz later on I will always think of this moment."

"I don't understand you," Max said. "You always say such strange things."

On the night of the silver wedding anniversary it turned even colder than before but the dining room, transformed by twenty candles in four bronze candleholders, had a festive air. A bottle of red wine stood in a silver goblet. The paper napkins were folded into little boats, and a grapefruit on a glass plate was decorated with small cheese squares.

Jettel wore a crown that was braided with stiff hands by Walter and Regina from a silver ribbon and she tolerated, satisfied by the rabbit stew, her husband's teasing with a sense of humor that she thought just as becoming as the ornament in her hair. The mood was good enough to unearth the first fight of their married life, seriously but without rancor, and finally, to undeniably clarify why Walter had not been allowed to eat lobster. Before they enjoyed the vanilla ice cream with hot chocolate sauce, someone mentioned the wedding night during which Walter had taken apart a radio that had just been given to them.

"Anyhow, I still found time to make your sister," he informed his son.

"And where," Max asked, "did you make me?"

"In a tiny room. We had to send the dog outside to have enough space."

"You were always crazy," Jettel said.

"So crazy that I write poems at night."

"What did you really do yesterday in the middle of the night?"

"I wrote a poem," Walter said, buttoned his jacket, and stood up. He climbed onto his chair, took a folded piece of paper from his pocket, cleared his throat, and started to read.

DEAR JETTEL!
For ten years in a row,
you now had to celebrate
your anniversary date
far away from Africa in the snow,
because your beloved husband made you leave the land
he could no longer stand.

Oh, how you complained back then,
and told all and everyone
how wonderful life had been
under Africa's beloved sun.

Germany at the time was full of dread;
there was much rubble, little bread!
Thank God those days are past;
there is no hunger here at last.
One can now buy everything and such,
and even — if one wants to — drink too much.

You have withstood the storm,
even have a house to call your own,
and in Frankfurt your husband got to be
an attorney and a notary.

Our daughter turned out to be even more:
She became a full-fledged editor,

and our son (also not a fool)
just entered his first year in secondary school.

You have achieved a lot I can tell
since you bade Kenya farewell.
I wish, therefore, that you may
be content for now and many a later day;
be healthy in your advanced years yet,
yours, and always affectionate,

Walter

Max helped his father off the chair, sat down himself, and was just getting ready to clap when he noticed the complete silence and then that his parents and Regina were crying. He felt a little bit of pride when he felt tears coming on, too. He became aware of the fact that this was the first time he cried with the adults.

18

In the late summer of 1957, the mystery of the heavyset, bald, red-faced man—who up to then had only been an occasional silhouette behind the house door—came to a surprising conclusion. When Walter and Jettel returned unexpectedly early from a doctor's visit in Rodheim, the strange two-ton man—who Max thought to be a spy and Regina one of those dubious characters who lately increasingly enlivened the reports of the local journalists during editorial conferences—was standing in the yard and smoking a cigarette. Since the long-delayed confrontation was now unavoidable, the cause of so many speculations introduced himself, reluctantly but not nearly as impolitely as expected, as Heini Kowalski from Neisse. Jettel's instinct had been right once again when she presumed that the silent man, who, it soon turned out, had had a key to the house for years and used it, too, would upset their lives some day.

Heini Kowalski was not a man to waste time at the decisive hour. Three days after meeting Else's employers he persuaded her to admit to them that she had had to carry the burden of a lie to each confession. As Walter had always suspected without voicing his doubts, she had not gone to the services regularly and had never gone to church lighthearted any more.

Her free afternoons, evenings, and eventually even her vacations had not been spent exclusively, as was assumed and often also maintained, with her recently deceased mother and her sister, but with a divorced man who had caused her enormous religious and pragmatic inner conflicts. The chance encounter that he had not planned, in spite of his energetic nature, now made Heini decide to end the time of deception and concern immediately. He resolved to take Else into his strong arms forever before the fall and told her in the direct way she appreciated most in him that he himself would give the explanations if she did not have the courage to do so.

After dinner Else confessed, her pretty, even face crimson and tear-stained, "I never would have married him as long as my mother was still alive. But everything is different now. The times have changed, Mrs. Redlich; you have to understand that."

"But you have a good life with us, Else. You are like one of my children."

"Yes, and I will never forget that, but I would still like to have a child of my own."

"Is his income enough for the two of you?" Walter asked.

"Not yet. Heini had to leave home and is only now starting to make more money. But I already have a new position. With the Americans."

"Wow! Doing what?"

"With a consul. Taking care of the children. He has two rooms free. We can both live there."

"Else, Else, what has happened to you? First you misuse the church services and now you want to live with a divorced man before getting married. You never would have had such ideas in Hochkretscham."

"But we are going to get married soon, Dr. Redlich, and the consul says that he is going to take us both along when he has to return to America."

"Well, that just goes to show how scarce domestic servants have become if one needs to import our Else with her beau to America," Walter said after he had calmed Jettel enough so that she was at least able to peacefully listen to him again.

"And what is going to happen to me?" Jettel complained. "You always promised me a maid when you shipped me back to Germany. Owuor never would have let us down like this."

"It was easier for Owuor. We did not even notice when he got married. That was nice. He had a new *bibi* come, sent her home to his other wives, and stayed with us. Someone like Owuor does not happen again, but you will get your maid, Jettel," Walter sighed. "It almost makes me happy that you haven't changed in all these years."

Else stayed until she was sure that Jettel would not be without household help. The farewell was marked by the heavy sadness and gloom of people who had learned to endure separation yet were unable to bear it. Only Max did not cry, but he asked Else to sing "Auf der Lüneburger Heide," his childhood song, and he was not hungry at night.

"Don't forget us, Else. And do not embarrass us at the consul's," Walter teased. "Remember that one does eat the mold in the Roquefort."

"I have learned more than that," Else sobbed into Heini's checkered handkerchief.

"What? That in our household my wife wears the pants?"

"No. That our pastor in Hochkretscham was not always right. Jews are good people."

"Just don't tell that to anyone, Else. People are not going to believe you."

Else was followed by Anna, who did not like the green beans prepared sweet and sour and with raisins. Jettel did not get along with her any better than with Emmy, who disliked children and men, who were in a hurry and became grumpy when the coffee after lunch was too hot to drink in one gulp. Hanna was so eager that she scrubbed the parquet floors in all the rooms on the first day, and on the second day she washed the snakeskin in the sun room with soapsuds.

On the third day she said, "I am not allowed to come anymore," and then before she could even be questioned about the suddenness of her decision, she added, "My father does not want me to work for Jews." Regina borrowed her mother's courage and her father's voice, and shouted "Out!" so loudly that the neighbors in the next house could hear it. At night, Jettel told the story over and over again and said admiringly, "Regina is a competent girl."

Max adored Maria. She lived with her parents; appeared every morning on time and in white shorts; sang the hits of Caterina Valente, whom he worshipped, too; and in spite of her domestic talents left no doubt about the fact that she expected her true talents to be discovered soon. Walter took exception to the open display of her naked, suntanned legs and even more to her illusions, which he considered unsuitable for a decent woman. He insisted, in spite of Jettel's protests, on letting her go.

With the blonde, blue-eyed Ziri, though, the warmth of a human being (she did not want anything but to be part of a community that was conscious of its own protective walls and its need for trust and familiarity) returned to the house. Ziri had lived with her mother in the countryside near Würzburg in recent years but was originally from the Sudetes. Walter and Jettel found that as reassuringly close to home as if she were from Upper Silesia. She was extraordinarily strong, laughed continually and without reason, and never mistook Walter's gruffness for insults. She very quickly understood that Jettel, although moody and demanding, was also quite capable of a motherly kindness and consideration that casual observers never would have suspected.

"We are a bit difficult," Jettel had vaguely hinted during the interview for which Ziri had appeared with an overstuffed suitcase and a basket full of apples.

"Even worse," Walter warned, "we are Jewish. Your mother may object to that."

"Why?" Ziri wondered, "should my mother object? She always says, 'God's garden is large.' My sister has a black boyfriend."

"Well, we should be all right then."

A week later Ziri moved, with the announcement that she had never sat alone at a table in all her life, from the kitchen to the dining room for her meals. This made Walter feel quite ashamed that during all the years of closeness he had never thought of offering the same to Else. Ziri played soccer with Max in the corridor, hid in closets during hide-and-seek, and boxed with him. She thought that Regina was too thin, so she always smuggled some extra butter into her food. Ziri also used Regina's lipstick and when she went home she borrowed the magic African belt with the tiny colorful beads.

Jettel instantly won Ziri's heart because she realized how well Jettel cooked and therefore did not set foot out of the kitchen while the food was being prepared. She was eager to absorb the fine urban lifestyle and was enchanted by the sentimental songs that Jettel had once learned from her mother's maid in Breslau and still enjoyed singing with a plaintive voice while she cooked.

Ziri had made up her mind not to marry a country boy but rather someone from the city, yet whenever she returned from Würzburg on Sundays, she brought Walter (for his sick heart) herbs from her mother's garden, fresh bacon, and stories of the country life that reminded him of Leobschütz.

"Ziri is like Owuor," Walter said, "only white and beautiful."

"Owuor was beautiful, too," Regina objected, and closed her eyes till her head found nourishment. "Owuor caught the sun with his teeth."

"Tomorrow," Jettel laughed, "I am going to bake a poppy seed cake with Ziri. She absolutely wants to learn that. So you have to go to the doctor with Regina. I specifically scheduled the appointment on her free day."

Regina had never been with Walter to Rodheim to see Dr. Schmitt. Initially she had been very suspicious when her father had chosen a tiny village, of all places, for his regular doctor's visits and only because he had heard at a meeting of Silesians that the physician there had the reputation of being a leading authority. Rumor had it that he had modern American medical equipment, which allowed him to diagnose heart diseases very precisely, and he was, therefore, able to treat his patients more specifically and efficiently than the experts in town.

Since there were many people from Sohrau in Rodheim, Regina immediately knew that Dr. Schmitt had to be from Upper Silesia, too. She did not trust his much-praised equipment and had even dared to ask if that alone made him better than the specialists in town. Walter had called her a condescending goose. At any rate, Regina saw, in her father's sudden admission that regular examinations were necessary, just the usual longing for the sounds and memories of home.

It was a wet, dark December day that reminded them of the journey to the Harz. Walter and Regina, comfortably warmed by the heat in the car and a swig from the small bottle of schnapps in the glove compartment, first talked about a complicated legal case that had been occupying Walter for a while. Soon, however, they were reminded by the street conditions of their adventures in "Römer's Hotel" and very quickly experienced the exhilaration of people who have overcome great danger and in retrospect use a magnifying glass.

The thought of how the four of them had been lying in bed together in their overcoats made them laugh so hard that they became hot and their shoulders started to tremble. They were not even able to restrain their euphoria when the picture started to fade. Walter drove the car to the side of the road, opened the window, and took such a deep breath that he started to cough. He silently stared into the gray fog for a few minutes.

"Sometimes," he said in a voice that had swallowed its cheerfulness too abruptly so that it would not threaten Regina's ears with a storm, "I think that that was the last time we were all happy together."

"How can you think that way? You have not been feeling too bad at all recently."

"I have become as superstitious as you and your mother."

"And what is your superstition telling you?" Regina asked while she hurriedly beseeched her own and crossed her fingers in her coat pocket.

"I have asked God every day for years to give me enough time to pay off the Rothschildallee and to wait till you are able to take care of your mother and your brother. I forgot to make a deal about an extension with him."

"Are you Faust? Did you make a pact with the devil? God is not limited by what we tell Him. He has His own opinions and does not let us suffer if our prayers are incomplete. You always told me that when I was a child. Don't you remember?"

"Oh, yes. It is good that you still remember that. I often reproach myself because I was not able to give you more. You didn't have a real religious upbringing. And I knew what was essential, but everything I believed died within me when they killed our family."

"Not everything," Regina said. "Otherwise you would not have prayed anymore and I would not be able to believe in God today. I still believe that He has been good to me."

"What have you been asking from him?"

"You know that quite well," Regina said. She smiled when she remembered her childhood prayers and added, "that you keep your job, *bwana.*"

Dr. Friedrich Schmitt, white-haired, rotund, and with a rough but friendly face, an overly distinct pronunciation, and the wit that Regina knew and above all recognized as the only medicine that would help her father, was originally from Gleiwitz. Regina liked him because he ranked sympathy higher than proficiency and took time to divert the patient from his physical condition and anxieties. She also noticed the unusual fact that the physician talked about his youth with the uncomplaining tone of people who find themselves free from any burdens when looking into the past.

"Well, shall we take a look?" Dr. Schmitt said.

"Do I have a choice?" Walter asked.

When the examination started, Regina was seated on a low stool in front of the desk and immediately felt the coldness of fear in her limbs. She stared at the doctor's concentrated face and uneasily examined the equipment that had been talked about so much during the last Silesian meeting. Her skin burned with the thought that she knew nothing that she ought to have known because she had assumed that the news of technical innovations was only the dream of some silly visionaries and that physicians were unable to look at the picture of a human heart.

The idea that the white-haired, fatherly man who stood less than three feet from her could precisely determine the state of Walter's heart, could talk about his conclusions with him, and in the end would even be able to realize what the future held, paralyzed Regina's mind and thoughts. Her fear did not leave out one of the wildest daydreams her imagination had ever created. She even remembered Owuor's stories of warriors who were larger than life and came at night to steal the hearts of good people. The victims were only able to defend themselves if they drilled their thumb into the right eye of the sneering attackers.

Regina forced her head into battle. She fought against the ghosts of her childhood, and against hopelessness, superstition, and rebellion. She was almost ready to close her eyes and to drink an invigorating draught from the cup of certainty, but she was unable to move her eyes from her father's naked chest. In a panic she got ready for flight and quick return. The flight was easy and soft, but she was unable to make the trip quickly back into the small room with the empty walls and small examination table. The fog in front of her eyes thickened.

As a child, Regina had often imagined that her father was Achilles: strong and courageous enough to hold out his chest to the arrows of his enemies without ever getting wounded. That time now seemed so long ago to her and yet so short. She had believed that she was able to look into her father's heart. She even knew that that must have been the case and that this look had given her the strength to love him without letting the sharp teeth of doubt into her head.

When Regina saw her father lying on the white sheet, he seemed so much smaller to her than in the dead days of Ol' Joro Orok and she regretted for the first time in her life that she had never told him about this. But she had never dared to mention the doubts that forced her love not to take the broad, comfortable way to its destination, but instead to take a small, grassy path. Regina realized with a despair that made her body rigid that it was too late for the truth.

"That doesn't look too bad," she heard Dr. Schmitt murmur. "We have to be satisfied."

"I am glad that at least you are satisfied," Walter said.

It was the irony in her father's voice—that familiar mixture of bitterness and amusement—that rescued Regina from the sharp claws of her fear. She closed her eyes for a short moment and moistened her throat, heard her own breath, and felt that her heart was beating more slowly again. She calmly tried to imagine what the physician might have seen. She understood, relieved and consoled, that she still had to forge a weapon to drive the despair back into its lair. She did not have to know anymore; she was allowed to trust. The warriors had not struck. They were blind and mute.

The gray shapes on the white piece of paper that the physician held in his hand did not tell of her father's kindness, his love for his family, his fanatic sense of justice, or his ability to forgive. Such a heart, she felt with renewed strength of her old confidence, would not be condemned to an early death by God. She almost felt a little sorry for Dr. Schmitt because he could only see what his equipment let him see. But she merely had to push the sigh back into her throat and the salt into her burning eyes with the practice of many years.

"Well, Regina," Walter asked when he put on his tie and while doing so watched her face in the small mirror over the sink, "what are you thinking about?"

"Sorry, I was just dreaming."

"My daughter, you have to know, is a master dreamer. She is even going to dream during my funeral."

"We are not there yet," Dr. Schmitt said, "if you live reasonably."

"That means for you doctors to do without everything that makes life worth living. What is the purpose of living then?"

"A dreaming daughter."

"I have another reason as well," Walter said in a voice that could only make the physician believe that the thought had just occurred to him. "I have to be at my son's bar mitzvah."

"What does that mean?"

"Let's call it the Jewish confirmation. With us a boy becomes a man at age thirteen. It is the proudest moment in a father's life. My father was not able to be there for me. He was fighting for Kaiser and Reich. I was very upset at the time. I have to pull through for another year and three months for my son's sake."

"You are still going to dance at your son's wedding," Dr. Schmitt said, "if you do without the cigarettes and the chocolate, and if you fight a little less."

It was good that you went with me," Walter said after driving silently for ten minutes. "I had wished for it often, but I didn't want to offend your mother. I am getting sentimental in my old age. I imagined that you could look into my heart."

"I could. Exactly. Just drive a little more slowly. There is a man under that big tree. And don't give him a ride. It is too dangerous in the dark."

"Since when does one leave people standing in the rain? Have you forgotten how we squatted on the edge of the road in Nairobi and waited for someone to take us along? I am not afraid of anything. Only of people who forget too quickly."

The hitchhiker was an old man with a long white beard, a black beret, a big rucksack (the kind that was used for amassing food during the days of hunger), and a wide coat that even the heavy rain had not been able to rid of the smell of onions and cold smoke. The completely filled rucksack was pushed into the back first and then the man quickly climbed onto the backseat, sat down remarkably straight, and sighed with relief. He was very small and had a slight humpback; his walking stick was so big that he had to hold it in front of him.

"Are you Rübezahl?" Walter asked, and accelerated a little too quickly. "I knew him well."

"I don't know," the man pondered. His voice was deep. "There is nobody who knows me anymore. So I don't spend any time thinking about who I am."

"Rübezahl after all. Where do you want to go?"

"It doesn't matter."

"Not at all?"

"The main thing is that the place has a jail."

When the exhausted man's clothes and beard stopped dripping, his tongue started to move. When he nodded, and he did so frequently, his head lightly touched the driver's seat and the beard tickled the back of Walter's neck. He did not tell his name, did not talk about the future, and laughed often but always without cheerfulness. He said he moved from village to village during the summer and lived outdoors. During the winter he tried to stay in jail at least for the night.

"During this kind of horrible weather," he said, "there is nothing like a good, warm cell and if I am lucky they even give me breakfast the next morning. But that hasn't happened a lot lately."

When he started his journey, he had dreamed of making it to Paris someday because he had heard about the bridges where one could comfortably spend the night with like-minded people. He was intrigued by the fact that he would not be able to understand their questions, but he never got further than Kehl.

"I liked being in France," he said.

"When?"

"During the war."

"During the war?" Walter asked. "Weren't you much too old then?"

"Not during the first one. I was allowed to go then. During the second war they put me into a concentration camp."

He could not be motivated to talk about a time for which, he said a little lower than before, he had been unable to find the right words for a long time now. His memory was no longer any good either and he was too old to torture himself with recollections full of blood. Regina turned around to meet his glance, but she was only able to see the outline of his head in the dark.

"I'm sorry," the man apologized. "I don't know what made me talk about the concentration camp. I only do that very rarely these days. Most people don't want to hear about it anyway."

"I do," Walter said, "and my daughter here, does too."

After the war he had stopped searching for lost traces. He lived off the things that were given to him and restricted his worries to the selection of jails that would open their doors to him. "It is not always easy," he complained. "The people in charge are becoming fussier all the time. They only want criminals."

"Don't worry," Walter told him. "You will have a bed in Preungesheim tonight."

"Preungesheim has been impossible for quite a while. The people of Frankfurt are especially particular."

"I know Preungesheim well."

Shortly before reaching Bad Homburg, they drank rye whiskey and ate fried eggs in a pub with Christmas decorations where they were the only guests. Regina wanted to call her mother so that she would not worry, but the telephone was constantly busy and she gave up. The man finally admitted that his name was Rübezahl and Regina apologized to her father after all these years. As a child she had always suspected that he had invented Rübezahl in the same way that she had fabricated her fairy.

"You are drinking your third schnapps already," she reproached Walter and took the glass from his hand.

"A man should be allowed to have a drink with a friend," Walter said seriously. "What I would like to know—" he asked and looked at the nameless man with a tiredness that had not been in his eyes before, "—did you never hear that you are entitled to restitutions for the time in the concentration camp?"

"Oh, yes," the man said, "but I didn't want that. Or do you believe that money can pay for a stolen life?"

"No," Walter said, "I don't believe that, but I would have liked to help you. I help a lot of people."

"I knew right away that you were a Jew."

"Why?"

"You did not drive faster when I mentioned the concentration camp but slower."

"At times one does not want to go on driving at all."

Fifteen minutes later Walter brought the car to a squealing halt in front of a shabby, small guesthouse in Preungesheim. He honked the horn several times, and then he said with an irritation that did not deceive Regina for a moment, "There you see what is wrong with jails these days. They don't even have guards."

"But this is not the prison."

"Oh, yes, it is. Believe me. I am an attorney and know my way around. Come on, let's just go in and straighten them out."

The old man reluctantly got out and followed Walter, who pushed open the door to a dark restaurant where a few guests made a lot of noise at a round table. The owner, who was wiping a beer glass with a soiled towel, lifted his head slowly, but when he saw Walter he put down both glass and towel, and said with delight, "That I see you again, Dr. Redlich. And so late at night. What brings you to our part of the woods?"

"Business. My friend here needs a room tonight and a good break-fast tomorrow," Walter said and handed him a banknote. "He actually wanted to stay in jail, but I told him that your place would be dirty enough, too."

The owner took the money and winked at Regina, "Always a joker, your father. That is what I like about him."

"He is serious," Regina explained. "He wants to help his friend. The man does not know where to go in the rain."

The innkeeper first looked at Walter, then at the old man. "For you I will do anything, Dr. Redlich. You also didn't ask a lot of questions when you helped me. Come along," he said to the old man, "I am going to show you to your room. If Dr. Redlich wants it this way, it must be all right." He put his hand on the old man's shoulder and pushed him out of the door. For a moment the two of them stood in the dreary light of a stale-smelling corridor. The friend of the one night waved before he turned, and Walter and Regina lifted their hands, too.

For a moment they lingered in the car in front of the dilapidated house and stared into the darkness.

"How come you know such dives?" Regina asked.

"Oh, the owner was once a client of mine and I helped him a little when he was in need. He has never forgotten that."

"It was probably not a little, the way I know you," Regina laughed.

"You are starting to sound just like your mother," Walter accused her.

"A strange day," he mused. "I can't even remember how it started. But it has somehow made me feel better. Rübezahl reminded me of the African people, whom I used to envy so much. No beginning and no end. What are we going to tell your mother? Where in the world could we have been for so long?"

"Lies are your department," Regina reminded him and raised her arm with the watch. "I am only an accessory."

They did not have time for the well-practiced game of great confusion. Jettel stood, pale and with red eyes full of tears, at the door to the apartment. "I always knew that the thirteenth is an unlucky day," she cried. "Schlachanska had a heart attack. He is dead."

19

THE FIGHT LASTED FOR TWO DAYS. It was in keeping with the cause and especially the shock. Except for regrettable eruptions, the tone was subdued, but from the start there was no hope of reaching a consensus through compromise. Jettel was against taking Max to Schlachanska's funeral. She argued passionately but also with uncommonly clear logic, which inspired her husband's opposition even more than usual, that Max was still a child and it would distress him too much to see Jeanne-Louise crying at her father's grave.

Max had confessed to his sister—imploring her not to tell anyone about his fears—how much the thought of Jeanne-Louise crying disturbed him. Since Walter did not know this, he was especially offended when Regina sided with her mother. He grumbled about women's hysteria being the greatest enemy of reason and missed no chance to point out that in any case his son, at almost twelve years old, was no longer a child and thanks to his father's foresight not a coddled one either. Besides, it was never too early for a man to get used to distress and to learn to clench his teeth.

"Looking at you," Walter complained, "one can see what happens when mothers bring up their children to close their eyes to life."

He did not come home for lunch on the day of the funeral but instead went to buy Max the pair of dark pants that he had needed for quite a while anyway. Trying to prove, though, that he was not totally lacking in sympathy like the dictator his wife and daughter took him for, he also bought Jettel the black leather gloves that he had refused to buy since the purchase of the Persian lamb coat.

"Someday," he said with satisfaction, "you will all be grateful to me."

Since the car, despite the cold weather and previous problems with the battery, started instantly, they arrived at the cemetery half an hour early. There were already so many people standing in the yard in front of the funeral hall that Walter assumed for a moment that he had been wrong about the time. Nervously he ran ahead with Max, and absent-mindedly greeted a group of women and after that with surprise several attorneys, whom he had not expected to see there given the circumstances of the judgment against Schlachanska.

Amused, he imagined the witty comments Schlachanska would have made seeing the people whose attachment only became apparent once more after the person involved could no longer notice it. His reflection gave Walter the kind of grim pleasure that always made his thoughts drift too far—he first remembered the pralines in the silver bowl of Schlachanska's elegant living room and then how he had stuffed them into the mouth of his drooling setter. Thus he did not see the small, bearded man—in a worn coat and big hat, running up to him with excited gestures—until he stood immediately in front of him and said with determination, "This is not acceptable. The boy has to leave."

"Why?" Walter asked, surprised. For a moment he thought that Max might have forgotten to cover his head and did not remember fast enough that that had not happened for years now. He became embarrassed when he noticed that he had run his hand over his son's head to feel if he was wearing his skullcap.

"Children are not allowed in the cemetery."

"We have been friends with the family for years," Walter explained to the man. "Our children grew up together. Joseph Schlachanska would be quite surprised if my son were not here today."

The man leaned on his cane, opened his mouth wide enough to indicate a laugh, and shook his head. "Not at all. Mr. Schlachanska was a pious man. He knew. Children who still have a mother and a father are not allowed in the cemetery."

"Since when?"

"Since there have been Jews, Dr. Redlich," the man said with the compassion of the educated for those who no longer know to think in periods of time that matter. "But in Frankfurt they disrespected the law until our rabbi came. Even our people brought wreaths for the dead."

"All right," Walter murmured.

He felt ashamed when he looked at the eager man admonishing him. The frail little man with the overly alert eyes and grand gestures reminded him of the men he had seen in the prayer hall in Sohrau. They had all been as devout as poor and his mother had often invited them home on Friday nights. He saw the white tablecloth with the poppy seed twist and the silver chalice that was passed around from one to the other and he was able to smell the chicken broth.

The thought that his mother's household had still been kosher and that she had been able to ask the most pious of the pious to her table made Walter melancholic. For a moment, which seemed very long to him, he envied the old man's steadfastness of his belief, which did not demand God to adapt to the changing times.

Sadly, Walter remembered that he had thought exactly this way the last time he had been at a funeral—in Nairobi when old Professor Gottschalk had died. It had been a Friday, and because of the Shabbat the rabbi had not wanted to wait until the daughter of the deceased arrived to begin the funeral. At the time, Walter was the one who understood the message. "Without the pious ones among us, there would no longer be any Jews at all," he had defended the rabbi, and almost all the people who heard him had called him a fool.

"All right," Walter repeated and held his hand out to the old man. "I am not a devout man, but I respect the laws."

He ran back to the gate with Max and wished with all his heart that at some later point in his life his son would be able to say the same. The thought that this might not be the case almost turned into a physical pain. But he said aloud, "You see, your mother is a smart woman after all. She has proven once again that she knows things that she cannot know."

He laughed but without a sound while he spoke, and then he pondered, still in a state of reverie and longing that he could not explain to himself, why all of a sudden all the bouquets, which he now saw everywhere and had not noticed before, were disturbing him. Obviously many of Schlachanska's non-Jewish clients had chosen to prove to him one last time that they held a different view from the judges in his case.

Walter decided to eventually enlighten his own clients about the simple rites of a Jewish funeral and the inappropriateness of flowers. He saw himself smiling ironically while he talked to his people from Upper Silesia and heard them say that they had always loved his sense of humor, but this time he was going too far with his jokes. He felt as if he had allowed himself some cheerfulness at the wrong time and with a small sigh released himself from his imagination.

"You better go home with Regina," he said. "I do not want to use Schlachanska's funeral to clear up whether we adults have to be half-orphans, too, before we are allowed in the cemetery. I am sorry, Maxele; now you will have to wait for my funeral to understand what I wanted to teach you today."

Regina and Max walked, first silently and later enjoying a really funny joke Ziri had made last night, along a wall that was overgrown with ivy. Regina noticed that Max no longer, as on the hike in the Harz, walked with small childlike steps next to her and also no longer played soccer with every larger stone. She was moved and quite receptive to the thought that this was a very suitable day to ponder the small signs of fleeting times.

Regina realized from her brother's firm gait that he was familiar with the path. Yet she was surprised when he stopped in front of the gate to the main cemetery and in a conspiring tone, which he only used with her and even more frequently in recent times, said, "We are allowed to go to the Christian cemetery. I know a bench very close to the entry."

"How?"

"I used to sit there with Else," Max told her, "when I was little."

"I thought you went to the Günthersburgpark with Else."

"Not on All Saints,' All Souls' Day, and Christmas," Max enumerated. "On Christmas I always went to church. To the crèche. Else," he giggled, "even let me hold the baby Jesus when I was really little."

"You should tell that to your father," Regina said, full of amazement.

"Else always said if I told at home that I had gone to church with her, I would fall down dead."

"I know that, too," Regina remembered, "only my Else was called Owuor."

"So you did not tell everything either when you were a child?"

"No, not everything. I lived in two worlds at the time and had a very hard time keeping the black world apart from the white world. I was always afraid Papa and Mama would be upset. I did not want to distress them."

"Neither did I," Max nodded. "You are the only one who I am never afraid will get upset. I can tell you everything." He drew circles in the wet soil with his stick and energetically drilled three holes into each one of them. "Did you know," he said without looking up, "that Schlachanska got a year and a half? Why did he never have to go to jail then?"

"You really should have asked your father about that. He could explain it much better to you than I can. The judgment had not yet been final. Papa thought the punishment was much too severe. How did you hear about it?"

"From Jeanne-Louise," Max said.

"Dear heavens. I thought she never found out. You didn't tell her, did you?"

"Nonsense. Some girl in her class did. I think it's great that Jeanne-Louise never told her father that she knew. One is allowed to lie if one loves someone, isn't one?"

"One has to, only I didn't know that you are that far already."

"Strange, I never want to lie to you and yet I love you, too."

"There are some people you don't have to keep anything from. That is an exceptional good fortune in life," Regina remembered, and saw Owuor's head, with his curls wet from the rain, appearing behind a dripping tree.

She aimed her eye at her brother's pupil. It was an old magic game — from an earlier life, not for children, and never for people who only grasped what they understood with their heads. Whoever lowered his eyes first, lost. But if four eyes gave up the fight with one movement of their eyelashes, the day would become one that never could be forgotten by either of the challengers. For the first time, Regina experienced the silent magic connection between like-minded people in this intensity with her brother. She looked at Max longer than the rules of the game permitted.

Her skin became warm when she realized that the old story of a love without escape had just started anew. When Cupid got ready to pierce her heart for all time, he still disguised himself as the cunning warrior of the Masai tribe and she was just as unable to defend herself as under the guava tree in Nairobi when her father had finally defeated her. Her brother, for whose birth she had once begged the great God Mungu, was no longer a child. He did not know it yet, but he already knew how to tie knots that neither of them would ever be able to sever.

"Come on," Regina sighed, "we have to go. How are we going to explain where we have been all this time? Nobody is going to believe that we spent the entire time sitting in front of unknown graves in the wrong cemetery."

They ran the last part of the way, but the car was already parked in the yard. An unusually large cardboard box was lying between the two trashcans. Max said, "*Oy vey*, there is going to be a fight. Papa bought a new gadget that Mama does not want." They did not have time to pursue their curiosity any further. On the staircase they heard their parents fighting.

"I am not going to have that thing in the house," Jettel screamed. "Everyone says that the programs only start very late at night. The boy will not want to go to bed on time anymore and in the morning he is going to be too tired to pay attention in school."

"Since when are you interested in Latin vocabulary, Jettel? And why does a twelve-year-old boy have to be in bed by eight?"

"He is only eleven. You always make him older when it is to your advantage. I am only interested in the welfare of my child. I just read the other day that a television is the devil's contraption if one has children."

"The Schlachanskas have had that devil's contraption for years. You always liked to sit in front of it. And Jeanne-Louise is still the best in her class. Television is no different from the cinema. Only that you do not have to wash your neck first if you want to watch something. Besides, our television is already standing there and it will stay."

The television set was the payment from a client, who still worked on the exchange basis, for Walter's success in a case that seemed hopeless from the beginning. The man was one of the oldest clients of the practice and owned a hotel in the inner city, had shares in a company in Tel Aviv, and mainly paid his fees with happily accepted invitations for Sunday dinners in his own restaurant or with grapefruit and avocados that he imported by the case from Israel.

Jettel had only decided to put up with the grapefruit, which were only available in a few luxury shops, after she found out that the Faffloks, who also regularly received the fruits that she considered unacceptably bitter, served them daily for breakfast and that they had resulted in a remarkable decrease of colds there. Her dislike for avocados remained, but Jettel had at least stopped rejecting them as poisonous green pears and throwing them in the garbage right away. She once even served the unwanted gifts, as the recipe in one of the progressive women's magazines suggested, with salt, pepper, and lemon juice. After the first night of heated debates, she also displayed an unexpected flexibility toward television.

It became apparent very quickly and definitely that the television, a light screen within a dark brown box that stood on the small living room chest that had been cleared for it, possessed unexpected powers that went beyond its original use. The unprepossessing device, on which a lamp and pipe-smoking gnome were standing, became a peacemaker in a marriage in which up to then fights about trivialities had even sapped the strength of the temperamental fighter who had initiated them.

During those days when the painful awareness emerged that the entire family had lost a loyal and unusual friend in Joseph Schlachanska—a cheerfully wise mediator of Jewish life and very unconventional advisor—the television diverted them, at least for a few hours, from the depressing feeling that life was once again and forever marked by a farewell.

It was just a coincidence that television began to cheer up the evenings at precisely the time as the agonizing depression after Schlachanska's death upset the daily rhythms. It was no coincidence, however, that Walter, Jettel, and Regina reacted with special intensity to a stimulus that they had known existed but had never attracted them.

The fascination of the gray pictures on a black-and-white background not only heightened their imagination in a very unusual way; but it also offered the possibility of repeating experiences that they had not thought about for a while, and in retrospect that made them as cheerful as people who find an old picture book in the attic and happily immerse themselves in the past. Jettel and Walter agreed that television affected them in the same way as the silent movies, which they now remembered with such joy and surprising clarity as if they were just coming out of the cinema in Breslau.

The news became the nightly high point that nobody wanted to miss for the simple reason that it was such a novel and almost comical experience to be able to see Adenauer and all the other important Bonn politicians, whom one only knew from fuzzy pictures in the newspapers or, at most, the weekly newsreels in the movie theater, close-up as if they were invited and welcome guests.

"Only that they are visitors you don't have to offer anything to and they don't expect to have a conversation with you," Walter cheerfully said.

"You finally had a good idea there," Jettel agreed contentedly. Jettel, who had never been interested in politics except when questions of Jewish life in the new Germany came up, now paid as much attention to the debates and parties in the Lower House of the German Parliament and complicated economic connections as to the gestures, facial expressions, and suits of the representatives.

Pictures of events abroad held a special fascination. They made the world bigger and reduced one's own world to a surprisingly small scale. A street in New York; a fashion show in Paris; pictures from Bombay, Tokyo, or Tel Aviv; even a dog in London's Hyde Park or the British queen in her carriage: all turned into an extraordinary panorama of foreign life, which one could be a part of by simply pressing a button.

One night the Suez Canal was shown on the screen. Jettel, Walter, and Regina jumped up as excitedly as if they were again on deck of the "Almanzora" that had carried them back to Germany.

"No camels," Walter reported.

"They are all on board, sir," Regina shouted, and the three of them enjoyed the old joke with such gusto as if they had waited for years to unearth it from the depth of a trench that had been dug too hastily.

They were not even embarrassed about their childish behavior in front of Ziri and Max when they momentarily allowed themselves the old, suddenly rediscovered joy of alleviating the sharpness of the real contours. As soon as the pictures started to flicker, Walter, Jettel, and Regina felt as if they had returned to the times when the radio had been their only connection to the world. They remembered—even Walter not without delight and melancholy—how they had pulled all the windows and doors open at the farm and the people from the huts had come together with their sleeping infants, goats, and dogs to happily listen to the small box's sounds that were unintelligible to them.

Max had his own pleasures. He loved the family dramas that
almost always featured a boy his age who thought exactly the way he
did. For the Schölermann family, with the attractive father, the efficient, understanding mother, and the loveable children, on Wednes-
days he crept in his pajamas to the door of the living room and lay on
the floor—the encouraging stories of the strength of love and harmony
were broadcast too late and his mother still insisted that he be in bed
by eight o'clock. The fear of discovery was, however, made worthwhile
by the surprising revelation that other families were not much different
from his.

"One day," Regina speculated full of hope after a broadcast about life
in Cairo, "we will also get to see Nairobi and Owuor will wave to us."
"Why Nairobi?" Walter asked, and his eyes betrayed that he, too,
longed for quite specific images.

"You don't seriously think that Owuor remained in Nairobi without us?"

"Wishing doesn't cost anything. You always told me that as a child."

A few days later there was no longer any doubt in Regina's mind that
she and her father had summoned fate in the old reliable way. She recognized the provocation too late. They had been too light-hearted and
had forgotten that wishes needed the protection of wise limits. The
hour of truth, therefore, transformed their careless high spirits into a
lethal monster with freshly sharpened teeth.

At the end of the evening news, there was a report about the murder
of a farmer. Walter was just about to complain that Jettel had not
bought the sausages from the Silesian butcher; the discussion about the
missing garlic diverted them from the events on the screen long enough
so that nobody noticed that it was Kenya that was in the news. Only
when the announcer's tongue stumbled when he tried to say Naivasha
did the word get its first outline. All three, still without any suspicion,
called it out to the man in the box as seriously as if the right pronunciation of the full-sounding syllables were of special importance.

The first picture was still only a shadow in a room full of laughter.
But then the charred walls of a burned house emerged from the gray of
the screen. A broken-down door lay across a bed of trampled carnations; the laughter stopped, drowned in the horror of uncomprehending
silence. On the closely cropped lawn in front of the house lay a dead

cow with its stomach slit. Bloodstained hair was stuck to a white fence. Black men in police uniforms and two white men in khaki shorts were standing in front of a jeep. A dog, which was not visible, barked. Small photographs of three blond children and a woman were shown. Walter got up and turned off the television.

"Naivasha," Jettel whispered. "It cannot be. It was so beautiful there."

"We went boating on the lake with Martin," Walter said. "I didn't even know that this had reached Naivasha."

"Mau-Mau," Regina swallowed.

They had all known about the war of the blacks against the farmers in the highlands, but without pictures the faraway stroke of lightning had not turned into the thunder of reality. It had always just remained a presentiment of transformations full of violence in a world that they knew as soft and bright. They had often and quite early heard about Jomo Kenyatta's fight against British colonial rule, had seen his photo in the papers, and—each on their own—had tried to interpret the features of the old, determined warrior who spoke of freedom and ordered murder. They had known the word Mau-Mau as the bloody slogan for rebellion and independence. They knew right away that it meant death, and even when they heard that peace was starting to return to Kenya, they did not dare pronounce this foreign word.

Walter was least able to explain his silence. The Mau-Mau uprising, in which even children had been killed by people who had loved them like their own, was at least a late confirmation for the farsightedness of his decision to leave Kenya. During recent years in Frankfurt, they had gotten a lot of mail from old acquaintances who had been forced to leave their farms and had wandered on to an uncertain future in America, England, or Israel. Even Jettel only rarely mentioned Kenya as the paradise she had been forced to give up.

But Walter was not concerned with the fact that he had done the right thing when he was one of the first to depart before the storm. The late confirmation of a foresight, which he had not had, was unpleasant to him. He only knew too well that he had never thought about a bloody war between blacks and whites in Kenya. In retrospect he felt only gratitude and recently also nostalgia for the country that had saved him and his family from death. He suffered more than he was willing to admit to himself from the idea that the old world no longer existed in which sun, wind, rain, and peaceful people had determined his life for such a long time.

Regina, on the other hand, always knew why she should not utter the word Mau-Mau. She would only be able to save the forests and fields, the mountains, the huts, the beloved people, the animals, and the wise God Mungu for her head and heart if she kept her lips closed. Now reality had caught up with her with a blood-smeared grimace that made her shudder. Regina drilled her fingers into her temples while she stared at the dark television set, but there were no answers to her questions and she had a premonition that in the future she would no longer know where to go on the days without light.

"I wonder if our house in Ol' Joro Orok is still standing," Jettel whispered, "and the outhouse with the three hearts and the beautiful kitchen under the big tree."

"Does it matter?" Walter answered. "We have had to part with so many things in life. We will also be able to get over the fact that another part of our memories no longer has a home."

Regina immediately switched off the small lamp on her night table after she went to bed. With the practice of many years, she was also able to put out the conflagration of the pictures, but her thoughts were like the most dangerous bushfires that always relight themselves with their own ambers—she felt too fervently that her ears had caught a word and had not yet passed it on to her head. She sat up in her bed and ordered, like a hunter who has lost the track, the pictures and sounds back once more. Only after wandering for a long time in a forest overgrown with vines did she emerge at that light spot where a lost person is able to see again. There the long-expected echo reached Regina's ears. Her father had spoken of Ol' Joro Orok and had said home.

She repeated the word, full of surprise, and yet she needed even more time than before to comprehend the message. Bewildered and yet liberated in a way that calmed her overwrought senses, she finally realized that Walter had gone on safari just like her. At the moment of this blissful discovery, she felt at first as if someone had pushed aside the big boulder that had hindered her view for such a long time. The happiness was short-lived. Then she understood, dismayed and with a sadness that first split her head and then her heart, why Walter had returned into the world he had wanted to leave in order to find a home again. In parting he had endured that sharp pain that never heals. The *bwana* had never reached home.

20

FOR HER FIFTIETH BIRTHDAY in June of 1958, Jettel wanted a trip abroad in late summer from her husband, and wanted Regina to accompany her. She was surprised at herself when she finally had the courage to make her wish known and was convinced that Walter would not even make an effort to talk seriously with her about this idea. Thinking about the long trip she had in mind seemed so unusual and, considering her husband's conservative views, even provocative to Jettel that she only dared to express her wish when she inadvertently found out that Walter was going to give her a new rug for the living room.

Whenever Jettel tried to talk about vacations, Walter would become irritable and insulting. During the disagreeable disputes he used to tell her that she had delusions of grandeur and he called her a spendthrift. Angrily he pointed out that he had truly gotten around enough in his life and certainly not voluntarily, and that he had only one wish: to see the Riesengebirge once again. The modern yearning for luxury, holidays, and foreign countries, which to Walter's consternation even gripped people who had previously never gotten any farther than their uncle's place in the country, struck Walter as a regrettable sign of the times, obtuse, presumptuous, and in his own case ungrateful toward a fate in which the word "departure" had a special meaning.

"Good God," Jettel accused him a week before her birthday, "I don't want to emigrate. I just want to see something different for a couple of weeks, and no Germans."

"And where is that supposed to be?"

"I was thinking of Austria," Jettel said, and angrily slammed her keys on the table.

She had anticipated derision, insulting remarks, even a big fight, but not the striking reaction she got. Walter slapped his forehead and smiled with such degrading irony that Jettel immediately planned to tell all the guests she had invited to the celebration not to come and not even to tell him about it. He was not even embarrassed to neigh so ridiculously and loudly that Ziri came running out of the kitchen with a meat knife in her hand so that she would not miss any detail of the unexpected merriment.

To Jettel's amazement, Walter slowly got up from his wing chair, saluted with élan, put his hand on her shoulder, and said almost tenderly, "You just go ahead, my dear, innocent angel. While you are gone, I will sit here all the time in my easy chair and think about what you said about the Austrians during our emigration. And when you come back, your old man will have killed himself laughing."

Regina's reaction the next morning surprised Jettel even more. She had initially only suggested that she wanted to go with Regina because she knew that Walter always had an easier time spending money if he thought he could make his daughter happy. Despite all the strategic considerations, which she was very proud of, Jettel had not really liked the idea that she might cause Regina a conflict that she would be unable to talk about.

In contrast to Walter, Jettel had, for years already, had a hunch that Regina did not spend her vacations, as she maintained, with a girlfriend in the Bavarian Alps.

She doubted, not without sympathy, that her daughter was willing to give up this part of her private life, which she protected so carefully and obviously also found satisfying, for a trip with her mother. But Regina agreed so spontaneously that Jettel in retrospect was ashamed for using a ruse, especially since she had been aware of its egotistical nature all along.

During the weeks after her birthday she asked herself, frequently and often quite self-consciously, if it had not just been Regina's good nature that had brought about the unexpected yes. But the closer the trip to Mayerhofen in the Zillertal came (Jettel was very proud that she had chosen the destination by herself and had made all the arrangements without Walter's help), the more she felt that Regina was not only looking forward to the vacation, but without a doubt also to being together with her.

Cheerfully, Jettel retrieved the song about the happy Tyroleans from the collection of her kitchen songs and in her afternoon coffee parties told the envious ladies, who were just experiencing difficult times with their adult children, that there was no greater joy for a mother than to take a trip with such a circumspect and caring daughter. Soon Jettel could not even believe that she ever could have been jealous of Regina.

Regina, on the other hand, was not able to explain to herself why she had had so much less patience and tolerance for her mother than for her father in the past. It seemed that with each day, beginning with the early start of the travel preparations, a little piece of reservation was chipped away between two people who had known each other very well at some point and had lost sight of each other through circumstances they were unable to explain.

Both first noticed the changes on the day when Jettel bought the shining, silver-gray evening blouse and Regina the tight black sweater. Walter—as usual—said "terribly beautiful" with a frown and both looked at each other and almost like conspirators started laughing sympathetically. They debated for days about shoes and sandals, and knee-high stockings and heavy socks; if they might need loden coats or even a dirndl; and in all seriousness, as if they had never lived on a farm, what they would do if a cow chased them across a meadow.

Jettel mentioned that this reminded her of the times when she had gone on vacation with her mother and sister. She now frequently used the word "resort" and talked about the elegant young men who had courted her early-widowed, beautiful mother. While she immersed herself, smiling, in a past she had not mentioned for years, she again looked very much like the coquettish, big-eyed little girl in the sailor suit on the faded photograph in the old tea tin.

Among the travel documents were two bright blue cardboard butterflies. On the day of their departure Regina and Jettel fastened them to their new white cardigans and giggled like young girls before their first date. The special Touropa train with the sleeper-coaches left at eleven o'clock at night. Walter insisted on coming to the station. He treated them to a porter and to Jettel's favorite ginger chocolates for the trip, and he created confusion in the compartment, which they only found after an excited search, by self-consciously asking the fellow passengers to treat his wife and daughter with special consideration since they had just been released from a psychiatric hospital.

"Take care of yourself," Jettel told him, leaning out of the window, "and eat well. Ziri knows exactly what she is supposed to cook for you. I gave her a special list for each day."

"That just goes to show what has happened to me. Aren't you afraid to leave me alone with a pretty young girl?"

"You know quite well that I have never been jealous in all my life. And go with Max to see Mrs. Schlachanska. She promised she would invite you."

"Of all people," Walter complained. "She always looks at me so reproachfully, as if she resents that I did not die instead of her husband."

"Just go. She is a good woman. And her cake is good, too."

"Don't fight with your mother, Regina. And on the way make it clear to her that Tyrol is in the mountains and not on the ocean," Walter called into the departing whistle, "and explain to her that the people there are Germans in disguise."

Mayerhofen in the Zillertal, accessible from Innsbruck only by bus, greeted its guests, who were exhausted from the long trip, with apricot schnapps in small, painted glass carafes; red geraniums in full bloom on the dark wooden balconies of the freshly painted houses; two cows festooned with flowers; a chapel in the marketplace; and sunshine on the meadows and new snow on the mountain tops. Regina complimented her mother so enthusiastically that Jettel instantly overcame her fatigue and mobilized an energy, unusual even for her, to explain to the surprised tour guide that she wanted to stay in the charming house with the pretty sign "Kramerwirt" or she would depart instantly.

Regina was greatly embarrassed by this display of motherly assertiveness and avoided looking at the man in the local costume during the negotiations. But he called Jettel "Madam" several times; admired her blouse; exchanged, after some initial hesitation but without any objection, the intended quarters for the ones she demanded; and then, even with a smile, made sure that her additional wish—to have the room that overlooked the marketplace, and not the smaller one with a view of the backyard—was also fulfilled.

"Don't put up with everything," Jettel laughed and sank in good spirits onto the bed with the red and white checked sheets. "Your father and you can learn a thing or two from me in that arena."

The first night they were served Kaiserschmarrn, which Jettel called scrambled eggs with raisins after the first helping, yet after the second helping, praised as one of those real Viennese specialties that she had learned to appreciate as a young girl. The newly arrived guests were offered a glass of wine on the house and were later invited to a small reception in the large restaurant. A bearded trio in lederhosen and green hats with long feathers played folksongs. Twice, at Jettel's special request, they played the song about the happy Tyroleans.

Gray-haired women in transparent white nylon blouses looked enviously at Jettel's freshly died curls and pointedly at her low-cut black dress with its pattern of luxurious red roses. The men, in suspenders that stretched across their tight shirts, hungrily scrutinized Regina's legs. Both of them enjoyed the glances, ordered a glass of wine that they drank from in turns, and made fun of the other guests, first whispering, but later speaking comfortably loud in Swahili. They even found words to express difficult concepts like "typically German" or "narrow-minded."

At the end of the night, they made friends with the owner's wife's dachshund and concurred that Walter was really a big fool because he always maintained that dachshunds were still Nazis. Before falling asleep they agreed that they had not laughed like this for years and had not felt this good either. They woke up when the rooster crowed and realized that they had not heard one since Ol' Joro Orok.

On the first card to Walter, Jettel wrote: "Of course, the Tyrol is a foreign country. We are reducing our expenses and this makes it possible for us to see so much that our heads are spinning." They saved the money they had budgeted for lunch by taking two rolls from the breakfast table, and by buying two bananas and milk, and spent the leftover money on a ride on the old-fashioned little train to Jenbach and bus tours to Innsbruck, Salzburg, the Tuxer Joch, and Großglockner.

Jettel, who at home avoided every exertion by referring to her age and her migraines, did not get tired on any of the trips, and was satisfied with everything, to Regina's amazement. Enormously popular with the fellow travelers, Jettel flirted with the men, who fought to carry her bag and to help her off the bus, and cared in a motherly way for unaccompanied older women. All of them told her their fateful life stories, were even more interested in Jettel's African adventures, and without exception sadly remembered Jewish friends they had helped in times of trouble.

With her new box camera Regina took pictures of her beaming mother in front of the Goldenen Dachl in Innsbruck, in the garden of the Mirabell Castle in Salzburg, and with a bag of Mozartkugeln, the famous Austrian chocolates, in the Getreidegasse. In view of the anticipated high point of the trip, they finally bought a small bottle of rum, which they thought especially inexpensive, at a kiosk.

They wavered for a long time over whether Bressanone, which to their surprise was also called Brixen, might already be "Italian enough" to satisfy their yearning, but they eventually booked the big, expensive trip across the Brenner with a one-hour stay in Bozen and three hours in Meran. Because the bus had a flat tire on the way, they were only able to take a quick peek and buy a pound of grapes at the fruit market in Bozen. In Meran, though, they immediately felt that they had arrived in the land of their dreams.

"We searched for it with our souls," Regina recited.

"You said that beautifully," Jettel said admiringly.

"There was a little bit of Goethe in it."

They walked on the splendid promenade in front of the elegant spa center, sat on a white bench in the glowing heat, and listened with delight to the spa orchestra playing waltzes. They sat in a cafe at the babbling Passer with its own palm tree and parrot, caressed the beautiful foreign word *espresso* with their tongue and the tiny silver cups with their hands, and were quite amazed that the waiter spoke fluent German. Still, they agreed that they had made their way into the heart of Italy.

In the shops under the cool, dark arbors they found a tiny glass horse with a blue mane for Ziri, and they were invited to taste wine but did not have to pay for the intoxicating mouthful of happiness. Both had red spots on their faces and in their ears they heard sounds that Regina identified as the call of the Sirens. They tried on straw hats and sunglasses and stared longingly at the certainly affordable shoes, belts, and handbags, which unfortunately were still too expensive for them. After the second espresso—this time they dared to take along the sugar in the attractive little bags—they decided to share the cost of a necklace of white porcelain beads with hand-painted pink and blue roses. Jettel paid fifty liras more than Regina and in this way ensured the right to wear the showpiece every Sunday and to wear it instantly. A soldier in an Italian uniform, who obviously did not speak German because he called Jettel *signora,* clicked his tongue and her cheeks turned pink.

With their last liras they bought Max a small, genuinely Italian policeman made of "really good plastic." He wore a blue helmet and twirled his arms in the wind. For Walter they bought two liters of Chianti in a moss-green bottle in a light-yellow woven raffia basket. They burned with excitement and joy at the thought that he had never seen anything so wonderful in all his life and would most likely not dare to open the bottle, even though the merchant had convincingly assured them that one could put a candle in the mouth of the bottle later on and that it would then be as beautiful as before.

Before leaving, they bought a big ice-cream cone with their very last coins and took turns licking it. Regina was allowed to pick out the flavors; she interpreted her mother's glances correctly and chose only chocolate, nougat, and mocha, even though she preferred vanilla and strawberry ice cream.

"I feel as if I have gotten years younger in Italy," Jettel said.

"You have," Regina confirmed, "but not only in Italy."

The bus had another flat tire in Brennerbad. The driver consoled the disgruntled tourists with red wine from his own supply. Only some overly critical older gentlemen disparaged the fact that a bus would have that many glasses, but no spare tire handy. On a meadow under an apple tree, Jettel articulated the thought that had occupied Regina since the second day of their trip.

"This really is," she said, "the first time that the two of us are so completely alone together ever since I was pregnant in Nakuru and was so desperate because I felt that the baby would be stillborn."

"And we are talking with each other the way we did then," Regina swallowed with the same heaviness in her voice. "I thought you had forgotten about that long ago."

"No. I often think about it. As young as you were, you comforted me very much then. I felt that you understood me as well as I understood my mother."

"And you don't think that anymore?"

"I am not so sure. You always take your father's side."

"No," Regina answered, "I don't. I understand you much better than you think, but I want to protect Papa. I always worry about him when he gets excited. Don't think that I haven't known for quite a while how difficult it is to be married to him. I am also aware that he often starts your fights."

"Most of the time," Jettel sighed, "we fight about you. You only hear us squabbling, but you don't know how things get started. Papa is obsessed with the idea that you are having an affair with your boss. Or that you cannot get over Martin and, therefore, do not want to get married. And then he gets terribly upset when I tell him that you are old enough to know what you are doing."

Regina felt the urge to embrace Jettel, but her parents' old fight for her heart made her as insecure as during her childhood. Her skin glowed, and she let her arms fall down.

"Thank you," she said quietly and caressed Jettel's hand.

"For what?"

"I should say that you understand me much better than I understand you. But I really meant thank you for the entire trip. I will never forget these days."

"I won't either. I had wanted to tell you that all this time. But I am curious, too. What is the truth? The story with Martin or your boss?"

"Both. And both not quite the way you think. You are a smart woman."

"That's what I always say," Jettel laughed, picked up a small apple from the grass, and threw it in the air, "only your father will never understand that. He just doesn't know anything about human nature. Still, I am looking forward to seeing him, even though I am already getting aggravated with him now. I bet he never makes Max go to bed on time."

She had hardly ever been this right. Walter would have considered it a sinful waste of his freedom to have Max go to bed before he did. Walter, who was often ashamed about his deep bond with Regina because he thought it unfair to Max, was in the process of getting to know his son from a new perspective. During the two weeks he spent alone with him, he realized that Max was no longer a child. He also recognized that Max had the same sense of humor as he did, the same appreciation for provocative jokes and earthy language, and even the same way of disguising emotions with a wryness that other people were unable to

understand. He was very happy about this accord. When he was together with Max he did not become tired as quickly as usual, nor did
he have gloomy thoughts. It gave him great pleasure that his cheerful,
intelligent son with his evident appreciation of language and irony so
obviously enjoyed their conversations.

Walter did not miss the opportunity on any day during the two
weeks to demonstrate to Max how refreshing, uncomplicated, and har-
monic life could be when men did not have to pay attention to women
and their tendency to busy themselves at the wrong moment with
things that spoiled a man's life. For the first time he developed the same
kind of close, twinkle-in-the-eye relationship with his son that he had
once had on the farm with his daughter.

When Walter had been alone with Regina at Ol' Joro Orok, he had
always tried to make life different from other times. He had allowed her
not to wash for a week and to stay up till she fell asleep in front of the
fireplace and was carried to her bed by Owuor. He now encouraged
Max to break away from any conventions, to do everything Jettel did
not approve of, and to talk about things that were usually not mentioned in his presence.

While sitting in the bathtub, Walter quizzed Max on the Latin vocabulary for the next day, and explained the Pythagorean axiom to him
with the help of a piece of soap, a brush, and a washcloth; after that they
turned to political problems, the nature of anti-Semitism, and what
Max had to do if he made his father a grandfather before his time. Max
was allowed to sleep in the marital bed and to accompany his father to
prison and to the office after school. There he increased his appetite for
life by studying divorce proceedings.

At noon they ate standing up at the shop of a butcher, on whose
behalf Walter had just filed for divorce and with whom he shared iden-
tical views about marital infidelity and pork chops. They bought curried
sausages at a stand, got cream-filled chocolate cakes for dessert, and ate
the cakes on a bench in the small park in front of the office. Walter once
asked his son if he did not prefer to spend his time with the other boys
in his class.

"No," Max said, "I am taking a vacation from the boys in my class."

Twice they sat on a scorching hot day under trees at the grand "Kai-
serkeller," and first embarrassed the waiter by taking off their shoes and

socks, and then even more when Walter pretended to have lost his wallet. He bought Max a bell that sounded like a car horn for his bicycle, and bought himself a chain so that his glasses could slide directly from his nose to his chest. The optician told them that such chains had only been available in America till now. They immediately realized that this was true because the people who saw Walter's suspended glasses stopped in their tracks and laughed surreptitiously.

Other than that there were the soccer playoffs. After two weeks of flickering pictures, screaming reporters, excitement, and constant fears about the well-being and success of his fabulous home team, Walter was sufficiently trained to denounce, in the same outraged volume as his son, all referees and players who endangered a German victory and German honor. Without expecting it, he was also faced with an immediate realization that would touch him deeply. It was the day of the enthusiastically awaited game between Sweden and Germany that would determine the entry into the finals. Walter initially enjoyed the duel in Goeteborg as if he had never been interested in anything else but free kicks, corners, and penalties in all his life. He rejoiced just like Max when the German team, whose players Walter had been able to name for a while now, succeeded in a surprise attack. But his concentration decreased earlier than in previous games   it had been a discouraging day with a lost case and a fight with a judge whom he perceived as insulting.

Even though he initially hesitated to disappoint Max with his inattentiveness, the pictures first lost their clarity and then their meaning. Finally, only his ears received nourishment. A force, whose attraction he was soon unable to resist, pulled him toward the never-forgotten sound of familiar noises. The longer the play went on, the more the driving, regular, and monotonous screams of "hcia, heia" of the Swedish spectators reminded him of the drums in the forest of Ol' Joro Orok.

Walter saw himself, when he permitted his eyes the journey for just a moment, standing at the edge of the large flax field. He also saw Regina tossing her hat into the air and lying down on the shining red soil to catch the message of the sounds, and he heard the black monkeys with the white manes screeching and afterward Owuor laughing. The echo bounded back from the mountain like a hollow thunder. The three of them were standing in the lightning, and they shouted with one voice into the woods, indicating that the drums had reached them.

"Heia, heia," Walter called out to the pictures and made his voice dark.

"You are not supposed to say heia," Max complained. "That is treason."

"High treason," Walter corrected him. "I only want to chase away the enemies with noise. That is what you do in a war. I still remember that from the locusts."

He was, however, unable to emerge quickly enough from a world that in retrospect had been able to lead him to believe in the fleeting harmony of life because he was young and healthy then. Simultaneously, with the memory of his still-unbroken strength, he again felt the heavy oppression of Africa and suffered, with freshly bleeding wounds, the yearning for the homeland that had expelled him, as if he had just recently had to leave Germany. Conflicting memories, each single one leading into a different direction, scorched Walter's senses. He groaned to extinguish the fire and with it the unsettling recognition that he had not found the home, which he had mourned in Africa, in Germany after all. Taken aback, he held his hand in front of his mouth so that the painful sound of resignation would not be repeated, but all of a sudden he realized that it was his son who had groaned. Relieved, he opened his eyes and looked at Max.

"That pig took Juskowiak out," Max screamed.

"Is he one of ours?"

"Papa, you know Juskowiak. How are we supposed to win now?"

Since the sound of the hard syllables fascinated him in a strange way, Walter wondered about the name Juskowiak. The time was long enough for another flood of pictures. He thought about Sohrau and his father's house with the linden trees. He saw streets, places, people, and scenes; thought finally about the Upper Silesian vote after World War I; and remembered how fanatically he had fought as a young man for his homeland to stay German. He heard himself talking persistently and obsessively about German culture and a German fatherland, and about loyalty, honor, and sacrifice. He tried to remember what he had felt when he said those words; tried to imagine the young men who had also devoted themselves to a lost cause, but he could not remember a single name, only the eagerness and the hate in the rough, determined faces. All of a sudden he envied the friends of those days, envied even the young man he had been, and envied the certainty of a conviction that their cause was the only just one.

"Fritz Walter got hurt. Man, he is out. He is limping off the field. The Swedish pig fouled him. This is unfair," Max shouted. "Look at this foul play, Papa."

Walter's eyes started to burn when he discovered in his son's red, swollen face the traces of fervor and hate he had just been thinking about. He did not like the mirror image of his own youth. He felt the need to finally protect himself from the misunderstanding that he now recognized as a lifelong illusion that made men blind. He felt compelled to tell the young man of those earlier days that home is only a dream, but he was no longer sure if he wanted to warn himself or his son.

"We only have nine left," Max called out. "We are lost."

It was the despair in the childish voice that drove away the ghosts. Walter noticed with relief how Max bit his lips and clenched his fists. He immediately made out the signs that troubled him even more than the look into the past. It was a moment of great release when Walter understood that his son had found the homeland that his father would never have again.

"Soccer," he said, "is really beautiful."

"But you have been asleep the whole time," Max complained.

"A father is never asleep. He is lost in thought. Remember that, my favorite son."

The game finished three to one in favor of the Swedes. Even in bed Max still repeated that the end of the German hopes amounted to a tragedy and that he was never going to be able to laugh again in his life. But he did laugh nonetheless when Walter in his pajamas twirled an umbrella, called "heia, heia," and suggested they should blacken their faces with shoe polish.

The next morning, two hours before the special train from Tyrol arrived, Walter and Max went into the Kaufhof, the department store for everything, to receive Jettel with a new saucepan. It was even higher and a lot bigger than the old stockpot that had remained in Leobschütz during the emigration, and it had gleaming handles and shone like a silver goblet. Walter lifted it on top of his head and the young salesgirl licked her lips and admiringly said, "You made a good choice. Genuine Swedish steel."

"Swedish steel," Walter imitated the high voice. He slammed the lid onto the pot and asked aloud, "Don't you know what happened? You don't seriously think that a decent German can cook his soup in a Swedish pot. I am no traitor to the fatherland."

With a voice that kept on getting louder, he shouted, "Heia, heia." The customers came closer and looked amused, curious, and sometimes admiringly at Walter. He yelled "Heia, heia" one more time into the room; this time the people who were standing around him chanted the calls with him and applauded loudly.

"That was a good job," Max praised him when he arrived on the platform with his father. "I don't have enough courage to scream that loudly in front of that many people."

"We Germans are not going to put up with everything," Walter giggled. "We are holding our heads high again."

The train from Innsbruck arrived two minutes early in Frankfurt, so Walter did not have time to explain to his son the difference between courage and high spirits nor was he able to tell him what he had wanted to explain to him the previous night after the last Swedish goal.

21

IN MID-NOVEMBER an unusually cold day ended an exceptional period of mild sun and warmth, which had made the early fall golden. With cutting wind, rain, hail, and an unexpected drop in temperature, this day of contrasts robbed Walter of all hope that he only needed to adjust to the change in weather in order to easily survive the winter through sheer willpower. As soon as he left the house he felt in his arm the sharp aches that he had learned to identify ever since his first heart attack. He had coughed so violently during the night that he was unable to stay in bed, and suffered till dawn in the wing chair in the living room. When walking, he gasped after only a few steps. Since he did not even have enough energy to make his objections known to Jettel, three days later, even though he was feeling much better just this afternoon, he sat in Doctor Heupke's consulting room.

There he stared so furiously at the asters in a light green marble vase, which made him think of an urn at precisely this inappropriate moment, as if the flowers and not the man behind the desk were responsible for the unsolicited message he had just received. Walter had considered the examination itself as much too thorough for his state, which he characterized once again, and as he thought quite descriptively, as a minor and temporary indisposition.

Walter was annoyed—even more than by the examination—by Doctor Heupke's latest suggestion, his serious tone, and his detached face. Walter angrily defined this facial expression as the established means of a professional clan, for whom he had nothing but disdain, to maneuver a patient from a state of temporary despondency into the kind of submissive attitude that in his opinion every physician since Hippocrates had misused for the credible practice of his healing powers.

Walter turned away disgustedly and for some time only concentrated on the big raindrops on the windowpane. When he finally turned around again, he lightly slammed his fist on the desk and clenched the other hand in his jacket pocket. He nodded and straightened his shoulders to indicate that an answer to the question put to him a few minutes ago had finally occurred to him. Relieved and all of a sudden reconciled to his fate, he realized that he still had enough power of resistance to defend himself with his usual heartiness. He liked the wordplay. He laughed, slightly amused, when he considered that it was especially appropriate for him at this moment.

"Not this time," he said overly distinctly. "Nobody is going to get me into your hospital anymore."

"But you know how it is. The whole thing is just routine," Doctor Heupke patiently contradicted him, "so that we can get you back on your feet again." He mobilized the big share of confidence he needed to smile unselfconsciously. At the same time he was amazed that he was still able to feel the same kind of sympathy for Walter that he had extended to him since his first consultation a few years ago. "A few days in the hospital," he stated, "will be good for you."

"That is what you said the last time, too," Walter reminded him. "Don't you physicians know when you have reached the end of your rope? You cannot implant a new motor."

"But we can correct your blood sugar level," Doctor Heupke enumerated, "and strengthen your heart. And make sure that you get some rest. I don't want any more than that. Why don't you," he suggested, "give a physician a chance for once to help a patient who has grown close to his heart."

"No flattery," Walter sternly disapproved. Even more than by the persistence of the physician, which, he noticed, resembled his own in the most irritating way, he was annoyed that Jettel had not only catalogued his symptoms with the kind of detail he would have appreciated a lot more in better circumstances, but also confirmed every sentence Doctor Heupke said with the hated comment, "That's what I always say."

"After Christmas," Walter triumphantly said, "I am going to have all the time in the world. But that is when the physicians go on trips these days and don't give a hoot about their patients."

"Not I."

"Of course, you are going to celebrate New Year's Eve at the bedside of your favorite patient."

"Don't worry about New Year's," the doctor promised. "You will get a break from the hospital then and celebrate with your charming wife. You can eat all the wrong foods you like, and I will start all over again at the beginning of the New Year and not say a word."

"I am going to think about it," Walter replied. "And only because you just made the first joke since we have known each other. But don't get your hopes up too high that I am going to loaf around here."

"And, please, don't get your hopes up too high either if you do not let us help you. And that is not a joke."

"Two in one day would have been too much anyway."

During the sleepless nights after the doctor's visit and on days that seemed without beginning and end to him, Walter admitted, at least to himself, that the improvement had been short-lived. Yet his stubbornness held on to the hope that his body would once again help itself. He was neither planning on going to the hospital nor thinking about the doctor's suggestions, but Jettel and Regina did not leave him alone.

For four weeks both of them threatened, implored, cried, and fought with Walter. They yelled at him and got yelled at in return, they reconciled with him, and they promised to visit him twice a day in the hospital and to tell all his acquaintances to do the same. They swore that they would bring him cigarettes and chocolates and would not object if he had files brought in from the office. Jettel appealed to his reason with just as little success as Regina tried to appeal to his sense of responsibility. As a last hope to persuade him to undergo the hospital treatment, she engaged Fafflok, but he, too, gave up. In the end it was Ziri who performed the miracle at a point in time when no one expected it. She changed Walter's mind with a single sentence.

"I always thought," she said a week before Christmas, "you wanted to be at your son's big celebration."

"Ziri is the only one of you women who has a brain in her head," Walter declared that night. "At any rate, a bar mitzvah can only be celebrated in the smallest circle if the father has just died. I have to make it through March. I owe that to my only son. Whatever gave you the idea that I was not going to the hospital?"

His surrender, which he now described with a grin as a game that anyone with the least bit of a sense of humor could have been wise to detect immediately, all of a sudden changed life for everyone. The quarrels with Jettel were about everyday banalities again and lost their sting. Walter teased Max and Ziri with his old gusto. Above all, he and Regina returned to the accord he had missed so much.

After the call to Doctor Heupke, whose sympathetic friendliness pleased him as if he actually deserved it, Walter's cough and mood improved with surprising speed. His choleric outbursts became less frequent; his insulting aggression was replaced by eccentric jokes that he greatly enjoyed. Regina even expected that he would soon come up with the suggestion that he need not go to the hospital after all, but she was wrong.

On good days Walter would whistle "Ich hab' mein Herz in Heidelberg verloren" after a breather on the third floor of the stairs and would call Ziri, whose name he was still unable to pronounce, Owuor. With increasing frequency, expectantly, and with ever more concrete plans that stood in striking contrast to his frugality and modesty, he talked about the bar mitzvah in March of the coming year.

He promised his son a celebration that Frankfurt would be talking about for years to come and promised his wife a new dress from one of those small shops that had recently become fashionable among the ladies. At night he drafted a long guest list that he happily expanded the next morning. For the most part it included the Jewish community, as well as colleagues, judges, district attorneys, and good clients. Also on the list were people from Upper Silesia and Walter's former fraternity brothers, several of whom had returned to Germany in recent years. Greschek was supposed to sleep in the living room and Grete in the conservatory. One night, he suggested that Martin should be invited. Regina objected, but her father was already too captivated by his idea to see through her game. He fell into the trap and wrote to South Africa.

For their anniversary he presented his wife with the pearl necklace that she had wanted for years. One day later, on Christmas Eve, he fought so violently with her—because she wanted to divide the carp and goose into two meals—that she threw the pearl necklace onto the kitchen table with a dramatic gesture and threatened never to wear it again and to stick the goose that Greschek had sent from the Harz into the oven without plucking it first. But Jettel's rebellion, which was as much a part of the holiday tradition as the honey gingerbread that she had baked on the farm even where there was no honey, could not dampen the mood in the long run.

"At Christmas," Walter used to say since the days of hunger were past, "even the Jews can eat their fill."

He maintained that he had learned that as a boy as part of his bar mitzvah instructions and always especially looked forward to the holidays. Even though Walter had taught his children early on only to identify with their own religious holidays (he did not tolerate any fir branches in the apartment and since their engagement had reproached Jettel about the Christmas tree in her mother's living room), he did not find it inappropriate to sing along with the Christmas songs on the radio, to admire the beautifully decorated tree at Fafflok's on the second day of Christmas, and to eat so much Stollen, the traditional German holiday bread, that he was getting sick.

It never would have entered his head to do without the herring salad, stuffed gooseneck, carp with beer sauce, and poppy seed dumplings, which reminded him of Christmas in Upper Silesia. He gained three pounds over Christmas and was in a good mood, even playful, when Jettel packed his suitcase for the hospital after the holidays.

Walter was familiar with the Holy Spirit Hospital from earlier visits. Above all, and this was much more important to him, most of the nurses knew him and this time again greeted him with a warmth that made him feel good. They had already learned that Walter's frequently rude ways were only a way to disguise his kindness, so they readily tolerated his teasing, crude jokes, and banter, showed understanding for his often unfair nature, and were never deceived by his brusqueness when he disliked some small thing.

The gray-haired nurses as well as those with firm hips and slim waists appreciated his free and easy compliments and generous tips. They found Walter amusing and were quite touched by the love that he showed for his family and his family showed for him. Above all they had the greatest respect for a patient who knew the head nurse well enough so that she visited him every night and had long conversations with him. On the last day of the year hardly any of the nurses missed the opportunity to wish him all the best in person.

Walter promised all of them that he would take care of his health, return with low sugar levels and poppy seed dumplings for the entire floor, and grumpily made them all promise not to tell of his generosity. He had asked the head nurse to provide champagne and open-faced sandwiches to a six-bed room at his expense and had slipped a student nurse, whose parents were from Ratibor, some money for a train ticket home.

Walter solemnly promised two physicians and the head nurse that he would take a taxi home, but after lunch he snuck out of the hospital, took his car from a side street, and drove home singing. Since his family did not expect him before the afternoon, he could not resist the temptation of frightening them even more than he would have done by just ringing the doorbell early. He unlocked the door to the apartment with a shout that only Owuor had been able to produce at Ol' Joro Orok when he wanted to hear a threefold echo from the mountain, threw his hat past Jettel's head onto the kitchen table, boxed Regina's back from behind, and sent Max to the corner drugstore to buy sparklers, streamers, party crackers, lead, and a sugar cone.

"You are getting more *meshuge* all the time," Jettel scolded and yet made him feel that she was happy. After a heated debate of three days, she had finally been persuaded to prepare the potato salad the way she used to make it in Leobschütz and not to leave out the herring that did not agree with Regina or Walter.

He tasted it standing up, wiped his lips smacking at the freshly washed kitchen curtain, lovingly called Jettel his "old woman," and gave her a kiss. "Too bad that Ziri cannot celebrate with us today," he said and pretended not to hear the giggles from the broom closet. He pulled her out, pressed her close, and sighed, "You don't know how happy you are making an old man."

"That's why I came today."

"Did you tell your mother that you are having an affair with your boss?"

"Yes," Ziri laughed, "but she didn't believe me."

"I am a very different father then," Walter said emphatically and looked at his daughter. "I would instantly believe my daughter if she told me something like that."

After dinner Walter insisted, although it was an especially mild day, on trying the *Feuerzangenbowle*, the punch with burned sugar, and the first five sparklers. Luckily for the further progress of the night, Jettel, after only half a glass of the much-too-strong alcoholic beverage, was no longer able to determine who had burned the hole in the curtain of the living room window and limited herself to a small series of complaints. Walter ominously accused his son and Max just as excitedly blamed him. Regina realized, with a touch of sadness that made her heart fly as fast as an arrow, that her brother had already mastered to perfection her old game of putting down false tracks without going easy on oneself in the process.

Following an old English custom, Regina had hidden a coin in one of the jelly doughnuts. It promised future health and happiness to the finder. But in a rather un-English way she had already undermined the English law of fairness and equal chance while baking. She had marked the fateful doughnut with a big raisin, quickly put a doughnut on everyone's plate and pushed the lucky one toward her father.

"Typical of the English," her father muttered when he spat out the fifty-pfennig piece, "that they consider it a sign of good luck if someone breaks his tooth on New Year's Eve." Yet it was obvious that he was immune to sentimentality but not to superstition.

When they poured the molten lead from a spoon into the water to tell their fortunes, Ziri retrieved a lump from the bowl that Walter graciously identified as a wedding carriage, but when Regina poured a very similar shape, he was not ready to extend the same generosity to her.

"Everyone can see," he said, "that this thing is a large suitcase. You most likely want to leave your old father forever in the New Year. Just like Hamlet's daughter."

"Lear's daughter," Regina corrected him. "Hamlet died a bachelor."

"Was he unhappily in love then?"

"Yes, with a girl from South Africa."

Jettel's lead figure was unanimously declared to be a lucky chimney sweep, Max's, after long deliberations, was only a spoon.

"A silver spoon," Regina enthused and made an effort to look like the fairy of her childhood days, "is the sign of the greatest fortune in a lead-pouring ceremony."

"Don't talk such nonsense," Walter contradicted her. "A spoon means that you, my son, will have to scoop up by yourself all the soups you will have gotten yourself into over the coming year."

He warmed his lead last, bent all the way over the bowl with water, and retrieved a small rectangular platform. Before anyone was able to look at it closely, Walter took it into his hand and said, "Nebbish, what was I supposed to get? This is a coffin."

Ziri crossed herself and turned pale, and Jettel and Regina became red and angry. Walter asked his son if he knew why women did not have a sense of humor. Max shook his head, rolled his eyes, murmured "long hair, little intelligence," got up, and embraced his father from the back.

Half an hour before midnight, Ziri went to the renters on the fifth floor to bring them their best wishes for the New Year and a taste of Jettel's poppy seed dumplings. She had been gone less than ten minutes when Walter, without anyone noticing it, called there and, with his voice disguised, asked for Ziri, whispering into the phone, "Come down immediately, Dr. Redlich just died."

Wearing a colorful paper hat made from one of the party crackers, Walter, giggling in the hallway, received the sobbing Ziri and the distressed young couple from the fifth floor. He had more trouble than anticipated in explaining the situation to Jettel, Regina, and Max, and he finally calmed all of them sufficiently so that they became willing to forgive him and were able to go into the New Year with dry eyes. Still, he kept insisting that in all his life he had never played a more successful New Year's Eve prank. At five minutes to twelve he sang the first notes of "Auld Lang Syne." His voice was strong and clear.

Regina stared at her father, frightened, and could not believe that she was hearing the long-forgotten sounds. She saw tiny stars, which melted into a spinning ball around her bewildered senses and then fell apart like a rain of fire. Her body trembled, her eyes burned, and she managed for only a moment to ban the salty grains from them before the pictures became ignited with the power of a hastily nourished bush-fire and became a burning forest. The old Scottish song, full of yearning, with its piercing melody that she knew since her days in the English boarding school, had always touched her. The memories now raged mercilessly in her head: scenes from a tropical night, the sounds of voices under the lemon and guava trees that were whipped by a humid wind. She had last heard the song in Nairobi on New Year's Eve of 1946.

At the time, the emigrants from Germany had clumsily sung "Auld Lang Syne," embarrassed to prove at least to themselves that after desperate years of searching for new roots, they had found a new home in Kenya and were no longer displaced people. With alarming clearness Regina saw the people, whom she had not thought of for years, standing in a circle and extending their hands to each other.

She heard them sing again and felt the pressure of hastily stifled laughter in her breast once more when the hard, throaty, German pronunciation reached her ears. Only Walter, who had learned the song in the British army, had made the old Gaelic words, the fleeting nostalgia, and the mystical romanticism resound. She had been proud of the splendid knight whose tongue, when it spoke English in this one wonderful moment of brief fulfillment, did not stumble like that of the foreigners.

Regina saw her father standing in a sergeant's uniform under Africa's fragrant trees. The three white stripes shone brightly on the sleeve of his khaki shirt. Walter was slim, and taller than most of the people standing around him. His eyes were clear, his hair full and black. He held Regina's hand and with the warmth of his touch he split her heart into two parts because she knew that he was unable to dream of anything else but the return to the Germany she feared. When she heard her father singing so forcefully in a language that was not his own, she had felt for the first time that he would neglect to protect himself from those memories that stole a man's peace forever before leaving. It had been one of those many moments in her life, and one of the earliest, in which the bond of love with her father became the demanding chain of inseparability.

The Frankfurt night sky turned as light as day, glittering green and burning red. The sound of church bells and muffled shots from saluting guns streamed in through the open windows. Cars raced and sounded their horns in the street. A dog yowled; pigeons flew up. Noisy children threw grasshoppers from balconies. A golden rain fell into the front yards and died down. Regina clapped her hands over her ears to protect herself from the sounds of the old world and opened her eyes wide. The flame under the burned sugar punch was glowing blue; the light from the lampshades of the six-arm ceiling lamp was pale yellow. Jettel's pearl necklace shimmered on white skin.

But the sparkler that Walter gleefully flourished while he shouted "Happy New Year" immersed his face with the malice of a lurking monster in the poisonous colors of transience. Regina saw gray skin; dark melancholy eyes and deep furrows on his forehead; bent shoulders that had carried, for too long, a burden for which their strength did not suffice; a slightly extended stomach; arms that had become thin; and white fingers with blue knuckles. The pain of recognition was devastating. Her father was a man marked by age and sickness. She knew that she would not be able to bear the truth much longer without having her eyes betray the fact that she was giving up the hope she owed him since the hour he himself had lost hope. But then Walter reached for her hand again—with the same warmth as in the long-dead days, with the same magic trembling in his fingers and as if nothing had happened since that night in Nairobi. The chain of love around Regina's body became heavy and hot. Walter awkwardly bent down to her, and his lips stroked her hair and touched her ear; she only cared that nobody but she should hear him say "thank you."

"What do you two always have to whisper about," Jettel complained.

"We didn't whisper," Walter maintained, offended. "Regina, please instantly tell your jealous mother what I just told you."

"He wants to have a piece of bread with gravy and did not dare tell you," Regina mediated.

In the late afternoon of New Year's Day, happily waving from the taxi and brandishing his hat from the window, Walter drove back to the Holy Spirit Hospital, strengthened physically by Jettel's roast rabbit and spiritually by a night that he thought of as carefree, stimulating, and extraordinarily successful. He told the cabdriver that he basically spent his vacations in the hospital and realized, a little taken aback but still in a good mood, that he had actually begun to think of the stay that way. The smell of the waxed floors in the long corridors reached his nose. He liked it. The warmth made him feel good, as did the nurses whose faces, still tired from the long night, lit up when they welcomed him. The head nurse had had a Christmas rose put into his room in a blue glass. He touched one of the blooms tenderly, opened his heart for a fleeting moment to its beauty, sat down on the freshly made bed, and noticed that it was no longer an effort to untie his shoes. When he got into his pajamas, he whistled "Auld Lang Sync" once more; delight in life made his temples throb.

With the fatigue he started to feel soon afterward came a satisfaction that his nature, which always fought against his failing body, seldom allowed him to enjoy. The twilight put him into a mild and confident mood even though ever since Africa he considered the time between day and night too long and dangerous. He closed his eyes and was fast asleep for several minutes. When he woke up, refreshed, he saw Regina's face, returned her look full of love, thought of Max's bar mitzvah, and resolved to make the time he had to spend in the hospital easy for the doctor and himself. He heard footsteps in the corridor and the clatter of dishes outside the rooms and enjoyed the familiar sounds in the same way as in the nights on the farm when he was able to identify the sounds before they began to trouble him.

The young student nurse (to whom he had given the money for a train ticket home) with the Frankfurt accent and the parents from Ratibor was back and thanked him with poppy seed dumplings prepared according to her grandmother's recipe from Hindenburg. He told her, with minute details that he greatly enjoyed, about a small swindler whom he had once defended in the district court and had been able to save from jail. The young girl in her starched uniform had very beautiful teeth when she laughed, but her glance and even more so her words told him that Upper Silesia had become a very distant land. He sighed; the chubby blonde asked him if he was having any pains.

"Not where you think I would," he diagnosed.

In the late evening the head nurse visited him with a brightly polished apple on a finely grained wooden plate. Her voice reminded him of his mother's, and her black skirt stood out in the white room of fears he wanted to forget, but he told her, amused again, about his New Year's Eve prank and how he had frightened everyone. "You know that people who are presumed to be dead live longer, don't you?" he recalled.

"I feel sorry for your poor wife," she said.

"I do, too. At least sometimes. But I have made up my mind to become a new person in the New Year. They still need the old drudge."

He so enthusiastically liked the concept of the new person who, by sheer willpower and a sense of responsibility, would manage to take control of himself, that he told Doctor Heupke about it the next day. The doctor recognized his chance and said, "Then you should stay with us ten more days. You will see how good that is going to be for you."

"Eight," Walter determinedly bargained with him. "I want to be home by January 9. In exchange I'll let you do everything to me while I am here."

He kept his word, followed the dietary prescriptions almost without complaint, took a long rest at noon, lived in tolerable peace with Jettel, and stayed far enough away from professional demands so as not to get upset more than once a day. At the end of the week, he felt strong and sure. In the afternoon he went for a half-hour walk with Jettel in the snow-covered park around the hospital. Although he had at first declared that he was not able to walk at all and that she just wanted to kill him as fast as possible so that she could spend his hard-earned savings on trips, he did not feel any shortness of breath or pain in his chest despite the cold. He eventually lost three pounds, and his face regained its contour and color. The high sugar levels improved, as did the mood of the doctor, who became so enthusiastic that he talked about post-recovery and a cure in Bad Nauheim.

"Only over my dead body," Walter said.

Regina visited Walter late in the evenings after work. She brought him newspapers and books and confirmed his long-held opinion that his gloomy daughter was much more cheerful in the editorial office than at home. She told him about colleagues, discussions, meetings, and the theater. For the first time, Walter was genuinely, and without his usual reservations and ironic remarks, interested in her work. He even went so far once as to call her capable and let himself get sufficiently carried away to admit that he did not think her job was as unsuitable for her, after all, as he had always maintained. He finally acknowledged something she had known for a long time, namely that he read the *Evening Post* in his office and liked her articles.

"I would have liked a son-in-law better, though," he immediately qualified his remarks.

"Don't fib like that, *bwana*. We agreed a long time ago on that topic. You would never have allowed any rival to have me."

"But I took away your freedom."

"You gave it to me."

They talked a lot about Ol' Joro Orok and Owuor, suppressed—amused that they were able to do so—the hard times of the past, and saturated the presence with a sadness that they would have been ashamed of in any environment other than that of the hospital. They enjoyed their long conversations, intimacy, and, above all, the knowledge that they were enough for each other. During the long hours of mutual understanding, neither of them managed adequately to hide their feelings so that the other did not realize how unswervingly their memories went to the much-loved people in Africa who accepted illness as God's will and were not afraid of the future.

"It is time I come home," Walter realized. "Looking back makes you weak."

He did not sleep well in the night before his release, and he woke up at five in the morning. His impatience and restlessness, and his yearning for work, duty and action, merit, and independent decisions had caught up with him. He needed family, home, and activity. He asked for his breakfast the moment the cart with the dishes clanked on the corridor, ate quickly, and got annoyed with the thin coffee and the egg that had been cooked for too long. He dressed, and he packed his small suitcase although Jettel was not coming till ten o'clock to pick him up. He stood at the window for a moment, counted the cars, fretted that his was standing at home, and rang for the nurse.

"Holy smoke, you are all packed already. The doctor wants to come and see you before you leave."

"He doesn't have to, I am going to send him a picture of myself."

"He is going to be here at eight at the latest. He specifically promised you that yesterday."

"And what does he think I am going to do here till then?"

"Now don't be so impatient on your last day here, Dr. Redlich. That is not going to be good for you."

"Waiting around will be even worse for me."

"It's not that long. Why don't you work on a crossword puzzle?" nurse Martha suggested. "You always like to do that."

"Just for your sake," Walter grumbled, "but under protest."

He needed some time to find his fountain pen and he searched for an equally long time for his glasses, sat down in the easy chair at the window, and opened the magazine, reconciled to the enforced idleness by the routine movement that already seemed like a part of everyday life to him. For a short moment the thought engaged him that nurses were much better at placating a discontented husband than a wife, and he smiled. All his life Walter had found satisfaction in the logic of crossword puzzles. They were in accord with his inclination to reach a set goal through perseverance and without emotions. He was fascinated by the fact that in crossword puzzles the outcome did not depend on chance. During the emigration it had struck him as symbolic that he did not know enough English to solve even a single puzzle.

He noticed that he was filling the empty little squares too fast, so he took a break to extend the pleasure for a while longer and looked out of the window. The clear light of the street lanterns matched his mood. The trees had become frozen during the cold night, but the first frost flower on the windowpane had melted already. When the second one began to drip, he bent over the paper again and kept on writing. It was so quiet in the room that the scratching of the pen seemed loud.

The alarm clock that had been set for seven o'clock rang piercingly. Nurse Martha came into the room. The hard linoleum did not dampen any of her firm steps. "See," she said, "now you have fallen asleep again with your glasses on your nose." As quietly as her heavy shoes allowed, she went to the night table to pick up the tray with the breakfast dishes, but her sleeve got caught on the small lamp and she had a hard time holding onto the tray. The small milk jar hit the coffee pot, the cup shattered noisily on the floor, and the pieces fell against the iron bedpost.

"I'm sorry, I didn't mean to do that," the nurse said and turned to Walter, alarmed. When he did not move, she started laughing. "You have to play your jokes with us to the last moment. Well, it is all right, Dr. Redlich; I know for sure that I have woken you with the noise."

She put the tray down and, still laughing, took the few steps toward his chair. Since his head was bent down, first she only looked at the small table with the open magazine. There were only a few empty squares left in the crossword puzzle.

Walter had not found the last answers before his death. He still had the pen in his hand.

22

IN ONE OF THE NIGHTS raging with the thunder of the black God in Ol' Joro Orok, far ahead of the time when it is necessary for a human being to gain everlasting vision, Regina had learned about the days of the final lightning. Those days armed themselves with a lethal axe and inflicted wounds that would never heal again. Whoever had suffered their pain was always able to count the scars and make them talk. None of the warriors of the dark, though, ever succeeded in ultimately taking away the hope of a child who still feels her father's hand on her shoulder. Now that day had come.

January 11, 1959, was a destroyer of life. One single strike delivered the decisive blow. Regina prepared herself to receive the foe she had feared for so long. When she caught the noise of her teeth, which clicked together like clubs with iron heads, she pressed her lips tight. She knew that if she wanted to show herself worthy of her father's legacy, she had to defend herself against the quick tears of sorrow with the same determination as a young Masai defending himself against the pain of his first wound. The discipline with which he had carried his burden was the recognition she owed him.

Far away, church bells rang from the world of life. The second day of the new era was a Sunday. After an icy night it brought low temperatures that had hardly ever occurred in the gentle mildness of Frankfurt winters and the air stayed rigidly frozen even at ten in the morning. Still, it became obvious half an hour before the scheduled time that neither the abnormal cold nor the biting, steadily increasing wind and certainly not the far ride many people had to make had been able to dissuade just one friend, acquaintance, colleague, or like-minded person, who felt the duty of being there, from coming to Walter's funeral.

The freezing people were assembled in small groups in front of the white cemetery walls, were congregated in the yard by the funeral hall, and stood under trees that guarded the first row of the snowed-in graves. Those familiar with the customs—those who did not have to suspect that they might offend some religious law unknown to them by some inadvertent movement with consequences they could not fathom—entered for a short while into a small, longish waiting room where each breath turned into a cloud of gray, damp mist. On a narrow white wooden bench, Jettel waited crying and Regina sat silently next to Fafflok. On the opposite side sat a few women in worn clothing and bearded men with alert glances.

Regina had never seen them before and Jettel had only seen them at funerals. The strangers, whose faces lacked timidity and whose many expressive gestures made clear that they were more familiar with death than life, talked to each other with a cheerfulness that matched neither their gray, furrowed faces nor the occasion. They made very abrupt pauses during their conversations, then looked thoughtfully at mother and daughter, and started to talk again as instantly as they had stopped. When they nodded, which they did frequently, it seemed as if they had practiced the uniformity of their movements for a long time.

Whenever the good silence started, Regina heard her brother's voice, which was reassuringly firm and very clear. For a moment she felt liberated from the prying glances that distressed her. She turned around and could even see Max if she dared to stretch her body and lift her head high enough. He stood in the next room with his tutor and practiced the prayer for the dead one last time. Even though she did not know Hebrew, it had become as familiar to her during the two days since the call from the Holy Spirit Hospital as if she had heard it all her life.

While holding her mother's cold hand, she tried to summon some ability to feel back into her own limbs to pass on pain and sympathy as required by the laws of daughterly love. But she was unable to steer her thoughts, which in an inattentive moment had stolen away from the present to the days without fear and death, into the right direction. The escape took all power away from her head and drained too much strength from her body.

Regina squeezed her eyes tight with a determination to turn the water in them into salt that would remain invisible once again and looked out into the yard. She saw the towering black hats, the wall of dark coats, and a never-ending sea of white faces, and her senses took flight again. She caught herself imagining that seeing so many people would have pleased her father and then she remembered how he had always said, cheerfully and amusedly, that nobody would miss his funeral for the simple reason that one did not have the expense of a wreath at a Jewish funeral.

She considered it a sin to enjoy a joke at a moment that required introspection, respect, and humility. She was ready to atone. Max came from the backroom. His steps were loud in the sudden silence. He sat down next to Regina and leaned on her shoulder. She finally felt the warmth she had been unable to pass on to Jettel before.

Distraught by regret and shame because she had so contentedly thought about her father's life and not his death, and moreover with a tranquility that she found strange and provocative, Regina let go of her mother's hand. Bewildered, she turned to her brother to claim the consolation of silent sharing, which flowed through her. She became aware that Max still had the same gentle eyes with the heavy eyelashes that had enchanted people when he was a child. But now, while premature knowledge overshadowed these eyes, another shade had been added— the kindness that had made her father the man he had been.

"Do you know when we can finally get out of here and go into the hall?"

"As the last ones," Max said. "Just think about it. We are sitting in the first row over there. I know that. Papa always promised me that."

He tried hard during the last sentence to have his voice laced with the sorrow that the ears of friends and, more importantly, strangers expected from him, but Regina detected the familiar, telltale sound of quickly suppressed levity and was aware of it, She bit her lips again to hold back the smile within before it became visible. Max was not able to get his father's jokes out of his ears either.

"Do you remember when he promised you that the first time?"

"When he had his first heart attack," Max recalled. "Do I have to be ashamed today because I laughed so hard then?"

"No, he wanted you to be able to laugh when you thought about him. Even today. He always promised me as a child that I did not have to wash my neck for his funeral."

"That is just as good."

On the way to the cemetery hall, her arm around Jettel and hand in hand with her brother, Regina noticed a large group of older people standing at the door, waiting uncomfortably. The men's black hats were conspicuously new; the coats looked as if they had lived through as much as their owners. The women, small of stature and plump, had hard features. The faces with the red eyes and the expressions of gloomy discomfiture were similar to each other. Even though Regina nodded to these mourners—whose sincerity she felt—to let them know that she thanked them in memory of her father, she was unable to remember any of their names. But without having to think for a moment, she knew the names of all the small towns and villages that had been their homes.

She was deeply moved when she saw the silent group. They had all come: the people from Silesia and Upper Silesia, those uprooted people with whom Walter had shared the memories of a naïve youth and the unappeasable longing for Breslau, Leobschütz, and Sohrau—these people alone with their idealized view of the past had made it possible for his lifelong dream of a homeland to become reality once more without having to admit that his illusions had died.

Regina noticed that many of Walter's much-loved compatriots held their hands folded in front of their stomachs as if they had to abstain from an action they wanted to perform. Yet she was unable to explain the associations to herself until a woman stepped up to her and whispered, "Dr. Redlich always said we were not supposed to disgrace him and come to a Jewish cemetery with flowers."

"He would have been happy that you thought of that," Regina whispered back to her. Again a funny thought prevented her from giving in to her pain. She remembered how Walter had told her that he had informed his people from Upper Silesia, whenever they came to his office or he went to theirs, about the rites of the Jewish burial and how they had all said, "How can one follow a gentleman like Dr. Redlich with empty hands on his last journey?"

Regina was so precisely able to imagine the hard sound of the Silesian voices, the surprised exclamations with the long, drawn-out vowels, and the brusque, picturesque expressions that she was able to hear her father talk. His voice was present enough to sharpen her senses. When the familiar sounds were supplemented first by wit and irony, and then by pictures that had been painted so long ago, Regina realized what her father had done for her.

He had been a wise man in the traditional costume of the fool. He had not rehearsed the future with his family out of some grotesque sense for the macabre, but only so that they would be able to stand the present without despairing. It was only Regina's body that was still trembling and only the cold that made it shiver.

Not all people, by far, found room in the large cemetery hall. They stood against the walls and in the center aisle. It was not possible to close the door; the ice-cold wind pushed up to the simple wood coffin. Regina tried to imagine her father in this coffin, but her head rejected the reality. She also told herself again and again that the thought that death had come to him so fast and without pain and premonition should console her, but she was only able to think of the lead being poured at New Year's Eve and the strange hoaxes of the night. Embarrassed, she squeezed Jettel's hand when the rabbi stepped to the podium.

He was a white-haired man of imposing height with a red face ready for anger at any time, arresting eyes, and the kind of voice that the most upright and eager of the biblical prophets were rumored to have. He spoke thunderously of the duty to preserve faith and tradition and said that, in spite of his liberalism, he had always found that commitment in his conversations with Walter. He called the deceased a contradictory man who had courageously taken on the emigration to a coffee plantation in South America, had loved his family, and had not been allowed to see his children grow up and follow in his footsteps. Regina stared into her lap, but then she lifted her head after all. She searched for her brother's look behind her mother's back. His shoulders were shaking, too, but he held a hand in front of his mouth.

"Just don't laugh when the rabbi mixes me up with someone else," Walter had often said. "He does that on principle at funerals. The main thing is that he says I was a good human being."

The staid speeches—by the representative from the bar association, who spoke of the now rare professional ethos of a "fair" man without ever becoming aware of the wordplay that his remark played with Walter's last name; the president of the Jewish community, who called Walter a man of the first hour and subtly transcribed his choleric temper as personal courage; and an old fraternity brother from the Breslau student days, whose address was interspersed with Latin expressions— often so strikingly resembled, word for word, Walter's ironic drafts that even Jettel had to smile once. She had sometimes looked like that on the farm when she had suddenly thought about her youth and had dreamed of her successes as a young girl. Rarely had she done so later on.

Regina remembered the days of her first life and became wistful. Even though she told herself that this was not the time, she started brooding about her parents' marriage. She asked herself if her father had at least realized in the short moments of Jettel's liberating laughter that his wife had more of a sense of humor than he was willing to admit. The sigh that Regina suppressed and also the tears that welled up seemed disloyal to her. Still, the question persisted as to why her father never could be persuaded to let go of any kind of prejudice. She was satisfied that her love had always been strong enough to be understanding of others in this respect.

The need for air and escape became unrelenting when the fraternity brother followed his Latin quotes with Greek ones. Regina's eyes, controlled for too long by a will that did not permit the display of actual feelings, were unable to distinguish one face from another. All of a sudden she saw Emil Frowein standing among the faceless crowd. She could not believe it.

He towered over most of the people there and it was obvious that he was one of the few who were able to understand the speaker. Regina had never seen him in such a stiff, black hat and she needed a moment to recognize him. She asked herself how he had gotten the idea that he should share this farewell, which could not mean anything to him, with her. She found no answer. The secretary had been the only one who was there when Regina had called in to say that she was not coming to work. The fact that Frowein had bought a new hat touched her even more than his unexpected appearance. She intended to tell him that when she was able to think, feel, and talk again.

It was now Regina who smiled when she remembered that her father had always said "Reiswein" when he talked about her boss. She had often been upset about it. She did not even understand why anymore, thought the altered form of the word witty all of a sudden, and realized that the clumsy joke was most likely the only thing that permitted her father to keep his distance and still talk about a part of his daughter's life that mattered to him.

It had never occurred to Regina to introduce the two men to each other. Frowein, she believed now, would have agreed in any case. Walter most likely would not have agreed. Yet Regina felt as if she should have at least tried to find a connection for the two chapters in her life. She was sorry about the missed opportunity; it seemed like too nasty a twist of fate that death was writing the epilogue that she herself should have thought of.

Frowein and her father were very similar to each other in their modesty, honesty, and integrity. Regina had felt from the beginning that this was why what had happened over and over again during the past years—when she had looked for dialog, confirmation, and loving care—was understandable. It made her sad that she had never been able to tell her father about the similarity between the men who shaped her life. Walter had longed so much for an explanation, and Regina had always been silent.

At this moment of passing thoughts that had nothing to do with her sorrow, her fear of separation, or the knowledge that all love has to die, Regina understood what had happened to her. She had not been able to get to the crucial word, to turn her head once more. When the call from the hospital came, she had not fared any differently than at the time when she had left the farm at Ol' Joro Orok without forewarning, without farewell, without a real last look at the house, woods and fields, people and animals, and had never returned again. This time, too, she had not been allowed to say goodbye.

With a despair that pulled her down into hopelessness with each new attack, she tried to relive the conversation of the last night, but she only heard bits and pieces of words that did not warm her and remained without meaning. Regina only knew one thing: She had not called her father *bwana* a last time, neither had he tenderly called her *memsahib*, and from now on nobody would share those conspiratorial words with her. The songs had faded, the magic was dead, and the game was over.

Owuor had extinguished the fire in the oven, just as he had done on the poisoned day in Nairobi, when he had left at dawn with the old dog on a rope and his belongings tied into a kitchen towel. Regina and Walter had sat in the kitchen. At that time, there had been a long farewell, one that fixed the images that had to stay in one's head forever, in form and color, with sound and scent. Had her father called a last time for the friend from his long wanderings as he often did when he needed something and nobody was around? Had he heard Owuor laugh one more time? Had he heard the echo bounding back?

Regina could not shake the memory of Owuor. She knew that she only had to close her eyes to see his face, but she did not dare give in to her longing. It was not good to go on safari with one's head as long as the body was still needed.

The hall was silent for a moment. An older man slowly went up to the speaker's platform. There he looked for a while for the paper in his coat pocket and touched his hat as if he wanted to take it off, but he remembered just in time that Jewish religious law requires one's head to be covered. He smiled self-consciously and blinked when he let his arms sink down. The man was speaking for the people from Upper Silesia. Regina initially just heard words without putting them together into sentences, but she forced herself to pay attention and soon realized that she had heard the speech once before.

She noticed it from the way the word "homeland" was emphatically stressed and how the short, thickset man with the steel-blue eyes said "Dr. Redlich": Walter had drafted the speech of the Upper Silesians in great detail and, as became evident now, almost word for word. The mixture of sobriety and unexpected sentimentality suited him. Regina heard her father laugh. Or was it Owuor? He had taught her that words were only good and right if one said them twice. The echo of Owuor's laughter had taught her to laugh.

The sadness became remote and soft. Regina felt consoled in a familiar way. It was not entirely true that one needed a long farewell so that one would not lose the love of one's life. It would not be any different with her father than with Owuor. He too could not leave her if she did not let it happen. Like Owuor, Walter had given her the gift of laughter. In another language, but with the same indestructible magic. Regina bent forward slightly and looked at her brother who, with the certainty of a well-prepared student, recited several of the words before the man from Upper Silesia uttered them. She realized that Max, too, would be capable of wit and sarcasm, but also of the love exemplified by his father. Only he did not know it yet.

The cantor rose and started singing the first notes of the prayer for the dead. Regina had often heard it during memorial celebrations for the victims of the concentration camps and she always experienced how this old complaint released tears in everyone whose heart it reached. Now the poignant melody, sorrow made rigid in word and music, in fervor, piety, and eternity, applied to her father. Her eyes remained dry. The farewell was already behind her. And ahead of her lay only the days in which she had to let just one scene enter her head. Her father stood in Nairobi under the guava tree, tightened the bow, and hit her heart with Cupid's arrow. Regina needed no more for a lifetime of love.

When she got up to follow the coffin with Jettel and Max, she became aware of many curious and critical glances directed at her; she lifted her head even though she knew that this was not the custom for those from whom death demanded suffering. This way she was able to hear two women discuss in detail why she was not married and Max had not cried.

"Nebbish," one of the women said, "they are too proud for either. The girl to get married and the boy to cry. And the boy is just about to have his bar mitzvah. That is the worst that can happen to a boy. To be without his father on the most important day of his life."

"I feel sorry for the mother," the second woman said. "She did not deserve this. Such a good, refined woman."

When Max, so different in his seriousness, spoke the son's prayer for the father at the grave, Regina was hardly able to hold back her tears. They were not for her father but for her brother, who much earlier than she had lost the protection and confidence of childhood. Full of protest and sadness, she thought about the bar mitzvah that now during the year of mourning would only take place in the smallest circle, and she took Max by the hand to console him. The pressure of his fingers was firm and warm. He had already started to take on the duty that he had been burdened with. He was not even thirteen yet.

Only when Fafflok, the thoughtful, taciturn companion of the last part of Walter's life, halting with grief, spoke the truest and warmest words of the day at the graveside, did Regina realize that her father, neither in a cheerful mood nor in one of his depressive moods, had never drafted Fafflok's speech. Regina gathered the reason. Fafflok had become his only friend in Frankfurt. Walter had only spared him, whose faith he respected like his own beliefs, from the macabre game.

Regina's memories wandered back to the beginnings in the foreign city; to hunger, hardship, and hope; to the first meeting with the Faffloks, the purchase of the house in the Rothschildallee, and Walter's obsession to leave his family a debt-free house. So many scenes, conversations, and emotions rushed at her that she did not see the woman in the headscarf coming up to her. Regina only noticed her when the stranger took a small knife from her handbag and cut into Regina's coat. Startled, she looked at her brother. His new dark suit, already bought for the bar mitzvah, was cut up just like Jettel's coat.

"One does that to spouses and children," Max whispered. "It is a sign of grieving."

"I didn't know that."

"I did. But I didn't think of it. Papa always told me to wear my old jacket to the funeral. He will be quite mad that I forgot."

"And how," Regina agreed.

"We'll know the next time," Max whispered.

"Are you starting to be like your father already?"

"Yes."

"That's good. That's the way it is supposed to be."

Two hours after the funeral the first visitors came to the Rothschildallee to pay their respects. Because the Sunday made it possible to follow tradition right away, it turned into a hurricane of condolences. There had never been this many people in the apartment—friends, acquaintances, and even strangers came to embrace and kiss the bereaved; to sigh, lament, and cry; to appraise the furniture and future; to give advice and remember their own sorrows. They pressed Jettel close, furtively and critically looked at Regina and Max, registered without exception that their eyes were not red from crying, and assured the sobbing widow that a husband's death was so much harder on a woman than the death of the father on the children.

Jettel nodded knowingly and judiciously, but said that she had good children who would never leave her and, like her late husband, would remove all difficulties from her path. They had had to give him their solemn promise. The people, who no longer whispered with dismay but openly demonstrated their active ability to take care of the sufferings of others, looked at Regina and Max again and nodded back. The most pious ones lowered their eyes and were quiet. Following the old customs, they brought soup, meat dishes, fish, fruit, and cake to the house. Whoever has to bemoan the death of a loved one should not be distracted from mourning through everyday needs like the necessity of supplying food.

"I like the pious ones the best," Max said in the kitchen, put a piece of gefilte fish on his plate, and eyed a cake.

"Your father used to say the same thing."

"Because he liked to eat as much as I do?"

"No. He always envied the pious people because they know where they belong. I do, too, by the way."

Jettel, in spite of her tears, composed and in a gray flannel dress with white ruffles—she had only found out at the cemetery that Jews do not wear black as a sign of mourning—kept on talking about Walter's last days, the unfinished crossword puzzle, and the happiness of her marriage. Her cheeks were pink. She was already in the process of weaving a new chapter in the story of her life.

"My husband," she reported, "fulfilled my every wish and even anticipated it. And he taught his children to do the same."

Regina envied Jettel very much, and not just because she was one of those rare women who did not look ugly in tears. She tried to imagine the future with her mother. She was not yet able to do so, but she was willing to take on the duty she owed her father. She was almost ready to smile at the thought of the embellished past that Jettel would now convert into a truth she would believe. Regina asked herself if Jettel was not going to miss the daily squabbles of her lively marriage; this time she really had to pull herself together not to smile. She was convinced that her mother would find new partners in her and, later when he was old enough, also in Max to continue proving herself in her fights against logic, insight, and any willingness to compromise.

The last visitors finally left the house in the early evening. Jettel asked Ziri to set the table. "We are going to live as we did before," she solemnly said. "I owe that to my husband. But I am not going to be able to eat a bite." She ate with a good appetite and sighed a lot. "He would have wanted me," she said, "to eat these sausages from the Silesian butcher. I got them especially for him."

After dinner she looked around and said reproachfully, but without malice, "I am surprised that the two of you did not shed a single tear. Several people approached me to ask if Papa's death did not affect you deeply."

"One can cry without crying," Regina replied, but her mother had never been able to recognize the regular repetition of words if they were not her own.

When Max had gone to bed, she went to his room the way she had done when he was still a child. He had often asked for new wallpaper, but Walter had been too careful with his money. It had been an old, protracted fight between father and son, and it would not find a quick end now with a mother who on the day of the funeral already considered herself an impoverished widow.

Regina stared at the pictures on the wall: peasant carts and busy horses; castles, trees, and babies in cradles; boys with balls, girls with dolls, and clowns with trumpets; men with goats and villages with church steeples and roosters crowing on them. She saw her brother lying on a white pillow in his blue and white striped pajamas. His eyes resembled those of the dolls on the wallpaper. His face was pale, his hair was dark, and the hand that reached for hers was too small for what it wanted to give.

"Do you remember," Max said, longing in his voice, "how you used to recite poems to me in the past?"

"That was because I could not sing. I did not expect you to remember that."

"I still remember everything," Max said, and after a pause he asked, "Don't you have a poem for today?"

"Yes," Regina said. "Do you really want to hear it?"

"Really."

She got a well-thumbed paperback from her room even though she knew by heart the text of Kurt Tucholsky's poem, which she had not been able to banish from her sorrow for the last two days. She only needed the book to hide her face. She pushed the small chair in front of the bed and began reading aloud without even looking at Max once:

> The world looks different now. I cannot believe it yet.
> > It cannot be.
> And a low, deep voice says:
> > "We are alone."
>
> A day without a fight—that was an empty day.
> > You dared.
> What everybody feels, but no one wants to say:
> > you said it.

Regina heard her father's voice simultaneously with her own. It was a parched day in Nairobi; she sat on the lawn burned by the sun, rocked the baby carriage, and recited verses from Shakespeare's *A Midsummer Night's Dream*. Max, six months old, kicked his naked legs and gurgled with pleasure. Walter stepped out from behind a tree in his khaki uniform and asked, "Well, Regina, are you stuffing your brother's ears with poems again?" The disapproval in Walter's voice had made her embarrassed, but she had continued in Shakespeare's voice, and her father had listened.

Regina shook her head as on the long-forgotten day and continued:

> Each one of us was your beloved guest,
> > who brought you joy.
> We carried everything to you. You loved
> > to laugh so much.
>
> And never any pathos. That was not part of it
> > in all that time.
> You were a Berliner and did not like
> > formality too much.

When Regina noticed that her voice was starting to become unsteady because she saw her father's face too clearly and his life and love turned into a surge of pain, she vacillated if she should read the last two verses she feared so much or tell Max that the poem was finished. His appreciation of language and beauty did not allow it.

"Go on," he urged.

> We are following, because we have to, on your path.
> > You are resting in your sleep.
> You have inflicted the first pain on me now.
> > It hit its mark.

You encouraged. Quietly took care. Laughed.
    If I am able to do anything:
It is all done for you alone.
        So please accept it.

Regina had learned the magic from Owuor at the edge of the flax field in Ol' Joro Orok in the blue rush of the long rains: Tears, if of laughter or sorrow, made one heart out of two. People whom this happened to would never be able to separate during their lifetime without having their hearts broken forever. Yet once before she had felt the weight of a chain that had been forged from love and she held back her tears. But only till she heard Max cry.